IN THE DARK

IN THE DARK

by

Meagan McKinney

KENSINGTON BOOKS
http://www.kensingtonbooks.com

KENSINGTON BOOKS are published by

Kensington Publishing Corp.
850 Third Avenue
New York, NY 10022

Library of Congress Card Catalog Number: 98-065850
ISBN 1-57566-371-6

First Printing: December, 1998
10 9 8 7 6 5 4 3 2 1

Printed in the United States of America

For my father, Richard John Goodman;
and for William K. Christovich
and his extraordinary wife Mary Lou Christovich
who have been so kind to me and my children.
It's great to know heroes and heroines exist
outside the imagination of this author and the pages of a book.

ACKNOWLEDGMENT

I *must* thank Kevin Carney, Administrative Assistant to the Chairman of the Board of Allstate Insurance, Northbrook, Illinois, and Burt K. Carnahan of Lobman, Carnahan, Batt & Angelle, attorney for State Farm Insurance Company.

Guys, I couldn't have written this book without both of you giving me an intimate peek at the insurance business. Thanks for letting me know Big Brother exists—as if we didn't suspect it already. The phone calls and interviews were priceless.

I hope the information I gave you helps your writing careers. I wish you guys every success in the future.

Meagan McKinney

PROLOGUE

A bank is a place where they lend you an umbrella in fair weather and ask for it back when it begins to rain.

—ROBERT FROST

Manhattan

"Sir. You know the rules. I'll have to ask you to sign in." Mabel Haskings peered over her half-glasses and stared her disapproval at the man.

He'd been coming in regularly to the bank for the last six months. The first time he appeared he'd been in the company of a slightly older woman who'd wanted to open a safety deposit box. Even now Mabel couldn't get over the shock of actually coming face to face with one of America's renowned heiresses. She herself had eaten bowls of Sugar Blum Toasties, and to this day she fed her dog Blum Bits for breakfast, lunch and dinner.

But it was one thing to buy a box of cereal, quite another to come face to face with the woman who bore the famous Blum name.

Mabel would never forget the day; never fail to recall the moment. Jacqueline Blum looked like any other customer at the bank. She was dressed in a rather outdated pink bouclé suit—thinking back on it, Mabel knew it had to be a Chanel—and she wore a wrinkled Hermès scarf around her neck as most wealthy women her age did in order to cover up the throat, the last frontier of the plastic surgeon. She'd come to the bank because she'd wanted to open a safety deposit box. So Mabel Haskings handed her one of the plastic Chase-logoed pens with which to sign her name on the deposit registry, and then Mabel had slipped the pen into her own purse that sat in the kneehole of her desk. It was the first time she'd ever requisitioned bank property, and even now she felt a little guilty about it, but it hadn't seemed right to throw the pen back into the desk drawer as if it belonged there. It no longer did. It had been touched by the illustrious Jacqueline Blum.

That had been Jacqueline Blum's only appearance at the bank. Mrs. Blum had opened the box, filled it in the private vault with her male companion at her side, then she'd gone back to her famous Blumfield Estate in Maryland, leaving behind power-of-attorney with the man in front of Mabel now, a man with whom Mabel Haskings wouldn't have trusted her Burmese cat, Georgy.

"Hello, Mr. Ferrucci, I'll be right with you." Mabel looked at his signature. As always it read *Jacqueline Blum.* She swore the man was even trying to make his signature look like Jacqueline Blum's.

Mentally shaking her head, she reached inside her top desk drawer and took out her keys. The safety deposit boxes had to be opened simultaneously with her key and the owner's. That was the built-in safeguard. However, it certainly seemed foolish to have all the in-place precautionary measures and then sign over the keys to the slimy character, Ferrucci.

Garry Ferrucci might be considered handsome to some women, but not to Mabel. She'd seen his type before. Oh, how well she knew it. Men who were handy at the Off-Track-Betting parlors—they wore fat diamond rings on each hand, Italian suits and slicked back yellow-gray hair. She'd been attracted to his type when she'd first come to New York, but once bitten, twice shy. She wouldn't be taken in by a man like Ferrucci any longer. Experience had made her wise and Garry Ferrucci was nothing but bad news. She knew if she looked inside his mouth, she'd find his tongue forked just like a snake's. And all that grease that kept his pompadour in place didn't come from a tube, no, he put it there just from the oiliness of his personality.

Jacqueline Blum was a fool to have anything to do with a man like Garry Ferrucci. Mabel speculated that the two probably had a relationship that was more than just business. It made no real sense, but that was how the rich were. Sometimes they were kooks, sometimes just hopelessly lonely and naïve, and sometimes both.

Mostly they made monumental errors in judgment and paid ghastly prices for them. Mabel wondered if Jacqueline Blum had ever had to; maybe she had, but that was the advantage to being the Blum Toasties heiress; no matter how burned she'd been in the past, Jacqueline had plenty more cash to fall back on. She could alway move on to the next disastrous project.

Indeed, as the saying went, the rich *were* different, Mabel mused as she led Ferrucci into the vault. She should count herself lucky that she herself didn't have that kind of money. After her disastrous engagement, there'd been no financial or emotional ability left in her to move on to the next loser. She'd now been loser-free for almost a quarter century, and was damn proud of it.

"Please place your key into the right lock, Mr. Ferrucci," she instructed, as if the man needed instruction. He'd been in and out of box 1329 for as many weeks as Jacqueline Blum had had the box.

The diamond ring on his right hand flashed when he turned the key. Mabel remembered it from previous visits. It said WINNER'S CIRCLE in gold and the letters were centered with a stone that had to be four carats. Mabel hadn't seen cubic zirconia as big as the diamond on Ferrucci's right hand, and it just enflamed her distrust of the man. Meeting Garry Ferrucci, she could finally understand why Tiffany's, the Fifth Avenue jeweler, had always, on a matter of taste, refused to carry men's diamond rings.

"I'll be right outside at my desk should you need me," she informed him, placing the large oblong metal box on the library table that sat in the middle of the vault. "Take as much time as you need, Mr. Ferrucci," she said with a smile she didn't feel.

Obediently she returned to her desk, but not before taking a covert look at the object Ferrucci placed on the green and gilt leather top of the table. It was a strange shape certainly. The only thing that came to mind when she spied it was that it looked like a stack of horseshoes cloaked in one of Jacqueline's wrinkled Hermès scarves.

Yes. They *were* different.

She took her seat at her desk and began another attempt at the memo she was writing to notify everyone at the branch about the lower-rate Chase bank card.

Her job was dull, dull, dull, Mabel thought. So was her life. For thirty-four years, she'd been buying the same smart suits at the same ladies' boutique in Ridgewood, New Jersey. Every day, she'd take the train into Penn Station and walk to the branch on Thirty-Seventh Street and Park Avenue. Not much had changed in the twenty-five years since Mabel Haskings had been first employed by the Chase Manhattan as a teller. The Pan Am sign had been removed from the Pan Am building; now Park Avenue didn't look as sleek and jet-setting as it had when Mabel was young and the world was her oyster. But it would all change next year.

Because next year it would be early retirement and a cottage in Pass Christian, Mississippi, right by the Gulf of Mexico. Mabel Haskings, Working Girl, would be leaving chic New York behind and returning home to her childhood memories of "the Pass." And she vowed never to look behind her. Her life had kind of been like the Pan Am building, at one time all new and sleek and optimistic. Then she'd been left at the altar. And after a few years of loneliness and toil at the venerable Chase Manhattan, her position as a New York bank teller didn't seem so glamorous anymore.

But the grind was going to end soon. She'd done her time; she'd paid her dues. She was fifty-five years old and she'd spent almost half her life in the same bank. Soon she'd be walking beneath the live oaks of her family's home. She'd go back to the heat and the stink of a Southern summer, but she'd drink iced tea, and go gambling, and wash her toes in the gulf. She couldn't wait.

"All done, Mr. Ferrucci?" she asked, seeing the man's shadow fall across her desk. She stood and followed him into the vault.

The strange silk-wrapped object was no longer on the table. The large oblong safety deposit box was the only thing around.

She lifted it and shoved it into the slot. For the first time since she'd opened the box for him, Ferrucci was leaving it heavier. Before, the only thing Mabel ever noticed was that the long metal box was always markedly lighter after Ferrucci made a visit.

"Your key, Mr. Ferrucci. Please place it in the lock on the right," she instructed like an automaton.

Ferrucci lifted his key. The locks turned. Box 1329 was "safe" once more.

"Thank you very much. Please visit us again soon." Mabel

watched Ferrucci leave. Perhaps she should have made another marketing effort to get the Blum accounts. Mr. Shingell had written her ten memos to make a plea to Ferrucci to have Jacqueline Blum move some of her money to Chase, but Mabel knew it was a worthless effort. Ferrucci wasn't about to listen to Mabel Haskings and her pitch about Chase Bank. She could talk until her face was purple but the Blum money was going to stay in the Regency Bank of Washington, and she knew it, and Mr. Shingell knew it. Because Jacqueline Blum owned the Regency Bank. She had her own bank branches in D.C., complete with their own vaults and safety deposit boxes.

It was one of the great mysteries. Why Jacqueline Blum would need to make the trip to New York to a small branch of the Chase Bank in order to open up a safety deposit box.

But like all great mysteries, Mabel told herself, this one seemed destined never to be solved. Jacqueline Blum's deposit box number 1329 at Chase was right up there with the twenty-three-year-old riddle of Mabel's fiancé who had broken it off with a smart, capable, efficient woman so that he could hitch himself to a stripper from Hell's kitchen.

They were the eighth and ninth wonders of the world, Mabel thought distastefully as she placed her attention once more upon the current bank card rate-change memo.

PART ONE

The Root of All Evil

CHAPTER ONE

Success and failure are both difficult to endure. Along with success come drugs, divorce, fornication, bullying, travel, medication, depression, neurosis, and suicide. With failure comes failure.

—Joseph Heller

One Week Later

Alyn Blum-Jones stared at the newspaper's headlines. A *Twilight Zone* numbness crept down her spine. She could hardly believe what she was reading:

BLUM CEREAL HEIRESS JACQUELINE BLUM
DECLARED MISSING

Townsfolk say woman last seen in Potomac boutique.

Authorities believe foul play is likely.

THE LONG VIGIL FOR THE RANSOM NOTE.

Alyn shook her head as if clearing it would make the words disappear. It just wasn't possible. She'd heard from Jacqueline only two weeks before. Everything was fine. The plans for Alyn to tour her aunt's famed stable were firm; Alyn was supposed to leave for Maryland tomorrow.

"Hey! You don't have time to read the paper! I've got a sick cat and two snarling Dobermans in the waiting room, and it's only eight in the morning." Her assistant, Joyce Abrams, plopped an overly full cup of coffee on her desk and went to the file drawer.

Alyn stared at her without really seeing her.

"You okay?" Joyce asked, her expression changing from efficient assistant to concerned friend. "What're you reading?" She went to the paper held lightly in Alyn's hand. Her eyes popped at the headlines.

"I just heard from her—do you really think someone hurt her?" Alyn fiddled with the temple pieces to her eyeglasses, which she held in her hands.

Joyce didn't answer. Her attention was taken by the article.

Alyn stood. She placed the thin wire-rimmed glasses on the bridge of her nose and swept back her thick ponytail of curly hair. "I guess I'd better not keep my clients waiting." She frowned. "But Joyce, if you find a free moment today, would you see if I can get an evening flight to Dulles? I think I'd better go down there and see what's going on for myself."

"You'd be the only Blum left, wouldn't you, Alyn?" Joyce chewed on her lower lip. "I mean, if something happened to your aunt, would that mean you'd get—?"

"I'd get nothing," Alyn reminded her. "My mother was disowned from the Blum fortune, remember? I told you that. Everything went south when she married my father and had me; it was the Blum name or him, and . . ." Alyn released a long tumultuous sigh. ". . . and she picked him."

"Poor little rich girl."

Alyn gave her a wry smile. "Yeah, yeah. But you know, a fortune like that makes you crazy. I heard all about it from Mom. Jacqueline had nothing to do all day, and no one but herself to please. That kind of egocentricity makes you cuckoo. I'm convinced of it."

"So you think your aunt was nuts? Maybe that's why she disappeared."

"I really don't think she was certifiable." Alyn's eyes darkened. "But how would I know? I never met Jacqueline Blum, remember?"

"You were going to. Tomorrow, in fact." Joyce's words faded to abysmal silence.

The headlines stared back at Alyn, their irony thick and bitter. Alyn found herself holding her breath. Finally the sentences came in one long exhale. "I don't know if she was crazy. All I know of her is what she told me on the phone when she called me after Mom's funeral. She said Mom had made the better choice. I mean—can you believe that? To be seduced and abandoned by the bum who was my father, the better choice? But Jacqueline had apparently always wanted a family, and she told me she was always jealous that my mom had had me.''

Alyn looked up from the paper. ''You know what, Joyce? If Jacqueline Blum was crazy, I don't care. I still believe what she said. Because Mom and I had a great life.'' There was more than a little more defiance on that last sentence.

''A great life, yes, but to the exclusion of half the human population,'' Joyce added.

''Hey, a dog loves you no matter what your bank account is, and he loves you if you get fat or wrinkled.'' Alyn laughed uncomfortably. ''Are you still trying to undo my mother's teachings?''

''Joe and I've been together for twenty years. When you find the right sub-species of male *homo sapiens,* I recommend them.''

''But don't you see? The Blum women were never good at finding the right ones. I guess I'm still carrying forward the Torch of Bad Judgment. You hated that last guy I dated, remember?''

''He was a clod. He bored you to tears.''

''Maybe I was the one who bored him. *He* quit calling *me,* if you recall.''

''Only because you're so dazzling. He couldn't handle you.''

''He told me I was uptight.''

''You have every right to be.''

Alyn glanced at her. ''Mom taught me more than I ever wanted to know about men. The older I get, the more I'm amazed at how strong she was to go it alone. But at least we had each other; meanwhile, Jacqueline had five husbands, none of them worth a damn. I'm glad you and Joe are happy, but give me a big ugly loyal mutt from the pound any day.''

Joyce smiled. ''Maybe you'll meet her after all. Maybe she's okay.''

''Sure. She probably just needed to get away, and nobody knows about it.''

Alyn again stared at the headlines of *The Boston Globe.* ''Five husbands, and Mom barely had one. Yet it seems like the same kind of loneliness. The same kind of yearning.''

''Just remember that you're not lonely, Dr. Jones. Not only do

Joe and I love you, but as we speak you have three clients drooling for you in the waiting room.'' Joyce handed her the files.

Alyn twisted her mouth in a wry smile.

''But let me know what I can do for you today, okay?'' Joyce patted her on the shoulder. ''I see you're worried. I think going down tonight is a good idea. I'll work on that plane reservation right now.''

''I never even met her. My celebrated aunt, and the only contact I ever had with her was a phone call and some letters. I can't believe now I might never meet her face to face. If she's really disappeared, for me it'll be like the great Jacqueline Blum never existed at all.''

''She kind of never did, Alyn. I mean, if your grandfather disowned your mother, Jacqueline didn't have to take sides in the battle. She could have kept in touch.'' Joyce's words were gentle but still reprimanding.

''Mom always thought it was guilt that kept Jacqueline away. Jacqueline had all the pie when she knew she should have only had half of it.'' Alyn looked at her. ''But you know, when she called after Mom's funeral, I don't think it was guilt at all. I think it was envy. Jacqueline didn't know Dad had left. She didn't know Mom had scratched out a living working at a drugstore. She didn't see the years of want and desperation that Mom had suffered because she had a child to support and no one to help her.

''Instead, I think Jacqueline pictured Mom and Dad deeply in love and living in that rose-covered cottage with their precious little child. And I don't think she could take it—because maybe what she said had been the truth. Maybe that *was* what Jacqueline really wanted so badly herself.'' Alyn shook her head. ''Oh, maybe her disappearance is just all a hoax. You know, like Agatha Christie. Maybe she'll turn up.''

''Maybe.''

''All those grocery store rags portray her as eccentric. Maybe she took off. Needed her space or something.''

''Possible.''

Alyn scanned the client files but her mind didn't quite register the information. Her thoughts were still on the headlines of the morning edition of *The Boston Globe.*

Quietly, she said, "But, Joyce, I've a bad feeling about this. People kill other people over ten bucks, let alone millions."

"I hate to even say it, but you may be right about that, honey," Joyce answered, her lips pulled in a frown.

* * *

The Masterlife Insurance Company headquarters took up a full twenty-acre industrial park along Peachtree Road in Atlanta. James Dunne's office was on the third floor of the Armisteade Building. As head of the Fraud Division, Dunne had his work cut out for him. Huddled around his desk were two other men in gray pin-striped suits.

"It's obvious," he said, laying his palms in a calculated position atop the Jacqueline Blum file.

"It may be obvious," answered his boss, Harry Fitzgerald, "but obvious isn't always proof. We need proof. That's why we've got to go up there and get some. Is the guy here yet?"

"No," said Dunne, "but he'll be here. We've heard he's the best. He can catch anyone."

"How does a bounty hunter become 'the best'?" Bo Parham, the youngest associate at Fraud, a newcomer to Masterlife whose trademark over-enthusiasm made Dunne sometimes wonder if Parham wasn't the reincarnation of a golden retriever, leaned on the edge of Dunne's desk. He stared raptly at his two mentors.

"This man Youngblood has averaged over a million dollars a year in returned bail bonds. If you're out there, he'll find you—at least that's what Atlanta's police commissioner told me." Dunne looked down at the thick file below his hands. He hoped like hell he was right. One misstep, and he might find himself working the grind again at Collision.

Fitzgerald nervously tapped a pencil on Dunne's desk.

"Hey, I hate to look stupid, but help me out here," Parham interjected. "The object is *not* to find Jacqueline Blum, isn't it? I mean, if we don't find her body within the year, we don't have to pay the policy, right?"

Harry Fitzgerald nodded grimly. His distinguished white head of hair gave him a paternal appearance that belied his renowned business ethics. Because of him, Masterlife was one of the most profitable insurance companies in the country. He was CEO *and* CFO, an unusual combination, but it worked. Masterlife was Fortune 500, and one of the reasons was because of the Fraud Division. It tickled Harry to death that—inside and outside of the corporation—they referred to Fitzgerald's pet division as the piranha-tank. The Fraud Division was his cherry on the sundae; often overlooked, but most profitable when well utilized.

"If something's happened to Jacqueline Blum in order to get Masterlife to pay the policy on her, the company doesn't have to do a thing until a death certificate is issued." Harry gave him a hearty-handshake kind of smile. "You see? If Jacqueline Blum's really a stiff by now, there's less than a year to produce the body and collect. Then our policy expires, and we're home free."

Bo looked more confused. "But why bring in this bounty-hunter guy if you don't want to find the Blum woman?"

"But we do want to find Mrs. Blum," Dunne answered with a veteran insurance man's calculated ring of sincerity. "We want to find her most desperately—alive, that is."

"And you think if she's still alive, Youngblood'll be able to track her down?" Bo scratched his head. Parham's expression was so canine Dunne almost wondered if the man was prone to using his foot for a head-scratcher.

"Precisely," Harry answered.

"But what if she's not alive? What if there's a body that turns up within a year?" Bo countered.

Harry stared at him. "Then we find our murderer before that, or we just pray the body never comes to light. Do you know what Masterlife will have to dole out if the death certificate is issued? Believe me, the profit margins will be slammed on just this policy alone."

Bo paled.

"Fitz," Dunne said, "I hate to ask this, but why wasn't the change in Blum's policy brought to my attention before now?"

"Paperwork glitch. The policy got filed without the proper investigation." Harry then tossed in, "Don't worry. The responsible party has departed this company."

Dunne could feel his anxiety level rise with his blood pressure.

The responsible party has departed this company. The words rang inside his head. "Listen, there won't be any paperwork glitches in my department. You can be sure of that."

"I know." Harry smiled.

Dunne knew his boss was sincere. Harry Fitzgerald was like most CEO's; as genuine and nurturing as a kindergarten teacher for the Hitler Youth.

"This thing should have been flagged. Especially when she changed beneficiaries, isn't that right?" Bo yammered.

"Certainly," Dunne answered, "but it's all water under the bridge now." He stared at the faxed headlines of the day's *Washington Post.* Jacqueline Blum was still front page news. Hell, she was still front page on the current *USA Today.* Her disappearance was a big damned mess, and he was in charge of it for Masterlife.

He gave a silent prayer to St. Jude. "Let's face it; unless this woman just walked off the edge of the world of her own volition, she was probably murdered, and a big part of her demise—if she is dead—was probably the policy. We need to find out what her will says."

"I'll contact her attorneys," Bo offered.

"Good. Now all we need is our bounty hunter to show up." Dunne looked at the door.

Harry stood. "He'll want to go to Maryland today. He can get started talking to Jacqueline Blum's friends, all of her social circle. I want to know why she changed the beneficiary to this life insurance policy, and I want to know why she did it only weeks before she disappeared."

"You say this man's able to track all this information down?" Bo looked at Dunne.

"Peter Youngblood's got the reputation for digging up information, bodies, and money." Dunne looked at Harry. "From what I've been told, he's also good at keeping them buried . . . if necessary."

Harry grinned. "I can see you've got this under control. Give my regards to Mr. Youngblood. If he's as good as you say he is, Dunne, you have my permission to offer two percent of the policy."

"Yes, sir. I'll call you as soon as anything new comes up."

Harry nodded and left the office.

"Two percent." Bo whistled. "That's more than four hundred

thousand. Not bad for some sleazy bondsman. Are you sure you don't want me to go after this case? I'll be happy to, you know. At least I've got an MBA. I'll bet this Youngblood guy's just some lowlife street character. I mean, how smart do you have to be to be a bounty hunter? He's not even a real policeman."

"I believe he was a policeman—some kind of homicide investigator—but don't ever mention it to him. Apparently it's a sore point."

Bo grunted. "Great. An ex-cop. Talk about a cliché. What a loser. Why don't they have me going to Maryland? I'm the one who can sniff out this kind of stuff. I mean, that's what I came aboard Masterlife to do."

Dunne was on the verge of getting irritated. "Youngblood knows what this is all about. That's why we decided to hire him. These are the kinds of games he plays every day. I was told he's the best by the highest authority."

"He'll sure as shit have the chance to prove it. Four hundred thousand smackers. That's a gross overpayment. It's not prudent for the company to pay that kind of money when they have competent persons on the payroll who can effectively—"

"Exactly, Bo. You're on the company roster. You get a paycheck, Youngblood doesn't. He gets zip if the case doesn't go his way. You want to take that kind of risk, be my guest. I'll call accounting and get you off the payroll immediately."

Bo frowned. "What's that supposed to mean?"

"I'm not a fancy MBA like you, Parham. I'm just some working-class grunt who rose from the ranks, but hey, I know the rules, and so does our bounty hunter. Youngblood gets his bucks only if we *don't* have to pay. He's the right man for this job. The *right* man."

Dunne paused. He looked at Bo and his irritation spilled. "Look at it this way, Parham, you don't need to get involved in this one because you're way ahead of the rest of us. Fitz loves you and you're next in line for a promotion. You don't need any more laurel wreaths beneath that fat white ass of yours."

Bo seemed to swallow a snarl. His face glazed over with an expression of corporate distaste, and he gestured toward the Blum file. "Who needs an MBA to figure this one out? It's Tinker Toys. Blum's life insurance policy is the reason she was killed. The previous beneficiaries were two men, relationship unknown. Ten days ago, Blum's attorneys wrote to Masterlife detailing Jacqueline Blum's new wishes that the old beneficiaries be canceled and the new one put into the policy. You don't need to be Einstein to get the answer to the equation of who mysteriously disposed of Jacqueline Blum."

"And what is the answer?" Dunne rasped.

"Alyn Blum-Jones," Bo responded, his gaze skimming the line of the life insurance policy entitled Beneficiaries.

"You think you know a lot, Parham, and maybe you do, but there's stuff about this case that you don't know, and have no need to know. So do what needs to be done and then back off."

"Is that really the best thing for Masterlife?" Bo smirked like a Freshman.

Dunne shrugged. He wasn't about to commit corporate suicide for a pudgy MBA from Emory. So, like an idiot, he said nothing.

* * *

"May I help you, sir?" asked the Masterlife receptionist on One. From her massive Eurostyle desk, she had to crane her neck to look up at the tall man standing in front of her.

"I'm looking for Dunne."

The receptionist's feather-rouged cheeks whitened. She nodded. Her gaze then lowered to the man's left arm where his muscles bulged out of his faded T-shirt. Just above the elbow was an exquisite tattoo of a cracked skull. A strange plant spilled out the top of it; one she couldn't identify. She'd never seen anything like it before, nor had she ever seen a man like this one—especially not in the reception entrance of dull Masterlife Insurance. He was tall, muscular and hard: hard of body, and if the cold gleam in his eye indicated anything, hard of mind.

"Do you have an appointment with Mr. Dunne?" The woman's hands trembled on the intercom button. Something made her nervous, and it probably had to do with the fact that the man looked like the type who was more accustomed to talking to someone behind bullet-proof glass than Italian *macchiato nero* marble.

She cleared her throat. "I really must ask if you have an appointment. Mr. Dunne is on the executive floor. I can't let you up there without prior approval."

He smiled. Something about him must have caught her off guard because her hand didn't hit the security button. Instead she stared up at him and mutely listened.

"There's a plane to Washington, D.C., leaving in an hour. If Dunne wants me to be on it, he needs to have his limo out front. Now."

"I'll—I'll give him the message." She didn't take her eyes off of him. Once he'd turned away, she had thoughts of summoning security, but she decided to call upstairs first.

"Miriam," she whispered into the receiver, her gaze all the while directed at the man slouched down on the thick marble bench near the main entrance, "listen, there's a man down here asking for Mr. Dunne, and he's got some kind of tattoo on his arm, and he said he's waiting for Mr. Dunne to call up his limo. The situation's a little weird so if you want me to call the guards—"

She stopped talking. Her eyes widened as she listened. "Okay. I'll ring the driver right away. Do you want me to tell the gentleman that Mr. Dunne will be right down? I'll do it now. Right away, I promise."

She replaced the receiver. With her eyes just as wide, she summoned the limo to the main entrance, then rose from her desk to tell the slouching man that the vice president of Masterlife was sprinting for the elevator in order to escort him to the airport.

CHAPTER TWO

Youngblood eased his tight shoulders and rested his glass of Johnnie Walker Blue Label on his bare torso. The scotch lingered on his palate like the taste of a woman. He tried to savor it, but it only left him with the wanting for more. Good scotch was like good sex. The better it was, the more he yearned for it.

He emptied the glass. Better to relish the desire for more than perish from a flood. He placed the crystal glass next to the mobile phone the very instant it rang.

"Yes," he grunted into the receiver.

"Did you get the job?" whispered a man's voice.

"Where the fuck do you think I'm sitting?"

"So you're in Maryland. In Blumfield."

"Yes." Youngblood glanced over to the bottle of Blue. But like a taste for sex, one had to be in the mood. His mood had suddenly soured.

"How much did Masterlife offer?"

"A little shy of half a mil."

"You know I'll pay you more—if this works out."

"I know," he answered woodenly.

"C'mon, Pete old boy. It's not often a person gets a chance like this. This is the daily double."

"I don't like playing both sides."

"Hey, look. I know how the police force screwed you. That's why I knew you were the man for the job."

"Yeah, fifteen years on the force and not one dickweed captain who would stick his neck out and tell the truth. But hey, what did I expect? I shoulda known I was the last good cop."

"But on this job you get to be the screwdriver and not the screw. Be happy about that."

"You'd know all about being the screwdriver, wouldn't you?" Youngblood answered bitterly. "I hear you made your first million running crack and your second selling a crack of the whip. Sure, keep up with the pep talks. I just might decide to do the right thing and pay you a visit and put you out of your fucking misery myself." He looked into the mobile phone, then grimly around at his surroundings.

"But you don't have one good reason to do the right thing anymore, Youngblood. And that's why you're mine."

Peter said nothing. His expression seemed chiseled out of granite.

The male voice on the other end seemed to hold his breath. "So, talk to me. What do you think of my plan?"

"I'm not going to kill anybody, if that's what you want to know."

"I'm not asking you to kill someone. I'm just asking for a little help. I mean, think of the chances of this happening ever again? I've got to find an angle on the situation. I've got to find some play here and take my turn at the wheel."

Youngblood was silent.

"Just keep your eyes on the money, Youngblood. It's so much money that the half million Masterlife is dangling out to you is going to look like a day at the track."

"I don't bet the ponies."

"If you go along with me, you won't ever have to."

"Just tell me what you want me to do."

"For now, report the situation to me. Tell me the details. Tell me about the girl. I want all the information about her you can get. Especially how involved she is."

"She's in it up to her ass as far as I can tell."

"Good. But I want details. I want to know all about her. Where she goes. What she does. What she eats. Who she questions. Who she fucks. I want to know everything. Is that clear?''

''Like a mountain stream. But what's looking like radioactive ooze right now is your motivation.''

''You don't need to dick with my motivation, Youngblood. All you need to do is report to me and take your loot. You understand?''

''I'm not a cheap whore.'' Youngblood grinned into the receiver. ''You can ask Masterlife about that.''

''You may not be cheap, but you're well worth the cost. Just do as I ask and the pot of gold at the end of the rainbow will be yours.''

''Rainbows and unicorns, a fairy princess and white castles in the sky. So how come everybody in this little storybook winds up dead?''

''Has Jacqueline been found? Do you know she's dead for a fact?''

Youngblood's mouth twitched with a smile. ''She hasn't been found but I know she's dead.''

''How do you know?'' the man grumbled.

''You're plotting, aren't you? You're building this house of cards on a whopper of an assumption, but it's only because you know what the odds are. It's twenty to one the woman's dead.''

''I want to know everything. Everything, you hear me, or the deal's off.''

''How come you think I'm such a lowlife bastard that I'd do anything for a few bucks?''

''Two reasons.'' The man laughed. ''One: it's not a few bucks we're talking about. Two: you're just a lowlife because you were made into one. You wanted to be a blue knight, and they screwed you out of a badge and out of your honor. What more do you have now? Nothing. Zip. Just a sweet need for revenge on the whole fucking world. So take your revenge, Youngblood. Think how good it will feel to screw back.''

Youngblood wiped his mouth on his knuckles. The need to tell him to fuck off was like an explosion in his gut, but the words wouldn't come. He couldn't deny his own living, breathing truth.

''I'll give you a call when I find something.''

"Don't sort it out yourself. Let me do that. I want to know everything about her."

Youngblood grunted and hit the END button on the mobile phone.

He went to pour another glass of scotch, but suddenly the taste for it was dead. As dead as the eighteen-year-old Vietnamese restaurant worker he was accused of murdering.

A shot of white anger flickered through him. What the hell was he doing freelancing out to that dirtbag? Even with all his years as a cop he'd never met such an amoral dick of a man as that guy was.

He lifted the Johnnie Walker Blue and felt the urge to smash the two-hundred-dollar bottle into the fireplace.

But he stopped himself. It would only burn. It would go to waste. Like he was.

He placed the bottle down on the table and poured himself another fine glass. And he comforted himself with the notion that as much of an asswipe as that guy on the phone was, Masterlife Insurance was probably an even bigger one.

* * *

The Delta Airlines flight #1946 from Boston arrived at Dulles just after midnight. Alyn rented a small red Geo from Thrifty Rent-A-Car and took off into the Virginia night headed toward the Washington Beltway.

Somewhere around Herndon it started to rain.

At first it was just a cold mist fogging up the windshield. Next came the clatter of hail. Finally, curtains of rain hit the car in horizontal blasts which pushed her into the dividing line. The shoulder of the highway and the brake lights of the car ahead melted into a graphite watercolor. Nothing was visible except the windshield wipers that clacked back and forth in a mocking metronome.

The Geo was little better than a tin can on wheels. Even without the bad weather Alyn had a devil of a time keeping pace with the frenetic interstate traffic that winged past at 80 mph. She wanted to kiss the ramp when she saw the Maryland exit for River Road. Her aunt's estate was at the very end of it, halfway to Frederick, but at least on the two-lane road she wasn't going to get run over by any eighteen-wheelers.

Alyn toodled past the intersection that marked the center of Potomac Village. The icy rain was still driving hard but at a slower speed, she didn't feel it knock the automobile as it had on the Beltway.

Soon she found herself in the countryside, on a road unlit by streetlights; where miles of rain-sodden hills were pockmarked with subdivisions pretentiously named after hunt clubs.

Four hundred and fifty thousand for a prefab colonial, and you too can count yourself among the horsey set, Alyn thought as she passed what she hoped was the runny lights of the last subdivision. She went ten miles more in the darkness and the rain, and settled into countryside of the kind Potomac had been in the pre-Kennedy years when it was just a bumpkin town surrounded by the emerald-lawned estates of diplomats and senators.

She was fooling with the Geo's radio when she realized she'd come to the end of the road. In the torrents of rain, she'd missed the gates.

Blumfield was almost a thousand acres. Jacqueline had written to Alyn proudly stating that hers was the largest "farm" near the District of Columbia. The estate was marked by a gatehouse of gray fieldstone and an enormous wrought-iron gate with the letter *B* in sterling silver that, according to her aunt's account, had to be polished every morning and every night.

Alyn pulled to the side of the road. She wiped the condensation on the inside of the windshield with a Kleenex but it only made matters worse. Now her line of vision was obscured with condensation and swirls of lint.

She released a groan of frustration. The car radio faded in and out as if it too were playing hide-and-seek with her. She clicked it off and cautiously turned the Geo around. Driving slowly, her nose pressed to the windshield, she tried to follow the fieldstone fence to the right until it met with the enormous Blumfield gatehouse.

At last it appeared, just as Jacqueline had described it. The gate's silver *B* shone in the Geo's headlights like the monogram on a giant's pinky ring. The gatehouse was the size of a small chateau, but no guard sat inside it. It was dark. She didn't know whether to be relieved or afraid.

Alone and in the driving night rain, she arrived at Blumfield with nothing to greet her but an intercom stand, and a buzzer. A driveway lined with budding dogwood and forsythia probably went to the house—if she could only get to the other side of the locked gate.

She parked the car and rolled down her window. The riotous storm was far-reaching and loud. No crickets competed with the sound of splattering rain, and Blumfield was so far from Washington that there was no hum of the city like Alyn had in her little house outside Quincy. The only things she heard besides the rain were the screech of the wind through the spring-bare tree branches, and the foreboding creak of the gate as it protested beneath the pummeling of the storm.

She braved the freezing rain and stuck her hand out the window to the buzzer. A camera she hadn't noticed before, which was mounted on the roof of the gatehouse, automatically turned to her direction. The lens retracted to focus. She didn't know whether to talk to the camera or the intercom.

But it was a moot point when no one answered her buzzer.

She pressed the lit button again.

Still no answer.

There was nothing for her at Blumfield but the cartoon eyeball of the camera lens staring down at her in the pouring rain.

She hadn't figured on no one being at the estate. Her aunt was missing, but it seemed that the servants should still be in the house. They should still be at their jobs until told otherwise. It only made sense.

She rolled up the Geo window and blotted the soaked door with her wad of Kleenex. Suddenly she realized how tired she was. She'd seen at least ten cats and seventeen dogs in her practice today. Her clothes still smelled of formaldehyde and rubbing alcohol because she hadn't taken the time to change before throwing her things into a carry-on and jumping on the shuttle to D.C.

Now it seemed clear that she'd reacted hastily. She wondered if she turned on the radio she might even find out that her aunt had turned up in Paris, or Manhattan, and everything was fine. And Alyn had come to Washington for nothing.

But she couldn't leave until she was sure. If Jacqueline Blum was right now sipping Dom Perignon at the Beverly Hills Hotel, then so be it. But she wanted to know that.

She released a deep breath and backed the red Geo out of the drive. In her mind she reviewed her options: she could go to Gaithersburg and see about a cheap hotel room and return to Blumfield in the morning, or she could do the smart thing and return to Dulles, go back to her practice in Quincy, and wait for news there.

Yet when did a Blum woman ever do the smart thing, she asked herself ruefully.

She was just about to back onto a darkened River Road when she heard the squeak of metal against metal. In front of her, the silver *B* was slowly sliding to the right. The gate was opening like the entrance to the Emerald City.

Like a cautious Dorothy, she hesitated, shifted gears and drove the Geo up to the gate. There had been no greeting, no questions through the intercom; whoever was behind the camera had now deemed her a worthy visitor.

The thought of why ricocheted through her thoughts like a bullet. She was a scientist and she possessed a scientist's mind. Every question had an answer. You just had to be dogged enough to venture forth and find it—sometimes through the dark and the rain, and at the mercy of strangers.

Steeling herself, she bumped the small car over the tracks of the sliding gate and stopped again. The hairs rose on her nape like the hackles of a canine.

The drive was pitch black and obliterated by a wall of rain. The road went only-God-knows-where. Someone of great importance could be waiting for her at the end of it, or someone evil. Perhaps the person who knew exactly what had happened to her aunt.

She accelerated to fifteen miles per hour and turned on the brights. She'd come to be of some help, to find out the answers to her questions and she was going to do that here. She couldn't do it in Quincy.

But she was filled with doubt and apprehension. Chances were her aunt was still missing, and it seemed likely that something dire had happened to her. The worst of it was that Alyn had never even gotten to know her famous relative. She'd had the temerity to attempt to solve a mystery about which she hadn't even the slightest clue. Jacqueline Blum was a total stranger to her. Her mother had mentioned her, of course, and Jacqueline had called after the funeral last year when Alyn buried her mother. But after the usual talk, even Alyn had figured the woman would never contact her again.

What a shock it had been to get Jacqueline's letter a month ago. The famous and rich Jacqueline Blum had been visited by the same apocalyptic horseman who'd run down her mother. *Breast cancer.* Suddenly Jacqueline wanted to talk about her sister Colette. She wanted Alyn to tell her all about her mother's struggles and triumphs. With one small mass of unruly cells, Jacqueline Blum had been thrown into the human race, and she had just now, fifty years after the fact, wanted to make those familial connections that one does when one is scared to death.

The note had been chatty and friendly, written by hand on the Blumfield engraved Crane stationery. It had clearly been an overture, and Alyn's curiosity had got the better of her. She'd written back and told her aunt all the fun details of the small animal practice she had, and all the anecdotal stories of her climb through veterinary school.

Again, Alyn expected to be blown off; again, a letter arrived in a thick cream-colored Crane envelope, this time while Jacqueline detailed the names of her treasured Thoroughbreds that lived in her stables.

Jacqueline and Alyn found they had a common love of animals. It seemed only natural for Jacqueline to ask her niece to visit the estate, and Alyn found she actually wanted to do it. Not only because Jacqueline Blum was one of the richest heiresses in America, but because she was the only relative Alyn had left in the world, and the sheer loneliness of life without her mother had finally driven her to accept Jacqueline Blum's very belated invitation of a week at Blumfield.

If only Jacqueline were here at Blumfield now. The two women could get to know each other, and maybe Jacqueline could tell

Alyn some things about growing up with Colette. Alyn deeply missed her mother. It had been over a year since the funeral, but the void was still there and probably always would be.

The road wound through rain-whipped elm forests and fields of limp hay. She guided the car over an organic bridge hewn from enormous crepe myrtle limbs that had to have been a masterpiece of engineering. Below her, she could hear the torrents of an overflowing brook, and between opaque walls of rain, she could make out the manicured rhododendrons that lined the hilly edges of the creek bottom. Even in a storm, she knew she was in a fantastic place. Blumfield clearly had had no expense spared in its design and upkeep.

A smeary light shone through the trees. She could make out the silhouette of a large fieldstone colonial house. She drove another quarter mile and turned into the driveway. No one was out front. The lights of the house were off except for a small lamp in the window of the second floor.

She parked the Geo in the circular drive. Leaving the car unlocked, she pocketed the keys and ran to the colonial's front entrance.

A huge lion-headed brass knocker graced the pedimented door. She lifted it and the echo sounded like a death knell. The boom rang all through the rain and yowling wind, but no matter how fiercely she pounded, it didn't seem to rouse the occupant of the house.

"Hello? Anybody home?" she called to the second-story window. "Jacqueline?" she tried to no avail. No one stirred.

She slammed the knocker again and this time found the doorbell behind an over-grown azalea branch. Ringing it several times, she swore she saw the curtains on the second floor move. Someone was inside the house. Someone had to be. The gate didn't open on its own.

"Hello . . . ?" she called through the pouring rain. Her violet polarfleece vest was soaked. Her leggings clung to her like Saran Wrap. Icy wetness shivered through her body.

Suddenly the front door swung open.

"Who the hell are you?" A man's gruff voice came from the darkened foyer.

"I'm—I'm Alyn Blum-Jones. I'm Jacqueline's niece. I came to see if—if she's been found." Alyn hated to stammer but it was disconcerting to be talking to a strange, shadowy man who clearly didn't expect her.

"Alyn Jones? Her niece?"

In a flash the outside lantern went on. Alyn felt as if she were put underneath a spotlight.

"May I come in?" she asked slowly, shivering. "I've come all the way from Boston tonight. I wanted to find out what's going on with Jacqueline." She squinted against the light. The foyer was still in darkness. The man was still only a shadow, but a large shadow at that.

"Come in," he said with the same harsh voice he'd used before.

She braced herself. There was no way to know what she was getting into. It suddenly seemed as if coming here to Blumfield to investigate her aunt's disappearance was the most impetuous thing she'd ever done.

She had no choice but to enter her aunt's home and deal with this man who'd answered the door. She was, after all, Jacqueline's only relative. She had a right to know what had happened to her aunt.

"I've come to see if Jacqueline's been found. I had a visit already planned but after reading the papers, I thought—well—I thought it best to come now."

There she went again. Stammering.

He shut the door behind her.

Nervously she leaned against it, not at all sure of her welcome.

He flipped on a light. His face was remarkably handsome for a man who had all the rough facial hair of an escaped convict and the chilling amber eyes of Blake's "tyger."

"Come back here," he instructed.

Hesitant, she followed his tall figure into a large room to the right of the foyer. He flipped on a switch. Suddenly she could see they were in a formal room.

"Is it wishful thinking to wonder if she's here?" Alyn asked, her gaze scanning her surroundings. By all accounts of the living room, her aunt lived well, but much more simply than Alyn would have believed. The reports on CNN detailing Jacqueline's opulent lifestyle made Alyn believe the woman would have had a bigger house and less casual furnishings than the damask slipcovered love seats and the pair of matching walnut highboys that flanked the fieldstone fireplace.

"She's not here."

Alyn's gaze riveted to the man who stood by the lamp. He was a good twelve inches taller than she with the kind of muscular build she figured could only belong to a steroid-pumped *Baywatch* extra. She knew how good his body was, because the man wore nothing but a pair of wrinkled flannel boxers in a pattern of black and green plaid. From his mussed hair and baleful expression, she realized she'd probably gotten him out of bed.

"Oh, I'm sorry. I didn't realize—well, the gate opened and I thought—well . . ." Her cheeks grew hot. It was bad enough waking the man up, but now she was going to make a fool of herself and blush.

"Jacqueline Blum hasn't turned up yet." He stared at her with the most wary eyes she'd ever seen. If the man were a little happier, she'd probably think him attractive—in a crude Harley-Davidson kind of way—but as it was, he left her cold. His only sign of emotion was a vaguely contemptuous lifting of the corner of his stony mouth.

"When was the last time you saw Jacqueline Blum?" he asked abruptly.

Taken off guard, she just shook her head. "I've never met her. Never even seen her."

It was not possible, but she could almost swear that the man knew who she was. The minute he held her gaze she had the distinct feeling in her gut that he didn't like her.

"That's sweet. You've never laid eyes on the woman and yet, here you appear, on this rainy night, the picture of altruism and concern. The timing's a little fortunate, don't you think?"

"Fortunate?" she repeated, confused.

He said nothing.

"Is—has there been any new information?" she blurted, unnerved by the rake of his malevolent eyes. She couldn't shake the idea that this man felt as if he were looking at Lizzie Borden.

"I was sent here to wait for a ransom note. As if there'll ever be one." He laughed. It was a most unpleasant sound.

Crossing his arms over his chest, he leaned against the built-in walnut bookcases. She then noticed the tattoo. Out from the crucible of a cracked skull sprang a plant that covered most of his thickly muscled upper arm.

She stared at it, and because of her pharmaceutical background, she knew exactly what it was. It was ghastly.

"So has there been any news at all?" She met his gaze, unsure if he would answer.

"Do you think there'll be a ransom involved, Miss Jones?"

"I don't know," she said, forcing herself to remain calm beneath the man's strange assessment of her. "All I know is that I came to help. I want to help."

"Have you come for a memento? A trophy? What about the best trophy of all, Miss Jones: Jacqueline Blum's complete disappearance. If we have no body, we'll never be able to tie this little murder up. There'll be no money paid, but then there'll be no evidence; and no conviction; and no"—his gaze flickered down at her arm—"lethal injection."

"What are you implying?" she whispered, her heart pounding in horror and sudden anger.

He seemed taken aback by her reaction; as if he didn't quite expect it. "Of course she's been murdered." His voice was stone hard.

Slowly she lowered herself to the love seat. It was stuffed with down, quite luxurious. Perhaps her aunt had known how to live after all. Alyn certainly hoped so, if Jacqueline had come to an untimely end.

"So are you a cop?" she finally asked, looking up at the half-naked man standing absurdly by the bookcases. Somehow she had to place him in this mess. He had to have some involvement at Blumfield or he wouldn't be the one staying in Jacqueline's house.

"Peter Youngblood." He didn't crack a smile. The gold eyes turned into slits. Studious, suspicious little slits. "What do your friends call you, Miss Jones? Alyn? Or do they call you Al?"

"My friends call me Dr. Blum-Jones," she said, her words cold against the derision of his.

"You're a medical doctor? That's right up there, isn't it? You must be one helluva egghead."

She could have knifed herself in the back just with the tone of his voice. "I'm a D.V.M., I guess not quite as highbrow as you'd suppose." She stood. "Are you a friend of my aunt's, Mr. Youngblood? Do you work for her? It's difficult not to wonder about you. You don't seem to be quite the person I expected to find here at Blumfield."

His expression was one of contempt, and Alyn couldn't shake the notion that the contempt was for her. "You could say I've been hired to look after your aunt's finances. If she returns I really want to give her some good down-home advice. Such as don't trust strangers."

"I'm sure she'd appreciate it." She gave him a derisive glance. He was a stranger, but for some inexplicable reason he seemed to know her. The way he looked at her, it was almost as if he knew more about her than she knew herself, and she couldn't help but wonder why.

"I really must know how the investigation is going. Who's the one in charge of the investigation? How do you fit into it? I came all the way from Boston to find out, so I really need answers." Her take-charge demeanor was a bit of a facade, but she hoped it would bring some information.

"I need answers too."

His words sent an injection of ice down her spine. It occurred to her again that if her aunt had been murdered, she could be talking to the murderer right now.

Against her will, she thought of the scene in *Psycho* when Norman Bates invites the shivering traveler into his back room for sandwiches.

"If there's been no news, I guess I should be going. I'm tired and I suppose I should get some rest so that I can talk to the police tomorrow. Let them know what little I know."

"You want to talk to the police? Let's call them right now, shall we? I know the FBI's number by heart." He walked to a portable black phone that sat on a desk by the bookcases. Picking it up, he gave her a dark smile.

"I don't really have anything to say that we need to call them in tonight. I just have her letters with me, that's all." She wondered why she sounded so nervous.

''Her letters?'' His gaze did a derisive scan of her face.

''Yes. She wrote to me. Just a few times, but I thought I should bring them to the authorities in case they might help.'' She looked to the foyer and front door beyond. ''They're in the car. I suppose if you think it's important, I'll get them and you can call the police now.''

He put down the phone, almost disappointedly. ''Why don't you let me have a look at them first.''

She glanced down at his well-muscled torso. Paranoia began to pace inside her. She was certainly no physical match for him. If he wanted to see what was in her letters before the police did, he would win the contest.

Instinct told her to mollify him. Show him the letters. They were rather unremarkable in any case.

Her gaze met his. Against her will, she could feel her face heat up again. ''I'll be right back.''

He said nothing. He only glared after her like a cat ready to spring.

She returned with her purse. Inside the pocket of her Coach handbag, she extracted her aunt's letters. She handed them to him. He'd never moved from the bookcases.

''These were so recent, that's why I thought to bring them.'' She looked at him and frowned. ''You're not some kind of police officer—or detective are you? You seem to know so much—''

''These are photocopies.'' He roughly handed them back to her.

''Yes, I didn't think anyone would need to see the originals.''

''A photocopy could be forged.''

''Yes, but these aren't forged. At least—I don't think so.'' Alyn looked down at the papers in her hand. She never thought that the letters might not have been written by her aunt, but Alyn didn't know Jacqueline's handwriting. Indeed, if someone had gotten hold of some Blumfield stationery and mailed the letters at Potomac Village, anyone who received them would think they were what they seemed.

Her paranoia broke into a gallop.

''Jacqueline Blum is missing. Only facts will find her.'' He stared at her.

She looked up at him, helpless and afraid. "Who are you?" she asked, the hair on her nape raising again. Peter Youngblood was a strange character. Here he was half-naked, making himself at home in her missing aunt's house, accusing her just by his eyes.

"I'm the guest who came to dinner, and now won't leave," he said to her just as softly.

"I need to go. I have to get to a hotel room. I'd like to get some rest, and I've got to go all the way out to Gaithersburg," she murmured, backing away from the living room.

"You can go to the mansion if you want to be put up here."

"This—this—?" She was back to stammering again. She wondered if her eyes could open any wider or if she could have looked more naïve. The house they were in was nice but it made sense Jacqueline lived in a grander building on the property. "This isn't Jacqueline's house?" she finished softly, almost defeated.

"Hell no." He laughed darkly. "This is just the guest cottage. The mansion's further up the road."

He gave her a cold smile. "Hang on. Let me get a shirt and jeans, and I'll take you there. There's somebody I want you to meet."

Holding her breath, she watched him leave the room. Suddenly the rain and the cold outside didn't seem as bad as where she was now.

CHAPTER THREE

"I can't stand it anymore, Georgy. I have to call," Mabel Haskings mused aloud to her tabby cat George III. She poured herself another glass of J&B scotch, then sat back in bed, her bleary gaze returning again and again to the phone.

George III meowed and rolled onto his back. Mabel scratched his tummy, an automatic gesture which she could perform drunk or sober.

"If I don't call, they may never know. And if something's happened to the woman, I'll never forgive myself. I've got to call." She rose out of bed and steadied herself on the phone table. Taking a deep breath, she dialed the police non-emergency number printed on the inside cover of the phone book.

"Yes, I would like to speak to someone about Jacqueline Blum."

There was a long pause. Mabel downed her glass of scotch and poured another. Her dreams had been left at the altar; now her soul belonged to J&B.

"Yes, I'm the one calling about Jacqueline Blum," she said when a man answered the phone. "To whom am I speaking, please?" she asked in her most sober bank teller voice.

"This—is—Detective Armstrong," came the halting reply.

"My name is Ms. Haskings. I'm with the Chase Bank Branch Number 383. I had to call you."

''Has the bank received a ransom request?''

''No, no, certainly not,'' Mabel said, warming up to her task with a little more J&B fire. ''We, at the bank, would have called you immediately if that were the case. No, this is just a concerned citizen who wants to give you some information about Jacqueline Blum.''

''Go ahead,'' came the distracted voice.

''Well, we, at Branch Number 383, have a safety deposit box of hers.''

Mabel waited for the bomb to drop. She paused and winked at George III who was taking the news well if his purring was any indication.

''Okay. And?'' Detective Armstrong could be heard in the background balling up paper.

''And that's the information. She has a safety deposit box at our branch of the Chase.''

Mabel was hard-pressed to take the exhale at the other end of the phone as concern.

''Look,'' she said, swallowing her exasperation with another jolt of scotch, ''I'm not a little old lady who's got herself confused. I didn't have to call. I just thought the police should know this.''

''Why do you think this is important?'' Armstrong asked, his tone impatient.

''Because it is important. We have her only safety deposit box in the whole of Chase Bank. Why doesn't she just open a box at her own damn bank?'' Mabel started getting angry. ''You know, I even have a pen that she signed her name with.'' Her gaze went to her bureau where the Chase pen was kept in a satin box. ''She used it herself.''

''All right. Fine. Is this Mabel Haskings I'm speaking to? Riverside Drive, Apartment 4B?''

Mabel stared at the receiver. ''Yes. Yes, it is,'' she said excitedly.

''Look, I've taken note of your call. I'll pass it along to the proper authorities. That's really all I can do, okay? Good night.''

''But—how—how did you know my first name and where I lived?''

''It's all on the computer when you call. At least we didn't have to work a trace.''

Mabel's eyes widened. "You thought you needed to trace my call? I told you we haven't received any ransom requests. I'm not a crook like that greasy Ferrucci character—"

"Thank you, lady. You have a good night." The phone clicked as Detective Armstrong hung up.

Mabel replaced the receiver. She poured another glass of J&B and held it with shaking hands. Men made her so mad. Her boss was like that. Dismissive. Curt. A Yes/No kind of guy. As cold as the North Atlantic. And he thought he knew everything, just like that stupid Detective Armstrong.

"It was valuable information, Georgy," she whispered as she crawled back into bed.

She took the last swig from her glass, then she passed out, the words, "They'll live to regret this," repeating on her lips.

* * *

Armstrong was on desk duty at the precinct until 11:00 P.M. As was his habit, at precisely 10:45 he went to the coffeepot for his last cup of the night.

"Any Bailey's Irish Cream to go with that?" his partner James shot out as he passed by.

"I wish," Armstrong grunted as he distastefully looked down into his Styrofoam cup. "Hey, I got some things to get out—would you mind? My kid's going to be in the school debate team tomorrow morning. I gotta get moving."

"Sure," James answered. "What do you have?"

"Here are the Olenda files." Armstrong piled them on James's desk. "And here are my faxes ready to go out now. The one to the FBI's kind of lame, but I figure I'd better pass it on anyway. It's info on the Jacqueline Blum case."

"Sure will." James grinned. He waved bye-bye to his partner, then he handed the files and the faxes to Lola, their secretary.

"Hey, he said for you to do this." Lola scowled. She scowled well, too, for it was one of her particular talents as a sixty-five-year-old Puerto Rican who'd married a GI.

"I'm outta here. I've got a stake out."

"You'll owe me for this. You'll owe me," Lola ranted, only half-joking. As it was she was drowning in paperwork.

"I'll owe you then." James cupped her cheek and passed his trademark game-show-host grin. Then he shrugged on his coat and disappeared.

Lola rolled her eyes.

Angrily, she snatched up the papers and took them to the fax room. She never noticed the Haskings memo that fell behind her onto the linoleum floor. Nor did the janitor when he swept it up and threw it away.

CHAPTER FOUR

"Who exactly is here at the estate handling the case?" Alyn asked as she drove the Geo along a wide picket-lined drive that wound toward the Blum mansion.

Peter Youngblood gave her a surly look. "What case?"

Alyn watched him in the dark of the car. He'd thrown on a pair of jeans over the Black Watch boxers and shrugged his shoulders into a faded blue T-shirt, but he hadn't done much more than that. His hair was just as tousled, and his feet were bare.

"What do you mean, 'what case?' " she said, pulling her gaze back to the night road. "I'm just curious as to who's here handling my aunt's disappearance. What authorities are involved exactly?"

He rubbed his jaw. "The police have her officially listed as a missing person."

"Okay. What else is going on?"

"Nothing. Everyone's been doing a real good job of sitting around with their thumb up their ass."

She shot him a contemptuous glance. "You know, it's none of my business, but if I were in need of a financial advisor, I'd hardly pick someone like—"

"Someone like me?" He grinned.

She trained her eyes on the dark roadway once more. "It's none of my business really."

"Damn right."

His words were like acid. She didn't like him, but what was really certain was that he didn't like her.

She took a deep, calming breath. "I only wanted to know what's been done about her disappearance. I'm concerned. I came all the way from Boston to find out."

"Jacqueline Blum is officially listed as missing. She hasn't been seen for seven days and ten hours. That's more than good enough for the authorities to list someone as missing in action, but until there's evidence pointing to a crime, they have nothing else to go on."

"Who first reported her missing?"

"Her majordomo."

"Was she close to him?"

He grunted.

"But surely the FBI, the police, s*omeone,* has some leads," she gasped. "A woman like Jacqueline Blum doesn't wander away for no reason. I can't believe every authority this side of the Beltway isn't crawling the grounds looking for evidence of foul play."

"You sound as if Jacqueline Blum is entitled to more attention just because she's a million-billion-zillionaire. Well, it doesn't work like that. A missing mother of four kids is someone who the police are going to burn up the roads to find, not some rich woman who just might have disappeared because she's bored and eccentric and can go anywhere she likes at any time for any reason and tell no one."

She gripped the steering wheel, exasperated. "I don't expect my aunt to receive special attention just because she's wealthy, but a woman is missing here. I don't think she decided to just walk away. She wrote me just the other week to plan my trip up here. Why would she do all that if she was planning to disappear? I didn't need the mystery if that's what her goal was. Neither does the public."

"Perhaps that's all this is. Maybe it's nothing more than a publicity stunt."

Alyn shook her head. "The last thing Jacqueline Blum of the Blum Cereals fortune needed was publicity. She couldn't sneeze without someone writing something catty about her. Why would she give them this fuel for the fire?"

"She's given it to them all right. She's disappeared without a trace. That's enough for the *National Enquirer* to do an eight-page spread, but not enough for the police or the FBI to do more than take note of her disappearance and file it away."

"So no one's doing anything about it?"

"I didn't say that."

He looked at her.

Even in the dim light of the car's interior she could see his expression and the harsh grim line of his mouth.

"It's unbelievable to me that a woman can disappear and the authorities aren't doing more than just noting it down like a bunch of bored secretaries."

"Jacqueline Blum's got three strikes against the authorities finding out what happened to her."

"Which are?"

He smirked. "She's rich, so she has the means to hide away if she wants to—there's no law against it, and the police know it; she could be an eccentric—I mean, hell, the tabloids write her up all the time as jumping from one inappropriate man to another, and that works against her when it comes to looking for motive of why she would want to disappear; finally, she's alone. She's got no one to miss her. That's a big part of the problem. With no one complaining to the police—with no little kids crying for their mommy—they don't keep her on their priority list."

"I'll keep her on the list," Alyn said quietly, her gaze wandering over the dark countryside in front of them. "I'll be her voice, if I must. This isn't right, what's happened. I know it. I think I can feel something terrible's gone on here."

He said nothing.

She could feel his stare like the lick of a serpent.

Finally he said in a quiet voice, "Sure something terrible's happened here. Jacqueline Blum's been murdered, and no one gives a shit."

"God, I hope not. Something has to turn up. If that's truly what happened, then somehow, someway, they'll have to find something."

"Oh, they'll find her body, all right."

She gave him a quizzical look. "Why do you say that? You sound so certain."

"She can't be declared officially dead until there's a body. C'mon. You knew that, Miss Jones."

She frowned. Everyone was nuts here at Blumfield. Maybe it was the water. He was talking to her like she knew way more than she did.

"No, I didn't know that, Mr. Youngblood, and I suspect if Jacqueline has indeed been murdered, she doesn't care much about proving herself officially dead."

"Ah, yes, the cruel paradox." He grinned again.

Alyn was more than relieved to see the lights of the mansion up ahead. Peter Youngblood made no sense. His humor was dark and inscrutable. She more than half wondered if maybe he had something to do with Jacqueline's disappearance. Everyone had to be suspect until they found out the truth. Instinct told her that the sooner she was rid of him, the healthier it would be.

"Here we are." He lept out of the Geo as soon as she parked it. He was like a kid ready to head for Disney World. "Have you met Hector Dante, Dr. Jones?" he asked with glee in his voice.

"No, of course not. Isn't it obvious I've never been here before?" she rattled on, trying to find her purse in the dark of the back seat.

"Oh, then you must meet him. He's your kind of guy. I haven't determined whether Hector was screwing your aunt or if it was Ferrucci, the stable master. Hey, maybe they both were." He smiled down at her after taking her arm. "And I use the word 'screw' in both a figurative and literal sense."

Oh, God, get me away from this lunatic. Alyn gave him a bright smile. "Well, let's meet him, I suppose."

They walked up the drive to the front of the mansion. To Alyn, the place looked as big as the Metropolitan Museum of Art. She counted five wings just on the right side of the building alone. They passed through a neoclassical portico held up by a dozen black marble columns and reached the gilt and mahogany front door which loomed like the entrance to Napoleon's tomb.

"You look pale, Doctor. Just think"—he smiled and swept his

hand along the panorama of Ionic columns—"one day all this could be yours."

"But I never even met her," she blurted out.

"No? Well, then it's not personal, is it?" He took her elbow and pressed her forward to face the front door.

With a confidence she surely did not feel, he rang the doorbell.

"Who is this Hector Dante?" she whispered as they waited.

"He calls himself the majordomo."

"You said that before. What is that?"

"Majordomo. It's a pretentious name for a butler. Hey! Maybe this all centers on that old cliché that the majordomo did it!" He squeezed her elbow just as the locks on the front door began to unbolt. "But don't count on it," he whispered ominously to her.

"Hector! My dear old friend. Look who I found at my cottage." He thrust Alyn forward as if she were a gun moll. "Auntie Jack just got a visit from her niece. Miss Blum-Jones here has been very worried about her."

Alyn came face to face with a short dark-haired man. Hector Dante was handsome with black eyes and aristocratic cheekbones, but welts of acne-cratered skin marred his features and gave him a street-meanness that even the costly cashmere robe he wore couldn't overcome.

"Who is this?" Dante demanded, in a thick Brazilian accent.

"Hector. I let her in. She buzzed at the gate." A woman's voice sounded out from behind him. She was a matronly figure in her sixties with artificial jet curls that had all the luminosity of a black hole. She clutched her wrapper to her chest and padded across the marble floor.

"Giselda. Go back. I'll take care of it then," Dante snapped.

Giselda scudded backward as if she'd been hit. She gave Alyn a gaze, then Youngblood, then she meekly nodded and retired into the rooms from which she came.

"This is Mrs. Blum's niece, Hector, old boy."

Alyn looked back and forth between both men. She still hadn't said a word. Propriety forced her to speak up. "My aunt invited me to Blumfield for tomorrow, but under the circumstances I felt I should come now and see if I can be of some assistance."

Dante stared at her. His gaze took in every feature of her face from her hazel eyes behind gold-rimmed spectacles to her mouth that had to have long ago worn away the coral lipstick she'd put on in Boston.

"Miss Jones, how good of you to come. Your aunt spoke highly of you." Dante bowed. Alyn almost believed him except for the poisonous glance he darted toward Youngblood.

"I know this wasn't expected. I really don't expect accommodation. There's a hotel in Gaithersburg. At a time like this I couldn't think of inconveniencing you—"

"He's the help, for God's sakes. How inconvenient can it be, right, Hector old boy?" Youngblood slapped him on the back like Hector Dante was some kind of Georgia redneck priming his fingers for the banjo.

"I'll show you to a room, Miss Jones." Dante ignored Youngblood and looked down at her empty hands. "Have you any bags?"

"They're in the car." She pointed lamely toward the red Geo. Inside she was numb, and more than a little fearful.

The majordomo looked across the portico and spied the tiny red car. He did little to hide the expression on his face. Clearly he was unimpressed.

"It's just a rental car," she mumbled when he was beyond hearing distance.

"Hector's my old pal. Don't be too quick to judge him. You and he have a lot in common." Youngblood watched her, arms across his chest, as he'd done in the living room of the cottage.

Alyn looked around her; anything to avoid conversations with Youngblood. The mansion's foyer had the *de rigueur* black and white marble floor, a magnificent curving staircase with bronze handrails, and a jungle of potted orchids tucked beneath the stair. The Joshua Reynolds—at least she was pretty sure it was a Joshua Reynolds—at the top of the staircase gave the foyer that museum feeling that the designer had gone for on the exterior.

"All the class Blum Sugar Toasties can buy, eh?"

Alyn shot him a withering look. "She had a lot of money. Is it a curse that she have good taste too?"

"Yeah. It sure was a curse," he said softly, enigmatically.

She stared at him. He was the strangest man she'd ever met. Even now he stood like a madman in barefeet on the cold marble floor, and he didn't even shiver. He was either made entirely of ice—or completely nuts—or he knew a lot more about the situation at Blumfield than she did.

"Well, here's good old Hector with the bags." Youngblood released a trademark sarcastic grin.

Dante glared at him as he passed through the doorway.

"Now you make sure and serve Miss Jones here breakfast in bed tomorrow," he called after the butler. "And don't give a worry in my direction, I'm doing just fine all by myself in the guest cottage. Just fine."

His grin widened, especially when Dante shot him a look from the top of the staircase that could have split an atom.

"I get the feeling he doesn't like me," Youngblood mused aloud to her.

Does anyone? She had to bite her tongue to keep from saying it.

"Good night, Miss Jones. I'll walk back. The fresh air will do me good." He looked around the magnificent foyer. "Especially after a visit to this place. I just can't breathe here. I don't know why."

"Good night," she said and watched him leave as if to make sure he really did.

He closed the door behind her.

She was left alone to face the huge curving staircase and the potted orchids. Even the steps of her Nikes echoed off the marble walls. Above, at the landing, the majordomo, Hector Dante, stared down as if she were the antichrist.

Personality was a funny thing, she suddenly thought, looking up at the dark man, and hesitating to take her first wary steps upon the stair.

Because, suddenly, as disturbing as Peter Youngblood was, she wanted him back.

CHAPTER FIVE

Fame is a vapor, popularity an accident, the only earthly certainty is oblivion.

—Mark Twain

"Breakfast will be served in the dining room at precisely eight o'clock, or Giselda may bring you a tray, which ever you prefer, Miss Jones." Hector Dante deposited her overnighter onto a mahogany luggage rack next to the bathroom door. Then he paused and stared at her with the same hostile gaze she remembered from the foyer. "Will you require anything else?"

"No, please . . . I'll come downstairs for breakfast. I don't want to be any trouble. I only came here because I was worried when I saw the newspapers. Perhaps foolishly, I guess I wanted to be of some help." Alyn watched him. It was obvious just by his poisonous expression that he couldn't wait to be rid of her. She wondered if it had to do with the fact that she was an uninvited guest, or that he had to work while his employer was nowhere around. Or something else.

"Good night then." He took his leave.

"Oh—ah—how do I get to the dining room?" she called after him.

He turned. "The easiest way from here is to go through Mrs. Blum's suite and take the rear stair. In her absence, we've kept her suite open. It's to the left."

He bowed, shot her another resentful look, then left for parts unknown.

Alyn looked around the unfamiliar bedroom. She knew she should unpack and get settled in; it was late. To remind her of that fact, the clock on the marble mantel chimed twice. 2:00 A.M.

But something outside her room beckoned her. She wondered if it wasn't just the need to connect with Jacqueline. Instead of wanting to tour her coldly decorated guest room, or the exquisite marble foyer, Alyn was drawn to what was personal in the house.

At first glance, there was little, but there had to be clues to Jacqueline's personality. Someplace in this monstrosity of a house, there had to be a room where Jacqueline escaped. A place where she succumbed to her humanity. Everyone, no matter how rich and pampered, had needs, and yearnings, and vulnerabilities. She wanted to know Jacqueline's. For some reason, Alyn was convinced that if she could just find out Jacqueline's weaknesses, she might know where she'd disappeared to.

Alyn went into the hallway as if driven by a force outside herself. To her left, a pair of ornate mahogany doors stood half ajar exposing a dimly lit hall, a sentinel-line of other doorways, and, at the end, a bronze railing that indicated a staircase.

She already knew what it was. It was Jacqueline's suite of rooms. The place most likely to reveal her hopes and fears, her desires and hungers.

Alyn walked toward it and slipped through the double doors. The hallway floor was gleaming Brazilian cherry topped with a faded antique pink Savonnerie runner forty feet in length. Satinwood and gilt beaux-arts sconces lined the doorless side of the hall; to the left three mahogany doors led into Jacqueline Blum's private rooms.

To enter would be snooping, she told herself as she stood frozen in front of the first room. Her aunt was probably dead, and Alyn Jones had no right to tour the personal suite of a woman she never knew.

But it wasn't just morbid curiosity that Alyn fought. The whole reason she had even thought to come to Blumfield was so that she could connect in some way to the strange ethereal woman who'd called after her mother's funeral. Jacqueline and Alyn were the last ones left. Alyn desperately wanted to know her last living relative; it seemed absurd to ignore Jacqueline Blum's existence simply because the woman's money had loomed over their lives like an oppressive South American regime.

Especially when the money had ruined so many things. Alyn wondered if she would ever forgive her grandfather for disowning her mother after Colette ran off to be married. His disapproval of the match had caused an enormous amount of damage. Sometimes Alyn didn't know which was worse: the fact that her grandfather's disowning her mother had led to Colette's predicted abandonment—or that her despotic grandfather had been proved right, and still that wasn't good enough for him to forgive and forget.

In the end, the Blum zillions didn't amount to much when compared to the love of her mother, but Alyn knew Colette was always hurt by the alienation. Colette hadn't just been stripped financially, but of her birthright as well. The whole sordid episode had been Alyn's second lesson in the character—or lack of it—in men. The first lesson, of course, had been taught by her absent father.

Now there might be nothing left of the last Blum woman but the ephemera she left behind in her suite the day she disappeared. Alyn desperately wanted to see the room. She wanted the emotional connection to her aunt that she now might never have.

Against all her mother's lessons of etiquette, she stepped inside the first open door. The gilt cove ceiling was sixteen feet overhead; below, spread out like the cover of *Architectural Digest,* was a set of Louis XVI chairs interspersed with silk brocade covered sofas in the same faded pink salmon color as the antique rug in the hall. Every painting on the wall, every swag of silk drapery, had been chosen to achieve the look of refined old money and deep seductive femininity.

The room had to be the sitting room, Alyn told herself as she gazed in stunned silence at the Gainsborough portrait that hung over the white Carrara marble mantel.

It was a breathlessly beautiful room, well executed down to the *famille rose* porcelains and the silver-framed photos of a young Jacqueline with Ronald Reagan or an older Jacqueline with Christopher Reeve or some other famous horsey-set personality. The room even had good intentions as shown by the brown cut-velvet throw artfully tossed across the back of one of the sofas; it was the perfect facade, the ultimate fiction; it was as if someone really did lie about this stupendous room with their Walmart slippers on their cold feet and the remote control in hand.

Indeed the room was exquisite. Exquisite, but cold and unilluminating. There was nothing personal in the room. Nothing that told Alyn about Jacqueline, and, perhaps, what had happened to her.

Disappointed, Alyn wandered to the next door. She couldn't help but wonder what a curious intruder would think of her own bedroom if she were declared missing. They might be able to look beyond the cabbage rose wallpaper and handmade quilts that said, "Unmarried Woman Lives Here," and they would see her veterinary journals piled on the table to one side of the bed and know that she had a lot of reading to catch up on. Her video collection in the knotty pine armoire said a lot more about her than she'd probably like. She was a Hitchcock groupie and had almost every film from *Blackmail* to *Vertigo.* Her one concession to heterosexual loneliness was a soft porn video her friends had given her as a joke present for her thirtieth birthday. It was entitled *Lord of Midnight.* She still had it in her armoire, and if push came to shove, she'd have to confess she'd watched it. More than once.

Looking around her aunt's sitting room, Alyn vowed right then and there to burn the damn movie. After she was gone, it was nobody's business who she was. Those details belonged to her; no one else had a right to them. For sure, when she got home she was going to make sure there was no evidence of her heart scattered about her home. She was going to get rid of *Lord of Midnight* first so that no one would ever know Mr. Right had never come along. And that she was stupid enough to still long for him.

Some things left behind could tell too much.

But not, apparently, in Jacqueline's case.

She walked into the adjoining room and found it just as soulless as the sitting room. It was the dressing room and bath. The tub was carved from a solid block of white marble. Alyn couldn't even imagine what it had cost. In boredom, she ran her hand along the polished curves and admired the gold dolphin that served as a spout, but all she could think of was: cold. Everything was cold. The green marble floor, the beveled glass enclosures where Jacqueline hung her expensive clothes, the vanity which was nothing but more marble and harsh Hollywood lighting. There was a certain Norma Desmond kind of glamour that tugged at Alyn's heart, but even Norma showed her humanity in little messes and tattered edges. So far Jacqueline Blum's rooms revealed none of these things. They were static; frigid.

The last of the three rooms had to be the bedroom where Jacqueline slept. Her soul was not revealed in the bathroom as Alyn's certainly was—already she cringed when she thought of the pair of snagged pantyhose she'd left to dry on the towel rack; the over-the-counter sleep aid she kept in surplus in the medicine cabinet because she was an animal doctor and a hopeless night owl; and, worse, the package of birth-control sponges that sat unused, their expiration date come and gone because if her knight had ever ridden by, he'd so far gone unnoticed in her relentless pursuit of her vet practice.

Alyn hated to think what the things in her bathroom told about her, but maybe it would be worse to have her home say nothing, as Jacqueline's did. Maybe the emptiness was worse than the embarrassment.

Dispirited, she twisted the gold doorknob and flicked on the lights to the bedroom.

She gasped.

Jacqueline's presence hit her like a bombshell.

On all four walls of the enormous bedroom were narrow little bookshelves richly trimmed in walnut and gold. The shelves were filled to the breaking point with paperback Harlequin romances.

Stunned, Alyn walked further into the room and turned around, unable to imagine how many books were around her. Each paperback spine was numbered and uniform in width, and there were thousands of them; they covered the room's sixteen-foot walls. On one wall the paperbacks were so yellowed they looked decades old while on the wall next to it, the Harlequins were so new the last batch hadn't even been opened from their mailer.

She slowly lowered herself down on an ottoman at the foot of the satin-draped bed. She couldn't take her gaze from the books even if she'd wanted to. They suffocated just by their volume. Her aunt's yearning was so obvious, so astounding, so obsessive that it tore at Alyn. She hadn't expected something like this. It took her by surprise. It was bald and poignant. Sad.

This was the fabulous Blum heiress's weakness. Jacqueline Blum practically had her own page in the *National Enquirer* to report on her latest affair, but for more than thirty-five years—the number of books proved it had to be that long—it looked as though, while her aunt had carried on in public, in private, the woman had nested herself in her bedroom and read the day away with a truckload of mail-order romance novels. Perhaps she'd used them to escape the hurt and rejection of all those nasty public affairs, perhaps she'd read them and felt some cold satisfaction the way Alyn had on a late Saturday night when all the warmth she'd had around her was the cheesy *Lord of Midnight.*

Maybe these romances were the cure for the heartless men who'd only wanted Jacqueline for her money.

And only wanted Alyn to break her heart like her mother's had been broken.

Alyn ran her fingers along the thousands of book spines. The oldest was a nurse/doctor romance that dated from 1958. The most current Harlequin sported a slick cover that had only the author's name, title and a small sprig of lily-of-the-valley. Times had certainly changed the covers and, no doubt, the content.

But the need hadn't changed. Jacqueline was a devotee to the point she'd even had her walls built with the special narrow bookcases in order to hold all her romances.

Alyn studied the spines again. Some looked so worn and overly read that they were falling apart. These had to be Jacqueline's favorites. If Alyn had a month, she'd love to lock herself in this same room and read all of Jacqueline's favorite novels. That might tell more about the elusive Jacqueline Blum than any formal investigation ever would have. It might reveal what was inside Jacqueline's heart. What she had wanted above all. What made her vulnerable.

A sick feeling gripped Alyn while she stood in the middle of the room, peeking at the intimate life of a woman she never knew. Suddenly all the numbness and shock of this strange trip and its strange circumstance gave way to a surge of anger.

Jacqueline was still a human being. She had money, but she had a flesh and blood heart that longed for love as much as any other woman's. As much as her niece's did, certainly. For though Alyn didn't read Harlequins, she certainly understood the need that had filled these four walls. She understood it too well.

Backing out of the room, Alyn returned to her own bedroom and tried to make sense of all she'd seen. Finally she succumbed to the exhaustion that hit her. She barely had her teeth brushed before her eyelids began to droop.

Snuggled beneath the eiderdown satin comforter, she closed her eyes and tried to fall asleep, but sleep didn't come.

She was haunted by the paperback palace of a bedroom, and by the dark angry looks of the majordomo, and, lastly, by the strange nut case who was staying in the guest cottage. But the biggest image in her mind was the stark absence of the woman who owned everything at Blumfield. The lady who should have been tucked in her own bed reading those unopened books and sighing for imaginary lovers.

Jacqueline Blum was missing. Gone. And now, for some reason, perhaps just seeing the intimate wantings of Jacqueline's heart, Alyn was suddenly convinced something terrible had happened to Jacqueline. And that Jacqueline wasn't coming back.

She tossed around in the bed and churned with newfound anxieties. It wasn't until she rose out of bed and checked and rechecked the lock on her bedroom door that Alyn could finally lay back in the bed and find her much-needed rest.

* * *

Alyn had a Hollywood wake-up moment when she opened her eyes, and looked around the strange bedroom. She actually said out loud, "Where am I?" and in seconds the entire tableau struck her as funny and she laughed.

So people actually did wake up in strange places and say those same cliché words. But they were effective. Especially when one was a little veterinarian and she'd opened her eyes to stare at a Renoir.

It was indeed a Renoir. She'd barely looked at it the night before. It was a rather small painting of the face of a pink-cheeked child.

But there in the lower right hand corner was the embryonic scrawl of the famous hand. Renoir.

Too strange. It didn't seem real to look at a wall and see a painting that most museums couldn't afford. Last night she had dreamed about painters and harlequins all dancing around Jacqueline in gruesome garish costumes. Jacqueline was dead and she was buried inside a tomb filled with rotting paperback romances.

Alyn sobered from the surprise joy of seeing the Renoir. It was already close to 8:00 A.M. She had yet to shower, and she sorely needed a fresh beginning to the day. For some reason, she instinctively knew it was going to be a long one.

Twenty minutes later, she walked down the staircase to the rear of her aunt's suite of rooms. The ends of her hair were still in wet ringlets from her hasty shower, but she didn't care. She pulled the unmanageable mess into a stretchy gingham ponytail holder. With a dash of lipstick and a navy cotton tunic and leggings, she was ready to see Blumfield.

"Good morning," she said cautiously to the majordomo.

Hector Dante stood in wait in the elegant breakfast room off the kitchen. The room, done in robin's egg blue chintz, had the same cozy feel of the guest cottage. But for the scowling woman in a gray housekeeper's uniform who poured a cup of coffee, Alyn might have actually enjoyed having breakfast there.

"Good morning, Miss Jones. The police have called. There's no new information, but they'd like to speak with you at nine." He seated Alyn at the only place set at the table. He then took the coffee cup from the woman and placed it to her right. Mumbling something to the housekeeper, Dante snapped his fingers and Giselda walked to the table with a linen-covered basket.

Uneasy, Alyn took a croissant from the basket and darted glances between Dante and the housekeeper. The woman wore care on her face in a veil of spider-web lines beneath her eyes and around her lips. Her pale complexion was lined like the crazing on Old Paris china. In her youth, she must have been beautiful; full lipped and voluptuous, but now the curves had turned into rolls, and the sparkle that had once been in her blue eyes now seemed as flat and dead as roadkill. She seemed much older than Dante but upon closer look, Alyn wondered if this were true. Dante could be able to hide his age well behind the smooth Latin skin and trim figure. Giselda had no such forgiving genetics.

"The cook is a disciple of Escoffier. What shall I tell him to prepare for you?"

Alyn's gaze returned to Dante. "Please, nothing. This is fine. I'm anxious to speak with the police. I have some letters of Jacqueline's to show them. I hope to be of some help."

A tray clattered to the polished floor. Giselda pleaded apology and cringed beneath the whispered curses of the majordomo. Alyn rose to help the woman, but Dante ushered her back to her seat.

"Please forgive Giselda," he said with acid in his voice. "The old sow is going through menopause. I never know what to expect."

A retort caught in Alyn's throat. The man's callousness stunned her, but she didn't quite know how to react. Upon first meeting, she wasn't feeling warm and fuzzy toward the housekeeper herself, yet she couldn't stand Dante's sexist, degrading language. Here was a handsome man who had clear advantages over this prematurely aging woman, and yet, there was no empathy, no kindness in his heart. Dante was just like every other man Alyn had ever known. Just like her father. Perhaps they beat their women with their tongue instead of their fists, but the lashing went just as deep, cut just as sharp.

This was why Alyn even now kept her lovers imaginary—as Jacqueline had done. Lovers were better on a cheesy porno tape in the bedroom armoire than in real flesh and blood where every word was a rejection, every action meant to deceive and wound.

She'd always promised her mother that she would never end up with a man like Allen Jones, her father. Her mother had been the perfect example for Alyn. Colette had given up all for love. And love had abandoned her. Allen Jones had married Colette just long enough to give his baby a name, then he'd hit the road when the payback hadn't come from Daddy. Apparently he'd always said that he and her mother just couldn't get along, but even at a young age, Alyn saw the ironic half-truth in his excuse; Colette couldn't get along without the one man she'd ever loved, and Allen couldn't get along without Colette's money.

Alyn steeled herself and locked her gaze on Dante. "Pardon me, but I don't believe every little mistake a woman makes is due to her hormones.'' She didn't waiver a muscle. Her shoulders and spine seemed forged of iron. She held Dante's stare with all the defiance of a teenager, and she watched him squirm.

''Miss Jones, I apologize at once.'' Dante bowed, but she thought it was only to hide his smirk. ''You'll have to forgive me, for I know Giselda and her moods only too well. You see she is my wife and we are much too used to each other.''

Wow. Another surprise, Alyn thought cynically. She had wondered why the woman would tolerate such demeaning behavior from another employee. Now she knew. It was called the marriage contract.

''Will there be anything else you require, miss? If not, I'll prepare the morning room for our visitors.'' Dante presented her with his fine mask of cultivated solicitousness. Alyn was already beginning to hate him, especially when Giselda, silver tray in hand, backed into the kitchen, a look of fear on her face whenever she glanced his way.

He probably beats her and cheats on her. Alyn frowned as she returned her attention to her breakfast. *Just like another Allen Jones. Mother always said the world was populated with Allens.*

''One last thing, Mr. Dante, if you would be so kind.'' She glanced over at Giselda and finally saw the gold filigreed wedding band which matched Dante's. ''I go by the title of Dr., not 'Miss.' I'd appreciate your addressing me that way in the future.''

''Of course, Dr. Jones. If I'd known you were a physician I would have addressed you properly from the start.''

Alyn opened her mouth to correct him, but didn't see the point. To announce she was only a mere veterinarian would be to give Dante a concession in his eyes, and she was unwilling to do that. Besides, there were only a handful of vet schools in the nation, and she'd had to have a solid 4.0 in order to be admitted to one. There was no way she was going to sell herself short of an M.D. when she was just as educated and paid much less.

''That will be most appreciated, Mr. Dante,'' she finished.

''Hector,'' Giselda broke in from behind them. ''Do you remember the police are to be here at nine? It's that time already, and I believe I hear the door chimes.''

Dante pursed his lips until they were nothing but a white line.

"Of course. When you're ready, Dr. Jones, I'll show you to the morning room."

She gulped her coffee and wondered why she was the one who was nervous. Just the mention of police had Dante looking anxious. He clearly wanted to perform his duties and get away. Even from across the table, she could see how his leg jumped beneath his black trousers. If he were a horse at the starting gate, he'd be frothing.

She slowly chewed the croissant. Her food went down like a brick. The atmosphere was charged with tension. She couldn't wait to down her java and get away from Dante. She wondered how her aunt had stood him. The only conclusion she could draw was that Dante must have a completely different side which he showed only to his employer.

"I'll take you to the morning room," he said stiffly when she rose from the table.

"Thank you," she answered, once again tagging at his heels like a scared puppy.

"I hear the door chimes now. The police are prompt, are they not, Dr. Jones?"

Alyn heard the faint bells of a Chopin refrain echo through the large foyer. From the entrance to the morning room, she turned to look and watched Dante allow three men through the massive front door. Two men she didn't recognize stood there, and she assumed they were the detectives who wanted to interview her; the other man she knew quite well. He was her companion of the night before. Peter Youngblood.

She backed through the doors. Frowning, she took a seat on one of the Chippendale settees scattered in various seating groups around the enormous room.

Detectives; she could understand why they were there. But there was no reason in her mind why Jacqueline's "financial advisor" had any business attending a police interview.

"Ms. Jones?" The first man entered the drawing room and whipped open a badge. "I'm Detective Harold Raney with the Montgomery County Police Department. With me is Special Agent Phil Trask. We're here to talk with you about Mrs. Blum's disappearance."

"Dr. Jones, if you don't mind." She nodded and held out her hand. Trask flashed a badge that said FBI. Her nerves twanged like fiddle strings. She'd never met an FBI special agent before.

The two men were in their fifties and balding. Trask was grayer and had more of a paunch, but they both had that suburban polyester jacket nice guy look. She trusted them almost immediately. In stark contrast to the way she felt about Youngblood.

He loomed over both men like the baboon that he was. And where the other men took their seats in the earthy manner of aging men: shifting belts and unbuttoning jackets, Youngblood merely slouched himself down on a priceless Georgian wing chair in one fluid motion, and started in with what she was beginning to recognize as *The Stare.*

"We're here just to do a routine interview because of the disappearance of your aunt, Dr. Jones," Detective Raney began. "Because we want you to answer all the questions, we have to let you know that you have the right to have an attorney present during this session—"

"An attorney?" she gasped. "Do you think I have anything of that much relevance to this—?"

"We have no charges filed against anyone at this moment, Dr. Jones. We just want to inform you that you have the right to an attorney present should you so desire."

"I don't know any attorneys," she said truthfully.

"Then you waive the right? May we have the interview now?"

She looked at all three men, two with their nondescript pleasant faces, the other with eyes that burned gold like a dragon's. Her nerves went from frayed to fried.

"I—I guess so," she answered hesitantly. There was much she had wanted to discuss with these two men but not in a defensive position. Now everything had turned on her.

"First, may I have your full name, your social security number, birthdate and driver's license." Raney wrote on a black leatherette pad. He was scribbling furiously, and she'd yet to say anything.

"My name is Alyn Blum-Jones."

"A - l - l - e - n?"

She shook her head. "A - l - y - n. I was named after my father. They feminized the name."

"I see." Raney kept writing.

She dictated the other pertinent information and waited for more questions. They weren't long in coming; she was only irritated by the source.

"Ms. Jones, why was your mother disinherited from the Blum fortune?" Youngblood didn't write anything down after his question. He seemed like the type who could remember everything. A mind like a trap.

"What does that have to do with Jacqueline?" She looked at Raney and Trask. She expected them to be annoyed that Youngblood was interfering. To her surprise they seemed to be waiting for her answer as breathlessly as he was.

"She was disinherited because my grandfather didn't like my mother's choice of husband," she answered in a flat voice.

"Why not?" Youngblood fired at her.

"Allen Jones was nothing much more than a redneck. My mother met him when her car broke down on her way to Martha's Vineyard. It was raining. She stopped at a farmhouse. My father answered the door. The rest is history, I guess you'd say."

"Isn't that a little strange that your mother would give up so much to marry a nobody?"

Alyn wanted to squirm in her chair. She wasn't used to being questioned about her family's history in a public forum, and she sure as hell didn't want to blurt out all of her mother's yearnings only to find them all tacked back onto her. Her mother imagined Allen Jones had loved her. And she was wrong. End of story. The only epilogue was that her daughter Alyn wasn't going to make that same mistake.

"She wasn't interested in money, I guess," Alyn finally answered. "I suppose she was just interested in love. That happens sometimes. Or so I've heard."

"Are you interested in money, Miss Jones?" Youngblood shot back.

She glared at him. "I'm a veterinarian. If I were interested in money I'd have become a neurosurgeon."

Youngblood slid her that grin that was half sarcasm, half amusement, and all contempt. "Of course you would have. But maybe you couldn't be one. Maybe your grades just didn't cut it . . ."

"Listen, I'll have you know"—she drew to the edge of her chair—"that becoming a D.V.M. is no picnic in the park. You have to study as hard as any other doctor—"

"Pardon me," Raney interrupted, "we didn't come here to discuss your qualifications as a vet, Dr. Jones. All we want to know is why and how your aunt disappeared. If you have any information on that, we'd love to hear it. Otherwise, this is going nowhere."

"My aunt wrote me a few letters. I photocopied them for you. Mostly she talks about her horses. I think that's where her interest in me came from. She was kind of obsessed with her stable."

She handed Raney the letters in her pocket.

"I can get you the originals if you think that might be of more use to you." She shot Youngblood an accusatory glance.

"This'll be fine. How long did you know your aunt?" Trask began scratching on his own leatherette pad.

"Not long. In fact I've never even met her face to face. I just had a phone call when my mother died, then these few letters came. There was talk of my visiting here to see her stables, but she disappeared before the date I was to arrive."

"Would you describe your relationship as cold, Dr. Jones?"

Alyn took a deep breath. She should have realized the interview would go like this. "It was neither cold nor warm. It didn't exist until the first phone call. Jacqueline Blum was as much a stranger to me as she is to the average *National Enquirer* reader. I have to confess that I was really surprised to get her letter because she'd shown no interest in me or my mother the entire time I've been alive."

"You must have resented that—to have such a rich famous relative snub you."

Alyn shook her head. "I didn't think about it much. I grew up knowing my family didn't get along. You can't miss what you've never had. My mother's sister was nothing more than a curiosity in my life. I'd heard about her from my mother and the social column in the newspapers, but other than that, I never thought much about her."

"How did your mother die, Dr. Jones?" Youngblood interrupted.

"Breast cancer," she answered coldly.

"Where?" Trask asked.

"Newton, Mass. Last November."

Raney jotted it all down.

Trask looked at her.

She caught Trask staring. Suddenly a chill crept up the back of her neck. "Hey, really—"

"And your father, Dr. Jones? Is he dead also?" Trask shot out.

"I don't know," she said woodenly. "I've had about as much to do with him as with Jacqueline."

"Why do you pronounce your aunt's name as 'Jahckleen' and not 'Jacqueline'? It's most unusual, isn't it?"

"My mother pronounced it that way. I figured she knew how to pronounce her sister's name. Is there something unusual in that? Should I have questioned my own mother's knowledge of her sister?"

"We don't think anything at this moment, Dr. Jones," Raney put in hastily. "We have to question everything. You understand."

Slowly she nodded. "I want to help, really I do. But I'm afraid there's not much more information I can give you. Jacqueline only wrote me the few letters, and I never made it to Blumfield for our visit. I was supposed to come here today in fact."

"What made you come now?" Trask began scribbling again.

"I wanted to come. I wanted to help."

"Help how?" Raney jumped in.

Alyn looked around the room and tried to gather her thoughts. "I had a bad feeling about her. I still feel like something terrible has happened."

"What makes you say that?" Youngblood interjected.

She glanced at him.

The smirk was still on his face even after the question.

"I feel that Jacqueline is dead," she said slowly.

"Why do you think that?" Trask shot out. "What, do you bill yourself as some kind of a psychic?"

"Yeah, Dr. Alyn Blum-Jones, Pet Detective and Psychic." Youngblood rose to his feet. Almost as if he were angry, he strode to the long silk-hung windows and stared off to Blumfield's tender green hills.

Exasperated, she turned to the other two men and said, "Really, I can understand your wanting to question me, but must Mr.

Youngblood be here? I can't see how Jacqueline Blum's financial advisor can shed any light on this case whatsoever."

"Peter, maybe you'd better leave us alone." Raney nodded.

Youngblood gave Alyn his signature dismissive glance, then he departed without another word.

"We think your aunt's disappearance is financially related, that's why we want to make use of Peter Youngblood." Trask shut the drawing-room doors in Youngblood's wake. "He's here freelancing the case for Jacqueline Blum's monied interests."

"Well, whoever these monied interests are, you can tell them the brutally obvious: money's definitely a reason for a wealthy woman to disappear off the face of the earth . . ." Alyn became pensive, suddenly heartsick from the memory of all those romance novels upstairs in Jacqueline's bedroom. Clearly, what her aunt wanted most was love. In the end, maybe all she got was betrayal.

"Really, have you no leads at all on this case?" she blurted out, a catch in her throat.

"You sound most sincere, Dr. Jones, for never having known the woman." Trask studied her.

She didn't mind. Now she didn't even care that they might suspect her. That was fine. Suspect everyone, she thought, because then you might catch the guilty one.

"My aunt and I had a lot in common. More than I first thought. I guess for all her wealth, I've come to see the parts of her that were wanting. I also can't shake the feeling that she's gone. And that she suffered."

"We think she's gone too. Most missing persons show themselves after forty-eight hours. Usually if they don't surface by then, it's because they can't. Because they're dead." Raney closed his notebook. "One last question, Miss Jones, did you kill your aunt?"

The question finally was out. It lay like a bloodstain on shag carpet. Intractable.

"N-no," she stammered, her heart beating against her ribs. The horror of the question stabbed like an icicle.

"Thank you very much then." Trask stood; Raney followed. "That will be all unless we uncover something further that you might help us with."

"Anything I can do." She fumbled through her purse for her

clinic's business card. Handing it to Trask, she smiled apologetically at the cartoon kitties drawn in lilac ink along with the header, "Dr. Jones Cures Cat-astrophies (even in a dog-eat-dog world)."

"Hey, that's cute—'dog-eat-dog world'! Ha! Very funny." Raney laughed as he looked over Trask's shoulder.

She shrugged. "It helps to have a sense of humor when you spend three quarters of a day looking in dogs' ears."

"We spend three-quarters of a day looking at dirtbags. I'd change jobs in a second for yours," Raney added.

She smiled at him. If they were Good Cop/Bad Cop, Raney was definitely the Good Cop. "Look, I hope you'll let me know how the investigation is going. I really want to help."

"We can't give out any information," Trask said.

She nodded resignedly. "I guess I'll have to keep up on things in the supermarket tabloids, like the rest of the world."

"When are you returning to Quincy?" Trask pocketed her card.

"I don't know. Maybe tonight. It's clear there's not much I can do. I doubt I can add anything more to the investigation than I've already done this morning."

Trask nodded. "Let us know when you leave."

Alyn frowned. "I will," she said quietly as they left.

CHAPTER SIX

If she was going back to Dulles that night, Alyn knew she'd better take a look at Blumfield. It might be the only time she'd ever see it.

After the interview with the police, she went back to her room, packed her overnight bag and left the mansion to explore. The first thing she wanted to see was the stables. Jacqueline's letters had brimmed with joy over the purchases of her million-dollar Thoroughbreds. Alyn was a veterinarian, but her practice was limited to household pets. She had never seen a million-dollar horse up close and personal.

She walked down the mansion's driveway through an alley of intertwining elms. The purple haze of redbud trees in the surrounding forest made the landscape look like a Monet. All was silent except for the caw of bluejays and the distant rumble of a car engine.

"Taking a tour?" She heard a familiar voice call out to her from a familiar black Ford Explorer.

Stiffening, she barely turned around. "Do I need a police escort for that? Are you going to fingerprint me?"

Youngblood laughed. "No. You only need my escort. Get in." The passenger door to his Explorer opened. He waited.

She stopped on the road and looked at him. After his easy

participation in the morning police interview, she really wondered about him. His professional status in the investigation was sketchy at best, but he sure was entrenched in the goings on at Blumfield, and she'd give anything to know why that was so.

"So are you admitting you're some kind of cop now?" she shot at him.

"No. I'm just saying I want to offer you my assistance in going to the stables."

She shrugged. "You needn't bother. I really don't need a tour guide. I can go see the stables by myself."

"All right. Go ahead if you want then. But if you're really trying to go to the stables, you're headed in the wrong direction. The road's behind the main house."

She abruptly began walking back to the mansion.

He backed up in the Explorer.

"It's three miles behind the house. You're still sure you don't want a lift?" he asked.

She stared at him as he hung out the driver's side window. The scene was ridiculous, having a stand-off in the road. She wondered if he was going to back that Explorer all the way to the house; he probably would.

"Are you planning to go the entire way in reverse if I don't get in?" she finally queried.

He cracked a smile. A strangely attractive one. "Yeah. You'd better be careful. I might run over you."

"Is that what happened to my aunt, you suppose? She got run over by some over-enthusiastic tour guide?"

The smile disappeared like an eclipse of the sun.

"You don't seem so anxious to talk when it comes to Jacqueline. Why is that?" she said, speaking her thoughts aloud.

"I'm not a big fan of homicide."

"What if she's simply being held by kidnappers? Maybe there will be a ransom note."

"The demands almost always come within forty-eight hours. Otherwise whoever did it didn't do it for a ransom."

"I suppose that makes sense." She shrugged. "I don't know much about criminal behavior, however. I guess I feel I should leave that up to the experts." She stood in the road watching him, knowing her eyes held accusation. She was only half surprised when he acknowledged it.

"If I'm the expert, does that mean you'll let this criminal take you to the stables?" He popped open the passenger side door.

Reluctantly, she slid in.

She hoped to take the ride in silence but even huddled against the door as she was, she couldn't escape the suffocation of his presence. He seemed to fill the inside of the Explorer like a bear. The top of his head brushed the glass of the sun roof and his shoulders pressed against the seat until it groaned.

In contrast, she seemed insignificant. Her petiteness had always lent her a youthfulness she figured would become welcome as she grew to middle age, but now she felt like a child strapped into the seat beside him. She was insubstantial and vulnerable next to him. Her only fortress was the strength of her mind. She prayed she would remember that if she ever needed it.

He peered at her from the corner of his eye.

She suddenly went from feeling frightened to feeling juvenile; she swore his glance was to check her out. He gave her a look that she'd seen in a hundred construction workers' eyes. She just hadn't expected to see it on the face of someone who looked like he ate live lambs for breakfast.

"You wear glasses."

Her eyes locked with his. She might have laughed at the obviousness of his statement, yet there was nothing even remotely amusing in the bleak lines of his expression.

"So what's your point?" She forced out a little smile. "Do you object to my seeing well? Or is there something else?"

"You didn't wear them last night."

"It was pouring rain. They wouldn't have been very practical without windshield wipers. Is it acceptable to you for me to be wearing contacts in such weather?"

She didn't mean to be sarcastic with that last comment but it came out before she could stop herself. He seemed off-balance at times—truly wacko at others—but then, when her eyes held his, he appeared all too sober. Even wary. And what made him hesitate? She could only find one thing around right now: a small woman who wore glasses.

"What is it? Do you have some kind of fetish thing for glasses?" She had to fight the urge to clap her hand on her mouth. It was all kinds of stupid to put such a question to a man who sported a tattoo.

"No." He didn't take his eyes from the road.

On either side were emerald fields of new hay and old growth hardwoods that probably hadn't seen an axe since the Declaration of Independence. It was a beautiful drive to the stables, but she couldn't tear her gaze off him.

He was pensive in profile, handsome actually, when his violent gold eyes weren't pinned on her. His nose was straight and well-formed like that of an English schoolboy, but his jaw was hard, and his mouth seemed cut from stone. He was a strange mixture of disarming and terrifying. And she found herself strangely attracted to him. Even now, she couldn't help but wonder if beneath his jeans he wore the flannel boxers she'd seen him in last night, and if the tattoo on his left arm—now hidden beneath a chamois shirt—was as gruesome as she remembered.

"You're staring, Dr. Jones."

She took an intake of breath. He hadn't even turned to look at her. He was like some kind of fly with a 360-degree field of vision.

"I just—I just can't think why you would remark about my glasses."

"They make you look . . ." His words trailed off into a swallowed whisper.

"How do they make me look? Do they make me look plain? Stupid? Ugly? What?"

She held her breath. Especially when those gold eyes turned on her.

"No, they just make you look . . . wholesome. Yes. Wholesome."

She studied him.

He most definitely didn't like the word he'd used to describe her. It seemed to leave a bad taste on his tongue, and he licked his lips like a cat who was furiously trying to clean them of the scent of a dog.

"I'm not so wholesome," she said in a low voice. "I know all kinds of things that I shouldn't."

"Such as?" His eyes went dead as if he already knew the answer before she did.

"For one, I've a background in pharmaceuticals. I know them very well, perhaps too well. I was going to get a masters if I didn't go to vet school."

"Is this knowledge just a by-product of your education—or do you use it for your own personal needs?" He smirked as if everything were falling into place in his mind.

"I'm a veterinarian. I know about drugs. But that doesn't mean I take drugs."

"What do you know then?"

She paused. "I know, for instance, that the plant tattooed on your arm can kill."

He downshifted using a little more force than necessary. "But it's a sweet death."

"Deadly nightshade isn't my poison of choice."

His gaze locked onto hers once more. "It's also called belladonna. 'Fair lady.' " He reached out and ran a rough hand beneath her chin. The friction of his skin was like a charge to a battery. It melted her insides.

"Yes, I know that," she whispered. "During the renaissance young women would ingest it to make them pale and to make their pupils large and dark. They poisoned themselves to become, in their view, more attractive to men." She watched as his eyes flickered down her body.

Finally his gaze again rested on her face. "You would look pretty if your pink skin were to turn white as marble, and if your hazel eyes were to turn large and black. They would appear to see everything. Everything," he added for emphasis.

She looked away.

The silence became sharp. She no longer wanted to show him up. In truth, he frightened her. She was relieved to see the Blumfield stable in the bend of the road.

The Blumfield colors were purple and gold. Alyn remembered seeing one of Jacqueline's horses in the Preakness once. The jockey's silks were stripes of almost black purple and gold lurex thread, a memorable combination.

The Blumfield stable was made that much more impressive by

its rigid adherence to the color code. A dozen stablehands, some currying colts, some just mucking out stalls, wore barn jackets of deep purple Gore-tex. Embroidered on their backs was the familiar gold *B* in the same style as on the gate. Even in the fields where Alyn watched Thoroughbreds trot through emerald grass, she noted they wore plaid Baker blankets specially woven of the Blumfield purple and gold.

"Pretty nice spread, wouldn't you say? I hear the stable building alone cost 20 mil, all paid for with insurance money after the old stable burned to the ground—with horses inside." Youngblood opened his door.

Alyn was ill. Jacqueline had mentioned the building of the new stable, but Alyn hadn't realized it was being constructed on the ashes of a previous one. She thought of the horses whinnying in terror as one by one they each succumbed to the flames. Ice ran down her spine; her stomach lurched.

She suddenly found herself reluctant for a tour, but she followed anyway, mutely stepping down from the Explorer onto the pristine new cobblestones of the stable courtyard.

"What do you want to see first? The overall layout? The mechanical exercise room? The indoor swimming pool—for the horses, I mean." He smiled grimly. "Or are you a detail person? Do you want me to show you the teak and mahogany trim on the interior of the stable boxes? Or should we go right to the best of the best, and I'll take you to see Wonderwall?"

"Wonderwall?" she exclaimed. "That's right. Jacqueline wrote me about Wonderwall. It was her most expensive horse. Five million, wasn't he?"

"Ten."

"Oh, I think I want to see Wonderwall first. I've never seen a ten-million-dollar horse."

In fact, she couldn't even imagine an animal of that magnitude of value. Certainly, she had none in her practice. She wasn't a racing fan, and the closest she ever got to famous animals among her clients was the SPCA cat that the shelter used in their commercial.

Youngblood smiled. He showed lots of teeth and very little pleasantness. "Let's go then. I'm glad to see you're always happy with the best, 'cause that's what you're going to get."

He placed a hand at her back and led her through the main stable doors. She shivered and wondered why his promise sounded much more like a threat.

"There he is." Youngblood's voice lowered to a growl. They stood in the octagonal end of the stable where the champions were housed. "Wonderwall" was engraved on a gold plaque which was riveted to the furthest mahogany stall door.

A dappled charcoal nose appeared through the iron bars to the side of the stall door. Alyn gently held out her hand and placed the flat of her palm on his muzzle.

She grinned. "I'm petting a ten-million-dollar horse." She rubbed harder, then poked her head through the open half of the stall door. "Wonderwall," she said softly.

The animal clambered through his straw bedding and stuck his head out the door.

"He must be eighteen hands," she gasped.

"Is that big?" Youngblood peered at the horse.

"Yep," she answered, already charmed by the Thoroughbred's sweet disposition. She'd expected a horse with nerves strung as taut as a ukelele's, instead she had this muzzling gentle giant with a coat of shiny dark gray dappled in melting snow.

"He's certainly beautiful. I can see why Jacqueline was so charmed by him. Her entire last letter was about Wonderwall. She called him her 'lover boy.' "

"Imaginary, I hope," Youngblood said drily.

Alyn didn't comment. Instead she thought of all the Harlequin romances shelved in her aunt's bedroom. It seemed most of Jacqueline's lovers were imaginary. The woman had had many husbands, but it was likely that one of them—or all of them—had caused Jacqueline to prefer reading romances alone in her room instead of venturing out into the world and risking hurt by her own lover.

"What makes this a ten-million-dollar horse?"

Youngblood's question caught her off guard. She scratched Wonderwall's face and up around the dark leather halter riveted with a smaller version of the gold name plate on his stall door.

"I really don't know. I suppose bloodline would have a lot to do with it. Maybe too the number of wins he's had at the race track. Potential in stud fees. Conformation."

"What's good conformation in a horse?" Youngblood seemed truly interested. He leaned against the steel bars and stared at her.

"You'd have to talk to a track veterinarian to get all those details. I'm just small animals myself. Cats and dogs—"

"I've talked to the Blumfield vet. He told me an awful lot. All about how this animal could stretch to the finish just like a Secretariat. Wonderwall's related, you know. Says that on all his papers."

"You've seen his papers?"

"Yes. He had to be well documented so that he could be insured." His gold eyes glittered ominously in a shaft of sunlight. "It wouldn't do to spend ten million dollars on a horse, and then watch him burn with his stablemates without the sufficient insurance to replace him."

Alyn moaned. "I hate to even think of that. How many animals were killed when the old stable burned?"

"Only five. Imagine that. Out of fifty Thoroughbreds, only five were in their stalls at the time of the blaze. But, of course, these five were the most expensive animals Jacqueline Blum owned."

"She told me she was heartbroken about that."

"Was she? I'd believe it. I think she must have been infatuated with the animals in here. I think no cost was too great if she found a handsome animal, and this Wonderwall fellow, he's pretty damn handsome, don't you think?"

"Yes."

"But is he worth ten million?"

Alyn looked at him. "You sound as if you're actually asking me that."

"I am."

"I'm not the authority."

"The authority already told me he's worth ten million. Now I want your opinion."

"I—"

"Take a good look at him."

She stared at Youngblood. There was no telling what he was getting at, so she decided to play the game.

She put her head through the open top door and counted off Wonderwall's assets. ''He's a big Thoroughbred, probably could stretch for a win pretty well if he wanted to. He's got nice conformation, I suppose.'' She studied the horse more closely. ''He doesn't look too special right now, of course, because he's relaxing in his stall, and I can't see his feet for the straw, but if he were outside I'd say—''

''Then let's take him outside.'' He took the lead shank off the wall.

''You can't just take this horse out of his stall. He's ten million dollars,'' she gasped.

''Yep. Ten mil and I'm going to take the old boy for a walk. Move out of the way.'' He clipped the gold-plated safety hook to the gold-plated ring under the chin of Wonderwall's halter. Then he released the stall door and walked the animal out of his stall.

Alyn couldn't even see Youngblood on the other side of the horse. Eighteen hands was six feet high and that was measured only from the top of the shoulder.

He walked the Thoroughbred back and forth across the octagonal pavestone floor of the stable. Alyn watched, mesmerized by the beauty of the animal. Wonderwall calmly took his time pacing. When Youngblood stopped, he stood tall, his ears rigidly forward like a well-trained show horse.

''How about the conformation now that you can see him?''

Alyn walked around the enormous horse. His feet were newly shod. Corrective heels were noticeable on his steel horseshoes, but that didn't necessarily mean much. She discounted it.

''He looks good,'' she said, running her hand over his front leg.

''But—?''

''But, what do I know about horses? I mean, he doesn't look swayback, he hasn't foundered, he doesn't have shin-splints. I don't really know what I can say bad about him other than he's wearing corrective shoes which is unusual, I suppose, in a horse you paid ten million dollars for. I guess I pretty much would have to say that a ten-million-dollar horse would come near to perfection, but hey, I hear even Fabio gets zits sometimes, so what does it all mean?''

''What are corrective shoes?'' he demanded.

"Again, I'm a small animal vet, but when we did our large animal stuff in school, we covered equine leg problems. Horses sometimes have to have special shoes made by the blacksmith. See? He's not wearing flat horseshoes—he's got heels."

"Show me," he demanded again.

She sighed. Bending over, she ran her hand down the rear tendon of his front leg. Obediently, the horse lifted up his hoof.

"See?" She pointed to the heels at each end of the shoe. "These things just take some pressure off his navicular bone. Sometimes they're used for that, but that doesn't mean he has that particular problem."

She glanced up. Youngblood was staring grimly down at the center of Wonderwall's immaculate hoof.

Alyn turned back to her subject. "But maybe they've found he runs better with heels. There were baseball players that went barefoot to games, so who am I to—?"

She stopped. Dumfounded, she stared up into the horse's loins.

"What do you see, Doctor?" he whispered rather wickedly.

"See?" she repeated, shocked.

In disbelief, she reached up and fingered the horse's testicles.

"What is it?" he demanded.

She shook her head as if to clear her vision. She probed the horse again, then said, "He's still got the sacks. He *looks* like he has balls, but they're gone. They're definitely gone." She stood and shook her head. "I don't believe it. This animal's a gelding."

"So that's what a gelding is."

She peered again beneath the horse's flanks. "He's a gelding all right. I can barely see the scar, so he was probably done young."

"No stud fees there."

"No," she whispered, a sick realization hitting her. "You know, I don't think this horse could possibly be worth ten million dollars. He's got corrective shoes, and he can't be put out for stud, and even if he could he'd only be good for stud if he wins big at the track, and he's still unproven there."

"But he'd make a ten-million-dollar crispy critter."

Alyn backed away from Wonderwall. The bile rose in her throat. "Jacqueline didn't know about this. I know it. I *know* it. She loved this horse. She told me so in her letter. She believed he was worth ten million because she paid it."

"She paid it but he wasn't worth it. Even I can see he has no balls. She never bothered to check under the hood, did she?"

"Oh, God." Alyn turned away. Suddenly all kinds of reasons popped in her mind for Jacqueline's death and most had to do with whomever convinced her to buy a nice saddle horse for the absurd price of ten million dollars.

"You know, there's a lot of crap going on around here, and I'm going to find out who's doing it, and I'm going to stop them."

She heard the whisper in her left ear, but she was numb. The words seemed to float above her as if she were in a dream. Somewhere there was a man who'd taken Jacqueline for ten million dollars. Jacqueline's disappearance had no concrete evidence of a crime, but standing right in front of Alyn was three-dimensional proof that bad things were going on at Blumfield.

Alyn wondered who the guy was. It was probably someone her aunt knew well and trusted completely. She couldn't get it out of her head that whoever had been close enough to her aunt to con her out of ten million dollars must have been intimate with her—because wasn't love the best confidence game of all?

She turned her gaze to Youngblood.

Her curiosity about him deepened. She knew very little about him. His finger was everywhere in the investigation, it seemed, but he had yet to produce to her a tangible reason for being around. She wondered who he really was, and who he was working for, and why he was investigating. And then she wondered how long she'd have to know him before any information about him would escape that locked-up personality of his.

He caught her staring. He smiled a slow, knowing kind of smile that left her feeling shaken. To protect herself, she immediately looked away.

The horror of how badly Jacqueline had been duped was multiplied every time she glanced at Wonderwall. He was a beautiful creature, with a gentle, tamed spirit. Not worth ten million dollars by a long shot, but she could see why Jacqueline had been so taken with him. And to think of him screaming and neighing in fright as flames licked up his gold-plated stall door was enough to make her want to vomit.

"Do the police know this?" she demanded.

Youngblood looked down at her. "They know your aunt was in a lot of shit. She was surrounded by crooks and thieves. I have a feeling before this is through, Jacqueline Blum will go down in history as one of the greatest fools of all time."

"She was lonely. She wanted . . . things." Alyn felt the sting of tears in her eyes.

"What 'things' could she want that she couldn't have?"

Affection, respect, commitment, love. The words echoed through Alyn's mind.

"Who did this to her?" she finally burst out, her heart sickened again by the thought of all those category romances on the shelves upstairs at Blumfield. It didn't seem possible, but maybe Jacqueline was even more hungry than Alyn was, and her betrayal was like a knife through Alyn's own vulnerable female heart.

"They don't know yet. They're looking into it."

"The men working here, they all had to know she was being defrauded. Who grooms this horse? Who's his veterinarian? Those two people, at least, had to know this animal was a gelding, and if they knew it, then they must have been a part of the scheme because they never told Jacqueline."

"How do you know they never told her?"

She shook her head. "In the two letters I received from Jacqueline, she was completely captivated by this animal. He was living breathing perfection. She didn't know when she wrote me. This horse had no flaws and that, I will swear to."

"You sound almost indignant, Doctor."

She met his gaze, surprised. "Of course I'm indignant. The woman was conned, and now she's missing. More than one crime has been committed here. Why aren't the police arresting people?"

"I guess you want your ten million dollars back."

"*My* ten million dollars?" she sputtered.

"Sure," he said coldly, his eyes the color of sunshine on ice. "Some might think you really feel for Jacqueline Blum, but here you wanted to see Wonderwall first. You wanted to see what you were going to have, and now you're disappointed because you're a veterinarian and not as easily fooled as your aunt.''

''This is absurd,'' she gasped. ''I'm not going to inherit Blumfield or anything. My mother was disowned from the Blum fortune, remember? When my grandfather died, the lawyers saw to it that Jacqueline couldn't give away any part of her inheritance to my side of the family.''

''But that wouldn't stop Jacqueline from giving her inheritance to you in her will.''

''She never even met me. Why would she give me anything when the Blum family has dozens of different charities and foundations to donate the money to?''

''You're the last Blum left. She had no children. She might have gotten sentimental and decided to leave her fortune to you.''

She sighed. ''Look, I really don't care if you believe me. I really don't. I've nothing to prove to you. I only came here to be of some help.''

''Yes, you've said that before.''

''But what I haven't said is what I've realized now. I can't be of any help. I think it best that I get back to Massachusetts. This should all be left to the police. There's too much going on around here. I'm no expert at fraud . . . or homicide,'' she added, her voice grim.

''You can become proficient at both those things very quickly. An instant expert. I know that.''

A shiver tingled the hairs at the back of her neck. She was in too deep, and way out of her element. She could see now that it was best to make a quick exit and not look back.

She quavered a smile. ''Hey, I'm just an insignificant person, a nobody, a little animal doctor who hands out rabies shots. I don't want money.'' She glanced at Wonderwall. ''I mean, look what it gets people.''

''You must want something,'' he said coldly.

The words came out much more fiercely than she'd wanted to show. ''I do want something. I want someone to care about what happened to this—this—*broken* woman.''

Silent again, she turned to walk away.

"I read your aunt's last letter. You know I think she really liked you."

He never failed to unbalance her.

She turned and looked at him closely. "But you told me my letters were no good to the investigation because they were copies. Now why do you believe them?"

"I'm not talking about the ones you have. I'm talking about her last letter. The one she left unfinished on her desk before she disappeared."

"The letter's addressed to me?"

"Yes," he said softly.

She absorbed this new information. The urge to get into the rented Geo and head for Dulles was suddenly eclipsed by the desire to read her aunt's last missive to her niece.

"Do the police have the letter? May I see it?"

"They aren't going to show you a goddamned thing. They're the police, right?"

"Right," she answered, her shoulders slumping.

"But I have a copy of it. I could show it to you."

She asked the questions burning in her mind. They fired like bullets at him. "So how come you're so chummy with the police? How come you're so privileged that you get to see all the intimate details of the investigation, and I don't? That's pretty strange for a financial advisor. And if you were Jacqueline's advisor, why the hell didn't you advise her against buying a ten-million-dollar horse . . . or were you the crook who sold it to her?"

He grinned. "There's no pulling the wool over your eyes," he commented sarcastically.

"So who are you?"

"I'm an investigator with the insurance company. Have you ever heard of Masterlife Insurance?"

"Everyone's heard of them. They're the ones with the cartoon tree in the rainstorm that the people take shelter beneath in the television commercials, right?"

"I don't watch a lot of TV but I think you're right."

"Didn't anyone ever tell those stupid ad people that it's dangerous to get beneath a tree in a storm? You might want to tell them from me that it's a truly bad commercial."

"It's a truly bad company." He grinned again. "That's why they're profitable."

"Well, then, you must be quite proud of yourself to work for them. Good luck in the investigation." She meant to stare him down at that point, but he didn't even look at her. His gaze was riveted to the other end of the stable. A shadow blocked the light at the other end. Even without turning, she knew someone had entered.

"Speaking of bad company, I see he's finally arrived," she heard Youngblood grumble.

Alyn turned around. Like a silhouette at the entrance to a cave, a man stood at the other end of the stable. All she could make out was that he was heavy-set and out of breath as if he'd been running.

"Garry! I didn't expect you. I thought you were in the village today supervising the feed deliver. I'd like to introduce you to Ms. Blum's niece. She's here overlooking her soon-to-be-acquired holdings."

She gasped and stared at Youngblood. Out of the corner of her eye, she could see the big man draw closer; she could hear the wheezing of his lungs as he tried to catch his breath.

"Alyn Blum-Jones," Youngblood gleefully announced, "I want you to meet one of Jacqueline's closest friends. He's the mastermind behind this new stable. Why, he was the first one to call for help when the old stable was burning. Meet your aunt's stable manager and all-around personal advisor: Garry Ferrucci."

CHAPTER SEVEN

"What are you doing here?" Ferrucci snapped. He glared at Youngblood, but his eyes kept darting toward Alyn.

"Just taking in the sights. Dr. Jones here wanted a tour. I felt obliged." Youngblood smirked.

Blood gushed into Ferrucci's face. He looked like he might strike Youngblood, but if he did, Alyn put her money on Youngblood. Not only was Youngblood younger by twenty years, he was also in much better shape.

"Get out. You're trespassing," the man snarled, particularly in her direction. He snatched up the leather lead chain on Wonderwall and began walking the animal back to its stall.

Alyn stared after the man. She found it impossible to believe that her aunt could have let this man run her stable. Ferrucci looked like some overblown lounge lizard with his thick diamond ring, ostentatious cuff links and slicked back hair. He was so out of Jacqueline Blum's class that they were in different galaxies.

"You don't like him, do you?" Youngblood whispered in her ear.

She looked up at him, startled. "No."

"Nobody else does either."

"Jacqueline must have liked him. Or she wouldn't have trusted him with her precious Wonderwall."

"Lust is blind, Alyn."

"You mean you think really—?"

"To Jacqueline, Garry Ferrucci was a younger man. A stud." He ran a finger along her cheek as if to drill the message home. "There was a lot of talk about them around the stable here. A lot of talk."

She turned away. Her heart twisted for Jacqueline. Ferrucci was a slimeball; she got that message in less than a second. It was absurd that Jacqueline even tolerated him, but somehow he must have seemed better than what she had. At some point, Jacqueline must have tossed aside all her imaginary lovers to seek out a warm body next to her. Alyn just hoped it had been worth the sacrifice.

She walked back through the stable, ignoring Youngblood's shadow behind her. Disturbing thoughts danced through her head like ghouls in front of a fire. Ferrucci certainly could have killed her aunt. He had all the motive in the world. Statistically, a woman was more likely to be killed by her husband or lover than by anyone else in the world.

Her heart mired in darkness, she climbed back into the Explorer. Before they pulled away from the stable, she vowed that no matter how lonely she got in her older years, she would never fall into bed with a man who wore diamonds.

* * *

Alyn curled by the blazing hearth and reread Jacqueline's last letter. The brilliant sunlight of the morning had faded to gray. A mist of rain slicked the windows. She'd found some teabags in the guest house kitchen and made a pot to sip by the fire. Outside the wind was blowing and it was growing colder. The news predicted snow overnight.

She hadn't been able to leave for Dulles as planned. After she'd exchanged acknowledgments with that repulsive lump of a man Garry Ferrucci, she let Youngblood drop her off at his cottage so that she might read his copy of Jacqueline's half-finished letter. Time passed and Youngblood had yet to return so she built a fire to ward off the falling temperatures. Now the tea had been drunk, the letter read, and still no sign of Peter Youngblood.

He was a strange man. Not as strange as Ferrucci, or perhaps just as strange, but in a different way. Youngblood seemed completely without morals. It made sense that he was the one recruited by the insurance company to protect their interests. He was an unlikely avenger but there was a bitter streak in him that could prove useful if one were looking for a mercenary.

She couldn't help wondering what he was all about. He'd had a past and from the tattoo on his arm it hadn't been a nice past. Still, he'd showed her Jacqueline's last letter. The document had stayed in his mind. Perhaps even touched his cold soul.

She looked down at the photocopy in her hand. The original was with the police. Firelight reflected off the paper, giving it a surreal glow, but perhaps it was surreal, an unfinished letter written by a doomed woman:

BLUMFIELD

Dear Alyn,

There's so much I want to tell you that the page won't hold all my thoughts. Before too long, I must tell you more about your grandfather and do my best to explain (but not excuse) why he did what he did to your mother. When you come to my beautiful Blumfield we'll spend our days in the stable and the evenings by the fireplace while I fill you in on all that you don't know. For some reason, in light of certain events, I feel compelled to tell you things about the family, so that if something should happen to me, there will still be one Blum in this world who knows about our family.

But before I make presumptions about your interest, I must first confess how dearly I want us to be friends. I want you to come here for a long visit and see all that I love, but I'm afraid—

Alyn closed her eyes. *I'm afraid—I'm afraid—* The words ricocheted through her mind like a bullet. She couldn't fill in the rest and it tortured her to imagine all the possibilities. What had Jacqueline been afraid of? Was she going to say, *I'm afraid the weather in Blumfield might be bad during your stay,* or was she going to say, *I'm afraid someone is going to kill me?*

A log fell in the fire, disturbing her thoughts. Alyn cursed the

English language for allowing gross ambiguities. *I'm afraid*— It could mean anything, or everything, or nothing.

She sighed and put down the letter. On a whim, she retrieved the other copies of Jacqueline's letters which were in her bag and compared them to one another. Pouring herself another cup of tea, she curled up on the couch and read each letter in turn:

BLUMFIELD

February 27th

Dear Alyn,

I know it will come as quite a shock to you to receive this letter, but I hope that you will read this in the spirit with which it was written. As you know, your mother, Colette, was my sister. We were never close and the family rift only served to make us strangers, but now I've come to see we were far from that. Colette and I shared the same parents, the same blood, and now, unfortunately, the same disease.

Last Christmas I had a lumpectomy in my right breast. My prognosis is excellent, with no side effects to the radiation, nor the surgery. In fact I only wish your mother had had such sensitive and caring people working on her when this terrible scourge struck her. She would have jumped right back into the world as I feel compelled to do. But such wasn't the case when your mother was stricken, and now how well I see her sufferings.

In light of this late but hard-earned empathy, could I be so forthright and ask you to write me back? Today I turned fifty years old, and I can't stop thinking of your mother, and now you. I must know who this last Blum is. Please take pity on an aging heiress who's known little in her life but the nasty chill of money. I will await your note with the most humble gratitude.

Your aunt,
Jacqueline

Alyn's hand still trembled when she read it even though the lines were memorized long ago. Jacqueline's letter had shocked her. It had brought back so much: her mother's butchery, her death, a daughter's loneliness, and finally a yearning to have a part of the family back, even if it meant putting her hand out to a stranger. A rich and famous stranger.

She looked down at letter two. Succinct and to the point, the note seemed hurried, as hurried as the Federal Express man who'd delivered it.

BLUMFIELD

March 15th

Dear Alyn,

You've delighted me beyond words with your kind letter! How much it would mean to me to have you visit Blumfield! I have a new Thoroughbred in my stable and I would be so excited to show him off to you. "Wonderwall"—my lover boy—cost me ten million dollars. He's the most expensive horse I've ever owned, but he's an exquisite creature and inside him beats a heart of gold. If only human men were made so well—I might actually remarry!—but instead I've learned to be a good heiress and stay out of the tabloids. I've finally smartened up—now I keep all my men a secret.

Please come to Blumfield as soon as you can. I must meet my sister's only child because I know I will see her in your eyes.

Your aunt,
Jacqueline

Alyn wondered how much was good-natured kidding in the letter and how much was the dark truth. When she'd received the second letter, she'd taken it in stride and noted nothing unusual. But reading it now, she found it ominous that Jacqueline was keeping her men a secret. Secret lovers had to be far more dangerous than imaginary ones.

She put the letter down and pensively tapped her fingers on her teacup.

"Any new revelations?"

She gasped. Youngblood stood in the doorway to the living room, staring at her. It was obvious he'd been there for a while.

"I didn't hear you come in," she said, catching her breath.

"I know. You were caught up in those letters. What's in them that holds your interest?"

"There's nothing that noteworthy . . . it's just that I was wondering what man she was seeing, that's all." She glanced at him, then looked away.

He smiled. "She liked secrets. Being rich and famous and dogged by reporters, I guess she felt she couldn't keep any."

He sauntered into the room and lowered himself to one of the plump couches. It was a strange feeling for Alyn to sit at the hearth looking up at Peter Youngblood. She wanted to rise and give herself a more dignified seat on the couch opposite his, but she was afraid if she did that she might look nervous or intimidated.

She was afraid. There was that line again, she thought. It could mean so much or mean nothing.

"I suppose I should get to Dulles. I'll miss the last shuttle to Boston if I don't leave right now."

"Consider yourself tardy. There's a storm coming. I doubt your flight will even take off."

She got to her feet using more nonchalance than was probably realistic under the circumstances. "Really, I'm sure it'll be fine. I've stayed too long as it is, and there's nothing more I can add to this mess."

"Do you want to stay the night in a vinyl chair at the airport or do you want the comforts of this place? You choose."

She twisted her mouth into the semblance of a smile. "Thanks for the offer but I really think I'd better take my chances and get to Dulles."

"No."

His terse command took her off guard. She wanted to give him a double-take. She certainly wasn't used to someone bluntly telling her no.

"What do you mean?" she almost stammered.

He calmly stretched out his legs onto the French-polished coffee table. "I mean no. You won't be taking your chances and going to Dulles. You'll be staying tonight at Blumfield."

She wondered if her hearing had failed. "I'm sorry but I still don't know what you mean. That majordomo doesn't want me around here another night, and there's nothing more I can give the police. I never even laid eyes on my aunt. It was a non-relationship except for these three letters. There's no more reason to stay here.''

''Did you know, when I left the police force, I became what's known as a bounty hunter. The insurance companies love to hire me because I can find out almost any information they need and I can do it quickly. That's why I was taken on by Masterlife to come here and size up the situation. I'm good at grabbing by the balls and not letting go. I mean, after all, that's my job. You see? I find these deadbeat jail jumpers and drag them back to the court and settle up. The money's out there—pretty good if you have the success rate I do.''

She really felt like she'd entered the cuckoo's nest. Youngblood was just plain nuts and it sure would benefit her to make as clean and quick an exit as possible.

''Wow. Impressive.'' She quavered a smile. ''And the next time we meet I hope you'll tell me some of your better stories, but right now, I really have to get the rental car back. My contract expires tonight, and I don't want all those extra charges waiting for me on the American Express bill, so if you'll just excuse—''

He stood. She never remembered him being so tall and so big. He was one big mass of muscle and hidden tattoos. She didn't want to look intimidated, but suddenly there was no hiding it.

''Hey look—'' she sputtered.

He laughed, clearly enjoying her fear. ''You know what a bondsman is?''

''N-no.''

''He's a jailor. He's given that right by the feds. A bounty hunter is going after the suspect to get the bond back, but he's given the right to be the suspect's temporary jailor until he gets the suspect to the court—whenever that may happen. You know, once I had to hold some asshole for two weeks trying to get the courts to cough up the airfare from Phoenix to Atlanta.''

''Really? How—how interesting,'' she stammered, ''but what does this have to do with the price of tea in China?''

''Hold on.'' He reached into his jeans pocket and retrieved a shiny black wallet. He took out a small card. ''We don't read the Miranda Warning to our suspects because they've already been formally charged with a crime. So what we bondsmen read is the

Supreme Court ruling of 1872, Taylor V. Taintor. Do you mind if I read it to you?''

She stared at him, sure he could see every millimeter of the whites of her eyes. ''Hey, I really can't stop you, now can I?''

''Great.'' He glanced down at the laminated card in his hand and began to recite from it. He looked like a little kid reading a *Dick and Jane* book except that he was no child but two hundred pounds of sinew and muscle, and he was beginning to terrify her.

''When bail is given, the principal is regarded as delivered to the custody of his sureties. Their dominion is a continuance of the original imprisonment. Whenever they choose to do so, they may seize him and deliver him up in their discharge; and if that cannot be done at once, they may imprison him until it can be done. They may exercise their rights in person or by agent. They may pursue him into another State; may arrest him on the Sabbath; and if necessary, may break and enter his house for that purpose. The seizure is not made by virtue of new process. None is needed. It is likened to the rearrest by the sheriff of an escaping prisoner.

''In 6 Modern, it is said, 'The bail have their principal on a string, and may pull the string whenever they please, and under him in their discharge.'

''The rights of the bail in Civil and Criminal cases are the same.''

He lowered the card and slipped it back into his wallet.

She stared at him, dead silent.

''Do you get what I'm saying?'' he asked.

She shook her head. ''No, I don't get it. I'm not a bail jumper, and yet, you seem to have me confused with one.''

''I'm just letting you know how I work. I'm pretty good at being a bounty hunter.'' He placed his wallet under her nose. ''American alligator. Costs a fortune, but I can afford it, you see. I'm a fucking success story.''

''That card may give you the right to hold a bail jumper, but I'm a free citizen, charged with no crime, and I choose to leave.'' She took a deep breath. ''To prevent me from leaving is called kidnapping. That's a federal charge, in case you didn't know.''

''Quite familiar with it. But I'm going to 'urge' you to stay here because there's a thin judiciary between what a bondsman can do in the line of duty, and what he can do just for the hell of it.''

She took a step backward and her calves bumped against the couch. A log sparked in the fire, fueling further tension to the room.

"I don't get it. Why do you want me to stay here? You've no bail bond to collect on me, and the police know I'm here. They'll find that out when I turn up missing—which I will surely be when I don't return to work tomorrow morning."

"You can call and let them know you won't be going to work right away. Those rabies shots you give out to the kitties can wait a few more days, I imagine."

"What purpose does this serve?" she asked, her heart pounding in her chest. She wondered if the sick fear that was drumming through her veins was the last thing Jacqueline felt before she disappeared.

"I want you to stay a few extra days because I've still got to find out some things before I know what's gone on here. And you're part of the puzzle, whether you know it or not."

"I'm not part of this. I swear I'm not."

"Oh, but you are. I just found out it's official. You stand to inherit everything in the Blum name. You have the biggest motive of all the dirtbags wandering around this place."

"What?" Her heart stopped in her chest.

"You stand to inherit all of the Blum billions. You're named in her will, and you're the recipient of her life insurance—but you knew that."

She dropped to the couch. Air seemed to turn her lungs to iron. She couldn't speak. Her mind was numb. Petrified.

"Yeah," he said softly, looking down at her, "you have all the motive"—his voice became harsh but barely discernable—"but none of the personality."

Her mouth felt as dry as a salt lick. "I didn't know any of this. Not any of this. And I don't want the Blum fortune. As far as I'm concerned, the Blums are cursed by their money, every last one of them, and I want none of their curse. I'm pretty happy without it."

"Spoken like a true heroine. Only riddle me this: you're the sole name on the Masterlife policy. No one else is going to get that insurance money but you, so who else has a bigger motive to make Jacqueline Blum disappear than you?''

She locked gazes with him, hers imploring. ''I don't want her life insurance. I just wanted to meet my mother's sister. I came here to see if I could be of any use to the investigation.''

''Yes, but you see my dilemma now, don't you? Masterlife doesn't want to find out that their client was murdered for her insurance money, and baby, Masterlife thinks the murderer is you.''

Terror froze her mind. She ran her hands through her scalp, loosening her hair from her ponytail. She probably looked wild, probably looked just like the homicidal maniac he thought she was—but she couldn't help herself. The anxiety of his accusation was like acid, dripping, dripping, dripping, until she went mad.

Her voice shook when she spoke. ''I can't tell you this more clearly, I had nothing to do with my aunt's disappearance. Nothing. I wanted to meet her. To get to know her. I've no other relatives. My father abandoned me before I was even born and my mother died last year. I've got nobody and suddenly Jacqueline Blum writes to me. It was intriguing. I wanted to meet her. I wanted to like her. I *wanted* a relative, not money.''

Tears suddenly welled in her eyes and streamed down her cheeks. She couldn't believe how twisted everything had gotten.

''You see my dilemma?'' He knelt in front of her and looked deep into her eyes. ''That's really the only question I want answered now. Do you see why I need more information from you? I'm being pulled on every side, and I can't make any decision until I know more.''

She gave a cynical laugh through her tears. ''What are we playing now? Good cop, bad cop?''

''Maybe, but you've got to stay here and answer my questions. Do you understand that?''

She looked down at him. It would have felt so good to lash out at him and threaten him with lawyers and even the ACLU. But she did see his dilemma. It horrified her to the point of nausea, but if what he was saying was true, she had to deal with it. There was now more she herself needed to find out, so his plan for her staying suddenly seemed like the only thing she could do.

''I have clients. I'll have to call Quincy and see if I can reschedule.'' She took a shaky breath. ''But if I stay I want to see a copy of that insurance policy. I want to know who the second, third—hell, even the fiftieth—beneficiary of that life insurance is. I think I have a right to know.''

He nodded. ''Fine. And make all the calls you need. But just tell them it may be a while before you can return to being Dr. Dolittle.'' Sobered, he rose and pulled away from her as if she suddenly bothered him somehow.

She dragged herself to her feet. Never in her life had she been so confused and frightened. Not even when her mother had died. Her mother had had a disease and it had killed her. A plus B equaled C. But this, this was a ball that came from left field at the speed of light.

She wiped her eyes with the back of her hand. Her hand trembling, she picked up the receiver and called Joyce at home. She prayed she could keep the terror out of her voice just long enough to tell Joyce how to handle things at the clinic.

CHAPTER EIGHT

Alyn's hand still shook as she lifted the glass of red wine to her lips. "I think under the circumstances I should go back to the main house and stay there."

"No."

She looked at Youngblood, again astounded at how definite he was with his answers. "But it looks a little strange, don't you think, to be residing in the same 'cottage' with you. That could be called fraternizing with the enemy."

"I fraternize with the enemy all the time. In fact that's my fucking job now." He poured himself a glass of scotch from the Johnnie Walker bottle on the mantel.

She wanted to say something sarcastic like, "Gee, you sound bitter," but now wasn't the time for wisecracks. Besides, she didn't want to know anything more about this man in front of her than she absolutely had to. Delving into his past would no doubt be like opening a Pandora's box and she had her own open right now.

"Your career choices aside, I really think it best that I ask Hector to provide me a room in the main house." She twirled the wine around in her glass, again making a lame attempt at self-confidence.

" 'Hector,' is it?" He laughed. "I'm glad you two hit it off. So, what, this place isn't good enough for the soon-to-be billionairess? You've grown fond of that Temple of Dendur down the road?"

She looked at him, confusion clouding her features. "No, that's not it at all. I just think it best that I stay in a neutral place. It doesn't seem prudent to be staying here."

"Neutral place." He chuckled again. "Did I mention that Hector and Garry were your aunt's closest advisors here? They were the ones originally named as beneficiaries to her life insurance—that is, until about a couple of weeks ago when she had her lawyers cross out their names and put yours in instead." He stood and walked to the cherry desk-bookcase, taking a thick pile of papers off of it. He plopped them in her lap. "Hey, sure, go stay at the main house. Hector would just love to see you meet with a freak accident."

Her quaking hand rested at her throat like a woman being faced with a noose. She looked down and realized he'd given her a copy of the Masterlife insurance policy. She read and reread it. "You're not even joking. They were the beneficiaries."

"Yep." He clinked his scotch with her wineglass. "And they are most put out by the fact that *Schockleen,* as you pronounce her name, was so befuddled as to do this to them in their hour of need."

"You mean that majordomo knew I was the one who replaced him on Jacqueline's life insurance?"

"Of course. You couldn't tell that by his warm greeting the other night when you arrived?"

She took two slow deep breaths. "I wondered why he didn't object to my arrival at the house. Here I was some stranger calling upon a woman who everyone in the world knows is not at home. I had no idea he knew who I was."

"I'll bet he was pretty damned surprised to see you at the door." He grinned. "I'll never forget the expression on his face when I introduced you to him."

"That's why his wife hated me."

"Giselda? She's a hard one to read. Maybe she hated you, but as far as I can tell she hates her husband worse. Dante treats her like a dishtowel."

"I saw that."

"And he was screwing your aunt right in the same house as his wife. How's that for marital tension?"

She stared at him, another wave of shock hitting her. "You're making that up. Jacqueline was doing Hector Dante?"

"I understand that women have always thought him handsome. He's been a bounder all his life."

"He is handsome. But—but—he's the help."

"Some cliché, huh?"

"How do you know this?"

"Word gets around. All I know is that Giselda didn't have too much fondness for your aunt because she was highly suspicious of her promiscuous husband and his penchant for the good life. Jacqueline always held a soft spot for handsome men and apparently Hector was one of them."

"And that man at the stable, Garry Ferrucci, he was written off the life insurance along with Dante?"

"Bingo."

"Was that why he was so hostile in the stable when he saw us?"

"Right again. Hey, have you ever thought of going onto a game show? You could win a bundle with a mind like yours."

She didn't appreciate the wisecrack. Her shoulders slumped and she turned grim.

Quietly, she asked, "Do you think Dante and Ferrucci killed Jacqueline?"

"They had less motive than you do, babe."

"That's not what I asked," she shot out.

He nodded. "I know."

"Did they kill Jacqueline?"

"At one time that crazy old broad had them inheriting the entire estate. She had no children, no husband. All she wanted was to leave her horses in good hands, and so she chose to give her money to Ferrucci believing he would take care of them, and she left Dante the other half, I suppose, in the hopes that he would always remember her."

She thought of the man they'd met earlier in the stable. Garry Ferrucci was fifty if he was a day, and overweight. His graying yellow hair had been sprayed into an Elvis pompadour which fitted with the chunks of diamonds on his fingers. His breath stank of cheap rum; his attitude stank of La Cosa Nostra. He'd glared at her in only a slightly less violent manner than he'd glared at Youngblood, and he'd told them in no uncertain terms what he thought of him snooping around his stable. ''Masterlife's next visit will have to be under court order,'' he'd shouted at Youngblood before three men in Blumfield purple and gold jackets arrived to make sure they made a hasty departure in the Explorer.

Alyn curled her lip in disgust. ''How could Jacqueline be so foolish? So blind? I know nothing about either man, but anyone can see Ferrucci is a total slimeball.''

''Who else did she have in her life? Everyone knew her father's mantra was that she would only be used for her money. Hell, he had her sister as a living example of Daddy's warning. So Jacqueline trusted no one; she *had* no one, and she handled everything badly.''

She turned toward the fire. Depression settled over her like a shroud.

Her own situation mirrored her aunt's in many ways. Her father's abandonment seemed at times to govern all her actions and judgment. She was never instructed right out in the open to not trust men, but she knew the guidelines anyway. Her own mother's bitterness had been a brilliant teacher. Colette never liked to talk about Allen. Not really. But the truth came out in small little parables that had formed Alyn. Once, at school in a parent/teacher conference, Alyn remembered her new teacher asking her mother what her husband did for a living. Not realizing Alyn was within earshot, Colette had answered, ''He gets away.''

It had meant to be funny. Perhaps the teacher had even laughed. Alyn didn't remember that part. All she remembered was feeling another thrust of the abandonment sword go through her heart. Her father, without lifting a finger to form her, had made Alyn into a cold fish. A woman who trusted no one; who had no one.

Which was why it had seemed so very imperative to connect with Jacqueline, to find out if there was a cure for the Blum affliction, or at least find comfort in the company of the fellow inflicted.

But that would never happen now. Instead, Alyn was just another Blum woman waiting to be victimized by her loneliness and bad judgment.

"Do you think Ferrucci and Dante might hurt me?" she whispered aloud before she could choke the fearful question down.

"I can't rule it out. They have no fondness for you, that's for sure. You've gotten in the way, big time."

"But I don't want to be in the way. I didn't ask for this."

"What do you expect when you're the heir to a billion-dollar fortune? Do you expect things to be easy? Do you expect everyone to say congrats and leave you alone?"

"Yes, because I'm not taking it. Not even if I'm named in the will. The damn money's cursed and I utterly reject the offer of it. In fact, I reject all offers. I want out of here." She stood and grabbed her coat and purse off the back of the couch.

His hand shot out and took her fleece coat by the collar.

"Did you kill your aunt?" he demanded.

"NO!" she cried.

"Do you know who did?"

"No!"

"Then do you think running back to Massachusetts is going to keep you out of harm's way? You'll still be leaving behind a lot of disappointed people back here in Blumfield." He leaned toward her. She could almost taste his breath as he whispered, "Keep your friends close," he yanked her to him, "and your enemies closer."

"I can't help with any of this. I can't do anything about it." She began to weep.

"Look . . . you can't just walk out of this unscathed." His words were more gentle than she expected.

"Is someone going to kill me?" She looked up at him, her face raked with tears, fear in her eyes.

"Maybe," he rasped.

"You?" She began to shake. "I mean, I know nothing about you except what you've told me. I guess you do work for Masterlife, but I've never checked it out for myself."

"Lesson One, then. You know nothing about anyone here. Keep it in mind."

"You're right. I shouldn't trust anyone. Not you. Not anyone."

"True."

"Oh God." She crumpled. Her head lowered to her hands and she felt faint. Inside, she was no longer Dr. Alyn Blum-Jones, confident and educated Doctor of Veterinary Medicine; instead, she was a frightened little girl again, just like the one who used to stay by her mama's hospital bedside until the nurse told her she had to go home.

In the back of her mind, she knew two strong arms had gone around her. Her instincts were to fight such contact; she wasn't used to it. But for some reason the fight had gone out of her. If Youngblood did mean to hurt her, she was giving him a helping hand by being so weak.

"I don't know what to say to you," he said gently into her hair. "You might just be a really good actress, and I might just be a fool, but I have to tell you, Dr. Jones, you're really twisting this in on me."

He held her against his hard chest and instead of wanting to flee, she surrendered. He was so warm, so big and engulfing. He made her feel safe and protected. She couldn't remember when she'd last been held like he held her. Nor when she last ever felt safe and protected.

He stared down at her. His large hands stroked the tight curls that had escaped her ponytail. "Look at you," he whispered. He touched the glass of her rimless gold spectacles. "You're nothing but incongruities. You've got the hair of a pixie and the glasses of an old man."

She locked gazes with him. "If I trust you I'll be as stupid as Jacqueline, and I can't do that."

"I know," he answered.

"But if I don't have someone to trust in this mess, I'll have no one to turn to."

"Your aunt was rich and men preyed on her."

"Technically I could be that rich now."

"Technically, you are that rich."

"You've already told me how much you like your job because of the money you make. You like money."

"I like money because that's all that's left for me to enjoy. I used to love being a cop. I used to love doing the right thing; being the hero. Now all I do is make money."

"I don't want Jacqueline's money. Do you believe me?"

He looked away. "You know, I almost do. Jesus, you have me

fooled. I swear you're so fucking wholesome. Not at all what I expected."

"What did you expect?"

He took her chin in his hand and tilted her face up to his. "I expected someone more calculating, more greedy, more evil, and someone much less . . . seductive to me."

He took her breath. She hadn't admitted to herself how attractive he was because he was someone who frightened her. But now, with his strange confession, she felt herself melt, and finally yearn. The loneliness inside her went from a cold ache to a heated one.

"This isn't the way to keep your enemies closer," she said, her lips quavering.

"Sometimes it's the best way." He leaned closer.

Before she could stop him, his mouth covered hers and she felt her body tremble from the moan that fought for escape.

It had to be the terror of the situation; the need for a sense of safety; the anxiety of not knowing what was ahead of her. If someone had told her that in twenty-four hours she'd be kissing Peter Youngblood with all the fury of a high school virgin, she'd have laughed until she cried. Now all she wanted to do was open her mouth and suck his tongue inside and hold him close so that no demons from the outside could sneak up on her.

He broke away. In a cold, matter-of-fact voice he said, "I think there's a little of your aunt in you after all. You both seemed to find the wrong people to trust."

She was devastated. She never let down her guard as she had just done with him. Now, to find him mocking her was shattering.

"Let me show you which room is yours." He walked to the foyer and out the front door. Her bag was still in the Geo.

She watched him go, her emotions tied into a knot. Her heart icing over once more.

* * *

Freezing. She was freezing. It was either her nerves or the damp cold of the storm, but here she was, four hundred miles south of Quincy, Massachusetts, and she swore she'd never been so cold in her life.

Alyn dug through her overnight case and zipped on the violet polar fleece vest. She rubbed her upper arms and stared longingly at the cold hearth of the fireplace in her bedroom. There were no servants in this house to light the logs and bring her hot tea. Just that terrible man, Youngblood, who was either the greatest threat to her safety she'd ever known, or her most merciful savior. She knew in the end he would have no middle ground. Without a doubt, Peter Youngblood took no prisoners.

She combed her shaking fingers through her curls and retied her hair behind her neck with a scrunchie. Polishing her spectacles on a tissue, she walked to the bedroom door. She had to resign herself to the evening; she would spend it talking to Youngblood. There was too much she didn't know about the situation to waste valuable time on her pride.

So he'd kissed her, and then made fun of her stupidity. She wasn't the first woman in the world to be made a fool of, and she'd never be the last. All she knew was that his warning was not in vain. If he was the enemy, then she would treat him like one.

A necessary evil. That's all he would be from now on.

She walked downstairs and sat once again next to the hearth. She could hear pots and pans clacking in the kitchen. Her first thought was that maybe she should offer to help him, but she immediately stopped herself. He needed no friendly companionship. Besides, if he was making dinner, she had no appetite, so why offer.

"I left some on the stove in case you want any." Youngblood sat down on the couch opposite her with a large plate of spaghetti and meat sauce.

She lifted her nose to it. With a chill in her voice that matched the one in her heart, she said, "I'm vegetarian, thank you."

"A vegetarian veterinarian. I guess that makes sense. It's kind of fun to say too." He slurped up a thick forkful of pasta.

"I like animals."

He looked at her.

"*Some* animals," she qualified.

He smiled and poured himself a glass of wine. "Kind of a pity. I mean, to refuse to eat only the animals you like. Sometimes they taste the best."

"I'm not too fond of pigs, but I don't eat them either." She hoped she sounded as icy as she felt.

"I'm not a pig. You like me enough not to eat me?"

"No," she answered.

He grinned but didn't look at her. "Good."

She poured herself another glass from the bottle. The wine made her feel warm and not so afraid.

"It's my turn to ask the questions," she announced, recurling up on the couch.

"Fire," he grunted.

"I want to know why the police haven't charged anyone with a crime. That Wonderwall is a walking-around monument to fraud, and Garry Ferrucci is a con man. Why isn't he being charged with something?"

"Do you hear anyone complaining about that horse? You hear someone bitching that they paid more than he was worth?"

"Jacqueline, even if she figured it out, might not be in the position to be able to complain."

"Exactly." He put his empty plate on the coffee table. "Go to the head of the class, Dr. Blum-Jones."

"So as I see it, everyone's in a stalemate here. This limbo could last through the end of time."

"No. Not forever."

"What do you mean?" she asked, staring at him from the top of her wineglass.

"Masterlife's only going to pay on their policy when they've proof their client is dead. They need proof of her death to collect, and whoever killed Jacqueline—if they did it for the insurance—knows that."

"But the only one who benefits from Jacqueline being declared dead now is me."

He lifted one dark eyebrow. "God damn, you're a rocket scientist."

Anger swelled inside her. "Yeah, I guess I am. Because I know something you don't."

"Which is?"

"Which is that I had nothing to do with Jacqueline's disappearance. So if I did it for the insurance, I'm stuck. I can't prove she's dead. I can't prove anything because I don't know what happened to her."

He lowered his head as if he were deep in thought. "Okay, let's go with that hypothesis."

"Yes. And let's just say Ferrucci and Dante are just as surprised as I am about Jacqueline's change of heart. They could have planned her demise months ago in an attempt to get her money, and were foiled at the last minute by her changing her will. Have you thought of that?"

"I think of everything." His eyes lifted. He scanned her face then his gaze lowered to a place somewhere below her chin. If he were one of her clients, she'd be recommending neutering right now.

She folded her arms across her chest. Hating to be self-conscious, she went on with her train of thought. "I think someone has done something terrible to Jacqueline. If I didn't do it, you've no choice but to go after Ferrucci and/or Dante. They have motive and nefarious painted all over them."

He said nothing.

"I really don't understand the police," she continued. "Wonderwall is no ten-million-dollar Thoroughbred, handsome though he is. Garry Ferrucci seems like the first person to start to investigate."

He rose and walked to the Goddard desk-bookcase at the end of the living room. He took three files from the desktop and walked back to the couch.

She grunted when he tossed the thick folders onto her lap.

"What's this?" she asked.

"The investigation. The first file is Ferrucci, the second, Dante."

"And this thin one?"

He lifted the corner of his mouth in a tight smile. "That's yours. We were most impressed. There's very little out there on you, Dr. Jones."

She held her breath and opened the third file. Inside were her transcripts from kindergarten at Churchill Elementary School all the way through Cornell Veterinary School. A copy of her birth certificate was there, along with her diploma and admittance into the American Board of Veterinary Practitioners. It came as no surprise to her to see her credit report and 1040 filings from the past ten years of reporting income to the IRS. But she wasn't expecting the last four documents.

Her mother's hospital records were carefully filed by date. The first document recorded her mastectomy and aftercare at Mercy General Hospital. The second clinically recounted her bout with the return of the cancer. The third record was her last trips to the emergency room. Her bones had become so brittle that she'd broken both femurs in one week just lying in bed.

Reading was agony for Alyn. Tears balled in her throat like a fist.

But the worst was yet to come. She knew what it would be before she turned to it. The death certificate. All too familiar. She remembered the time and place, and forever it would be etched upon her memory.

She closed the file and put it aside. Quietly, she said, "Your file's incomplete."

"It is?" He raised one eyebrow.

"You don't have anything about my father in there. You've left him out."

He didn't say anything for a long moment. "I thought you never knew your father."

"Yes, but he still exists—at least I think he does—and he's a part of me. It's a big omission to leave him out of my file."

"Agreed," he answered grimly.

Ferrucci and Dante's files were next for her to go through but she hadn't the heart to open them. It was blasphemy that she and them were all put in the same investigation. Ferrucci's file was more than an inch thick; she didn't need to be a mind reader to know that most of the documents in it would be court records of how he and his kind had yet again evaded the law through lack of evidence.

"You're not going to read the others?" He rested his wineglass on his chest and stretched his legs out onto the couch.

"Would anything in there surprise me?"

He snorted. "Nothing new in there, that's for sure."

"Then I think I'll take these two files to bed and see if reading about their monotonous revolving-door brushes with the law cures my insomnia."

He glanced at her. Amusement gleamed in his eyes. "The police can't convict on a theory. They have to have proof—in every case."

"Speaking of lawyers," she interjected, "I know what I'm going to do tomorrow. I'm going into Potomac Village, find the first flunky who's got a shingle hanging out front of his office, and I'm going to get myself unwritten out of Jacqueline's will."

"Why would you do that?" He seemed sobered immediately.

"I'm not going to do it to prove my innocence. I don't have to do that. I've never been charged with a crime. I've never committed a crime." She shook her head. The scrunchie slipped at the back of her neck and a few curls fell into her eyes. "No, I'm getting myself written out of this mess—to save my life if need be."

"I don't know if you can write yourself out of a will that has yet to be validated with a death certificate."

She released a deep breath. Two more small curls fell into her eyes and she brushed them away with all the patience of a toddler.

"You look tired."

She studied him. "I was up late last night."

"Then I invite you to go to bed early tonight."

"But I've got to clear this mess up so that I can get back to Quincy tomorrow."

"I don't think anything's going to be cleared up until Ferrucci and Dante are caught with their fingers in the cookie jar."

"But what if that doesn't happen?"

"I'll make it happen—and I'll catch them unless you're the one I should be going after." His voice turned dark. "And if I find that out for certain, I'll catch you. I promise."

"How can you entrap these two? It won't hold up in court if you do—at least that's what I thought."

He leaned his head back against one of the thick down pillows on the couch. "The police can't use entrapment. Yeah, it gets thrown out of court then, but I'm not the cops. Not anymore."

She opened her mouth to ask about why that was, then she thought better of it. There was no use in riling this man while she was stuck in the same house with him.

"So do you have any ideas about what to do next? Any advice?"

Her questions sounded more sheepish than she'd have liked but she was still afraid. She saw Gary Ferrucci's amphibian green eyes every time she closed hers.

He turned his eyes and stared at her. "The only advice I'd give you right now is to watch your back."

"How do I do that?" she asked.

"You let someone else do it for you."

She looked away, worry clouding her face. "I—I really don't have anyone watching out for me. If you're saying to hire a detective or something like that, I'm not sure I can afford it. You see, I do a lot of work for the humane society and I don't make that much money."

"You've got billions, trillions and zillions coming to you. I have no doubt someone would do it and bill you later."

"I suppose you're right." She slumped against the couch. Deflated wasn't the right way to describe her. Stomped was more like it.

"Remove your glasses."

She looked at him, but said nothing. A strange tingle ran down her spine.

"Do it."

She kept her gaze trained on him. Slowly, her hand rose and she pulled the spectacles from her nose.

"Just as I thought."

"What?" she asked in a low voice.

"You look younger without them. You look twenty-five with them and twenty without them."

"I'm thirty-one."

"I know."

She looked at the folder with her name on it lying to the left. She felt violated but strangely comforted at the same time. He knew a lot about her, but he also knew a lot about the situation at Blumfield.

She held his gaze for a long moment and wondered again if he would be her salvation or her doom.

Slowly, she said, "I suppose you know everything."

"Everything that matters," he answered, closing the conversation with a cynical smirk.

CHAPTER NINE

It was midnight. The Masterlife Insurance building was lit up like a beacon in an industrial park sea. The night cleaning crew, a little mini-United Nations, went through the offices like dervishes, some pushing dust mops, some emptying wastepaper cans.

James Dunne ignored the onslaught. His hunched-over-his-desk silhouette appeared through the mahogany blinds of his office, bathed in the light of his green glass desk lamp. He shuffled through his files and drank coffee from a Styrofoam cup. And he tapped pencils on his desk until the points broke and he reached for another one. Everyone in Fraud knew when Dunne was uptight; his secretary would be busy in the morning sharpening a new box of pencils.

The phone rang on his desk.

He grabbed it like a lifeline.

"Harry, I swear to you. I'm onto it. The lawyers are meeting now." He listened for a moment, then said, "I'll call as soon as they've reached a conclusion. And I'll inform Youngblood. Yes, he's at the estate. He'll let us know if he leaves or if anything changes." Dunne listened into the receiver, and then nodded. "I'm onto it. Remember, I was the one who discovered this loophole." He paused again. The muscles in his shoulders visibly loosened.

"Thank you, Harry. You know I'll come through for you." He nodded again and hung up the receiver. Then he stared at the phone waiting for it to ring again, to give him the answers he sought.

* * *

Alyn didn't remember hearing the phone ring. She slept deeply, without interruption, until the knock on her bedroom door woke her.

Sitting bolt upright in the strange bed, she clutched at her robe and called out, "Yes?"

"Blum's lawyers have called. They've got some news." Youngblood's deep voice boomed through the door, chilling her.

"I'll be right there." She stumbled in the foreign room and searched for the lamp. Turning it on, she squinted against the light and searched for her slippers. They were nowhere to be seen, probably kicked beneath the bed. She hadn't the wherewithal at the moment to get down on her hands and knees to find them, so she padded across the cold wood floor, tied her terry bathrobe and opened the door.

He stood in the bedroom hallway looking almost as she remembered him from the other night. He wore another pair of flannel plaid boxers, but this time the boxers were wine-colored, and he had a gray sweatshirt pulled over his chest.

"They're contesting the will."

She pulled a hank of hair out of her eyes and tried to focus. "Who is 'they'?"

"Ferrucci's brother's a lawyer. He says the Blum estate was held in trust specifically to never be placed in your mother's hands—or her offspring. Do you know anything about this?"

She nodded. "I told you my mother was disinherited. I suppose this doesn't surprise me."

"Well, apparently, they want to invalidate Jacqueline Blum's last will. If they succeed everything could revert to Ferrucci and Dante if Jacqueline is declared dead."

No words would come to her.

"Angry?" His gaze studied her face.

"No," she breathed.

"You might have lost everything."

"I didn't want it," she answered emphatically. And it was true. The idea of being saddled with that kind of a fortune seemed like more of a burden than she could bear. A weight was lifted from her chest just by knowing her life might continue as usual.

She suddenly frowned. "But I guess I have to say I don't want Dante and Ferrucci to get everything. That positively nauseates me."

He stared her down. Even in the dim upstairs hallway, accusation and suspicion glittered in his eyes. "Since Masterlife's insurance policy was purchased with Blum money, they might be able to make a claim saying the trust implies that you can't be named as beneficiary to her life insurance. This would invalidate her current life insurance also. You'd get nothing of the twenty million. It would all go to her two trolls."

She knew he was waiting to see a reaction. Anger. The need for retribution. Perhaps even despair.

Instead all she said was, "Well, I guess there goes my credit line for a bodyguard."

He hesitated. Then he laughed.

His smile was all snarling white teeth, but it was infectious. She chuckled too. "But then, maybe I should be glad I'm getting out of this mess," she interjected. "Maybe now I don't need a bodyguard."

The laughter died from his expression.

Her grin dissipated like fog in the night. "What is it?" she asked, her voice sounding small and afraid.

"I think maybe you need someone watching you more than ever now."

"Why is that?" Bewilderment hardened her expression. "Their lawyers are getting me removed from the loop. You said so yourself."

"Jacqueline Blum hasn't turned up dead or alive."

"So?"

"So this is still a murder as far as I'm concerned. And I'd bet Jacqueline Blum's life on the fact that the one that has the motive to murder is the same one who's to inherit."

"But you thought that was me."

"Yes." A muscle bunched in his jaw. "But Jacqueline only named you as successor a couple of weeks before she disappeared. Somehow she had to have been tipped off that Ferrucci and Dante were no good. She probably figured they were dangerous and that's why she kept the changes to her estate a secret. Ferrucci and Dante probably didn't know anything about Jacqueline changing her will or her life insurance until they were confronted with it. I'll bet they were mightily surprised to find you messing things up."

"But I'm messing them up no longer."

"You could file against them."

"But I won't," she said adamantly.

"Their lives are pretty fucked up right now. The police are crawling all over this place and until there's a body, there's no will, no life insurance. They sure as hell don't want everything tied up with you in probate if they went to all the trouble to murder Jacqueline."

She swallowed a clump of fear. "God, if it's so obvious they did this thing, why can't the police arrest them?"

"No evidence. No body."

"Should I go back to Quincy and just keep quiet?"

"Do you think whoever killed your aunt is going to let a little veterinarian stand in the way of their riches? The impending litigation alone is enough to make someone want you out of the picture. You could make their lives hell and don't they know it."

She looked at him. Terror made her body go rigid. "Can't I just tell them I don't want the money."

He laughed. She took that as a no.

"I have no money to pay someone to protect me."

His hand lifted and he stroked the skin beneath her jaw. "Are you what you seem?" he asked.

"Yes," she whispered.

"Then I'll see that you're protected. I'll be the one to watch over you."

"Can you get these guys?"

A smile tipped the corner of his mouth. "Before they get you?"

"Yes," she choked out.

He chuckled. "I can try. You can't ask for more than that. Especially with the rates you pay."

* * *

Alyn tossed and turned all night. Her dreams raged and floated through clouds of thunderbanks. She awoke minutes before dawn, a thin film of perspiration covering her body.

She rose and went to the bath connected to her bedroom. Just like in the main house, the guest cottage bath was outfitted like a five star hotel's. She had no trouble finding shampoo and all the other toiletries to freshen up. After a fifteen-minute shower, she was a little more alert. But no less rattled.

It still made no sense to her that she should be in the middle of the situation at Blumfield. She wondered what Jacqueline had been thinking naming her—a niece she'd never even met—to inherit the bulk of her estate and life insurance. Jacqueline knew better than anyone that Alyn and her mother were legal pariahs to the Blum fortune.

It made no sense to Alyn except that Jacqueline had had her will and life insurance changed as a matter of desperation. She'd changed it because the way it had been written had suddenly become unpalatable to her. Perhaps Jacqueline had discovered she was in a rat's nest. The horse Wonderwall kept springing to mind. Perhaps Jacqueline had belatedly discovered the fraud. Or perhaps she was just dogged by suspicion. Perhaps in a hasty, ill-conceived moment, she'd changed her will and life insurance to protect her from Dante and Ferrucci, little knowing she was doomed anyway.

Alyn towel-dried her hair and pondered the bitter irony of the situation. If Dante and Ferrucci had done something to their boss in order to speed up the will, they were probably more than surprised to find out things had been tampered with. Peter Youngblood was right. As soon as there was a body, they'd have some evidence of a crime, which could ultimately point to the culprits.

But until then, it was a free-for-all, with Alyn in the middle of the game.

She went to the window and raked her fingernail across the

frost-laden pane. Her thoughts were dark. She longed for the warmth of the sun but it was slow in rising.

The rain had turned to ice overnight. A late winter storm had left every black branch, every tender green bud, dripping in iridescent ice. Alyn held her breath as the first glow hit the horizon. Mesmerized, she watched the fields and woods below her window come to life.

It was a beautiful sunrise. The glow turned from purple to orange to pink. Starlings and house wrens tweetered in the bare trees adding a symphony to the masterpiece. In the distance a group of tawny deer picked through a crushed field of winter rye nipping at whatever they could find.

Alyn nearly wept at the beauty of her aunt's estate. Blumfield was all she had imagined and yet even more. Its vulnerabilities were something she'd never expected; they made her heart ache. And her heart ached now, thinking how afraid she was, how blind and impotent she was against the unknown forces which had disposed of Jacqueline.

All she knew for certain was that she yearned to see yet another beautiful sunrise at Blumfield—or anywhere for that matter. She knew she just wanted to stay alive and healthy so that she could continue to see sunrises for all the years yet to come.

CHAPTER TEN

It is not enough to conquer; one must know how to seduce.
—VOLTAIRE

"When I have some news I'll call you. I already told you that. I don't need you ringing me at all hours wanting an update." Peter spoke into the cell phone with the same bored exasperation he'd use if he were talking to the cable company.

He listened to the person on the other end, then interrupted. "—Look, she just got here. If you want more information more quickly than I can get it, take over. Bulldoze her. And good luck."

Listening again, he closed his eyes and leaned back in the bed. Finally he interrupted again. "—Then you're going to have to wait until I get it for you or hire someone else. That's the way it is. Get it?"

He hit the END button, leaned off the edge of the bed and slid the phone as far across the room as he could.

The tension showed in the hard lines of his expression. If he took one more interrogation, he was going to shove that cell phone into a certain dark place where no one would ever hear it ring again.

Heaving a sigh, he let his mind wander. It went where he couldn't stop it. His thoughts went to her.

It wasn't like him to think about a woman too much. When he was on the force, he'd always been consumed with *the job*. He'd never had the time to connect with someone. But his days as a homicide cop were sure as hell over. Now he had lots of time to obsess about a female.

He lay in bed watching the morning light creep into the room. She was next door; he could hear her rise from her own bed and walk across the floorboards of her room.

Her name was unusual. Alyn. Just like a man's name, but there was nothing masculine about her. She looked like a little girl with her soft wheat-colored curls and her overly large eyes, eyes which he thought had a shade of green to them, especially when she stared across the spring grasslands of Blumfield.

She had a nice smile too. It was secretly inviting. It drew him in, especially when she looked at him with those eyes full of yearning and hesitant curiosity. Of course, she rationed it around him, but the few times when he'd made her grin, he felt as if someone had opened up his gut and tickled him with the point of a knife. She was all threat of pleasure, and all promise of pain. The light of her pretty mouth never quite overcame the gloom in her eyes, and that in itself became a challenge: to see what might rip down the sadness that veiled her like a cocoon.

He turned on his side. Willfully, his mind escaped the chains he held on it and began to fantasize about the woman in the room next door.

He pictured her rising from the bed, her hair loose and messy and slept on. Perhaps she was wearing just a T-shirt, white like her sheets, but it would be a man's T-shirt. It would fit her in a very different way than it fit him.

She would be still warm from the nest of her bed. Sleepy-eyed, she'd stretch and tantalize him with the loose bell-shaped hem of the T-shirt. It would rise, rise, rise until a shadow appeared between her legs, then she'd lower her arms, and the shirt would fall around her again, too big across her delicate shoulders, just barely big enough across the chest.

In his mind's eyes, he watched her walk across the floor. Her bare toes would dig at the rugs scattered along the way to the bathroom. As she walked, the T-shirt would reveal more and more hints of the curve of her waist, the fullness of her breasts, but it would still cover her. He was still unable to see her.

She'd go into the bathroom and turn on the shower. All he'd

be able to see now was the back of her. Slowly, perhaps because she was still not awake, she would pile those incredible curls on top of her head with a barrette. She would be sloppy about it and some curls would escape and grow tight in the rising steam of the shower. Then he would get a glimpse of the vulnerable softness of the back of her neck. That delicate place between the tendons where the hair went from thick and long to short and babyfine.

He groaned and thought back to a time when he was fourteen. He was the cleanup crew at a machine shop. The place was plastered with lewd pin-up calendars and centerfolds of big-breasted women. Skin was everywhere, and for a time he really enjoyed the view.

But there was one man whose bench he cleaned every night who didn't seem to go for all the sleaze. Peter knew nothing about the guy—had never laid eyes on him because he worked during the day and Peter worked at night—but all this guy had stuck to the wall was an 8 x 10 black and white abstract photo.

Peter might have never noticed it at all except that it stood out among all the garish Kodachrome. He still remembered the night he'd stopped by the guy's bench to really look at the photo. At first he couldn't make sense of it. It just looked like some kind of sci-fi amalgamation of light and dark. Dawning came upon him like the awakening of manhood.

It was a close-up of the back of a woman's neck. Her hair blended into the dark background. He could make out shadows where her fingers held her heavy mane out of the way of the camera lens. The shot was of dark hair and white skin erotically melting together until they became one.

He'd spent an hour staring at that photo, immersing himself in the sublime eroticism of it. All the skin mags in the world couldn't come close to matching the fascination he'd had for the back of that woman's neck. It was art. And now the back of Alyn's neck was art.

His thoughts trailed back to the shower. He could even hear the water running.

In his mind's eye he pictured her again. He'd still see nothing but the back of her as her feet would shuffle a towel in front of the bathtub. She'd use a leg to test the shower and the water would run down the back of her smooth calf, warming it.

She'd pull the T-shirt over her head and tossed it toward the hook on the door. It would miss and fall to the floor but she wouldn't see it. She wouldn't turn.

He might see a bit of her face in the mirror over the sink. Her expression would be relaxed, but internal. She'd wear just the simple enjoyment of the bodily pleasure of bathing. Her nude back would be the last vision of her before she disappeared behind the translucent shower curtain.

He'd stand at the bathroom door watching her. Her shape would be silhouetted in the curtain, the details blurred by the running water. She'd run her hands up and down her front rubbing herself with soap, immersing herself in the hot, cleansing experience of the water. He'd watch her like a man obsessed, even his tongue savoring the forbidden view of her behind the shower curtain.

He rolled onto his back in the bed. One long deep breath, and he succumbed once more to his imagination.

Entering her bathroom, quietly so that no floorboard would squeak, he'd pull down his boxers and throw them over the puddle of her T-shirt. The noise of the hammering shower would mask him slipping in behind her. There, in the shower with her, he'd watch her again, watch how she held her face to the showerhead, her shoulders low and relaxed, her neck slick with drops of water.

She was so vulnerable, so unaware of him. He enjoyed the anticipation, marveling how her whole mind seemed to be focused on the water raining down on her forehead.

His gaze would lower. He'd ache to put his hands on her narrow waist, he'd admire the lush curves of her ass, the shapeliness of her legs, the smooth hollow of her back right between the shoulder blades.

It was a real fantasy now, he thought to himself. A woman would shriek and hit the ceiling if she were surprised in the shower. But in his mind, he reached for her. His one hand covered her eyes; his other hand reached around her waist until his arm pressed her back against him.

She startles at the touch, but she doesn't scream; she shows no real fear. She seems to know immediately that it's him, and in a moment, he feels her relax against him, surrendering herself because it was his fantasy, and deep down, she's wanted him too.

He explores what he has yet to see. His hands rub down her front, a groan emanating from his chest as he revels in the weight of her breasts, the narrowness of her waist. His thumbs bump across her delicate ribs, his palms rest in the feminine curve of her belly just below her navel. She still hasn't turned to look at him, to completely submit. He wonders what will coax her.

But then she turns her head to him and tilts her mouth to his. He kisses her and she tastes of soap and water and warm sweet woman . . .

Peter sat bolt upright in bed. Next door the shower was sharply turned off. He cursed and looked down at himself in the bed.

He was hard as a hammer. A dark spot appeared on the front of his boxers—a little pre-cum just to taunt him. Just to add a little sharpness to the ache of wanting something he couldn't—shouldn't—have.

What he needed was a shower of his own.

He stumbled to his bathroom and flipped the water on high. He didn't even bother with the hot water handle.

The water was like icicles on his skin. The heat of his body washed down the drain and left behind only the memories.

He wanted no more tender thoughts of her but they creeped in even with the ice of the shower. To feel for her would be dangerous. Too many people wanted her gone and were willing to pay for it. He knew that only too well.

If he became her protector he'd be putting himself right in the middle again. Certainly he was no coward, but he was no longer the whipping boy like he'd been at the department.

He hung his head and let the cold water flow over it.

He didn't want to be attracted to her. He didn't want to be her savior.

But the possibilities should she be left to fend for herself were sickening. He couldn't stand by and do nothing. He felt something for her. As dangerous and stupid as it was, it had happened, and he'd have to deal with it. So whether he was the one contracted to do the job or not, he vowed to screw them all.

He would not see her dead.

* * *

Alyn dug into her handbag and pulled out her Sears credit card. The windshield of the Geo was covered in a thin layer of frost. She scraped the driver's side clean, then ran the wipers until her visibility was passable. Once in the seat, she started the engine and took off down the road.

The main house stood frozen in silence as she drove past. No cheery morning lights lit the windows, no fires burned in the house's twenty chimneys. Inside, she pictured Hector and his wife having coffee in the stainless steel kitchen, no words being spoken between them. There would be only glances exchanged—his would be of contempt for the woman he married who had committed the unforgivable sin of looking her age, and hers would be vaguely frightened, half-hidden behind a mask of inferiority and rage.

Alyn turned the car to the road at the back of the house. If she recalled correctly, a few miles down and she would be at the stables.

The stablemen with their purple and gold jackets were out in force with not a soul idle. Like drones, they attended to their work, barely looking at her when she parked the car in the cobblestone courtyard. All around her, there was activity, as the men worked like Stepford wives in their aim to please. They were either too engrossed in currycombing a stallion, or mixing the day's feed, or halter-training a foal to even notice the stranger among them. Alyn thought the whole tableau almost chilling. The men's need to function seemed to supersede even their humanity. All around her, there was no emotion, no visible opinions, no talk. The message seemed to be: Just work and get the job done. And the men practiced it like it was the Eleventh Commandment.

She stole into the stable and took a quick tour of the animals—if that could actually be done in a building that apparently had fifty stalls. At last she came upon the octagon end. She could see Wonderwall still in his stall, his head bobbing up and down as he munched his morning hay.

"Hey there," she said softly.

His nose poked through the bars. The gold-plated buckle on his leather halter clanked against the steel.

She stroked the warm gray velvet of his nose. The words she

uttered were nonsense, but as she'd learned in vet school, the tone was everything. Wonderwall responded by itching his forehead against the smooth mahogany molding that bumpered the interior of his stall.

She smiled at his antics. He might not be a multimillion-dollar horse, but he was a lover boy. She'd have loved to own him herself if he were somehow attainable for the likes of her.

"Are you the center of this storm, Wonderwall?" she asked him quietly as he went back to foraging through his hay. "I think you're a masterpiece, no matter what. Jacqueline had good taste and you pretty much fit into the ideal, even if you can't pass those things on to your offspring."

She tweaked his forelock and laughed when his nose shot through the bars for another stroking. Cautiously, she placed her cheek against his muzzle. He nudged her and she exhilarated in the puff of his warm breath against her face.

"I'll have to come back with an apple next time, won't I?" She rubbed her knuckles down his long forehead. "Or are you a sugar man?"

"Definitely a sugar man."

She whipped around at the strange voice. Blood thrummed through her veins, injected with a healthy dose of adrenalin.

"Hello," she said, knowing her cheeks had to be as white as a dead woman's. "I hope you don't mind my admiring the horses. I was up early and took a drive—"

"No, no, go right ahead. We're very proud of the work we've done here." Garry Ferrucci gave her the kind of dark, slimy smile that could have graced the face of Saddam Hussein. He walked into the octagon with his cold green eyes centered on her.

She didn't know how to respond. The man's fury at the last meeting had been supplanted by insincere propriety. But to make small talk and exchange pleasantries seemed to be the height of fraud, especially when she had every reason to suspect this man in the death of her aunt.

"So you're Jacqueline's niece." He smiled. His teeth were crooked and stained with tobacco.

She noted that he pronounced her aunt's name the way her mother had. *Schockleen.*

"Yes, but when shall I ever meet Jacqueline?" Her words were taunting. She wasn't as afraid of him as she thought she'd be. He couldn't do much harm to her—if he even wanted to—with that army of purple and gold clad drones working around the stableyard.

He sorrowfully shook his head. "A terrible thing. If only we knew what happened to her."

Bullshit, she wanted to utter, but kept her mouth closed.

"Are you here for a long stay? I wouldn't think you'd be too fond of the place having lost it all just yesterday." He smiled.

She was shocked at his frankness, but she supposed someone who'd gotten away with murder wouldn't worry about public opinion. Her own lips twisted with sarcasm. "Yes, I understand it was your lawyer who saw to that. Thanks."

"I hope you're not angry. I just felt a moral obligation to follow Jacqueline's wishes. A man has to have integrity, you know."

"I love that word. *Integrity*. It sounds so strong, so noble, and yet I've never known a man who used it to describe himself who had any."

He gave her a double-take. "I couldn't just stand by and watch an interloper foil Jacqueline's last desire. What kind of man would I be then? What kind of friend?"

"If you're referring to my aunt's ill-conceived desire to give all that she owned to you and that majordomo, I think I best remind you that her *last* desire was that her estate go to her niece. So perhaps we shouldn't speculate. Too much speculation could lead us down roads we might not want to walk."

He stared at her. His face was raw and freshly shaven but she suspected such personal hygiene was performed by him only once in a blue moon. He stank like a rider on an Atlanta bus in the middle of August.

A grin cracked his mouth. "For all I know, you could have had something to do with my dear Jacqueline's disappearance."

She took a calming breath. "Dear? Was she dear to you then? I'd think otherwise."

"I've known her for years." He waved at the interior of the stable. "All this she acquired through my experience and knowledge. We met at the track maybe ten years ago.'' He paused and looked at her meaningfully. ''We shared a common love . . . of horses.''

She felt ill. Suddenly, she could see that her aunt and this man had been lovers. She couldn't fathom what Jacqueline saw in him, but Garry Ferrucci would have been a man who knew something about horses, and perhaps with the same interests, the sexual bond just developed.

And Jacqueline, with her room full of romances, might have paid for her own romance with her very life.

''Money makes a cold lover.'' Her words were filled with acid.

''Do you know that for a fact? Your love affair with it wasn't even as long as a day, if I recall what my lawyer told me.''

She snorted. ''I never held this estate, and if it had been willed to me, I wouldn't have taken it. I can think of better uses for money than just the pursuit of hedonism. You'd better hope I never get anything of Jacqueline's because it will go to charity, and you can just kiss it goodbye.''

''Such conviction. Such *integrity.*'' He smiled again and looked just like Hannibal Lecter in front of a plate of fava beans. ''I'd hate to see such an idealistic young woman fall prey to the lure of money—''

''It won't happen.''

''No? Perhaps something else, then.''

She glared at him even though her stomach held a cold ball of fear. He was threatening her, but like the slime he was, he knew just how to couch his language in vague words so that she wouldn't be able to make anything of them.

''Blood is thicker than water, Mr. Ferrucci. I never really knew the meaning of that before, but it's all clear to me now. And you know what? Blood can be thicker than money too.''

She faced him like a challenger. ''I think I would have really liked my aunt if I'd ever had the chance to meet her. I don't have anyone else in my family but her, and now she might have been taken from me. It angers me, Mr. Ferrucci. The money can be taken away, and so can the water, but when you take away my blood, you go too far.''

He was silent. He merely stared at her with those snake eyes of his.

"I think I need to find out what happened to Jacqueline Blum. I realize that I take her disappearance personally—and you know what, Mr. Ferrucci? For all her riches and fame, I do believe I'm the only one who does take it personally. And that saddens me. And it makes me yearn for vengeance."

"You stupid girl, stumbling in here like a fly in a web." Ferrucci's anger that seemed buried below the surface now leaked through the cracks.

"Is it your web, Mr. Ferrucci?"

"You'll find out. Very soon. I do believe you will."

"Are you threatening me?"

He laughed. "You think you almost had us, didn't you, you little bitch?"

She stood silent and icy, unwilling to comment.

He gave her one last look-over. He sneered and then tipped his hat. "Goodbye, Miss Jones. It was nice meeting you."

She watched him walk away, his pants hitching with his gait, the long swept-back gray hair brushing the neck of his tweed hacking jacket. Despair crept into her. He was guilty. Obviously guilty. He'd done something to her aunt, and yet without proof there was not—nor would there be—any justice.

CHAPTER ELEVEN

There ain't no such thing as a no good woman. Every no good woman was made no good by a no good man.

—Bessie Smith

Alyn pulled the Geo up to the front of the guest cottage. Youngblood was waiting for her in front of the Explorer, keys in hand. He looked angry.

"Where have you been?" he snapped, his eyes flashing.

She was in no mood for an argument. Her hands were still trembling from her run-in with Ferrucci. "I went for a drive."

"Where?"

"To the stables." Her own anger rose. "What's it to you?"

"Do you want protection or don't you?" He glared at her.

Her insides crumpled. All she saw was Ferrucci's sneer and look of blood-red hatred on his face. "Yes," she whispered, "I want someone to protect me."

"Then you will stay where I can watch over you."

She locked gazes with him. Tears unbidden filled her eyes. "Ferrucci threatened me. I'm of no account to him whatsoever, and yet, he threatened my life. I swear he did."

"He'll do more than threaten if he gets the chance."

"I don't want him to get the chance." Fear and resentment filled her. She didn't like being terrified. She hadn't asked for it, that was for sure. All she wanted was a little jaunt down to Blumfield and to offer some help. Now she was neck-deep.

"Look," she began, "I—I sure can't pay you to protect me. I

can't even swear I can do what you say because I've my practice to return to and I've got responsibilities. You have to know this."

"If you were dead, who'd take care of those responsibilities then?"

She could feel the blood drain to her toes. "I guess someone else would." She tried to hide the fear in her eyes. "Do you think I'm really going to be killed? But aren't I insignificant?"

"The only living relative to Jacqueline Blum is never going to be insignificant. Particularly to anyone who desperately wants to avoid legal hassles and police scrutiny."

"You frighten me when you talk that way," she said, her voice low and trembling. Her resentment over her situation built anew.

He stared right into her eyes. The tension between them was as volatile as nitro.

"Good," was all he said.

* * *

"I'd like to make a police report. I've been threatened." Alyn held the phone receiver and looked around her bedroom desk for a pen. One was in the top drawer along with a Blumfield engraved pad of paper.

"The man's name is Garry Ferrucci. F - E - R - R - U - C - C - I. He's here at Blumfield. I believe he's the stable master." She listened into the phone and nodded. "Well, what he did was imply that he was going to hurt me."

She frowned. "No, he didn't in so many words but—"

She listened some more. "Yes, but—" She closed her mouth, the corner of her lips curled in a futile twist. "All right. I understand. My name? Alyn Blum-Jones. I'm staying here at Blumfield. I'm Jacqueline Blum's niece." She smirked. "Yes. All right. If he says anything more concrete, I'll call back and file a report."

She replaced the receiver. The luxurious damask-hung bedroom seemed to close in upon her.

It had probably been naïve of her to think to make a report on Ferrucci, but her anger grew by the second. Everything was so obvious here at Blumfield, but yet the police did nothing because the schemes all seemed to fit outside their guidelines. Her respect for law enforcement in general was declining. The boldest crimes seemed to go unpunished. All she had to do was watch *Geraldo Rivera* to know that.

She paced. The sun was beginning to set. Outside her window, the oak trees were blackening to shadow. The whole day had gone to waste.

Youngblood had questioned her about Ferrucci's conversation, then he'd told her there was nothing anyone could do about it. She'd taken to her bedroom, half in anger, half in exhaustion. Suddenly the stress began to tell upon her. She'd lain down on her bed in order to collect her thoughts, and the next thing she realized, she'd slept until four in the afternoon.

She'd arisen with the grand idea of filing a police report on Ferrucci.

Now she felt as stupid as a stump. There was nothing to do but go downstairs and seek Youngblood's advice once more.

Her hair was a slept-on, knotted mess, but she paid it no mind. Stuffing the curls into a barrette, she tied up her hiking boots and trod downstairs.

The smells of cooking wafted in from the kitchen. She followed them and found Youngblood at the Jenn-Air, grilling a two-inch thick sirloin.

"Hungry?" he asked, grinning.

"Not for that," she answered, perching on one of the island bar stools.

"There's peanut butter around here somewhere." He didn't look up from the grill.

"Thanks." She smiled wryly.

"Did you have a good rest?"

She almost choked. "How did you know?"

"I checked in on you."

She could have sworn he looked as uncomfortable as she felt. "Is that one of a bodyguard's duties?"

"When you didn't come down, I just wanted to make sure you hadn't decided to make another field trip to the stables."

"Believe me, I'll never go there again. Not even to see that beautiful horse."

"That animal's days are numbered anyway."

"What makes you say that?"

"I have a funny feeling that horse will die in another fire. That way there's no evidence that Jacqueline wasn't sold a ten-million-dollar horse." He flipped the steak.

She lost all her appetite. "But they wouldn't dare try it. The authorities would be all over them like flies to the honey pot."

"You forget that most criminals are pretty damn stupid and lazy. The fire worked beautifully once; they'd try it again without another thought."

"I can't just sit by and wait for those animals to be torched. I can't and I won't."

"What're you going to do about it?"

"Why can't the animals be sold off now? I'll bet even the illustrious Wonderwall would make an exemplary show horse. And if they don't get the price they say they're worth, we'll just have to take a tax loss on the leftover estate."

He smiled and plopped the steak onto a Portmerion plate. "Do you really think anyone here is going to let you hold an auction so that those horses don't mysteriously burn up in a stable fire? Do you think they'll give you the right? That they're even that humane? Do you think they treated Jacqueline with the same mercy?"

She was immediately humbled: she felt exactly as she did on the phone to the police. "No, I guess you've got me. I'm being naïve again. I'm just assuming people care . . ." Her words trailed off into pensiveness.

"But did I tell you I called to make a report on Ferrucci's threats?" She put on a sarcastic bright facade. "You know what they told me? He didn't really threaten me. Not technically. If he didn't come right out and say he was going to kill me and how he was going to do it, it just doesn't merit checking into. Did you know that?" She nodded. "Sure you did. You used to be a cop."

Sighing, she finished with, "God, this stuff isn't my milieu. Murder and fraud and conspiracy are pretty much out of the scope of your average vet. I'm really sorry."

"How about some dinner then?" He suddenly seemed angry about something but he didn't talk about it. Instead, he placed his plate on what had to be the kitchen table—even though it was a huge cherry provincial piece that seated twelve—and he sat down to eat alone.

"I'll make something in a minute. I have to go to the car and get my laptop. I figure I can set up the computer and e-mail Joyce to give her whatever instructions I can on my current patients. Is it okay if I set it up in the living room? I noticed there were two phone jacks in there."

"Go ahead," he answered, his attention—like the brute he was—given to the slab of charred flesh on his plate.

She shrugged on her raincoat over the violet polar fleece vest. It wasn't raining, but the wind had kicked up and shattered the ice on the bare branches overhead.

The Geo was parked to the right of the Explorer. It was dark; the only light was from the front door. She opened the passenger door and reached in for her laptop. The black bag was on the floor, right where she'd left it.

She lifted it, then suddenly grimaced.

"Eck." Her hand found something cold and slimy dripped on the leather handle of the case.

"What the—?" She placed the case on the concrete drive and walked toward the Williamsburg lantern that lit the front doorway. Her hand was covered with a smear of cold black. She thought at first a bird might have been trapped in the car and left droppings everywhere. But then her hand hit the beam of light from the front door. Her palm was smeared with red. Bright red.

A scream gurgled in her throat. She stared down at her hand until the red blurred in her vision. Without even thinking, she stumbled through the front door and ran for the kitchen.

"Peter! Peter!"

Her throaty cry roused him from the table. He stared at her face, then down at the hand she held out in front of her.

"My—my car," she stammered. "This was on the handle of my computer case."

"It's blood."

"For God's sakes, I know that," she blurted out. "But what kind of blood? Whose blood?"

He didn't answer. He strode to the living room. On the desk

was a mahogany case. Inside, he removed a Colt .45 pistol; the gun seemed big enough to kill a polar bear.

"Hey . . ." she said weakly, following him.

"Stay here."

"But it's my car. I think whatever it is, the message is for me."

"No doubt." He turned. His eyes were frozen gold. "So stay the fuck here, *comprenez?*"

She clung to the doorway, hating him at that moment, and yet needing him like she'd never needed anyone.

The minutes ticked by.

One.

Two.

Three.

Finally he showed up back in the foyer, his face grim.

She choked. "Please say it's animal blood. I love animals but—"

"It's animal blood all right. Ferrucci's. He's laying in the back of your Geo, his brains blown out." He looked at her; all his anger surfaced. "You're in deep now, Alyn. You just called the police to tell them he'd threatened you, and now we're going to have to call them to tell them he's lying in your car, executed by a bullet to the back of the head."

She had no comment; she made no move to protest.

Numbly, she watched him walk to the desk, pick up the phone and punch 911.

"This is Peter Youngblood at Blumfield. I need some cops at the guest house right away. There's been a murder."

He stared at her, doom in his eyes.

Her breath sucked out of her lungs like the crash of the Hindenburg.

CHAPTER TWELVE

Mabel danced the key in front of her eyes. It was the end of the day, time to go home, but she wasn't ready to face the empty apartment and dinner in solitude. Instead, she made her mind up to do some extra work that had been building up on her desk.

She picked at a bagel left over from breakfast, ordered another cup of coffee from the employee cafeteria, and sat with her favorite news rag, *Tattletale.* It was a juicy mixture of *USA Today* and *The National Enquirer.* For those who couldn't tune into the salacious daytime talk shows, they could catch up on their astrological forecast and read the latest prurient journalism concerning the missing Blum heiress.

But the key kept drawing her gaze. Finally, in exasperation, she took it into the vault and shoved it inside one of the keyholes of box number 1329.

But the master key was useless without Ferrucci's key.

Nothing was going to open Jacqueline Blum's security box without both keys used in tandem. Even dynamite wouldn't penetrate the steel casing. The only way to open it was with Ferrucci by her side.

The police wouldn't listen to her. They had more than proved they were all nincompoops. The only way to discover the secret inside Box 1329 was to somehow lure Ferrucci into opening it with her. Maybe if she could find out the contents, she could persuade those idiots at the precinct that something fishy was going on at her branch of the Chase.

She went back to her desk and drummed her lacquered nails upon the blotter. Nervous, but mad from the desire to know, she finally scrolled through her computer and found the number listed on Jacqueline Blum's application for a security box.

The phone was heavy in her hand as she dialed the number in Maryland.

"Hello?" she said softly into the receiver.

"Hello," answered a man's smooth voice, timbered, perhaps, with a slight Latin accent.

"Yes, this is Mabel Haskings from Chase Bank, Branch Number 383. I'm calling in reference to a security box Ms. Blum opened several weeks ago. Would it be possible for me to speak to Mr. Garry Ferrucci?"

"Garry Ferrucci?" the man repeated. "Ah—he's not available at the moment. May I help you?"

Mabel shook her head. "No, I'm afraid I can only speak with the owners of the box. I know it's unlikely, but, well, I suppose Jacqueline Blum is not available—"

"Certainly not. Have you not read the newspapers?" he interrupted.

She released a sigh. "Yes, I'm afraid I have."

"Then you know I cannot possibly reach her because we do not know where she is."

"Of course. But you could at least tell me how I might get a hold of Mr. Ferrucci? It's that much more imperative that I speak with him, given Ms. Blum's disappearance."

"He is not available at this time, but I will be more than happy to deliver a message."

She paused. Perhaps it was instinct that made her hesitate. But curiosity burned like an inextinguishable flame inside her, compelling her to open the flood gates.

Finally, she said, "Yes, would you please tell him to call Ms. Haskings at Branch Number 383 of the Chase Bank?" She closed her eyes and held her breath. "Could you also tell him it's a matter most urgent that I reach him? We fear our security boxes have been compromised. We're asking all our customers to come into the bank and move their belongings to our new bank vault while we do a lock check.''

''I see. Well, Miss Haskings, I will be sure Mr. Ferrucci gets the message.''

She wondered if it was just her imagination or if she truly heard a tinge of malice in the man's voice.

''Thank you very much.'' She put down the receiver.

Garry Ferrucci would be at her desk at 9:00 A.M. the following morning if he had something in that box he was worried about.

And if he never showed up?

Mabel shrugged. Then her curiosity would be assuaged. If Ferrucci never showed up, there was clearly nothing incriminating in Box 1329. The police wouldn't have to be convinced, and she could forget about it.

It would be as simple as that.

* * *

''I don't own a gun. I didn't kill him. You saw me. I was sleeping this afternoon.'' Alyn's voice was on the edge of hysteria.

''I can't give you an alibi. You were in your room too long, alone.'' Peter rubbed his chin. Together they sat opposite each other on the slipcovered couches. The whine of a siren could be heard in the faraway silence of the night.

''Should I call a lawyer?'' A tear streamed down her cheek. ''I have to confess I don't know any. I never thought I'd need one.''

''Ferrucci was one helluva bastard, wasn't he?'' he murmured bitterly. ''Just like him to fuck your life up too.''

''But who killed him? And why in *my* car?''

''To make you take the heat, is why.''

''But I had nothing to do with it,'' she said, shivering.

''Who has it in for you other than Ferrucci—?''

''Hector Dante,'' she interrupted.

''But then why kill Ferrucci?'' He scowled. ''Those two are together in everything as far as I can tell. Now Dante has to operate without a partner. Big disadvantage if you're trying to scam the police and the insurance companies."

"Maybe if Ferrucci was screwing my aunt out of her money using horses like Wonderwall, Dante might have been worried about being implicated. He's certainly off scot-free from penalties in that scheme because with Ferrucci dead, Dante has no connection to the two. All he has to do is let Jacqueline be declared dead and he can collect all the benefits for himself."

Youngblood stared at her as if she were on to something. "Dante must have somehow listened into your call when you called the police. He knew then he could set you up."

Alyn wanted to put her hands over her ears as the sirens came closer. She heard the cars stop at the Blumfield gate. Someone at the main house—probably Dante—opened the gate without pause. Within seconds, the two squad cars pulled into the guest cottage driveway.

"C'mon." Youngblood held out his hand.

Alyn placed her shaking one in his. "I've never been questioned by the police, and now I've done it twice in as many days."

"I think you'd better get used to it," he said as he led her outside to the flashing blue lights of the police cars.

* * *

"The gun was a Beretta. An old one. Maybe even an antique. It should be easy to match once ballistics gets finished." Detective Harold Raney lowered his voice. His cigarette glowed red in the darkness of the cottage driveway. "You know, Youngblood, this looks pretty bad for the girl. First the insurance issue, now this guy being executed in her car."

"She knows nothing about guns; she doesn't own a Beretta. Besides, she was inside the house with me. I don't see how it's possible for her to have done it without me in on it."

"Were you in on it?"

"No," Youngblood answered, ice in his eyes.

"But you didn't hear the shot?"

"You know they used a home-made silencer. Beads of Styrofoam were everywhere. C'mon. The coroner's going to find it imbedded in the wound."

"If the guy's got enough of a wound left to even examine, maybe he'll find it." Raney smiled bitterly.

"Who's doing the powder tests?"

"They're doing them now. She ought to be done."

Peter nodded.

"Are you vouching for her? Was she really with you the entire time? Are you going to be her alibi?"

Youngblood stared at Raney's face beneath the faraway street light, the glowing end of the cigarette like a third eye. "I'm going to do better than provide her with an alibi. I'm going to find the guy who did this, and I'm going to bring him to you."

Raney laughed. "No, shit? Well, hey, go for it, Youngblood. But I got to tell you, if your girlfriend fails the powder tests, she's coming with me."

"She won't." Peter turned away and walked into the cottage.

CHAPTER THIRTEEN

Submit to the present evil, lest a greater one befall you.
—PHAEDRUS

Alyn sat at the kitchen table, nursing a cup of tea. Her heart quickened when Youngblood's shadow fell across the door.

"Have the results come in yet?" she whispered.

"They just radioed Raney's car. Negative. From beginning to end, all the tests show there's no gunpowder residue on your hands."

She slumped down in the chair. Suddenly she realized how cold her tea was. It had been hours since she'd first made it.

"Are they going to go after Dante?"

Youngblood took the chair opposite hers. "I'm sure they'll question him, and take some tests. What that'll prove, I don't know. We have to figure out why he did it, then go for a confession."

"By means of what? Extortion?" By now she was so out of her mind she was only half-kidding.

"I'm not ruling out any means to an end." His eyes met hers. "That's why I succeed."

"What about me? I might really have you fooled," she said quietly. "I might have just killed that man."

"Yeah." He still stared into her face. She could barely breathe beneath the weight of his gaze.

The intensity of his eyes didn't flinch with his words. "Don't think I haven't thought it."

"I wouldn't ask you to lie for me." Tears burned in her throat. "But I swear to you, I was in my room all afternoon. I didn't leave it. I swear I didn't kill him."

"I know," he said, lowering his head to hers.

"I wouldn't make you lie for me," she said again.

"I know," he answered, his mouth so near to hers, she swore he might close the distance between them with a greedy, worshipful kiss.

"What do I do now?" She barely breathed the words. They meant more than the obvious and he knew it.

Slowly, he straightened. He grabbed a glass from the cabinet and poured some scotch.

He looked at her, and she looked at him.

"Want some?" he offered.

She nodded. The fiery liquid was just what she needed to digest the fear that seemed permanently lodged in her gut.

He found another glass. Bottle in hand, he motioned toward the living room and the comfortable sofas.

They each took their own couch. They were like enemies in a face-off with the coffee table and the bottle of scotch as the neutral ground.

"Drink it slow," he warned, shoving a quarter-filled glass of amber drink toward her.

"I'm not quite in the mood to savor right now." She tried to keep things light, but there was no way to do so beneath his scrutiny.

Her mouthful of scotch went down like a cannonball.

She swore he almost smiled when she tried to squelch a cough.

"I said take it easy." His eyes narrowed. He leaned back and brazenly placed his feet on her couch.

She edged over toward the curved arm of the sofa. With his feet next to her, there was no shaking the feeling that her territory had been compromised.

"I hope this isn't your best," she commented. "I'm not much of a scotch drinker. I don't know if I can quite get all the nuances."

She swirled the glass and a smile tipped her lips. "It's strong, but I already like how it makes me feel. Yes. I think I really do."

"You have to learn how to appreciate the taste." His gaze locked with hers. "Put some in your mouth. Just a tiny bit. Drink it like you're breathing it in, and then hold it there like you're holding your breath."

She put her lips over the thick rim of the crystal glass and ever so gently took a sip.

His eyes were nothing more than slits of gleaming darkness as he stared at her. "Now wash it over your tongue, let it soak into your gums. Does it tingle?"

She didn't take her gaze from him. Mutely, she nodded.

"Come here. Don't swallow."

Like an automaton, she rose from her seat and perched on the cushion next to him.

"Tilt your head back toward me."

She didn't move. The taste in her mouth changed from burning alcohol to mellow and peaty. Perhaps she was beginning to appreciate it. She still hadn't swallowed.

His hand rose to the back of her neck, stroking the fine hairs there. She stared at him.

"Tilt your head back," he said softly.

She did as she was told.

His palm, callused and warm, rested on the exposed vulnerable hollow of her throat. He seemed to relish the texture of her skin. His thumb brushed against her ear, searching for the sensual pleasure of her pulse.

She sat perfectly still, frozen by the shock of his hands around her neck. She wasn't afraid, but she wasn't comforted either. His touch both threatened and worshiped.

Finally he whispered, "Swallow."

She relented.

The scotch slid down her throat. The volatile liquid seemed to evaporate right into her veins. On an empty stomach the alcohol hit her quickly. In seconds, she was warm, satiated, and relaxed. Too relaxed.

"Another taste?" he rasped into her ear.

She almost slumped against him.

"Yes," she said softly.

He leaned forward. She thought he was going to give her some from his glass, but instead he took a deep sip of scotch into his own mouth.

She waited for him to finish, eagerly anticipating his next instructions. He swallowed; she felt a pang of jealousy that she didn't have the courage to wrap her hands around his neck and experience the intimate ridges of his neck as he'd explored hers.

His hand cupped her jaw. Strong, warm knuckles bumped down her throat. She thought it was an invitation to take up her glass, but he stopped her. His hand clasped her outstretched one and pulled it between them.

She held her breath.

Slowly he bent toward her. As if wielding a power she'd never knew existed, he drew her to him as easily as gravity pulls on an apple.

She tilted her head up and unconsciously beckoned with her mouth.

His lips pressed against hers.

She succumbed.

The kiss was of the darkest jungle. With his hands around her neck, caressing and pressing, he erotically sent messages of possession. She might have fled in terror had it been anyone else touching her, but she discovered she wanted this. Because she wanted *him.* She not only wanted his invitation, she wanted his conquering.

He still held some scotch in his mouth; she silently pleaded for it. He gave her a taste and set her mouth on fire. Want built inside her like the rise of a roller coaster. The taste of scotch would never be so fine again.

"You feel it seep into the warm cavern of your mouth?" he whispered against her hair.

She moaned.

"More?" he rasped.

"More," she demanded, her voice throaty with pent-up sexual desire.

"Do you deserve such a fine liquid?" He ran the back of his hand over her cheek.

"Please," she whispered, almost hating him at that moment—as one hates a captor.

"Upstairs for the rest," he taunted.

Her hand reached for a glass, either one, but he drew it away and pulled her off the couch.

"What about the scotch?" she asked.

"Is this about scotch?" His gaze was solemn and, yet, mocking.

She looked away, unable to face him.

And wondered if her every thought, every feeling, every desire, was written on her forehead for all the world to see—or was he someone special? Did just he see it?

He took her hand.

Reluctantly, but at the same time willingly, she followed.

* * *

She and Youngblood trod the stairs.

Alyn watched his back and trembled from want and fear, but she made a conscious adult decision to go along.

The first compelling reason for her compliance was that she was lonely. Yet not just any man would do for her. She'd decided a long time ago to wait a lifetime for her needs to be assuaged. What she truly wanted was a soul mate. She wanted someone as strong and willful as she was.

Looking at the dark-expressioned man on the stair above her, she wondered if for the first time in her life she might have found her match.

He led her to his bedroom and closed the door.

She wanted to speak, to slice into the heavy tension that had built between them, but he wouldn't let her. The ferocious animal that seemed to lurk just beneath his surface emerged. He pushed her against the wall and covered her mouth with his.

She took his kiss deeply, not caring how he pulled at her T-shirt and unfastened her bra.

His hands filled with her breasts. She looked at him, amazed at the emotion that tightened his features. Lust made him hard but something gleamed in his eyes, something warm and—she prayed—caring.

He yanked on the snap of his jeans.

She placed her hands on his waist, hoping to hold him back.

"Don't," he said, pushing her hands away.

"But wait—" she whispered.

"No." He grasped the waist of her jeans.

"Now?" she questioned breathlessly.

"Now," he grunted, yanking down her jeans, yanking down her panties.

"I want to be made love to—" she gasped.

"Next time," he emphasized. He ripped open his fly. The sound sent shivers down her back.

"But isn't there time now?" she whispered, hardly daring to look at him.

"I want you. All night." He set his teeth. "But first, take the edge off. Take the edge off . . ." He shuddered.

"Like this?" she asked naïvely, her breath coming hard as his hand slipped between her bare thighs.

"You're just like I imagined. All female, aren't you? Soft, and warm, and tight." He shut his eyes.

She moaned as he pressed her against the wall and lifted her to him. Every nerve in her body went taut as he filled her. Her buttocks slapped against the wall with his rocking motion that quickly turned fast and furious. Her back arched as if to ward him off—or bring him nearer—she couldn't decide. That he was pleasuring her was certain, but even when her release built and crumbled and built again, she wasn't sure if she hated him for his haste or loved him for his passion.

Only one thing was clear to her. He'd proved beyond a doubt that he was as strong and willful as she was.

He finished with one last deep thrust and fell against her. Their bodies slid against each other, slick with sweat.

Slowly, tenderly, she felt him lower her. Her feet found the ground, but her knees were weak and knocked together. He kissed her. His lips silently begged for connection, but she was still rattled, hardly able to do more than go through the motions.

"Look at me," he whispered, kissing her nose, her forehead.

"I—I can't," she exclaimed. She pushed him away and slid her unclad leg into her panties and jeans.

"Look at me," he demanded, pulling up his own jeans.

"No," she whispered, unable to meet his gaze.

She made to leave, but he took her arm. She pulled it from his grasp, barely hearing the words, "Stay tonight."

She went to the door, emotion like a tight cold ball in her chest.

"What are you afraid of?" he said harshly to her back.

She paused. He hadn't hurt her. Maybe he'd been a little crude when she'd wanted perfume and seduction, but what did she expect from a man who had a tattoo of belladonna on his arm? Nights of wine and roses? Out of the question.

No, she had to decide. She was afraid of him because he was first and foremost a man, something she had little experience with and little trust in. But so far, he'd proven himself to be her only ally at Blumfield. And she was crazy attracted to him. It was a volatile combination, and she was at the turning point with it. She now could either run from the mess at Blumfield, and run from him; or confront her demons—no, *embrace* them.

There was still no way for her to meet his gaze.

But she turned back to him.

She offered him her mouth, and he took it. The kiss was almost sweet. The tender kiss of two lovers who meet all too infrequently.

He led her to his bed.

Grasping her face in his callused palms, he kissed her again and lowered her to the mattress.

Perfume and seduction were silent promises that rode on his every kiss, but her mind stayed tangled in thoughts of the jungle, and her soul remained haunted by the shadowy specter of primeval man and woman locked in violent surrender.

CHAPTER FOURTEEN

With sleepless, strain-reddened eyes, Alyn watched another dawn filter into a bedroom at Blumfield. She'd lain awake most of the night, because the bed was unfamiliar. It was Peter's bed.

The promises had been kept. Seduction had followed seduction until she was sated beyond reason.

Still, she knew she had to tread carefully around him. He was dangerous. Alyn didn't trust many people, and her sense of self-preservation cried out not to trust him. She'd had few boyfriends in her life. Certainly none that lasted more than a month or two. Inevitably they would do something that would rattle her and she would push them away and be done with it.

But Peter wouldn't go so gently. He was ferocious, passionate, opinionated and infinitely powerful. The kind of man who could completely seduce a woman into the safety of his strength.

But even so, his emotional and physical strength was like a sheer cliff, towering and inpenetrable one second, causing her to free fall the next. She knew not to trust it. Though her hands and nails might be bleeding from her hold onto his jagged edges, she could only continue to hang on. She had met her match; certainly he hadn't taken what she wasn't willing to give. But his intensity, his greed, his single-tracked pursuit proved he existed way out of her field of comfort. And he would not go away just because she told him to.

Yet besides his lust, she needed his friendship. She needed *him.* He might be the only one who kept her out of jail.

A door below her slammed. She turned and surprised herself with the empty space in the bed. Peter was gone.

Grabbing a sheet, she wrapped it around herself and went to the window. Youngblood was on the driveway, approaching his Explorer. He was leaving.

She dashed for her clothes and dressed the entire way down the stairs. The front door was deadbolted; it took a moment for her to find the key, but when she at last freed herself from the cottage, the Explorer was just a dot on the road leading to the main house.

* * *

Hector Dante and his wife stared at the Montgomery County police officers who carried boxes wrapped with red evidence tape out of Garry Ferrucci's apartment attached to the stable. A stream of blue uniforms like ants marching to the nest loaded the boxes into a police van.

"They were here before I got the phone call. There was nothing I could do," Dante said under his breath.

Giselda's face was wiped clean of expression. "I asked if I could help. I told them I was the housekeeper, but they said no one would be allowed into Mr. Ferrucci's apartment until they were through with the investigation."

"We've got to get that key. If they find it and go to the safety deposit box before we do—"

"Maybe they won't find it," Giselda interrupted.

"Jesus Christ, don't be an idiot."

Giselda lowered her head. While Dante walked away in disgust, she fiddled with the gold Byzantine chain she always wore around her neck.

Attached to the center was an alloy key with the number 1329 stamped on its face.

* * *

Youngblood walked to the end of the stable farthest away from Ferrucci's apartment and the half-dozen technicians who were scouring it for evidence. He stopped at Wonderwall's stall. It was clean but empty. The Thoroughbred was pacing in the paddock.

Cell phone in hand, he pounded in the number and waited for an answer.

"Yes," came the terse greeting.

"Jacqueline Blum's stableman is dead—he was found shot in her niece's car." Youngblood's eyes went dead. He showed no emotion, no interest.

"Who did it?" came the question.

"Not you. That's about all I do know."

"Did she—?"

"I doubt the girl had any involvement. I'm just calling to tell you that things are turning on themselves here. I'll need more money for this bullshit or I'm out of here."

"Whatever it takes. I told you that before."

"I want to know how this mystery's going to end. You never explained it all to me. I want to know all that you expect of me. I want the details now—like what I'm supposed to do with the girl." A muscle in Youngblood's jaw began to bunch.

"I'll tell you when the moment is upon us."

"Not until then?" Youngblood didn't bother to hide his snarl.

"Not until then. Call me if there's anything more."

Youngblood punched the END button on the phone. The muscle jumped again in his jaw. He stared at the stable building for a long time deep in thought.

But soul-searching and ambivalence weren't going to get him through the thing, and he knew it.

And neither would they keep Alyn safe.

* * *

Alyn found Peter standing by the empty stall. His back was to her; she was spared for a moment the awkward morning-after silence.

But then, as if he could sense her presence, he turned and looked straight at her.

''Hello.'' His jaw hardened. If he were embarrassed about their liaison the night before, he didn't show it.

''Hello,'' she answered softly. The picture of them both entwined in bed came unwanted into her mind. To cover her self-consciousness, she gestured to the other end of the stable. ''I see the police are still here.''

He nodded. ''You'll be happy to know Montgomery County's finest is on the job.''

She tried to smile but it was difficult.

''They'll probably be finished in the apartment soon.''

''Do they have any idea who did it?'' Her nerves stretched taut. She couldn't deny that she was terrified. What had happened to Garry Ferrucci could happen to her. That much was obvious.

''As far as I can see they have no ideas at all.''

She tried the light approach again. ''Have you any theories?''

His gaze locked with hers. ''I think I'd need a flow chart to figure who's got it in for who around here. This place is nothing but a house of games. Nobody's who they seem.''

She chewed on her lower lip to keep it from trembling.

''Are you who you seem, Alyn?''

She met his stare.

''I want to know about you. All about you,'' he said.

''There's really not much to tell. I'm very dull.''

''Did you hate Jacqueline for inheriting while your mother was disowned?''

''No.''

''Tell me about your father.''

''Him, I hate.''

''Why?''

She took a deep breath. Still, she couldn't meet his gaze. ''He abandoned my mother before I was born.''

''What do you know about him?''

''Not much else. My mother didn't ever talk about him. She destroyed everything that reminded her of him when he left. I wouldn't know him if he passed me on the street.''

He looked at her.

She finally had the nerve to look back. "Jacqueline and her money were never what I envied. It was all those little girls on the playground being pushed on the swings by their daddies. That's what I envied."

"He was probably a mean son-of-a-bitch. You were probably better off without him."

She laughed though she felt like crying. "That's what my mother always used to say if she ever said anything."

He took her by the hand and began to lead her through the stables.

She mutely followed.

Inside the Explorer, they rode in silence past the forensics team picking through Ferrucci's apartment. Back at the guest house, Alyn saw the tail lights of the police tow truck taking her rented Geo to the compound.

Peter yanked up the emergency brake to park. Before she could open her door, he said, "You know Ferrucci was Jacqueline's lover."

She shook her head. "I don't want to believe it, but it explains a few things."

"Certainly not her taste in men."

"The Blum women have terrible taste in men." She flicked him a glance. "But that explains why he was able to take such advantage of her." Alyn couldn't get those bookcases of Harlequin romances out of her mind.

"Jacqueline Blum found it hard to stay away from the men. As was outlined in every grocery store tabloid from here to Seattle, she had as many lovers as she had diamonds. And none of them proved to be worth a damn."

"But she was pretending to herself. She was seeing things in them that weren't there. They were only imaginary lovers. None of them ever really loved her, and that was the problem. That was why she searched." Even Alyn was surprised by the quiet conviction in her voice.

"You sound like you speak from experience." His eyes glittered as he watched her.

"I guess deep down I'm a Blum woman. Just like my mother and my aunt before me."

She suddenly was aware that she'd said too much. Holding her hurt deep within her, she unlatched the vehicle door and walked into the guest house alone.

CHAPTER FIFTEEN

It was almost an hour later before Alyn got herself out of the funk she was in and joined Peter in the kitchen. Deciding what she needed was either a stiff shot of Jack Daniels or coffee, she opted for the latter and went scrounging through the cabinets for coffee filters.

Youngblood sat at the kitchen table and watched her.

She couldn't take his stare anymore. "Okay. Confess. What's going through your mind right now?"

His gaze slid down her figure, then he looked away as if he were somehow in a state of deprivation. "I'm thinking that Ferrucci had every reason to want Jacqueline to disappear, and Hector Dante had every reason to want Ferrucci out of the picture. And two plus two equals four." He rubbed his unshaven jaw and returned his gaze to her.

"I don't like him at all," Alyn added.

"Dante's a prick. So what else is new."

"Did Hector Dante murder Ferrucci?"

Peter lowered his head and heaved an exasperated sigh. "Ferrucci knew who it was. Somebody was with him in that car. There was no sign of a struggle at all."

"What would they be looking for? I don't have anything of value in my home, let alone in that rented car."

"You have the letters. I think they'd be interested in Jacqueline's letters to her long-lost niece even if they hadn't disposed of Jacqueline. They're paranoid. They'd damn well want to know what Jacqueline was writing to you about."

"You think someone convinced Ferrucci that a copy of those letters might be in my Geo?"

"It's only speculation, but something drew him into that car. It's obvious he was shot there."

Alyn shivered. She would never look at another red car the same way again.

Slowly, she said, "My instinct tells me to go back to Quincy and forget all about this place and hide."

"He'd find you. There was a reason Ferrucci was shot in your car. Whoever it is wants you covered with the stink of this place too."

She turned on the coffee maker and watched the water drip into the pot. The silence became oppressive. There were no other sounds than the grandfather clock ticking in the foyer and the sound of hot water streaming into Pyrex.

The doorbell chime was enough to send Alyn straight to the ceiling. Peter gave her a cautionary glance before going to the front door.

Hector Dante stood in the late afternoon gloom of the portico. He said nothing, only motioned to be allowed to enter.

Youngblood nodded to the living room.

Her heart pounding in her chest, Alyn followed them.

"And to what do we owe the pleasure of this visit?" Youngblood bit out.

Dante glanced between Alyn and Youngblood. He curled and uncurled his hands. There was a small line of perspiration on his upper lip even though it was cold outside.

"I had nothing to do with his death! You know that! *Nothing!*" he burst out.

"The cops riding you? Is this what this is about? Well, hey, we don't give a rat's ass—"

Dante outstretched his hand to implore Youngblood. "I don't care what the police do. I just don't want to end up like Ferrucci.

So, whatever you want, it's yours. There's no need to go for me next. I'll give you what you want. Exactly what you want.''

Youngblood paused, as if he were unsure of what to make of Dante.

''So give it to us.'' Alyn was amazed at her composure when she herself was as terrified as Dante appeared to be. But she wanted answers, and Dante clearly knew more than they did.

''I don't have the key but I can identify it for you. It's got to be in one of those boxes the police took out of Ferrucci's apartment.''

''Tell me about the key,'' Youngblood demanded. He glanced at Alyn as if unsure whether she was really following the conversation or not.

''Jacqueline opened a safety deposit box in a New York bank. Ferrucci kept the key.''

''What was in the safety deposit box?'' Peter walked further into the room, seemingly mesmerized by Dante's story.

''I don't know.''

''You don't know?'' Peter laughed. ''But yet you know he was killed for the key.''

''He said the box contained our 'insurance policy,' whatever that meant. I'm figuring Dr. Blum-Jones is the most interested in insurance policies. Are you not?'' He turned to eye Alyn.

''Did Ferrucci handle Jacqueline's death . . . or did you?'' she whispered darkly.

Dante stared at her.

Peter stepped between them. ''C'mon. Cut the bullshit. Tell us finally what happened to Jacqueline.''

Dante continued to stare. ''I had nothing to do with her disappearance. In fact, if the truth were known—well, if it were known, she and I—we—we were—'' He licked his lips, fear glittering in his dark eyes.

''You were lovers,'' Alyn finished for him, putting the equation together.

He didn't deny it. ''Giselda was able to look the other way. But not Ferrucci. He never liked me intervening in his operations there at the stable. He had his own scams built into Jacqueline's affections. He didn't want competition.''

''So you were both named in Jacqueline's will because—''

Dante lowered himself to the couch. "Because she imagined we both loved her."

Because you were both her imaginary lovers.

Alyn looked at the man. Silence permeated the room.

She tried to digest this latest information. Her aunt had had two lovers at Blumfield, maybe more. Intrigue layered upon intrigue. She wondered who else was out there who had a reason to want Jacqueline dead besides the man in front of her and the one who was already cold in the morgue.

"I'd give you the key if I had it, but I don't," Dante vowed.

"You really believe we got rid of Ferrucci, don't you?" Peter contemplated their guest. "I suppose it's no wonder you think you're next."

Dante looked up. His naked expression asked only one question. "Am I?"

Nervously, he asked, "If you killed Ferrucci for the key, you can have the damned thing. I've never known what he kept in the box, and I've no need to know now. All I want is out."

Youngblood laughed. "And so here you are, pissing in your pants just because you think we might have the goods on you. If you were an accessory to murder, Dante, I'll find a way to nail you. I won't need a .45 to do it either."

Dante scowled. "I don't have the key. I've looked everywhere. It's got to be in with the police evidence they took from Ferrucci's apartment. That's why I'm here. To save myself. You can get it back, Youngblood. I'm giving it to you. I don't know what's in the box."

Peter snorted. "What makes you think I can get at it?"

"You used to be a cop. At the very least you can find out if the police have the key in their possession. And that way you'll know I don't have it. That I'm not worth killing." Dante began to tremble.

For the first time since Alyn had laid eyes on the man she began to feel the human side of him. His fear seemed as real as the unused coffee mug she still held in her hand.

And his terror was most definitely centered upon her.

"I'll think about it," Peter hedged. He eyed Dante with all the indifference of a rattlesnake. "But before I do anything for you,

I want to know if you had anything to do with Jacqueline Blum's disappearance."

Dante's glance turned violent.

Alyn was so shocked she took a protective step toward Youngblood.

Dante blathered, "Ferrucci was the detail man. He was the one who first took Jacqueline for her horseflesh. I would have been happy with less than he wanted. I told him we might kill the host."

"Did you?" Youngblood asked.

Dante refused to answer.

"We've got to find out what's in that safety deposit box." Alyn looked to Peter. He locked his gaze with hers.

"We'll have to go to New York. Which bank?" he asked Dante.

"Chase. The branch at Thirty-seventh and Park."

Peter smirked. "You can leave if that's all you have to say. If we need you, we'll call you, don't call us."

Dante eyed Alyn nervously. "I told them the pampering would end. I told them I never wanted to be a part of this."

"Who is them?" Alyn asked softly, not expecting an answer.

She never got one.

CHAPTER SIXTEEN

Politics is the gentle art of getting votes from the poor and campaign funds from the rich, by promising to protect each from the other.

—OSCAR AMERINGER

Jacqueline imagined they loved her. That was the crux of her insanity, the ongoing fantasy that the men in her life could feel love, and even more, bestow it upon a woman for her soul—maybe even just for her flesh—and not just for her bank account.

Alyn contemplated this dark thought during the entire plane flight to La Guardia.

Youngblood sat next to her. She wondered when she was going to get back to Quincy and if she shouldn't do it sooner rather than later. Chasing down this mystery was not only getting time-consuming, it was taking her down roads she wasn't sure she should go.

She glanced over at Peter. He was the road with the main danger sign. She knew very little about him. Getting him to reveal himself wasn't going to be easy. She had the feeling that he would tell her anything if he thought it advantageous to do so. If not, she could put a gun to his head, and he would stay clammed up even until she pulled the trigger.

"You're looking at me strangely," he commented, adjusting his tall frame in the leather seat of First Class.

She worried her lower lip. "I was just listing all the things I know about you." She studied him. "It's a short list."

"Good."

"Somehow I knew you'd say that. Or, at least, that you'd think it."

He stared down at her. "What specifically do you want to know?"

She shrugged. "I don't know. It's kind of like you can't form the questions until you have more of the answers."

"I was born in Atlanta right on the cusp of the Civil Rights movement. That was back when it was a sleepy little nowhere town. My mother worked as a secretary for *The Atlanta Constitution.* My father, well, he was, shall we say, your classic no-good alcoholic."

Silence slithered between them.

The attendant came by with a tray of hot towels.

Alyn used the time to contemplate her next question.

"Is that why you decided to become a cop—because your father was less than upstanding? Kids always rebel against the parents. Even I did and I adored my mother." Alyn grinned. "She wanted me to marry a rich doctor and have eight kids. She wanted me to have all the things she thought she didn't have—like a stable home and lots of family. But I kind of disappointed her. I didn't even get out of school until I was thirty—and so far no rich doctors have asked for my hand."

"A lot of doctors are sons-of-bitches anyway," he added.

Her smile deepened. "Yeah. Tell me about it. Everybody hates lawyers, but you know going in that lawyers don't care about you and all they want is your money. They don't hide behind this Hippocratic oath thing—or should I say hypocritic oath—hey, maybe that's where the word came from in the first place!"

He smiled. It was the first time on the plane.

"Was it that funny?" she asked softly.

"Don't take this the wrong way, Dr. Blum-Jones, but sometimes you're very good at being a blonde."

She picked up a lock of her hair and began to twist it in her fingers. In a wispy voice, she said vacantly, "Turn ons: Whipped Cream. Turn offs: International Terrorism."

He slid his hand to the back of her neck and pulled her toward him. Quickly, but with an unexpected quirk of emotion, he kissed her.

"Are you trying to tell me that you like dumb blondes? You and the rest of the male population? Who knew!" she gasped.

"I'll admit I have a side of me that's all pig. But I have other sides too." He looked down at her.

"Pigs are okay. More intelligent than we give them credit for, and they make great barbecues." She grinned. "It's just that no one wants one all the time."

The attendant went through the aisle and handed them each a glass of champagne. "Dinner is coming," she said in a perky voice. "We're having pork tenderloin in Marsala wine."

Alyn smiled into her hand. Peter had to look out the window. The attendant went about her duties.

Sipping her champagne, Alyn repositioned herself in the roomy leather seat. "I've never been in First Class before. You sure you're not a rich doctor?"

"No. I'm even richer than that. I work freelance investigations for the insurance industry."

She noticed his grimace. "Masterlife, right? How much are they paying you in order so that they might avoid paying Jacqueline's policy? A lot, I'll bet. I mean, we could probably be flying on the Concorde right now courtesy of Masterlife if that plane made the Washington-New York shuttle, right?"

"Masterlife isn't paying me to cover up Jacqueline's death."

"Oh no? If it's homicide they could hold the killer accountable for the policy payment. They could try him in civil court for wrongful death, and tie the thing up in litigation for years. They might never have to pay." Her thoughts raced. "Or, of course, they could just make sure she's never found . . ." She suddenly stared at him.

He glanced at her.

"What?" he snapped.

"The most economical way to solve this problem for Masterlife is for you to find out what happened to her and see that her body never surfaces. That way, they have no lengthy litigation, no one to pay off."

"It's more complicated than that."

"Are you denying that they're paying you to make sure she's not found?"

"I'm not confirming or denying anything. All I'm saying is that it's more complicated than you think. You've complicated things just by your existence. They didn't realize she had any living relatives until she mysteriously changed her will—and the powers that be at Masterlife somehow missed that incident until she turned up missing.''

''I guess they would really like me out of the picture.'' Her stomach turned to lead. ''I don't suppose I should trust Corporate America anymore than I should trust some thug on the street.''

''You'd probably be wise not to,'' he murmured.

''Who do you trust, Peter?''

''Myself.''

''But I don't have a cop's nose for treachery like you do. I don't know if my judgment is any good. I question everything.'' She was quiet for a moment. ''I question you.''

He locked gazes with her. ''Good,'' was all he said before the attendant brought their dinner.

* * *

The plane landed at La Guardia at ten sharp. Alyn and Peter took a cab to Manhattan. They pulled up to a little hotel on the East Side, near Gracie Mansion.

The Brownley was in a class onto itself. It had only ten suites and prided itself on service and anonymity. Alyn had never heard of the place but she had no doubt when they checked in that each suite was occupied by probably the most rich and famous people in the world.

''Who does your travel arrangements?'' she whispered to him as they took the ornate turn-of-the-century beaux-arts elevator up to their rooms.

He grinned. ''Getting used to it? I probably should make you stay at the Salvation Army just so you don't get any inheritance ideas.''

The bell captain manually opened the door on five. He held two skeleton keys each tied with a large red silk tassel. ''You're in the Jackie O. Suite, Dr. Blum-Jones.'' He walked to a discreet cream-colored door and inserted the key.

Alyn gave Peter an arch look. ''How appropriate,'' she mumbled under her breath.

The bell captain opened a panel to the left of the door, revealing a liquid crystal screen. He stood back and said, ''May I encode your door, Dr. Blum-Jones?''

She hesitated, then walked up to him.

He nodded and gently motioned to the screen. ''If you would be so kind as to place your hand on the screen so that we might read your fingerprints?''

She looked at him for a moment. Her hand fit on the screen. A second later a green light lit up beneath it.

''We have presidents staying here. We guarantee security.'' The bell captain smiled and closed the panel. He turned the skeleton key and held open the door.

''How does this work?'' she asked naïvely.

''The knob reads your fingerprints.''

She studied the silver-plated knob. ''But this thing looks like it's been on this door since the place was built.'' She gestured to the ornate skeleton key. ''And why bother with that when the door will open just by reading fingerprints?''

''Charm,'' he said with a smile and allowed her to enter.

Peter walked in behind her. The bell captain took his leave but not before informing them that their luggage had been brought up the service elevator, and the valet had already unpacked their clothing. He excused himself, then left them alone.

Alyn marveled at the space and elegance of the suite. Jacqueline Blum would have been as at home in the place as Jackie Onassis. The sea green silk taffeta draperies were the perfect foil for the handpainted Zuber wallpaper depicting old New York. Aubergine tassels and maroon wool damask upholstery complemented not only the backdrop of the walls but the budding foliage of a spacious rooftop garden through a double set of French doors.

''Like it?''

''Unbelievable,'' she answered.

Peter walked to the French doors. ''See out there? See the greenhouse structures?''

She peeked out the beveled glass of the door nearest her. ''You mean all the Victorian wrought iron? It's gorgeous. They did a marvelous job restoring this property. John Jacob Astor would have loved this place if he hadn't gone down with the *Titanic.*''

''All manufactured for that effect, but not that purpose. The glass in the greenhouse is high tech. Not only is it bullet-proof but it bends the light. If a sniper were to sight someone sitting on this patio he'd have an impossible time actually hitting him.''

''No kidding?'' she said, again studying the aged and patinaed structures. ''I really just thought all that was a vestige of an old turn-of-the-century greenhouse.''

''Nope. This place is impenetrable. The walls are steel, the doors are steel, and you need a matching fingerprint to enter.''

She turned to him and said, ''So did you pick this place out, or did they?''

''If you mean Masterlife, they know nothing about this hotel. I picked it because I know that it's the safest place to stay in New York. The President of the United States stays here.''

''I'm hardly the President of the United States.''

''I know,'' he said under his breath. ''But you're worth more dead than alive, and I've promised you protection.''

''I've certainly got that here,'' she answered, her fingernail pinging the steel French door painted to look like wood.

''It's late. I'll let you get some rest. My room's over there.'' He pointed behind her. ''Tomorrow we'll pay a visit to the Chase branch and see if we can find out anything.''

''Will we accomplish much without the key? Hector Dante spoke so convincingly, I felt sure the police had carted it off with the rest of Ferrucci's belongings. I was grossly disappointed when you told me they didn't have it. Were they lying, do you suppose?''

He smirked. ''The cops could have been lying, but the minute you think they might be, it's easy enough to catch them. Conspiracies never quite threaten me like they do some others. I don't believe anyone can organize and coerce more than three people at a time—let alone a whole department.''

''How your cynicism rages. You'd think you were a public servant at one time.''

He smiled. This time it even reached his eyes. ''I'm really beginning to like you, Alyn.''

She smiled back. ''That's because you know all about me. I just wish I knew more about you.''

The smile died in his eyes. ''You shouldn't go searching. You might not like what you find.''

"I only want the truth. Could it be so terrible?"

"The truth is subject to interpretation. That's why the world is full of hard-working overpaid lawyers."

She giggled.

He looked at her one last time. She almost thought there was a strange yearning in his face.

But then the moment fled. He closed the door to his room and she heard him turn on the shower.

CHAPTER SEVENTEEN

The nightmare might have come from the change in pressure during the flight to New York, or even the Dramamine she took beforehand, but all night Alyn had the same dream time and again. She was being chased by a man in a black hood. The man hid his features behind a thick felt hood which revealed only his eyes. Like an executioner, he pinned her arms and dragged her to a hangman's scaffold. Then, just before the noose was around her neck she broke free and snatched the hood from his face.

"I know you!" she cried out, terrified.

Then she awoke.

The third time she had the dream, she must have called out in her sleep. She opened her eyes, struggling for real within a strong grasp. Her hands flew to the face of her captor but then a familiar voice soothed her.

"It's me. It's all right. It's going to be all right."

She went limp and fell against him. Unconscious of the tears that still streamed down her cheeks, she breathed in and out until she felt the horror ebb like a receding tide.

"Some nightmare," he cajoled, stroking her unbound hair.

"Yes," she gasped, still clutching him.

"Who was it?"

She squeezed her eyes shut. "I don't know. It always ended

before he could kill me, before I could put a name to the face." She lifted her head. The tears were suspended on her face like the rivulets of a frozen stream. "I—I thought—I feared—it was—"

"Me?" His mouth twisted into a wry grin. Even in shadow she could see the flash of his handsome white teeth. "I haven't sunk so low that I'm offing little veterinarians for the insurance biz."

"I guess my fear is—that whoever got Aunt Jacqueline, has something to do with me. But I'm helpless. I don't know what's gone on around me. I feel like we're playing Ten Little Indians and I'm number ten. But who is it? Who's killing everybody?"

"I don't know. That's why we're here. To find out."

"I wish I knew what happened to her. I feel like a part of my soul has disappeared with her. There's no one left on earth for me. No one. All my family's gone if she's gone."

"You never even knew her," he said.

"I never even knew her," she repeated, her voice betraying her heart's mourning.

A muscle tightened in his jaw. "Some say you can't miss what you don't know, but I don't think that's true. I see in my own life that there were a lot of things I never really knew, but idealism is like a poison. It lures you into the belief that things are the way you want them to be, not the way they are."

The bitterness in his voice cut into her. "What was it, Peter? Why did you quit being a cop?"

He took a moment. "Friends, I think. They call themselves such, but in the end, you're expendable. Like starving men, they'll be the first to cannibalize you and feast off your bones."

"How did they feast off your bones?" she asked quietly.

He shook his head, but the darkness seemed to lure him into trust. Slowly, he began, "I was a rookie cop out to save the world—I didn't know anything. I used to like going to this Vietnamese restaurant in my neighborhood, and to make extra money I worked the security detail at night. It was a small little operation, a grandfather, his son and wife and their teenage children all pitching in. Thahn Nguyen was sixteen and he—he was really excited about driving a car."

His voice grew thick. "I did a double shift that day, then went to the restaurant for a late dinner. They'd been robbed a couple of times before so they were always glad to see me. I was sitting at this little table near the front door and I realized they hadn't come out with my meal. Soon some of the other patrons were wondering where everybody was. So I got up and went into the kitchen.

"I saw . . . well, I saw . . ."

"You saw what?" she whispered.

"I saw my partner Ramsey emptying the cash register. Thahn was standing in front of him helpless while Ramsey held a gun on him. The rest of the family was locked in the freezer."

He rubbed his jaw, obviously agitated. "He would have shot all of them, I know, because he did security detail with me and he knew the Nguyens as well as I did. He would have had to kill them all because they had recognized him, but he didn't because I walked in and caught him stealing from the cash register."

Peter's breathing became harsh and shallow, as if he were trying to physically purge the memory from his body.

"Then what happened?" she asked, touching him softly on the arm.

"Ramsey turned the gun on me. It was one of those freak things. Five seconds elapses, and the whole world's gone nuts. Ramsey turned his gun on me. I reached for my weapon, and so did Thahn—they must have kept a gun in the drawer under the meat counter. Thahn got the gun. Ramsey saw it coming and he aimed. Thahn and Ramsey blew each other away a nanosecond apart. And here I was. Standing there, holding a gun that had got off one shot right into my dead partner's side. Afterwards they said I had to have been in on it. The Nguyens didn't trust me. Hell, they thought I had orchestrated their youngest son's murder and been thwarted in my plans to silence them too. I really couldn't blame them, but the investigators claimed I shot Ramsey so he wouldn't talk. He was my partner. He was as crooked as they come, and I had no idea, and no one believed me."

Alyn squeezed his arm and leaned her forehead against the muscled strength of his shoulder. "It could have been worse. You could have gone to jail unfairly convicted of committing a crime. And now, at least, you do other work. And clearly it pays well from what I've seen."

He turned to her and lifted her head from his shoulder. "Don't you see? The department was in on it. Ramsey was a rogue cop causing nothing but trouble to his superiors who were on the take in the local crack trade. The Nguyens' restaurant was the way they were laundering money, and they put me with Ramsey from the first because they knew when Ramsey fucked up, I'd have the shit all over me too, and then they could get rid of Dudley Do-right and the rogue cop all in one fell swoop."

"I thought you didn't believe in conspiracies. Too complicated for the average bear, or something like that." She searched his face in the darkness.

"No, I don't think you can get a conspiracy together. But this only involved three people, me, Ramsey, and the Chief of Police."

"Reginald Berre?" she gasped. "The one in the news?"

"The same."

"I heard about his conviction in drug trafficking on CNN. So it was he who set you up?"

"He had the power and the motive. I was expendable. Me and the entire Nguyen family."

She shook her head. His story was tragic. Somehow he'd survived the ordeal but he'd obviously been scarred by it.

Hesitantly she touched him. A light caress, nothing more, but he reacted to it. He took her in his arms and held her to him, whispering, "Right and wrong—truth and lies—mixed forever that night. Life will never be so simple again."

"Life was never simple," she answered, looking up at him in the darkness. "You just hadn't found that out yet."

"Something very good inside me died after that, Alyn. Without it, I'm dangerous," he whispered harshly.

"An independent contractor without conscience, without morals, would be very much in demand. Particularly from big business." She stroked his beard-roughened cheek more to soothe herself than him. "So have they hired you to kill me if I should stand to collect Masterlife's policy?"

It seemed as if every muscle in his body turned to concrete. No longer wanting her answer, she tried to extract herself from his embrace but it only grew tighter.

"Why ask questions like that? Where does it get you? Is there any way to answer it except with a denial—which could be true or false? Why back me into this corner?''

Her voice trembled. ''I only asked because I don't want you to think I'm stupid. I found out early on that life wasn't simple.''

''No, it's not simple. It's not,'' he answered, staring at her in the night darkness of her bedroom.

''I don't think you would hurt me. Not really,'' she half-sobbed, hating the way his body remained rigid and angry against hers.

''You can't say that, Alyn. You don't know it. I don't even know it,'' he finished quietly.

''The man who has as much self-knowledge as you've revealed couldn't hurt me. You question your coldness, Peter. You hate it inside you even as you let it rule your life. That man wouldn't hurt me.''

''Why not?'' he tormented, shaking her.

''Because that man knows I'm harmless.'' Her words grew thick with unshed tears. ''And he knows I've laid my trust in him.''

''Alyn, you speak like an innocent,'' he said bitterly.

She took a deep breath and gathered up all her bravery. With a whisper-soft kiss, she said, ''But sometimes we need an innocent.''

''Why?'' he bit out.

''In order to disarm us.''

He took her face in his hands.

She broke off the kiss and for a long moment they simply stared at each other, she nearly lying atop him, he clutching her tightly to his chest. Finally he brought her head to his and he kissed her. His tongue moved so deeply she swore her moan came from her very soul.

''Disarm me then. Disarm me,'' he pleaded as he rolled on top of her.

''I will,'' she promised as she lifted her head for another kiss. And then another. And another.

* * *

Mabel Haskings was an odd little woman, Alyn thought while she and Peter waited the next morning at Chase Bank. Alyn watched the woman eyeball them from the other side of her desk for almost fifteen seconds before she would even answer their greeting.

"I can't give you any information about our customers. That is Chase policy, and I'm sure if you banked here at Chase you would appreciate the same security." She peered at them over her reading glasses. Mabel Haskings was handsome in her sturdy serge suit and fuchsia charmeuse blouse. She was the type of woman Alyn had always believed epitomized the 1950s working girl: Ms. Haskings oozed capability, organization, and fashion-smarts. The only thing missing was that particular sort of confidence of the era, that perky subservience which said, "I'm a woman who knows her place, and *loves* it!"

Mabel Haskings seemed to have none of this, and by her very dissatisfaction, Alyn began to like her.

"But we've come for some rather unusual information," Alyn wedged in. "My aunt was Jacqueline Blum. Perhaps you've heard of her?"

"Everyone has heard of her. I understand she's missing."

Alyn didn't miss the disgruntled look that crossed Ms. Haskings's features. Alyn added, "We think she's got something inside the security box here at Chase that may shed some light on why she disappeared."

"Have you told the police about this theory?"

This time Peter spoke. "I'm working with the police on this case for Masterlife Insurance."

Mabel looked at him from over her glasses. "If you'll pardon me, you don't look like an insurance man."

She seemed unimpressed with Youngblood's worn jeans and faded gray thermal Henley T-shirt. Alyn was glad that his long sleeve covered the tattoo.

Youngblood leaned forward in his seat. "It's a whole new world out there, Ms. Haskings. I don't have to look like anything."

"Well, you're wrong about that—" she countered.

"You'd have opened the security box for us if I'd have arrived in a Hugo Boss suit?" he asked, incredulous.

"No. I can't open that box under any circumstances short of a court subpoena or by the direct wishes of the owner. I just meant that it's *not* a whole new world out there. No, it's the same as it always was. Same old people, same old plots, same old world. Only the names change.''

Alyn felt the woman's bitterness like a stinger. She looked at Peter. His mouth was a hard line.

''We think the man who opened the box with her had something to do with her disappearance. His name was Garry Ferrucci. Does that seem familiar?'' Alyn asked.

Mabel Haskings's face was wiped clean of emotion. ''I really can't answer any of your questions. Our customers have a right to their privacy whether they're missing or not. So if I may walk you out . . . ?'' She stood and clutched a ledger against her chest like a shield.

Alyn looked at Peter. He nodded acquiescence. Ms. Haskings escorted them through the lobby.

Once at the door, Alyn expected the woman to have the security guards make sure they left, but instead, the woman breezed past the guards and went with Alyn and Peter into the exterior lobby.

A line of weary people waiting to use the ATM didn't even look up.

Alyn was about to follow Peter out the door when she felt a brush at her elbow.

She glanced over.

Mabel Haskings whispered casually in her ear. ''There's a small cocktail bar behind the Waldorf-Astoria. It's called Clancy's Midtown. I go there every night at six o'clock.''

Alyn stared at the woman. Mabel Haskings's meaning was clear when Alyn looked past the woman's brittle professional smile and ice-etched face. Her eyes implored a meeting.

Stunned, Alyn watched the woman disappear inside the bank.

''What was that about?'' Peter asked her once they hit the sidewalks.

''What are you doing at six tonight?'' she asked.

''I don't know. What?'' He lifted one eyebrow.

''Well, Peter, I know a place where I think we can get a really good scotch.''

CHAPTER EIGHTEEN

Clancy's Midtown was a small hole-in-the-wall cocktail bar that hadn't seen a profit since Sinatra and Martin were in the Rat Pack. Decorated in early "Mack the Knife," the place boasted lime green plastic chairs clustered around tables lit with hip paper lamps à la *The Jetsons.* The cream and black linoleum floor was now a monochromatic gray; the cracked orange vinyl tufting on the bar front oozed foam rubber like effluvium. An overweight bartender contributed to the stale air with a cigarette that dangled from the corner of his mouth. The background was a hockey game on ESPN.

"So what can I do you folks for?" he asked in a thick Bronx accent.

"Two scotches," Peter said, "straight up."

The bartender poured a gold liquid from a bottle of Glen-something and passed it over. Alyn took a seat at the corner table so she could watch the door.

"I'll bet that woman's been hanging around here since the place was new." Peter had a gulp of his scotch and perused the decor.

"I hope she shows up. She was really uptight, wasn't she?"

Peter shot her a wry grin. "Bankers. They've got reasons to be uptight."

"She definitely knows something or she wouldn't have wanted

to meet with us." Alyn's gaze locked on the vinyl-padded door to the bar. It opened and Mabel Haskings walked through it.

Alyn stood. Peter took another sip of his scotch.

Mabel walked toward them as if she were in a trance. She looked behind herself more than once; her eyes held a frightened expression.

"Thanks for meeting with us," Alyn began.

"Drink?" Peter asked.

"J&B please," she answered woodenly. She took another glance around the place. The bartender nodded a greeting. He brought the J&B before Peter could even order it.

The three of them sat at a table in the dim light. Alyn wasn't sure how to begin.

"Jacqueline Blum was my aunt. My only living relation. She's missing, and I feel somehow that the security box she opened at your branch of the Chase Bank may have something to do with her disappearance." Alyn gave her a steady look. "Can you tell us anything at all about the security box?"

Mabel nearly inhaled her drink. She placed the empty glass at the corner of the table nearest the bartender.

"It had everything to do with Jacqueline Blum's disappearance," she began, "but the police don't care. They just think I'm some kind of rambling old lady. You know, there was a day when I could get the attention of any man I chose . . ."

The bartender brought J&B number two.

"You've spoken with the police?" Peter asked gently.

Mabel clutched her glass like a talisman. "I called them when I heard Jacqueline was missing. I told them it was extremely odd that a woman of her financial calibre whose own company included seventeen branches of the Regency Bank of Washington was going to open a puny safety deposit box at our branch of the Chase."

"What did they say to that?" Alyn prompted.

"Not a damned reply at all. I called again and left a message but I guess my information wasn't good enough for them." The older woman smirked. "The world's just not the same. Why, in my day, not only did the police respond to a phone call, they *sent* a detective. You talked to a real live human being. Now it's computers this, voice mail that. Push one to automate, two to end a conversation that no human is ever going to hear because it lies lost in the black hole of cyberspace.''

''Why do you think Jacqueline opened the box at Chase?'' Alyn held her breath, waiting.

''She didn't really open the box.'' Mabel drank scotch number two. ''That hideous man Garry Ferrucci did—oh, sure, Jacqueline Blum signed all the forms and authorized everything in her name, but Mr. Ferrucci had that woman on puppet strings.''

She motioned for the bartender, then edged up to Peter and Alyn as if getting chummy. ''You know, I never would have guessed him to be her taste in men, but those lonely wealthy women really amaze you. Remember all the husbands Doris Duke went through?''

''Mr. Ferrucci is dead, Ms. Haskings,'' Peter announced.

Mabel Haskings seemed as if she'd been hit in the jaw. ''Dead?''

''He was shot.''

''Really? How about that? I thought his type lived forever.''

''Even his type can't survive a gunshot to the head. He was murdered.''

Mabel gasped. ''I never would have imagined—but maybe he was some kind of mobster. Maybe they got to him.''

''Who's they?'' Alyn queried.

''You know, all those shadowy types a man like him hangs out with.''

''Do you know any of those other men?'' Peter asked.

''No, I'm just assuming Garry Ferrucci was a cheesy aspiring goodfella. What else would he be?''

Peter sighed.

Alyn could tell he was exasperated, but she wasn't ready to give up. No matter how useless Mabel Haskings's assumptions were, she was still their only lead—and so far, the woman had certainly confirmed that Garry Ferrucci had a key to Jacqueline Blum's Chase security box.

''Do you think it would be possible for us to see the form Jacqueline filled out?'' she asked.

Mabel violently shook her head. ''I shouldn't even be meeting you here. I've got my pension to think about. I'm retiring soon, you know. It'll be expensive for them—I've been with the bank for years. They don't need a reason to fire me now."

"We just want something we can trace to my aunt. Anything. Please."

Mabel looked at both her and Peter. "If you want to find out more about Ferrucci, I certainly can't help you by showing you anything which concerns Chase Bank—"

The woman paused, then seemed to be wanting to say something more.

Both Alyn and Peter stared at her.

"Do you think there's some information we could find out about him that isn't tied to Chase?" Peter nudged.

J&B number three in her grasp, Mabel nodded. "I know Ferrucci's involved in some kind of business here in the city."

"What kind of business?" Alyn asked.

"The reason I know this isn't because I've been snooping into the records. Oh, no."

"We believe you. I've no doubt that you're a person of *integrity.*" Alyn shuddered while she said it. There was that word again. God, how she hated it and its hypocrisy.

"I suppose I can tell you this because it had nothing to do with the bank's relationship with Mr. Ferrucci." Mabel looked around the bar. It was still empty and until 1959 came around again odds were it was destined to remain so.

"The last time the man showed up at the bank, he placed something in the box," she explained. "It was wrapped in a silk scarf. The thing was kind of horseshoe-shaped. He left my area but then returned a moment later and asked to use my phone. Of course, I let him. I gave him a bit of privacy, but you know my desk is just a cubicle, really. Open to anyone who passes by.

"I couldn't help but overhear his conversation. It was something about money he was owed. Mr. Ferrucci said that if whomever on the other line didn't hand over what was due him then he was going to make sure the guy on the other end never owned any more nightclubs in New York or anywhere else for that matter."

Peter shifted closer to Mabel. His eyes glittered with interest. "Do you have any idea who he called?"

Mabel rolled her eyes. "I really shouldn't be telling you this, but what I know of Mr. Ferrucci has nothing to do with Chase. I feel I'm only helping in the investigation by letting this out. And the police just don't seem to give a damn about my information."

"Please go on. Please," Alyn assured her.

"Well, after Mr. Ferrucci left, naturally I had no idea who he spoke to. But just out of plain curiosity—I confess I'm a tabloid reader and fascinated by the rich and famous—that's how I knew Jacqueline Blum when I saw her that first and only time at the bank—well, I—I have to admit I hit the redial button and found out."

Peter laughed.

Alyn wondered what the expression looked like on her face. She was clearly impressed by the woman's ingenuity even if it could be classified as snooping.

"You were able to trace his call from your desk phone?" Peter asked, clearly pleased.

Mabel nodded. "Yes. It was grossly unprofessional of me. But I really was curious. I thought I might get Blumfield Estate or something. I didn't, of course. It was a local number."

"What number did you get?" Alyn held her breath.

"Well—I got some sort of nightclub, I guess, from what Mr. Ferrucci said. All I know is that when I called the number, the man on the other end identified the place as The House of Wax. Yes, that's what I believe he said. I hung up then without saying a word."

"Did you keep the number?" Peter drilled.

Mabel drained her glass. "I wished I'd kept the number, but I felt bad having snooped. I worried I might get into trouble." She looked furtively at Alyn. "Hey, I hope you find your aunt. I really do."

"Thank you," Alyn answered softly.

The woman stood and wavered for a moment while she gained her balance. "I really must go. Georgy is waiting for me. I don't stay out past seven hardly ever."

Alyn assumed Georgy was Mabel's husband. She extended her hand.

Mabel shook it.

Peter stood and towered above both women.

Mabel didn't shake his hand. She seemed far too intimidated by his size.

"Please tell your husband we hope we didn't keep dinner waiting," Alyn called after her.

Mabel looked back, confusion darkening her face. Then she left the bar without another word.

Alyn sat back down at the table. The bartender cleared it. Peter waited until they were alone.

"Ever heard of this place?" she asked.

He shook his head. Punching in his cell phone, he waited for Information.

"I'd like the number for The House of Wax." He paused. "Yes. W - A - X. That's right." A furrow appeared on his brow. "No listing? All right. Thanks." He ended his call.

"Maybe she didn't get the name right." Alyn worried her lower lip with her teeth.

Peter looked to the bartender. "Do you have a phone book in this place?"

The man grunted. He opened a drawer behind the bar and lifted out a battered and stained Yellow Pages with the cover torn off.

Peter stood and took it from him. He thumbed through it.

"Hey, maybe it's some kind of museum," she mused. "They have those, you know. In London. In New Orleans—"

Peter didn't answer. He closed the phone book.

"Maybe it went out of business."

He looked at her as if he'd forgotten she was there.

"Are you ready to go? We've got a club to visit."

"But I thought there was no listing," Alyn said, unable to hide the surprise in her voice.

He flipped open the phone book to Night Clubs. His finger scanned until it landed on a particular listing.

Alyn leaned over the phone book.

Aloud, she heard herself say, "Oh my God. You mean it's called The House of *Whacks?*"

CHAPTER NINETEEN

If we could read the secret history of our enemies, we would find in each man's life a sorrow and a suffering enough to disarm all hostility.

—Henry Wadsworth Longfellow

The club was just north of Hell's Kitchen. Alyn and Peter took a cab but they could have walked.

Alyn was quiet the whole ride. She'd never been inside a place like she knew she was going to now. She couldn't get the ad for the club out of her mind. The writing was circled with a bull whip. It said in red letters:

The House of Whacks

"More bang for your buck."

The whole entire cab ride all she thought about was the scene in *Pulp Fiction* where Bruce Willis meets the Harley leather boy, Zed.

"You're looking very pale." Peter hid the smirk in the corner of his mouth.

"I'm just not used to going to places like this."

"Scared?"

She looked at him. "I'm not sure."

"I'll protect you."

"Yeah, but who's going to protect me from you?"

"A whip and a chair," he said as the cabbie stopped in front of a closed electronics store.

The club's street entrance was a simple wooden door that led up to the apartments over the out-of-business electronics store. The hallway was dark, painted with faux granite to mimic a dungeon. An overweight balding man in a black T-shirt and jeans perched at the top of the stairs, waiting like a déclassé gargoyle.

Peter trod up the stairs with Alyn behind him. He reached for his wallet and grunted the question, "How much?"

The man eyed him up and down. "If you want to contribute to the playing, it's twenty-five a couple. If you came to just watch, it's fifty."

Peter glanced back at Alyn.

She stared at him, too busy praying under her breath that he had a fifty on him.

"We're actually here to see Ferrucci. Is he around?" Peter handed him several bills.

The man added the money to the wad that was stacked in his shirt pocket. He counted out change and said, "Why'd'you want to know?"

"We were in town. We just thought we'd look him up."

He eyed Peter. "You'll have to talk to Chloe about him. Ajax tells her most everything."

"You don't know him?" Peter asked casually.

"Nope. If he was ever here, he's gone now."

Alyn had to bite her tongue in order to keep from asking the man to define the expression *gone now.*

"Thanks." Peter grabbed her hand and led her inside the darkened club.

The back of the bar was draped in shiny velvet swags. Crystal sconces lined the four walls. The nightclub had a cheesy manufactured Victorian decadence to it that would have done Disney proud. The only things missing were the sound effects. Those came slowly, crescended and faded. The crack of a whip preceded moans that emanated from an adjoining chamber.

"Know where Chloe is?" Peter said to the bartender. He then pushed a twenty-dollar bill onto the marble bar top.

"She's in there," answered the skinny twenty-something man,

a slacker with more piercings on his face than a brass-studded barstool.

Alyn hesitantly followed Peter to the room from which the whipping sounds originated. Her very breath choked her when she came upon the scene.

A nude man was buckled into a leather harness and chained onto a cross on the wall. Behind him, a man in a black leather helm was beating him with a thick-handled cat-o'-nine-tails. The handmaiden to this scene was a sleek black transvestite the size of RuPaul. She wore a cotton-candy-pink bouffant wig and a satin merry widow in a black blood color that could only be described as Marquis de Sade red. Whenever the chained man crumpled beneath the lashes of the whip, she ran up to him and soothed his reddened skin with a rabbit-fur chamois. The scene would have been funny if Alyn had not been so utterly horrified by it.

Peter, however, looked almost amused. He walked up to the transvestite when the whipping resumed, and said something to her. She nodded and laughed, touching his arm as a woman would do who found a man attractive. Putting down the chamois, she motioned to the helm-clad inflictor and left for a barstool.

Drinks ordered, Alyn perched next to Chloe and sat silently while Peter asked the questions.

"We're looking for Garry Ferrucci. We thought he hung around this place."

Chloe sipped on a pink martini. If the question rattled her, she didn't show it. "I heard Garry's dead, baby. I got to tell you that. You won't be seeing him here no more."

"No kidding?" Peter fingered his scotch glass. "So how'd you find that out?"

"Ajax told me."

"Who's Ajax?"

Now Chloe finally looked surprised. "Child, you don't know who runs this pimpdaddy land? Why that be Ajax."

"Ajax? That's the name of the guy who owns this place?"

"He owns lots of places." Chloe suddenly slid Alyn a glance of a woman sizing up the competition. "Who's this Miss Thing witch you? This here your girlfriend? I tell you, you two could have some fun playing in this sandbox. I got lots of toys, and I'll be happy to help. I take Visa *and* American Express."

"I'm not sure how much playing we'll be doing tonight," Peter answered, biting back a grin.

"You a vanilla girl, child?" Chloe finally addressed Alyn.

"Vanilla?" Alyn repeated, unsure of the question.

Chloe turned her attention back to Peter. "I know you aren't."

"What gives me away?" Peter's face was clean of expression.

"What gives you away? Why, by those eyes, of course, you bastard. You just look at a woman and your eyes say you want to top her."

He laughed.

Alyn looked at both of them, bewildered. They were speaking an entirely new language. Again, it would have been funny if she hadn't been so shocked. Who knew there was S&M jargon. She supposed every group really *did* have a convention.

"Did Garry work in this place?" Peter asked after a moment, sipping his drink.

Chloe made a moue of her purple-lined mouth. "Hell no. Alls I know is that he worked for Ajax. Like we all do."

"Tell me more about Ajax."

"Why, that's the man. The M-A-N, if you get my drift. His motto is, 'I own you,' and don't I know it." She took a Virginia Slims out from a pack on the bar. The bartender lit it for her. She blew smoke in Peter's direction, but eyed Alyn.

Alyn finally found her sensibilities. Gathering herself, she said, "When we last talked to Ferrucci, he was having an argument on the phone with someone here. It was something about money. That's why we thought he worked here or something."

Chloe laughed the deep throaty laugh of a drag queen. "Baby, Garry Ferrucci didn't work at nothing. He was a two-bit operator from the race track who showed up out of the blue with a deal Ajax baby said he couldn't resist. And that's alls I know."

Alyn couldn't understand it. She blurted out, "But this makes no sense. Why did he need a deal with Ajax? He worked for Jacqueline—"

"Girl, who died and made you Cunt? Let me tell you, Ferrucci didn't work for her. Not the way I saw it. He was over here working for Ajax, doin' what Ajax told him to do. Garry Ferrucci was about as much her employee as I'm Pamela Anderson-Lee."

"Can we talk to Ajax?" Peter asked, glancing covertly at Alyn.

Chloe blew more smoke. "He comes here sometimes. But you're not likely to see him. He owns a lot of businesses. You know The Plush Pussy? That hip retro club over the Chanel Boutique on 57th Street? He owns that, too; fuschia fur lampshades and all."

"What's his real name?" Alyn asked.

Chloe coughed back a laugh. "Child, if I knew that, I'd be sucking on his dick, too. I don't know nothing about the man 'cept we all work for him, and when he says 'Jump!' we say, 'How high, massa?' "

Peter slipped her a couple of bills.

Chloe looked down at the cash in her hand and her eyes gleamed.

"What was that for?" Alyn asked him when he pulled her back to the entrance and its awaiting gargoyle.

"She looked like she could use a new pair of pantyhose." Peter nodded a farewell behind him.

"You remember my name, sugar!" Chloe called back to him, smiling at the money in her hand. "It's Chloe Orgasma! *Chloe Orgasma!* You remember that name when you ready to dump that vanilla life and come lookin' for some excitement, child!"

Peter grinned out the side of his mouth. He grabbed Alyn's hand, and they were out of there.

* * *

"What does one wear to a nightclub called The Plush Pussy?" Alyn called from her bedroom of the suite.

"Something that shows skin. Something black," Peter answered from the rooftop garden.

She walked outside. It was a warm night and the breezes were sensual against her barely clad body. "Like it?" she asked, spinning around.

His eyes and the expression within them were hidden in shadow, but she swore she saw a slight gleam of appreciation hidden deep within the darkness.

"You look fantastic," he whispered.

"How like a man to say such a thing, especially when I look like a shameless slut."

She wore an old serviceable black skirt which she'd hiked up six inches with a wide patent leather belt. Her black bra showed through the sheer blond silk of the blouse which she *always* hid beneath a conservative wool blazer. A last minute stop to Saks Fifth Avenue, and she bought a black garter belt and stockings which went with the *de rigueur* black high heels that she had packed just in case there might be a reason to dress up at Blumfield. Now that aspiration seemed almost laughable. The expectations of her trip seemed absurd. She'd gone to Maryland to see if she could locate her aunt; now here she was in Manhattan with a man she hardly knew, going to a nightclub she would have recoiled reading about in *Time.*

"Are you wearing panties?" He stood up, and therefore, towered over her.

"What you mean to ask is: Am I a complete and total and absolute slut tonight?"

He laughed. "Enquiring minds want to know."

She tipped the corner of her mouth in a grin. "I'll never tell." She then backed through the French doors, grabbed her purse, and touched up her lipstick and powder.

He followed her to the elevator.

She had to admit he looked sexy in a pair of gray tropical weight wool slacks and a black polo shirt. He might have even looked tamed if not for the too-closely-cropped hair and the tattoo which she knew lay covered below the jersey on his sleeve.

But to tame him would require, in his words, a whip and chair. A collar and a leash.

Maybe even iron padlocks and keys.

No, he was a hard nut to crack.

And she was not at all sure she was up to the challenge.

CHAPTER TWENTY

Love is an angel disguised as lust.

—Bruce Springsteen

The Plush Pussy was probably the most déclassé martini joint on the East Coast.

But it was done at great expense.

Alyn didn't know a lot about Manhattan real estate; however, it certainly seemed to her that the commercial space above the Chanel Boutique on 57th Street was not about to go for small rent. Yet instead of designing a club that might draw the Sherry-Netherland kind of crowd, The Plush Pussy was the kind of club one might find in the no-man's land of downtown America after the Wal-Mart opened on the highway.

It was intentionally seedy, with fake leopard-skin upholstery and nylon-nightie lampshades. Bottles of Night Train and Thunderbird lined the back of the bar as if to profess a big wino/derelict crowd. Brad Pitt and Trent Resnor were said to use the club as their watering hole, and Alyn didn't doubt it when she saw the groups of emaciated stick girls in their combat boots, tattoos and acetate slips that only *looked* like they'd bought them at the Salvation Army. The place was so intentionally manufactured one had to wonder at the intelligence of the clientele. It was a wanna-be flop house, but no wino was ever going to wander into this club with a $100.00-a-head cover charge and twenty-dollar shots of cheap vermouth. She didn't respect the patrons—they were all trying a little *too* hard—but she did find herself begrudgingly admiring the mysterious Ajax. He had obviously tapped into a fad that was making him money hand over fist.

Drenched in the beat of the latest Moon Mix techno sound she leisurely scanned the crowded club, and all the while she resisted the urge to run to Clancy's and tell them to move their whole operation—ripped vinyl and all—over to Trump Tower.

Hell, Clancy'd be a millionaire overnight.

"I think we're a bit conspicuous," Peter shouted in her ear above the current din of The Lords of Acid.

Alyn shrugged. "We tried. But I can't help looking like an unoriginal 'working girl,' and you look like my Georgio Armani pimp. I didn't know we were supposed to wear black vinyl hip-huggers and be loaded up on ecstasy." She rolled her eyes. "Amy Vanderbilt, when will you get the dress code right?"

He chuckled and grabbed her hand. Not bothering with ordering drinks he led her to a table where they could further scope out the place.

"Who do you think would know the most about Ajax? The security guard to your left or the one covering the manager's door?" he asked.

She looked to her left. If there was a security guard amongst the crowd of young drugged-out sleazes, she had a hard time isolating him until a skinny man in the crowd lifted his hand to his ear and appeared to concentrate. She then realized that the guy, dressed like he was going to a high school rave, was wired like a Secret Service agent.

"I say we talk to the one guarding the manager's door. At least with him we have a chance of finding out who the manager is. The guy near me doesn't look like he knows his own name." She glanced at Peter.

He nodded. "C'mon."

They wove through the crowds and the thick beat of music. Peter had to yell in order to ask for the manager. The guard seemed to size them up, then he opened the door and allowed them to enter.

Behind a large desk, appearing very much like Bugsy Segal, was a man in a double-breasted suit. He looked up and greeted them with a surly expression. "What do you want?" he asked.

Peter took a relaxed seat on the orange leather couch in front of the desk. The manager's rudeness didn't seem to bother him at all. Alyn on the other hand had ready a knee-jerk apology and a desire to leave.

"We're looking for Ajax." Peter stretched out his arms along the couch's back. Alyn took a seat next to him.

"Who the hell are you?" the man demanded.

"We knew Garry Ferrucci. He told us that Ajax owns this club. Is he here?"

"Nobody sees him. Not even big shots like you," snapped the man.

"What's your name?" Peter asked.

"Mr. Blue."

"Well, Mr. Blue, we want to speak with Ajax. It's about a little matter of evidence he left over at Ferrucci's apartment. If he wants to talk about it, he can reach me here." Peter tossed the number of the hotel onto the coffee table.

"Don't hold your breath." The man glowered at them.

Peter grinned and stood. "If he doesn't call by tonight, we'll be going to the Feds."

He took Alyn's arm. She didn't bother with a farewell. She didn't think Mr. Blue was the creep's real name anyway.

* * *

"What a day." Alyn curled up on the couch in the suite. She'd changed into a large, very unsexy sweatshirt and leggings. Now she scanned the old headlines of the morning's *USA Today* that had been left on the coffee table.

Jacqueline Blum. Poor Little Rich Girl Likened to Doris Duke. Another Sad Ending for an American Heiress?

She grimaced at the article. Her heart sank as she read her aunt's biography. It seemed in the end not one man had ever really loved Jacqueline Blum. She'd had five divorces and one annulment. Even her father hadn't really loved her. He'd used her to manipulate his own emotional agenda, such as shunning

Alyn's mother when Colette had gotten into trouble. Jacqueline had bounced from one tawdry love affair to another in an attempt at finding happiness. But the only men who'd ever made her happy, who'd never disappointed her, were buried inside the yellowing pages of the hundreds of paperback romances she'd kept locked in her bedroom.

Alyn leaned her head against the silk damask pillows of the couch. Dark thoughts enveloped her. Exhausted, she watched the play of light on the rooftop garden as Peter moved about in his bedroom.

He was a darkness all his own. Tomorrow she had to call Masterlife. Until she found out a little more about him, she wouldn't feel truly comfortable. The trip to The House of Whacks and The Plush Pussy proved there were more things in her universe than certainly *she* had ever dreamt of. It disturbed her how well he understood the more sinister yearnings in the human heart.

He walked through the living room dressed only in a pair of worn jeans and flannel boxer shorts that peeked over the low-slung belt. She spied on him from the couch as he went to the bar and popped the top on a jar of macadamia nuts.

Already they were acting like an old married couple. It comforted and bothered her all at the same time. It didn't seem possible she had known this man less than a week. But it seemed she had known him a very long time. He knew so much about what drove her, what stopped her, what frightened her.

He looked up at her.

Their gazes held.

"Without a doubt you are attempting to eat nuts that ounce per ounce are more expensive than the platinum sold at Tiffany's." She arched her eyebrow at him. When in doubt, use levity.

He smiled. Irreverently he shook the contents of the jar into his mouth.

"Heathen," she whispered.

He sank down on the couch next to her. "Want some?"

She peeked into the near-empty jar. "Oh, I am not worthy." She moaned but she took a handful anyway.

Crunching the nuts, she found herself admiring him.

His proximity always did something to her. It had to be hormones, but she'd always think he was handsome. The hair on his chest was just enough to entice her fingers, his muscle-toned torso was perfect, even all the way down past his navel where the dark hair began to thicken again before it disappeared beneath the band of his shorts. He was the alpha male. Annie Liebovitz would give her soul to photograph the likes of him for a Calvin Klein ad.

But he had two flaws; both self-inflicted. The first was his gaze. His eye color was breathtaking; an intriguing mixture of gold that was like the spark off a candle flame, but it was the expression in his eyes that consumed her, frightened her, and yet, left her greedy for more of him, wanting the possession and desire he seemed to hold within them.

The other flaw was the tattoo on his arm. She didn't like the imagery of the belladonna plant bursting from the cracked skull. It was voluptuous death spilling out onto life when death shouldn't thrive and blossom; death was supposed to wither, grow skeletal, and disappear. To go away. There was no joy to be found in its triumph.

But somehow Peter found some small joy there or he wouldn't have endured the pain of having dye injected into his skin.

''What are you thinking about?'' he asked, his thumb barely caressing her cheek.

She lowered her eyes, away from the tattoo. ''I'm thinking about how much I don't know—about how much Jacqueline didn't know.''

''What don't you know?'' His hand cupped her chin and lifted her head to his.

''I don't know about men. It seems Jacqueline didn't either.'' She met his gaze. Her own had to be filled with trepidation.

His grasp grew tender. ''What do you want to know?''

She looked around, anywhere but at him. ''I don't think one man can answer all my questions. I want to know about my father. I want to know why Jacqueline, with all her experience with men, picked such losers.''

Her gaze slid to his arm. ''I want to know why a man such as you would mark himself the way you have.''

''You're asking about this?'' His forefinger tapped the tattoo. ''You knew what this was, didn't you?''

She nodded. "The belladonna's a metaphor, but for what? For death, of course. You celebrate death with that picture."

"No. Not celebrate," he answered grimly.

"Why then have it?"

"To accept it. To surrender to it. Rebel against it . . . . to *inflict*—"

Her breath constricted with the sudden fierce beating of her heart. "No. Not inflict. Definitely not that."

"You don't know."

"What happened to that young man was not intentional. It was an accident. An accident. You can't inflict an accident upon someone. It's not possible."

"You can't inflict an accident, no, of course not. But an accident can certainly become an affliction."

"But you wouldn't hurt anyone intentionally."

He turned to her. "How do you know that? How do you know that I didn't kill Ferrucci?"

His body tensed in anger. "You say you know nothing of men and that you don't trust them, yet you blindly trust me. Have you ever interviewed someone I put in prison? A bondsman has total authority over his capture. *Total authority.* The bond jumper has no Constitutional Rights. I can do what I like with them until I bring their broken bodies to jail."

He ran his fingers through her hair on either side of her scalp. Pulling her down onto him, he said, "Do you really want me to teach you about men? Do you want me to explain all the ugliness, all the pain? I can, you know. I've been there."

She took a deep breath and stared at him. He was so close she just had to exhale and her lips would touch his.

"But is there nothing a man can offer but ugliness and pain?" she whispered harshly. "From what my mother and Jacqueline went through, I think I have to believe there is nothing else."

"Still, you don't want to. I can see it in your eyes."

She conceded with only a slight shake to her head. "I guess I can't help it. There's a tiny hidden part in me—just like there must have been in Jacqueline, who embraced all those Harlequin romances—who still wants to believe in Prince Charming. No matter how bruised and wounded, I still want to believe there's a special man out there. One who'll worship me and make me into the princess I long to be."

His expression hardened. "I'd like to be the one to show you that man," he said, almost like a reprimand.

A knot of tears seemed to choke her words. "I—I just don't see how you could. You know too much of the ugliness. And you know it too deeply. You even knew about that twisted club and what they do there."

She tried to hide the revulsion on her face, but she did a poor job of it. "I—I even think you know *why* they go there."

"Yes," he whispered, like a hissing snake.

"Do people really go there for pleasure? Is that possible?"

"Yes."

"But what kind of pleasure?" she gasped. "I don't understand it. It makes no sense."

"It's release," he said, slowly, pointedly. "They go there to accept, to surrender, to rebel . . . to *inflict.*"

"No," she moaned. "I don't understand."

"You don't want to understand. Because it's darkness I'm talking about. It's night. It's the shadowed landscape of the human soul. But like Jacqueline, if you don't understand it, Alyn, it can sneak up behind you and devour you. Wipe you off the face of the earth."

"I can't understand a world that makes no sense."

"But it does make sense. You just have to look into the mirror. See the shadows in your own soul."

"I don't have any."

He smirked and looked her dead in the eye. "You're lying."

A tingle ran down her spine like cold drops of rain.

"You can't fight what you refuse to see, Alyn. That was exactly Jacqueline's problem. Are you to end up like her?"

"No," she refuted, shaking her head.

"Then see your shadows. Understand them. Accept them."

"No," she said again.

He stood so quickly she almost tumbled off the couch.

In horror she watched as he removed his belt from his jeans.

"What do you think you're doing?" she gasped.

"If I took this thing and put it around your neck, what would you say to that?" he demanded.

She gave him a frozen glance. ''I would tell you to go to hell. I'm not your thrall.''

Without a word he looped the end of the belt through the buckle and slipped it over her head.

''Do you see this? If I pull on the strap you come with it.'' He gently tugged.

She had no choice but to rise to her feet.

''Do you like it?'' he whispered against her hair.

''No,'' she spat.

''But what would you say if I said I liked it? What would you say if I told you the feeling it gives me is exquisite—that control is the best sexual game of all?''

''Let me go,'' she said woodenly.

He pulled her to him by the neck. With sweet roughness, he kissed her.

Against her will she felt herself warming. It was hard to resist a man she was violently attracted to, who was vowing to take away her choices and responsibilities, and forcing her toward pleasure.

He slowly unthreaded the leather belt from the buckle.

Free again, she stumbled backward and glared at him.

He laughed and threw the belt to her.

''Your turn,'' he said.

She looked down at the mahogany-colored belt. The leather was still warm where it had pressed against her vulnerable throat.

''C'mon,'' he dared.

''I don't want to do it,'' she said adamantly.

''You just don't like that side of yourself. Because you're afraid of it. But it makes you weaker that way. So go ahead. Look it in the eye, Alyn. Go. Do it.''

''I won't,'' she gasped.

He took her hands. He forced her to loop the belt through the buckle again.

''I won't,'' she refuted when he placed the noose around his neck.

''Go ahead. Tug,'' he whispered harshly, his eyes glittering like ancient gold, his hand holding out the end of the belt as if in supplication.

''I don't like these games.'' She shook her head and stepped back.

''Take a taste. Indulge.'' He went to her. With both hands wrapped around her one, he forced her to take the end of the belt.

''Tug,'' he bit out.

She closed her eyes.

''DO IT,'' he growled.

She let out a low cry. With her better judgment receding like the tide, she tugged on the leather belt.

He fell into her, his balance upset by the stronger force of the garrote.

She was shocked by the slam of his body into hers.

She stared up at him.

He eyed her, taunting her with a wicked gleam of understanding.

''So now you decide. Do you like it?''

She refused to answer. Her every emotion was in turmoil.

He shook her. ''Do you like it?''

She turned away.

His hand lay gently on her small shoulder. ''Just tell me. Admit it and it will teach you what you may one day need to know.''

With tears choking her, she said, ''I don't like it—but I understand it now. I do understand it. And I hate you for making me understand it.''

He wrapped her with arms of tender steel. In a soothing voice, he whispered, ''Don't hate me. I want to protect you. I don't want to just show you the ugliness in the world.''

He took her chin in his hand and forced her to meet his gaze. ''Oh, God, could you ever look beyond this bitter man and see the man you seek underneath? Could you ever do that?''

A trembling sob erupted from somewhere in her soul. Slowly, she put her arms around him and she held him closer than even he held her.

She shivered and almost hated herself. If he was lying to her, if he was scamming her just to dominate and humiliate her, then he was brilliant because she utterly believed him. She'd never known greater intimacy in all her life.

With one long tug at her hand, he led her into her bedroom.

Before she could even shudder, he'd yanked down her leggings and panties, and knelt before her, hungry and demanding.

She tipped her head back and held his to her, and suddenly she didn't care if he taught her twisted games. All she wanted was him, and if she could have him, then she would play. Because nothing else in the world mattered, not shadow nor light, not good or evil. The only urgency was to ease the burning loneliness inside her, and now she finally understood she could only do it with him.

Indeed he'd taught her much, she thought as her mind was swallowed in pleasure. In the end, it didn't matter who held the leash, imaginary or not. Because he was most definitely in control of the game.

The diabolical game.

PART TWO

The Judas Kiss

CHAPTER TWENTY-ONE

If you pick up a starving dog and make him prosperous, he will not bite you. This is the principal difference between a dog and a man.

—MARK TWAIN

The phone ringing was as obnoxious as the scratch of a harlot's nails across the hood of a new Porsche. Peter turned his bleary gaze to the clock. It was midnight.

"Hello?" Alyn said sleepily from her side of the bed. She'd picked up the phone and now lay back in the twisted covers still damp from their lovemaking.

It was dark in the bedroom. Not even the glimmer of city light could penetrate the thick silk drapery.

"Who is this?" she asked, stiffening beside him.

He slowly sat up in bed. He knew what was coming. So much of everything already made sense. It was only a matter of time before all the details were out and his suspicions proved correct. His only fear was the future, and how Alyn would take the cruel betrayals that were sure to come.

"How do you know who I am?" She struggled to a sitting position herself.

Even in the darkness, he could make out the worry and fear on her lovely face.

Gently, he took the receiver from her.

She relinquished it and held onto his arm instead while he dealt with the caller.

"We want to meet with you," he said, not even bothering to ask who was on the phone.

He listened while the man gave him directions as to when and where they should meet. Grunting assent, he closed his eyes as if memorizing the time and place, then he hit the OFF button and lay back on the bed.

"I think that was the man named Ajax," she whispered.

He stroked her hair as she snuggled for protection against his chest. "Yes."

"He—he seems to have gotten the message we're looking for him."

"Yes." He didn't offer more.

"Do you think he's dangerous, Peter?"

He laughed mirthlessly. "Yeah. I think so."

Heavy fearful silence drifted across them.

He closed his eyes. He hated silence. It made him think and he didn't want to think. Because there was so much to think about; the future; right and wrong. Cat and mouse. The morning was sure to prove ugly.

He'd had no business getting involved with Alyn. It made him weak and vulnerable. At first he thought she was just a money-hungry manipulator, but now that he believed differently everything was bound to shatter. Now he saw her fragility, her loneliness, her confusion at the evil world around her. And all he wanted to do now was protect her. Even if it cost him.

He took a deep breath and silently cursed the silence. He didn't want to think or squirm. He just wanted to sink himself into the warm naked woman next to him, the one with the frightened innocent face, and the shameless hungry lips that even now searched for his weak spot.

But she was looking much too low to find his heart.

* * *

Alyn couldn't understand why Peter was so particular about what she wore to the meeting with "Ajax." He insisted that she wear her hair in a ponytail away from her face. Her clothing had to be plain and dark.

Dressed in washed navy linen pants and tunic, she again asked him why he was being so difficult. She went to put on lipstick, but he pulled her hand down and placed the capped tube back in her handbag.

"I don't get it." She faced him.

He stroked her cheeks with his thumbs as he did often when he looked at her. "I want people to see your face."

With that, he took her by the hand and they left the hotel.

They were to meet the mysterious Ajax in the American Wing of the Metropolitan Museum of Art. Alyn walked with Peter through the rooms of English furniture, medieval armaments, heart-stopping Manets until they came to the displays of Louis Comfort Tiffany glass windows. They were in a cavern of a room which had been specially built to display the facade of an eighteenth-century American bank building.

Peter eased himself down on a bench in the courtyard space in front of the bank.

She looked at her watch. "We're really early. Can I poke around while we wait?"

She expected him to nod; she was shocked when he took her hand and forced her down on the bench next to him.

"I know who Ajax is," he said so quietly she almost couldn't hear him. "At least, I'm pretty sure I know who he is. I didn't figure out what his angle was until recently."

Her eyes widened. "Why didn't you tell me this? Who is he?"

She nervously looked around. There was no one in the entire room but a young mother and her sleeping child. Still, she kept her voice down. "I don't understand. Why tell me this now? Here?"

"Because you would never have come here to meet him if I'd given you any ideas about who he was."

He didn't look at her eyes. "Look, I could be wrong. But there are things you don't know about the situation. There are dangerous people out there you've never even contemplated. You don't see things the way I do. By my perspective."

"Which is . . . ?" she said warily.

He finally met her stare. "Which is from me. The man who's out for hire to anybody and everybody. You think I'm on the books working for Masterlife? You think I'm some kind of freelance cop out working for the good guys? Well, you're wrong. I'm working for them—and everybody else in between—and not one little fuck in the line is a good guy."

He drew his face closer. The planes of his cheeks grew hard. "But these guys don't make all that money by working aboveboard. Whether they're white-collar paper-pushers for Masterlife or sleazy club owners, the path to their happiness is money, and they will ruthlessly get rid of any obstacle in their path."

"And I'm somehow blocking the way," she answered woodenly. She could barely muster the words through her fear.

"Masterlife does *not* want to pay this policy off. And they're willing to pay a guy like me under the table to see to it they don't have to. Believe me, they don't care the way it's done as long as there's nothing on the record that shows their involvement."

His eyes grew cold and hard. The way she remembered them.

"Think, Alyn. These insurance companies, they have every risk outlined in actuary tables to the dime. They can pay twenty million to some long-lost niece of Jacqueline Blum, or they can get rid of the obligation altogether. Make the obligation 'go away' before they have to pay it, or make sure the body of their deceased client never comes to light—whichever works best."

He studied her, his gazing raking up and down. "These guys are bad people, Alyn. Evil. They are the ultimate in corporate Nazism. Their Final Solution is the manufacture of money and the eradication of debt. You understand? Statistically, to Masterlife, you're nothing but several pounds of calcium, lipids and protein. On the tables your uninsured life is worth less than one hundred dollars of cheap organics. These guys—these dark-suited monsters in Atlanta—they don't care about one hundred dollars."

Her stomach tightened. She wondered if she were going to be sick. "Are—you—telling—me—that—you—you've been hired—by Masterlife to—?" Her breath came in hard gasps. The entire room seemed to swirl in a bleeding mass of stone, glass and sunlight.

He put his arm around her waist.

She knew she should brush it off, get away from him until she could think, but she was too stunned to do anything but think of her next intake of air.

"I took their money . . . but I didn't agree to do their job." His face was taut with dark anger. The emotion was like a shadow that now covered it. "There's no honor in the men around you, Alyn. You suspected this; but I *know* it. I know it because I'm one of those men. But I—I—I *want* to believe in something good."

He looked down. "I *want* to believe. And that something good, I've discovered, is you."

She broke away. Frozen tears burned her eyes. "What kind of creature are you, Peter Youngblood? Would you have done the job if you hadn't decided you wanted to sleep with Masterlife's hit?"

He grabbed her arms. Forcing her to the bench, he said, "It's not like that. I'm not an assassin by trade. They picked me because I promised to get the job done. I took it because I knew I could make sure Jacqueline Blum was never found."

"But how could you promise that?" she snapped.

He shook her as if to drive his words home. "Because I put all bets on the fact that you had your aunt killed to receive the inheritance. If I could solve who killed Jacqueline then I could keep the body buried—so to speak—away from the investigators. No body; no money.

"But then I saw you, talked to you. I realized you couldn't have done it. So I had to reframe this whole mess. When Ferrucci was shot that really threw me—but I just turned everything around again. Ferrucci and Dante probably ran scared after they knew your aunt changed her will. They were facing the fact that they'd get nothing after probably planning Jacqueline's murder for months and speculating on every possibility except the one that confronted them at the end: being found out for the dirtbags they were by their benefactoress. And that's where I was bested by the mystery of Jacqueline Blum, until . . . until I came here to New York and realized who Ferrucci would work for. Hell, this guy would be Ferrucci's insurance policy. I've no doubt he'd seek him out."

She must have lost her mind. She could barely follow what he was saying through the running terrors in her brain.

When she forced herself to be calm, she came to the last obvious question. "Ferrucci didn't need another job. Jacqueline might have written him out of the will, but she hadn't fired either Ferrucci or Dante. Why would Ferrucci propose to go looking for a job when he already had one? And a good one?''

''Because there's always a better one, especially for an entrepreneur like him.''

He took a deep breath. ''Are you listening finally, Alyn? Are you putting these pieces together? Masterlife wasn't the only player in this game. And they all were willing to ante up to me to get the job done. I just didn't know why until now.''

Her gaze locked with his. She ran through the scenario again and again, but the key remained elusive. Every time her logic went through the maze of the facts she came to a blind end.

''Time's up,'' he said gently, his gaze looking behind her. Something akin to recognition fired in his eyes. ''Go ahead, Alyn, turn and meet your nemesis.''

A chill of premonition crept slowly down her spine on arachnid legs.

She turned to face a man who stood several yards behind her, staring at them. He wore black slacks and a cocoa brown polo shirt. He was a handsome man, older than Peter by twenty years at least, but he'd kept his well-toned body, and he'd kept his well-drawn features, the best of which were his hazel green eyes.

Her eyes.

She choked.

He seemed to recognize her the instant she did him. Shock and anger tightened the handsome face her mother had sacrificed herself for. His lips thinned to a narrow white line, then he spun on his heels and he walked away as fast as he could without attracting the bored notice of the security guard posted at the entrance to the wing.

Alyn rose to her feet as if to follow him. The man was like a beacon, a ghost within her psyche that had just been made flesh.

She called out to him, her voice making a guttural primeval cry that spoke only anguish and yearning, but the man didn't turn around. He disappeared around the corner.

She took a step toward him but Peter grabbed her hand and stopped her.

''You understand now?'' he said.

She fought his hold. She had to have another look at the man, that animal who possessed the genetic makeup that was uniquely her own.

"I need to know," she cried, but Peter wouldn't relinquish his hold.

She twisted her arm, but still the manacle grip remained. Tears flowed down her cheeks as she finally spat, "How did you know he would be the one?"

Peter's mouth was grim and tight. "I deduced. I only talked to him on the phone—never saw his face, or knew exactly who he was. But when I figured it out, I knew who it would be. He'd be the next one in line to inherit if you got the estate. I had a hunch, and now that I've seen him, I knew I was right. I knew it was him."

"Alan Jones. My mother always referred to him as A.J.," she sobbed.

"A.J. Ajax."

She lowered herself to the bench.

It would take an eon for her to assimilate the shock of seeing that face; the one so much like her own. Never had she dreamed she would ever look her father in the eye. Never had she imagined he would be so handsome, and so heartless.

"When I was a little girl," she sobbed quietly, "I always knew my father would one day see me with his own eyes and love me. I wanted to find him for as long as I can remember. I always knew when he looked at me, he would forgive me for my birth and love me."

It was all she could do to keep herself from rocking on the bench like a wounded animal.

"Your mother took her knocks. She knew in the end he was bad."

"But I always hoped," she wept. "I always hoped." She wiped her tears with the heel of her palm. "And even if I discovered him to be bad, I never thought he'd want me—want me—*dead,*" she ground out through bitterly clenched teeth.

"But he was the next one in line, Alyn. Dante and Ferrucci knew it. When Jacqueline changed her will at the last minute, their original chances vanished, so they were desperate to make a deal. They already had a dead heiress and no one to pay. When they found out you were incorruptible, they went to the next in line and offered a settlement: proof of Jacqueline's death for a chunk of the estate. Ajax—the underworld hustler of their dreams—heard the terms, and obviously, he bit."

"But what about the lawsuits blocking my right to inherit? They instigated them," she spat, bewildered.

"Red herrings. As soon as Ferrucci could lock in his deal with Ajax, the suits would have all been dropped. I'm sure of it."

"Then that man would see me dead," she said coldly.

"Yes," Peter hissed.

She swallowed a sob.

After a long cold moment, she said, "So will he? Even now that he knows I know he's in on this, I've ruined his plans. He's got to know he can't inherit now that I know he's waiting in line. I'll see the money go to the animal shelter before he'll ever see a dime."

"I think he gets it, Alyn. He didn't look too happy to see you, and to see you with me."

"Does he know what happened to Jacqueline? Was he a part of it?"

Peter released a dark laugh. "After the fact. Ferrucci and Dante were written out of the will before Jacqueline was missing. She outmanuevered them but before they could be informed they were trumped, they pulled the trigger thinking they were going to inherit."

Alyn was very quiet. She thought of her aunt and her hollow parade of lovers; she thought of her own mother, and that hazel-eyed fiend who'd served as the donor to her gene pool. Alan Jones was just an imaginary lover too. Because in reality, he loved no one. No one.

With a frigidness that forged her will into steel, Alyn rose from the bench.

"C'mon," she said.

He seemed surprised by her newfound determination. "Where are we going?"

Her face and the expression on it must have been carved from marble. "I'm not sure who I should trust right now. All I know is that I'm going to find Jacqueline's body. But first I'm going to a lawyer and draft the donation of my estate to the Society for the Prevention of Cruelty to Animals. That'll screw all of them. Including you if you're in on it."

She looked at him, half-expectantly, half-contemptfully.

"Aren't you going to let me deny that?" He seemed only vaguely kidding.

She didn't see the amusement in his words at all. "What use are denials now? I can't believe anyone. All I know is that I've got to protect myself. I need you to help me, and I'm not giving you a choice, Mr. Youngblood." She slid him an acid smile. "You *used* to work for Masterlife and Ajax. Now you're working for me."

His eyes gleamed with unfettered anger. "Is this your way of putting the belt around my neck?"

She smirked. "I don't need the belt. I've got charges for conspiracy to commit murder, and you and Masterlife are up to your hairy fat balls in the debris. You'll either be working for me, Peter Youngblood, or I'll be pressing charges and filing civil suits, and you and Masterlife will be praying for a bullet."

He eyed her with a new respect, even some self-deprecating amusement.

She walked away, knowing he would follow.

Behind her she heard him say, "I see you're finally getting the hang of topping."

She smirked stiffly and wondered if this was how it felt to have your heart ripped out and watch it go splat on the wall.

All she said was, "Yes. Vanilla no more."

CHAPTER TWENTY-TWO

Alyn had to get inside that security box. She had to know what Ferrucci had been hiding in there. Without it, there was probably going to be no other clue that might lead to solving Jacqueline's disappearance.

"You'll never get into it without the key and a proper ID," Peter told her back at the hotel.

She chewed her lower lip. "Why did Ajax show up? Did he want that evidence you spoke of at The Plush Pussy, or did he believe already that the evidence was the key to the safety deposit box?"

"I think he was looking for the key. We're all looking for that."

"Okay. So what's in the box?" She raised her eyebrow at him. "Money?"

"Hell, no." She couldn't believe how savvy she was becoming. Less than two weeks of bizarre trips and threats to her life, and she was thinking like Sherlock Holmes.

"It's evidence in the box," she told him. "I've no doubt about it, and if your thoughts are traveling the same road as mine, you have no doubts either."

He smiled like a pleased tutor. "Okay. Go the next step. What's the most valuable or damning evidence these men could have?"

She locked gazes with him. "Valuable? Or damning? Or both?"

He grinned at her as if she were his prize student. "Let's say both."

Her eyes widened.

Suddenly everything made so much sense.

* * *

Okay, so it wasn't completely true, Mabel thought, her hand trembling as she dialed the main branch downtown. *But a person's security box was just that, secure. Especially at Chase where they had years of integrity behind their name.*

There was, however, one flaw to the system.

No one could access a safety deposit box without the co-key that was always in possession of a bank official. But that didn't rule out the bank having the ability to control its own boxes.

Mabel knew she was technically acting outside the guidelines. She was supposed to be notified by the main branch before she refitted a box. After fees were past due, the bank had the option to repossess the box and—as a by-product—hold onto its contents. They did this by popping the second lock and replacing it with another.

She was not following the rules. Mabel chastised herself.

But the fees *were* overdue.

Garry Ferrucci *was* dead.

And now, after so much time and publicity, what were the odds that Jacqueline Blum herself would trot into the bank and want to visit with her valuables?

Nil, thought Mabel. No one gave a damn about that poor Jacqueline Blum, least of all the police. Mabel was still smarting over their dismissal of her evidence.

But she herself would find the truth even if no other fool in the world would.

If she took it upon herself to empty the case, she might not be able to go to the police with her evidence. But at least she herself would have the satisfaction of solving the one burning mystery of her wretched boring career at Chase Bank. She alone would know what nefarious secrets Garry Ferrucci had deposited in Jacqueline Blum's box.

Mabel would then retire to the Pass and muse over her knowledge, insignificant as it might prove to be, but still, it would be hers alone. *The National Enquirer* would never know it; the FBI would never know it. It would be Mabel Haskings's dirty little secret which she would take into retirement. And with it, she would thumb her nose at the rest of the world that had treated her so poorly.

She walked to the vault and found the locksmith already there. She showed him the paperwork on Box 1329 and instructed him to pop the lock. It was accomplished in a matter of seconds.

Mabel opened the door with the bank's key, slid out the long gray metal box and went with it to the table in the center of the vault.

Protocol said she was to send the contents of all repossessed boxes to the branch vice-president, whereby, he or she would keep them until the owners came for them.

But this time, Mabel was going to act on her own.

She sat down.

Without even peeking, she pulled back the metal lid and dumped the articles into a manila envelope. Casually, she returned the box to 1329 and told the locksmith to refit it. He went to work.

She took the envelope to her desk and left it there to sit nondescriptly until the bank closed and she could stuff it inside her purse.

* * *

The J&B was going to taste sweet tonight, Mabel thought as she opened the third deadbolt on the door to her walk-up apartment.

She shut the door behind her and placed her purse and the shopping bag full of dinner on the counter in her kitchenette.

Easing her feet into her terrycloth slippers, she went through her evening routine like a robot. She slipped off her dress and hung the garment on a wooden hanger. Then she wrapped herself up in a ratty lavender chenille bathrobe that she had bought at Irene's House of Fashions in Brooklyn Heights, circa 1967.

The scotch poured, and dinner warming in the oven, she put her legs on the mauve wool plush ottoman that matched the rest of her living room furniture and clutched her handbag to her chest.

Tonight was going to be anything but routine.

Excitedly, she opened her purse and brought out the bulging manila envelope. The heavy clank of metal was only barely muffled by the silk scarf balled up in the center of the package.

As if she were a little girl reaching inside a Christmas stocking, she placed the first treasure in the palm of her hand.

The very brilliance of it made her gasp. Eighteen large paisley forms fashioned out of flawless diamonds interlinked to form a bracelet. It had the name of the jeweler Harry Winston invisibly written all over it.

The next piece out of the manila envelope was a necklace to match the bracelet and a large brooch centered with a diamond the size of her thumbnail.

Mabel knew Jacqueline had to have sets and sets of priceless jewelry, but somehow these pieces must have been set aside as special. She speculated they might have been given to Jacqueline as gifts. In that case, their sentimental value would even overshadow their huge monetary one. And perhaps that was why the woman had separated this ensemble from the rest of her collection.

Mabel was then not surprised to find an old notecard with the bold penstrokes of a man who was used to handing out his autograph. The writing said:

For Jacqueline—
You, only you, and again, you.
With love,
Phlip

Mabel was stunned. Obviously the note was from Phlip Kearney, the film star.

She never expected to peek inside the life of the rich and famous, and now here she was, reading love notes from Phlip Kearney and running $500,000 worth of diamonds through her fingers. The tabloids still speculated that Jacqueline carried a torch for the man—even though Phlip had left her in the sixties for blond bombshell Ann Marie and now had been long in the grave. The jewelry had probably been from him. And maybe the tabloids were right. Jacqueline had saved it for some reason.

She dug through the envelope again and pulled out two tiny gold lockets. Inside each were the engraved words "Daddy's Girl."

She studied them and felt a hard knot of tears in her throat. These had to have been made for Jacqueline and her sister, Colette. The necklaces were so tiny and delicate that a grown woman could have worn them around her ankle.

They'd been made in the heyday of the Blum family, when John Harrington Blum was a handsome young millionaire with a beautiful wife and two little girls who were the darlings of the media. It was before his wife died, before he grew harsh and cruel, before all the tragedies that were to come.

Humbled, Mabel put the lockets beside the ensemble of diamonds.

She'd expected to find riches in the safety deposit box, but not the sad unfolding of one woman's heartaches. It made her almost hesitate to look at the last article in the envelope, the heavy U-shaped piece which was wrapped inside the Hermès scarf.

But she couldn't turn back. These treasures were for her eyes only. Jacqueline had never known dull little bank teller Mabel Haskings, but their heartaches had been similar, their stories pretty much the same.

Sighing, she slid the balled-up scarf out onto her lap. The silk twill was in the classic Hermès colors of maroon and olive. It had figures of show-jumping on it, along with snaffle bits, leather bridles and blue ribbons. It was definitely of an early vintage. Mabel speculated that it could have come from the Paris period in the seventies, when Jacqueline had taken a notoriously cavernous apartment off the Place Vendôme.

She began on the fat knots that held the ball of silk together. The object within had a strange bumpy ridge on one side of it and when she flipped it over, the underside was polished smooth.

It could have been a piece of jewelry but it was too big and awkward. The closer Mabel got to it, the more she was convinced the thing was some kind of piece of machinery—half of a cog, or something of that nature.

She flushed with excitement when the last knot was untied.

Whatever was hidden inside the scarf had to be a very real clue to the solving of the mystery of what had happened to Jacqueline Blum.

Out of respect for that, Mabel said a silent prayer, then flung aside the scarf.

The object tumbled into her lap.

The first second was filled with curiosity. Mabel looked at the thing and didn't quite place it.

Then her eyes widened.

She became paralyzed with horror.

Her only sensation was the warm metal taste of blood in her mouth where she bit her tongue in an effort to muffle her scream.

CHAPTER TWENTY-THREE

Alyn was living a nightmare. The man she was sleeping with—perhaps had even fallen in love with—was one of the predators. Her own father wanted her dead, and could be planning her murder even as she took the cab ride with Peter back down to the Chase Bank.

Jacqueline and Colette had had their betrayals, and now it did seem that the legacy had been fulfilled. Alyn Blum-Jones could be counted in as one of the victims.

Peter's hand rested on her knee. He did that a lot. He liked to caress her, touch her quietly when they were out in public. It was like their own private language. With one silent stroke he invoked memories of their lovemaking and left her with very little doubt that he demanded possession of her. And now she understood that possession could be achingly sweet . . . or a long dark tunnel to hell.

The cab pulled up to the curb at Thirty-Seventh and Park. It was near lunch hour and already there was a stream of office workers running through the revolving doors beneath the Chase sign.

Peter made no conversation as he paid the cabbie and pulled her out of the cab. She followed his lead. What else could she do. She was determined to solve the mystery surrounding her aunt even more than he was, because now she knew with a certainty that to find Jacqueline might mean the difference between saving herself, or dying too.

Peter went into the bank first.

He'd been quiet; that last night she'd swore he was so morose that they would forgo their ritual of lovemaking. She'd gone into her room and slipped beneath the cold delicate covers of her bed. Then she lay in the dark for more than an hour, awake and suffering. Not knowing what would ease her pain.

But he'd come to her finally. When she'd gotten sleepy, she felt his large form ease himself down onto her mattress.

One displeased word from her and she knew he would leave for his room. So she said nothing, and he held her, and they kissed. And made love. And then she knew that at least she could feel warm and secure for eight hours, if not the rest of her life.

Mabel's desk was empty. A young boyish-looking teller was placing a stack of papers on her desk.

"We're here to see Ms. Haskings," Alyn told him. "Has she left for lunch already?"

"She's not in today," the man said, eyeing her.

"Is she ill?" Alyn looked at Peter. A sick knot formed in her stomach.

"I dunno. Maybe. I've heard the woman's never called in sick in her entire career here. We call her the Triassic Teller because she's been working at Chase longer than the president."

"Thank you," Alyn said softly, her mind a thousand miles away.

Again she looked at Peter. The teller walked away.

"Is she dead, Peter? If we go look for her will she be missing too?" Even she could hear the rising hysteria in her voice. "Did Ajax get her and maybe next he'll get—?"

"Miss Galloping Paranoia. You don't know that," he interrupted. Placing his hand in the small of her back, he said, "I'll find out where she lives. Let's go get something to eat; I'll call a couple of old friends on the force. They can ring us back with the address before our soup's delivered."

* * *

Mabel Haskings's apartment was a small walk-up on the West Side. It seemed very little to show for years of dedication to a huge international banking concern. Alyn hoped Mabel's retirement proved to be more fun-filled than the dreary dark hallways that led to the non-descript door of 3B.

Peter knocked loudly.

Immediately they heard bumping and skittering from the other side of the door.

"Someone's definitely at home," Alyn said.

"Mabel Haskings? Mabel Haskings. This is Peter Youngblood and Alyn Blum-Jones. Remember us? We spoke at Clancy's. We looked for you at the bank today."

There was more bumping and shuffling. The peephole beneath the doorknocker blackened, then showed light once more.

"We were worried about you," Alyn called out. "They told us you've never taken a day off. We thought—well, we would really like to talk to you again about that deposit box if we could."

Slowly one lock unbolted, then another, then another.

The door creaked open and a face appeared.

Alyn caught her breath. The creature before them couldn't be the same woman they had talked to at Chase just the other day. That woman had worn a classic, if somewhat dated, wool suit and sensible Ferragamo pumps.

This woman was nothing more than the shadow of the banker they'd seen; her face was death-mask white, her eyes were shadowed in the heavy bruise-colored purple of an insomniac. She wore only an ancient tattered bathrobe and her hair stood on end as if it had been frantically pulled on all night.

"Are you feeling okay? Are you ill?" Alyn asked, moving in front of Peter. This version of Mabel Haskings didn't require intimidation. Clearly something was terribly wrong. Mabel Haskings needed help.

"I—I can't tell you—" the woman said in a harsh dry sob.

"Tell us what?" Alyn asked, taking the woman's arm and leading her to the couch.

"You can't come in here. Really, please, you must leave," Mabel protested.

"We want to help—"

"How did you get my address?" the woman exclaimed in a fit of paranoia.

"Please, calm down. Can I make you some tea? We just want to talk to you." Alyn looked at Peter.

He took a seat in the chair opposite the couch. His gaze was pinned on Mabel. "We got your address through a friend of mine who's a cop. If you're frightened you might want to tell us what's going on. It's best to trust someone."

"I can't trust anyone. I *am frightened.*" Mabel buried her head in her hands.

"Please let us help you. Please," Alyn said, softly touching the woman's trembling shoulder.

Mabel lifted her head and looked at Peter. "So are you a policeman?" she asked with an edge of hysteria.

Alyn intervened. "No, he's just a friend of mine. He's helping me look for my aunt. Remember? Jacqueline Blum was my aunt."

Mabel swung around and locked her gaze on Alyn.

"Yes, that's right. She was your aunt." Tears began to flood her eyes and tip down her creased cheeks.

"Oh, please tell us what's wrong," Alyn begged, hysteria creeping into her own voice. "I just know this has something to do with Jacqueline, and this mystery has so many twists and turns, I'm afraid for everyone."

"I'll be next," Mabel said numbly. She rose from the couch and stared out her small window to the derelict brownstone across the street.

"What makes you think that?" Alyn asked.

Mabel didn't turn around. "I know it. Because I'm the only one outside of the victim and her killers to know she's dead."

"You know Jacqueline Blum is dead?" Peter said.

Mabel nodded.

"How do you know?" Alyn rose and stood next to her.

"I know because—because—" A renewed flood of tears hit her. She momentarily became incapacitated by them, but then, as if invisible arms had shaken her, she righted herself, wiped her eyes with a Kleenex, and said, "Wait here. You may as well know. Someone else should know."

She walked into her bedroom and came out with a small pink box.

Upon closer inspection, Alyn found it was a little girl's jewelry box, the kind Woolworth's used to sell back in the 1950s. This one was covered with quilted satin vinyl, and it had obviously been treasured because the only sign of wear was on the seams, where the glue had finally given out.

Mabel held the box in her lap. Tears came anew but this time they were silent as she gazed at Alyn. "I shouldn't have done this. My life is over. I'll never get my retirement now. It's just that I didn't think anyone would ever know. The police didn't care about the deposit box. That sleaze Ferrucci was dead; Jacqueline Blum was missing; I figured by the time anyone came looking for the contents of the box, I'd be long gone and—"

"You opened the box," Peter interrupted, his eyes locked onto her every movement.

"I—I opened the box." Mabel released a silent shudder.

"What did you find?" Alyn piped in.

"I thought I'd find jewels, discover some kind of secret." The blood drained from her face. "But never did I think to find—to find—"

Peter circumvented another bout of tears by taking the box from the woman's lap. "May I open it?" he asked.

Mabel seemed to shrink away from the pink box. "Yes, yes. *You* open it. You look at it."

Alyn held her breath.

Peter looked at her.

For a long moment their gazes held. She knew they were on the precipice of something, but whether they'd all be saved or go into free fall, she didn't yet know.

He opened the latch. The ludicrous sound of "Hello, Young Lovers" came tinkling out from its interior.

Without even seeing it, Alyn knew there had to be a plastic ballerina spinning to the music inside. It was a ridiculous thing to see in a man's hands, particularly a man whose stone features only revealed his revulsion by the darkness that passed over his eyes.

"What is it?" Alyn whispered even though she knew she wouldn't be heard over Mabel Haskings's sobs.

Peter looked at her. The expression on his face told her to stay back, but she had to know. She had to see for herself.

She rose from her place on the couch. Moving as if in slow motion, she placed a grip on Peter's meaty shoulder and looked inside the innocent pink box.

She'd seen a thousand of them before. Not many nestled inside an expensive scarf, nor many *homo sapiens* ones, of course, because she was a veterinarian. Yet Darwin was pretty much on the mark when it came to skeletal comparisons. Lower mandibles were similar. Even the human ones.

Alyn found herself back on the couch. Without even thinking, she took Mabel's quivering shoulders in her arm and hugged her.

Yes, it must have been quite a shock for the woman to have found that piece stuck inside the scarf. Not what the lady had expected at all, Alyn thought.

She herself, naturally, didn't like it, but she was a medical doctor. Things like that didn't shock her.

Didn't shock her.

Peter crowded next to her on the couch. Without a word, he merely stared at her, his eyes full of concern, his touch gentle and reassuring against her cheek.

"It's Jacqueline." Alyn nodded. She was all but talking to herself but she didn't care. "That's their treasure all right. Dental records adequate for even the worst forensic dentist; enough evidence to prove her dead, but not enough to prove how she died."

"It'll be all right, Alyn," Peter said roughly.

She stared at him while Mabel still cried against her shoulder.

"How will it be all right? I'll be next." Alyn looked down at the sobbing woman. "Or she'll be next." She felt the tears rising in her throat. "But at least she won't be murdered by her own damn father."

The tears started down her own face, cathartic saline rivers that brought feeling back into her ice cold soul. She crumpled into herself and barely felt the arms that went around her.

"I won't let him."

Peter's words were like the finest Toledo shield, but she couldn't believe him. Her aunt had been cut down. Her own biological father was somehow involved in the butchery. Now this man, this mercenary, this bondsman, this thug-for-hire was going to be the one to trust? Not possible.

"Alyn, look at me. Do you hear me? I won't let him." He tipped her head up so that she would face him.

She stared at him, numb and afraid.

"I won't let him," he rasped, his eyes fired with anger.

"And why not? What's in it for you?" She knew her own eyes, red though they were, had to look as frosted as a winter dawn.

"Because you're mine."

She looked away. He'd failed to convince her.

"Because I—I care about you." His words suddenly seemed desperate.

She remained unmoved. Quietly, she tried to hush and comfort Mabel, who was still overcome.

He jerked her chin up so that she would look at him again.

"Because I love you, and nothing but your own choice or a damn cruel God is going to take you away from me."

She stared deep within his eyes. It didn't seem possible, but the emotion appeared to be there, tucked in the shadows, afraid to come out, but more afraid not to. He'd had a similar expression in his eyes when he spoke of his days at the police department. It was a genuineness she didn't see very often, a sincerity that was honest even though it was cynical and filled with pain.

She rested her head upon his shoulder.

In one quiet gesture, she surrendered completely to him. After all, she had no other choice, and she knew it.

They made a strange trio, she thought darkly; she and Peter and Mabel sitting on the couch huddled like bears in a den.

But it didn't matter what they looked like or did. Mabel was terrified and so was Alyn, and Peter was going to help them.

And if he betrayed them?

Alyn closed her eyes and burrowed her cheek against the place in his chest where his heart beat most fiercely.

If he betrayed them, then it was all over. Because she loved him too, and she would go to her grave to be with him.

Even if he put her there.

CHAPTER TWENTY-FOUR

Hector Dante had never liked the new stable.

The paving stones from Italy were an expensive detail; the octagonal wing where the prize horses were kept was an architectural marvel. Still, the place haunted him.

Even now he could hear the shrill whinnies of the animals as the flames engulfed them. He'd never known he was an animal lover until that sickening moment of no return. But there'd been no other way to go.

Garry had sold the animals to Jacqueline. She—believing they were worth what she'd paid for them—insured them for a fortune, and then the animals had to be destroyed before someone figured out the million-dollar horseflesh was nothing but a few particularly handsome Thoroughbreds rejected by the track.

Jacqueline had been easy to fool. She desperately wanted to be part of something alive and apart from her cold riches. The stable made her feel like she had a purpose; in addition, it was the kind of hobby that required the employment of lots of men. If Jacqueline Blum had a weakness for horses, it was quadrupled by her weakness for men.

The scheme was perfection. They torched the stable, collected the insurance money, bought another below-par but esthetically pleasing animal for an astronomical trumped-up bill of sale, then they split the profits all around. The delicious millions.

But now, as he'd been told and told and told and *told,* the pampering was going to end.

Dante released a deep sigh.

He walked to the other end of the x-shaped stable and inspected the progress of the new wing. It was identical to the octagonal-shape building where Wonderwall was housed. Jacqueline had been anxious to increase her stable. The foundation for the new wing had yet to be poured when Jacqueline disappeared.

But it had been poured now. And was as hard as concrete should be.

He rubbed his Guccis against the herringbone pattern of the paving stones set in the concrete foundation.

The new wing certainly looked beautiful; never mind that all the stone work was terrible on a horse's feet, Jacqueline insisted everything be beautifully paved—and neither he nor Ferrucci was about to argue with her, because there weren't going to be any champions coming out of her stable anyway.

A door creaked. He whipped around but no one was there.

It was past 2:00 A.M. No one except the construction workers were in this wing of the stable anyway, and they cut out at five.

It must have been a ghost, Dante told himself, almost laughing aloud. Again he rubbed one of the pavers with his shoe. Jacqueline must be walking about in spite of all the concrete that bound her, forever tying her to her beloved stables.

He shuddered. Indeed he'd never liked the new stable, and now he was utterly revolted by it. A worthless monument to greed and vanity was all it was. And now—unknown to the public—it was the Taj Mahal of Maryland.

There had been some very real affection between himself and Jacqueline. The affair had gone on for years. Maybe he could have been Mr. Jacqueline Blum—but Giselda would never give him a divorce, and Jacqueline never considered the possibility.

No matter how hard he tried, she told him she would never remarry. Her husbands had all been a disappointment to her, she'd said. Not one of them had ever truly loved her. She couldn't take that chance again.

Oh, but she should have taken the chance one last time, Dante thought bitterly.

Had they married, they might have actually endured.

But in the end, she'd left him no other choice but to go along with Ferrucci's schemes. Hector Emmanuel Dante was not the kind of man to live without money. And if he spent his days playing majordomo to a rich and lonely heiress, he spent his vacations in his homes in Rio de Janeiro and Paris, and that beautiful lodge that Giselda didn't know about in Vail.

Hector Emmanuel Dante was entitled to a certain kind of life, and when the small life he had—when even that was about to end—he protected himself.

And that's when he'd helped Ferrucci kill his own lover.

He heard the creak again.

He turned, and this time he couldn't dismiss it. The hair stood on the back of his neck. He spun around, but the eight corners of the stable wing were in darkness.

He knew he made an easy target beneath the work light the construction crew had left on. The thought sent a shiver down his spine.

They still didn't know who killed Ferrucci. In the end, even he'd dismissed it as some kind of revenge killing for one of Ferrucci's sleazy deals. Garry Ferrucci was known for making enemies, but not Dante. His only real scheme had been Jacqueline, and no one knew about her except Ferrucci—and—and the man in New York—that guy who'd worked his way up the porno empire until he had enough money to buy all those fancy New York City clubs. But thank God Ferrucci had been able to dig him up. They'd never have been able to make a deal if not for that sleaze when they were written out of the will.

But all those machinations were in the past now.

Dante had finally decided it was time to *partir*. Exit.

Giselda and he had their reservations on the Concorde for 6:00 A.M. They would manage with their fortune made from Ajax's payoff, and Ajax could deal with the rest of the bullshit. It was all his, and good riddance.

Hastily, Dante took one last look at the place. He kissed his hand and waved irreverently to the floor, where he'd buried his hopes and his dreams . . . and his lover. He then made for the exit.

But a figure stood in the shadows, blocking his departure.

Dante stopped. Nearly along with his heart.

The figure moved into the wedge of light cast from the construction wing.

He lashed out. "Jesus Christ! What are you doing skulking around here?

"Are you trying to give me a God-damned heart attack?" he shouted, the recognition instant.

"Absolutely not," came the answer, before two silented shots were fired; one at Hector Dante's head and the last one at his crotch.

CHAPTER TWENTY-FIVE

Peter carried the silk-wrapped package into the suite of the Brownley and placed it on the coffee table.

They'd left Mabel at her apartment; the woman had refused to go until her cat was settled in with a neighbor. Mabel seemed much relieved to have the Hermès scarf and its contents gone, even though she was still terrified to stay alone. Alyn promised she could stay in their suite as soon as she was ready to go there.

The little silk bundle seemed to grow larger on the table. Alyn was revolted by the thought of it, but she couldn't think of anything else. That the mythic Jacqueline Blum had been reduced to a small piece of U-shaped bone, dried-up flesh, and a set of lower teeth, didn't seem possible.

"You know, it could be someone else." She looked at Peter who was sitting in the chair.

"Do you doubt she's dead?" He lifted one eyebrow.

"No. But maybe that thing there—" She nodded to the bundle. "Maybe it's someone else."

"Would you kill some street hustler and save his jaw in a safety deposit box for posterity—just cuz?"

His logic was hard to refute.

"No," she answered. "I would only save the jaw from someone whom I wanted to prove dead. The rest of the body—if I had murdered someone—I'd dispose of so there would be a minimum of evidence."

"Exactly."

"Where is the rest of her?" she asked solemnly.

Peter took her chin and kissed her mouth deeply.

From any other man she might have felt violated, angry, even tempted to slap his face, but not him. Not any longer.

The whole situation had left her with a dead space inside where her heart used to be. Her mother was gone, and now, so it seemed, was Jacqueline. She had no family left except her father, and he could be lurking around any dark corner with a .357 magnum pointed in her face. There was very little Peter Youngblood could do to make her reach inside the crypt that had been her heart and make it beat again. Unless he was a miracle worker.

"I think Ajax—I mean, my father—knows where Jacqueline is. I think I should meet with him. Talk."

"He doesn't seem like the strike-a-deal-with-the-cops type."

"No," she answered. "So I guess it's good I'm not a cop."

He crossed his arms over his chest and looked at her as if she were a truant child. "You think you're going to have a meeting with Ajax?"

"He'd take a meeting with me. He knew who I was. He knew I was his daughter."

"Yes, he did. But that doesn't mean he still doesn't want you dead. And now that we've gotten proof of Jacqueline's death, he wants to be next in line. You're in more danger now than you've ever been."

"Not if I can tell him what I've done with the money. That it all goes into a charitable trust upon my inheriting it, and stays there even after my death. That should defang him where I'm concerned."

"He knows we have this figured out. Do you think your life is worth his spending even a weekend in jail? Think again, woman."

She fought the terror rising in her throat. Her father was merciless. And she above all in the world except those he might have looked in the eye and exterminated, had to know this. But did that cast her immediately into the role of coward? Victim? She'd face Satan himself now in order to prove she was her mother's daughter and not her father's.

"I'm going to meet with him," she said evenly. "I'm going to tell him that I've got the evidence of Jacqueline's death and that he cannot win this game of tic-tac-toe. Then I'm going to the police and let this house of cards fall to the floor."

"Spoken like a brave little virgin. And what do you know of the big bad wolf, little girl? I'll tell you—nothing. You know he's out there right now setting up protections. If that means snuffing you and me, no problem."

She walked to the window and paced. Her mind was so full of anger and terror and despair that she could barely form a sentence.

"So what do we do?" she finally gasped. "Do we go to the police and say, 'Here's an old jawbone we found. Don't ask how, but we think it belongs to Jacqueline Blum. And hey, could you call Masterlife insurance for me? Great. Have a nice day.'

"Yeah. That ought to keep us alive until the next outing episode of *Ellen.*" She released a caustic laugh. "No. I've got to confront Ajax. I've either got to get him in jail, or be at the mercy of his hit men the rest of my days. And I refuse to live my life that way."

"Look, this isn't about winning and losing and noble speeches." His words were razor-sharp. "This is about *alive* and *dead.* This is about being around to have dinner or becoming some worm's dinner. Get that into your skull."

"You think I don't know that?" She spun around and faced him. "That was my father in that museum. Not yours. My father."

He rose. "Yes, and the little girl in you is still thinking, 'If only I could show what a well-behaved child I am, if only I could talk to him and make him see me as his daughter, if only I could make him love me, then maybe he wouldn't kill me.' Wake up, Alyn. Wake up. You're planning to meet with a cold-blooded killer who's already sold you out. He doesn't care about Daddy's little girl."

She took a deep intake of breath. The thought of screaming at him crossed her mind, the thought of hitting him—no—flogging him—would have been so exquisitely sweet at that moment.

But he was right. Peter had reached right down into her dead space and ripped out the last tiny debris of hope. Now there seemed little reason for her to exhale when she'd only have to repeat the cruel procedure again, and keep living.

Stiffly she turned toward the window. The room seemed suddenly frigid, so she wrapped her arms around herself, and said nothing.

He came up to her from behind.

Slowly, like a cautious bear, he placed his hands on her upper arms. He leaned her back into his chest. She was warm finally, but she felt nothing. And she vowed she would stay that way.

"What a couple we make, Alyn," he whispered roughly against the top of her head. "Me, a man who has faith in nothing, and you, a woman who has faith in no man."

She said nothing.

The brutally obvious needed no comment.

"So what would please you?" he asked, his voice insistent. "What do you want out of this screwed-up life, Dr. Blum-Jones D.V.M.?"

The words came out before her head knew she'd said them.

"I want someone to love me."

His hold on her arms grew even tighter as he seemed to struggle with his own demons.

"So could you love me, Peter?" she whispered, suddenly disarmed and defeated. "Could you be my friend, and stay by my side? Will you squeeze my hand at the birth of our child? Laugh with me when I'm old? Fight when I fight, weep when I weep, love me even when all the world has walked away and abandoned me?"

She was silent for a long moment. They both were.

Finally, she left the warmth of his arms, and went to the bar. She needed a scotch. Maybe he needed one too.

The phone rang.

Peter was still facing the window. He had yet to meet her gaze or answer her questions.

She chalked it up to male cowardice. It was easy to tell a woman you were hired by a big corporation to get rid of her. It was another thing to tell her that all the meaningless bullshit of sex had finally landed an atom bomb in your heart.

She picked up the phone. To her surprise, she knew the voice on the other end well.

"Joyce! How are things at the clinic? God, it seems so far away and long ago." The wistfulness in Alyn's voice was genuine.

"The good doctor herself! How are you? I've been worried about you, darling. Not only are we losing business to Dr. Smithings, but with all that's going on at Blumfield, I'm just sick thinking you might be getting into the fray."

"Blumfield?" Alyn looked up at Peter. He had finally turned around. His gaze was now riveted to her.

"Yes, haven't you seen the news?" Joyce's words over the receiver were filled with trepidation.

"No, what's happened?" Alyn answered, running to the armoire where the room's electronics were held. She had CNN on before Joyce could utter another word.

"Jacqueline Blum's butler was found shot in the stable. Murdered. The authorities believe there might be a connection to Ms. Blum's earlier disappearance."

"What?" Alyn asked, her vision glued to the screen of the TV as the anchor commented with a forensics specialist who'd been to the scene where the majordomo was found.

"They're pretty sure the butler was shot with the same gun as the one who shot the stable man. It really has everybody freaked out. Nobody seems to know what's going to happen next."

"Oh God. Let me go, Joyce. I'll have to call you later, okay?"

"Sure. But let me know you're all right. I've been really worried. I haven't had you off of my mind for a second since you left."

"Don't worry about me. I'll be fine. I promise I'll call my next available moment." Alyn put down the receiver.

She looked at Peter. "Hector Dante was found shot to death in the Blumfield stable. The preliminary ballistics test reveal it was the same gun that killed Ferrucci."

Peter whistled under his breath.

Alyn was silent for several long moments. An idea germinated in her head, and she suddenly became more and more sure it was the path she must take.

Without warning, she blurted out, "I'm going to talk to Ajax."

"What do you think that will accomplish?" By the expression on his face, he didn't seem to like the idea at all.

"I just know I have to find out what happened to Jacqueline.

Call it a filial duty, call it whatever, but I think I know the way to do it.'' She grew pensive again, then picked up the phone receiver.

When Joyce answered the phone, Alyn said, ''Hey, it's me again. Listen, could you do me a big favor? You know Renny? Yeah, he's a little dusty, but never mind that. Here's what I want you to do . . .''

She gave Joyce the specific instructions all the while under Peter's puzzled and disapproving gaze.

When she hung up the phone, she wasn't surprised to hear him ruminating about dizzy, unpredictable blonds.

She tried to walk past him.

He grabbed her hand. ''What the hell are you up to?''

''I'm going to confront Ajax.''

''You could get hurt.''

''You mean I could die.''

His grip tightened. ''Exactly.''

She stared at him. ''I'm still going to do it.''

The corner of his mouth twisted in a wry smile. ''Then I guess I'll be going with you.''

''You don't have to.''

''Yes, I do.''

''How so?'' She didn't really need the patronizing reply she expected, but she was prepared for it.

As always, he shocked her. ''I'm going with you because that's how I'll answer your questions once and for all.''

Her heart seemed to stop beating.

Deep within her soul, in the cold grave that was once the home of her dreams, a small seed was planted.

Perhaps he couldn't really love her . . . yet. She could understand that. They'd known each other for days, not years. It took more than sex and adversity to create love.

But the days had been long, terrifying, and raw. They had produced emotions that even surprised her.

So maybe there was hope for them. Maybe, if they kept at it, the feelings they both wrestled with would be tamed. Understood. And nurtured.

And maybe, just maybe, they would *both* live to see that day.

CHAPTER TWENTY-SIX

The package arrived from the Quincy Small Animal Hospital precisely at ten o'clock the next morning. The bellboy presented the Federal Express box to her. Alyn unwrapped it in private.

Finally, she showed it to Peter.

He seemed impressed. They were now ready to go.

Alyn predicted Ajax would take her call. She told him they would be at the bar in the Algonquin at four o'clock. He didn't say whether he would be there or not; he just listened. But Alyn had no doubt she would see him.

The Algonquin was an old prestigious hotel off Fifth Avenue, with black turn-of-the-century wainscotting and heavy William Morris-style tapestries. The bar was dark and popular, but at that time of the afternoon there were few patrons.

Alyn picked a table in the back. Nervously, she placed a lavender Bergdorf Goodman shopping bag in the middle of the table. Then she played with the paper cocktail napkin.

Peter simply sat back in his chair and surveyed the others in the bar like a bodyguard for the president.

When she had a pile of shredded napkins, Ajax entered the bar. He was late, but Alyn would have waited all night to have the chance to talk to the man. She had so many things to ask him.

He was hesitant. The emotion in his eyes was hooded by the shadows and smoke of the bar. Uneasy, he sat down opposite Alyn.

She still couldn't help but think he was a handsome man in his *nouveau-riche* Versace suit and tie. There was a coldness in his face, only apparent if one looked very hard. Certainly the Blum women had their esthetic judgment in men honed to a fine point. If only their character assessments were as sharp.

"You called me." It wasn't a question begging for an answer; it was a demand, a threat, a statement.

Alyn was caught by his gaze. She looked into those eyes exactly like her own, and she found she couldn't speak.

"We told you we have something you want," Peter answered, his expression hard with animosity. "The *proof.*"

"What exactly is your proof?" Ajax didn't remove his eyes from Alyn.

"Why, it's the contents of one safety deposit box Ferrucci held with Jacqueline Blum at Chase. We might have some other things too, but those are to be negotiated later."

If Ajax was stunned, he didn't show it.

He turned to Peter and said, "What makes you think I would be interested?"

"Because you hired me, that's why. And you sure as hell were interested in Ferrucci's key to it, so we figure you've got to be interested in the contents."

"Do you have the key?"

"We have something better than the key," Alyn finally said, looking straight at him. "We have the contents."

Ajax took a moment to absorb this information. He stared down at his well-manicured hands and said, "How do I know you're telling me the truth? You could be bluffing."

Alyn couldn't believe him. In a cold voice, she answered, "But I was taught better than to lie, you sleaze."

Peter put a hand on her knee. Just feeling the iron sinews of his fingers made her stronger.

Ajax looked around, nervously assessing the other patrons around them. So far, none of them seemed to notice the tense threesome sitting in the far corner of the back. "I'd have to see what you have first. And I'd have to know how you got it."

"We've got the contents. Never mind how we did it." Peter leaned forward as if to give emphasis to his words. "But one of the things we have has some very fine teeth."

Ajax seemed to take this revelation like a punch in the gut. Cautiously, he said, "Why don't you turn it into the police?"

"Because we want to know where the rest of her is," Alyn hissed.

Peter nodded. "We want answers, so spit them up. If you slime out of Jacqueline Blum's murder, you won't be able to for Ferrucci's and Hector Dante's. Your mistake there was leaving behind the bodies."

The man stared at the both of them.

Quietly, as if he were sure they'd never listen if he shouted, he said, "I didn't kill Dante and Ferrucci. If you report this to the police, I'll see them pin those killings on the real murderers no matter what I have to do."

"Give us a break." Alyn curled her lip in disgust. "You think we're going to believe you didn't kill your two henchmen after Jacqueline was good and gone? How stupid do you think we are?"

"I don't think you're stupid, Alyn. Not stupid at all. Because your mother wasn't stupid, was she?"

Ajax's words sliced right through Alyn. Without even knowing why, she said, "My mother must have been a little stupid or she never would have gotten mixed up with you."

He seemed angered by the words even though he had to have expected them. "It's too late now I suppose, but just for the record, it wasn't me who left your mother, it was the other way around. I wanted to help her but she was too proud. Once her father disowned her, she was ashamed. She said she felt she'd misled me into believing she had money."

Alyn laughed. The bitterness inside her was like a poison. "Oh, you were the good one, huh? You were going to stay with her and the baby and do the right thing, were you? You must think the whole entire universe is peopled with lobotomized idiots. Next you'll probably say how much you love me—that is—how much you *did* love me until you realized you could snuff me and get your hands on the Blum fortune that way."

"You don't have to say such things. It's ugly, Alyn. It doesn't flatter a beautiful woman to hear such things come out of her mouth.''

The hatred inside Alyn grew. She could just picture this man chastising her mother that way. He was the kind who would say anything to anybody to get what he wanted. He was the Grand Manipulator, and because her mother had been sheltered and naïve, she'd believed his lies.

But not Alyn.

Alyn was a woman of the world, savvy, educated, and cynical. As much as it was a temptation to want to find a place for herself in her father's heart, she at least knew he didn't have a heart.

With that absolute knowledge, she was way ahead of the game.

''This little father-daughter talk is really touching, but I say we get on with business,'' Peter said. ''Now let's discuss what you're going to do for us once we hand over the goods.''

''What I'm going to do for you? Why nothing, of course. The police should have this important piece of evidence. I can't believe you two would interfere with the law the way you have.'' Ajax tapped his thumbs on the oak table and waited for a response.

''You'd love for us to turn it in, wouldn't you?'' Alyn said. ''Jacqueline Blum would be declared officially dead, you could then knock me off and get everything.''

It was her turn to lean into the table for emphasis. ''But I got news for you. I just had *my* will done. Everything I own is going to the United Way and the Humane Society. So go ahead and take your best shot, Daddy. Because a lot of good things are going to come out of my death, none of which include making your bank account any fatter.''

A muscle in Ajax's jaw began to twitch as if he were agitated. ''Ferrucci and Dante approached me with the job already a done deal. They approached me. Me. It wasn't my idea. They were the ones who were going to go after you.''

She rolled her eyes. ''You're right. None of this was your fault. You were going to keep your hands clean and just stand around and wait to collect. My God, what a fine upstanding citizen.''

Ajax stood. ''I think we've concluded our meeting.''

Peter jumped to his feet. ''We want to know where Jacqueline is.''

The man stared at both of them. "I don't know. And it's certainly none of my business, now is it?"

"We could make it your business," Peter interjected.

"By going to the authorities? And what evidence do you have to implicate me?"

"We want to make a deal."

Ajax laughed. "A deal? What kind of deal could you make?"

Peter opened up the Bergdorf Goodman shopping bag and withdrew the bundled Hermès scarf. He unknotted it and laid its contents out for Ajax to study.

Ajax gasped.

With the blood thrumming in her veins, she coaxed, saying, "Here she is. Jacqueline Blum. All they need to make a positive ID and finalize her estate. We could, in theory, leave the thing here in your hands. You could see it go to the authorities and this mess could be off our backs forever."

"What do you want in return?" Ajax asked, finally looking up.

Peter answered. "First, we want a bargain that if you take this thing with you, you'll leave Alyn alone. She wants no part in your games, and she wants to go back to her life knowing that she's safe. She's changed her will, so if you harm her, you won't profit.

"Next, we want to know where Jacqueline is. Alyn wants to give her last relative a decent burial."

"I'm her last relative," Ajax snarled.

Peter nodded. "Which brings us to the final part of the bargain." He retrieved a document from the lavender shopping bag still on the table. "If you agree to all of this—if you will leave Alyn alone and not harm her—she will give you this."

Ajax took the document and thumbed through it. He looked up and said, "This is a signed lifetime refusal of any claim to the Blum estate."

"Exactly." Peter's smile was like the snarl of a wolf. "You won. For the price of Alyn's life, you win the Blum estate as next in line. Because Alyn's mother always fantasized you might come back and do the right thing, you were never divorced. With this document, you'll be the next in line."

Ajax seemed to mull it over. "I really don't understand why you're doing this."

"Because we don't want to worry about Alyn's health; we'd rather worry about yours." Peter gave him another smile.

Ajax eyed him, all while wrapping up the jawbone in the scarf and redepositing it within the Bergdorf Goodman bag. "I'll take the deal." He grabbed the signed papers in front of him and turned to Alyn. "You go back to your life, and you have a good one, kid."

She was waiting for him to give her a pseudo-affectionate knock on the jaw.

It was surreal. He walked away like a fox in the night carrying off the prize rooster.

Alyn leaned back in her chair and closed her eyes. Suddenly she was exhausted.

Peter's hand, warm and large, slid beneath her hair and massaged her neck. "You were wonderful. You kept your temper; you kept your distance. It had to have been hard. Christ, the guy's your father. I can't believe how well you handled this."

She wiped away the tears just coming to her eyes. It had been difficult. The little girl inside her had kept wanting to scream, "Why won't you love me?" But the cautious adult that she was kept the little girl safely hidden. And now the little girl was crying tears of sadness, and yet, relief that the scary man had left.

Peter kissed her.

She opened her eyes and looked at him. His expression was as it always was when he looked at her; it both threatened and worshiped in the same moment.

He caressed her cheek. "You're never going to be safe until that man is either locked up or dead. We've got a lot of work to do. Let's go back to Blumfield."

She ached to touch the hard planes of his face, to see if she could soften them with a caress.

But for some reason she kept her hand at her side. Something inside of him still frightened her, and the more she got to know him, the more she began to believe that it was simply because he knew things about the world that she had yet to experience. And dreaded experiencing.

"What's it like to kill a person?" Her words were low and reverent.

They frosted over the expression in his eyes. ''You live with it. What you did becomes part of you. Sometimes you're lucky to find someone who forgives you for it, and it's ironic, because you know deep down you could never forgive yourself.''

''I don't think I could kill my father. Not even in self-defense. I look at that man, and all I see are my eyes, and my expression, and my mother's blind love for him.'' She straightened. ''Even if he went after me, I don't think I could do it.''

''That's why we're going back to Blumfield. We'll get him the right way, the legal way. If just to make sure you don't have to confront him again.''

''He walked away from us thinking we're fools to trust him,'' she said softly.

Peter's voice was harsh. ''Good. Because he's the one walking away with a document not worth the paper it's written upon; not to mention, a jawbone from a very dusty bulldog specimen you got from a veterinary supply house.''

CHAPTER TWENTY-SEVEN

Peter and Alyn arrived back in Blumfield just in time for Hector Dante's funeral. Giselda Dante wept next to the empty urn while the priest read aloud the Catholic Mass for the Dead in Latin.

The coroner had not yet released the body, so a facsimile of Dante's ashes was scattered to the wind. Jacqueline might not have wanted her majordomo's ashes to feed the front lawn of her mansion, but it was a moot point. Hector Dante, for all intents and purposes, had made his last appearance at Blumfield.

When the ceremony was over, Alyn was struck by how grieved Giselda was. Dante had probably never treated the woman well, but now she seemed genuinely desolate without him.

Giselda's tears only reminded Alyn of her mother. No matter how sick Colette had become, no matter how broken and defeated, she still asked for her husband to be by her side. With the morphine overtaking her, Colette's betrayal had been as recent as her last memory.

Alyn wondered whether, if her mother were alive and healthy now, and knew the things Alyn knew about Ajax, she would still call out for her lover from her sickbed.

The old sadness seeped inside.

She wondered if she would ever be so needy as to lay on her deathbed and the only thing keeping her heart beating one more beat was the pathetic hope that the man she loved would somehow arrive and tell her he loved her too.

Perhaps it was a disease Giselda and Colette had. The worse they were treated, the less they demanded, the less they expected. So the tiniest gesture became monumental. A deathbed visit became the heaven they sought, not the relief of the afterworld.

She glanced at Peter. He made her weak. But it was a weakness that was offset with strength. She didn't believe him to be a liar; he'd told her too many unsavory stories about himself for her to believe he was glossing things over. His job for Masterlife, the Great Satan itself, was nothing to be manufactured in order to gain the trust of a lover. So maybe that was why she believed him. Maybe the ugliness of it all was the strength. The truth, no matter how ugly, did set you free, and maybe Peter was her phoenix rising from the ugly ashes of her truth.

But her mother was taken in by Ajax's lies. Ironic, when, even as far back as Alyn could remember, she knew her daddy wasn't really going to show up and save her mother and herself. Colette knew about the lies, and yet she chose to have hope anyway. And, it appeared, so did Giselda. That was the sickness.

But Alyn's every instinct told her she couldn't build a life with a liar. And her instincts also said Peter Youngblood was no liar. If he said he would be at her side, then he would be there. Until death.

And that, Alyn thought as she watched Giselda being led away by the priest, was the difference between two kinds of weaknesses and two kinds of women.

* * *

The New York Police Department took break-ins in stride. Detective MacAfee stood in the entrance to Mabel Haskings's apartment, jotting down all the information he thought relevent. He was only disturbed by this one because the owner hadn't been located.

But she'd probably show up.

Usually in cases like this, when the victim was not a drug dealer or into anything too weird, they just showed. The station would hold the missing persons report for forty-eight hours like they were required to, and then they'd get the phone call that the bewildered owner had arrived back from visiting Aunt Jane to find her apartment sacked.

But there were details to note down and file in any case. It was best to go through the motions, even when you knew everything would go exactly as you'd seen a hundred thousand times—everything would be written down, the insurance money would be paid to the victim, and the robber would walk unless he did something stupid like accidentally lock himself in his next victim's bathroom when he decided to take a piss.

"What made you decide to come here?" he asked, finishing an interview with a shaking middle-aged woman who apparently was the victim's friend. Cops were everywhere in the trashed apartment, shifting through the detritus of what had been a nice little walk-up before it had been ransacked and smashed to smithereens.

"Mabel's never missed a day of work since I came to Chase, and that's been over nineteen years. She hadn't called in sick and I—I—was worried." The woman looked around the room. Every piece of mauve plush upholstery had been knifed open to reveal the cotton batting and horsehair. All the books were off the shelves, on the floor mixed in between the shards of glass and porcelain, all that remained of what once had been a very decent collection of Dresden figurines.

"Do you think she's been kidnapped?" The woman put her hand to her mouth as if to hide the horror.

Detective MacAfee shook his head. Still writing in his little black notepad, he said, "She's probably out of town and the message got lost. This looks like a regular chance break-in. See? The door was simply kicked in. They do it all the time."

The door hung by one hinge. Two out of the three deadbolts hadn't been locked.

Still the woman wasn't satisfied. "You really must go looking for her. This just isn't like Mabel. I'm very worried."

"Do you think you could come down to the station to give a report?"

The woman nodded.

MacAfee shrugged into his old London Fog. "Okay, we'll get a squad car to take you down there. Then we'll write up a missing persons report."

"Yes. Yes, I would like to do that. I am truly worried. We've got to find her. If just to tell her about this . . ." Her words dwindled as she surveyed the catastrophe around her.

MacAfee nodded.

What he didn't say was that filing a missing persons report with the NYPD before the forty-eight hour limit was about as likely to locate a person as mailing a Christmas list to the North Pole.

But he let her have her moment.

Then he whisked her away, out the door, and down to the waiting squad car.

CHAPTER TWENTY-EIGHT

"He was a short man. Balding. You know, the kind that sweeps all the greasy bangs over the bare spot as if people can't tell. His clothes were nothing wonderful. To sum it up, he looked like a thug." The desk sergeant for the 29th New York Precinct shifted his hefty form in the chair. "You know he coulda handed me a bomb or something, and I woulda never noticed. There were a thousand people going at me that night at the desk."

A detective picked up the Ziploc bag that held the evidence. "He said nothing about Jacqueline Blum? You're sure?"

"He could have said this jaw belonged to Hitler when he handed me the box, and I wouldn't have gotten it. I was just too busy."

The detective picked up another bag. Inside it, in Forrest Gump handwriting was written the name: Jacqueline Blum.

"The press is going to go nuts on this. I mean, did the guy really think he had Jacqueline Blum's jawbone? It's a helluva risk walking into the police station just to play a prank. It must have meant something to him—or whoever might have hired him," the desk sergeant said.

"It would be important to whomever wants Jacqueline Blum to be declared dead."

"Yeah," said the desk sergeant.

"Well, let's get the press involved. How about a big article in the *Times*. Let's rattle the woodwork and see if this cockroach crawls out again."

"You think maybe you want me to call?" The desk sergeant asked hesitantly.

"No. I'll do it. This way I can take the heat and leave your name out of it." The detective looked at the harried policeman. "I feel an obligation to protect you, Sergeant. After all, you're the one who greets the public."

* * *

"Mrs. Dante? It's Alyn. I was wondering if there was anything I could do for you?" She knocked again on the door.

After a minute, the older woman answered.

Alyn didn't know what to expect, but the malevolent expression on Mrs. Dante's face wasn't it.

"What do you want?" Giselda asked, her head barely visible through the crack in the door.

"I just thought I might bring you a cup of tea. We haven't seen you since the ceremony, and I was a little worried you might not be feeling well." She held up the small wire tray in her hands. "I figured you must have been married to Mr. Dante a long time. I'm sure things are difficult for you right now. I just wanted to help."

Alyn suddenly felt awkward. Here she was comforting a woman on the death of her husband who was probably one inch short of the devil, and whose death probably saved Alyn's life. It was a strange predicament, knotted further by the fact that this woman, by the expression on her face, despised her.

"I didn't ask for any tea."

Alyn nodded. "I know. I just thought—"

"Fine. Bring it in here. Put it on the bed. Thank you. Now go."

Alyn did as she was told.

She gave the woman one last look, then Giselda shut the door of her suite.

Alyn found her way back from the kitchens to the mansion's foyer. Peter was waiting for her there.

"That was odd," she said almost to herself.

"What?" He grabbed her hand.

"Giselda Dante has two tickets on the Concorde in her apartment. I saw them on the coffee table as I put down the tea tray. Man, those are expensive tickets. I don't know how, but I think Hector Dante must have left her pretty well off."

Peter's eyes darkened. "With what, I wonder."

"Probably pay-offs from Ajax, insurance money from the barn fire, I would imagine. Do you think the police could trace the Dantes' bank accounts to his?"

"They could try. But if Dante's got a wad of money, I doubt it's sitting in an account in this country."

"You know, she still seems pissed off at me. I guess my appearance really ruined everyone's plans." Alyn chewed on her lower lip. "But if I were her, I sure as hell'd hate my incompetent husband. Dante should have known Ferrucci's plans were going to backfire. You can only torch a stable once without attracting the wrong kind of attention. I mean really."

"It worked once. The greedy often get lazy."

Alyn narrowed her eyes. "You know, I'd really love to see more of Giselda's apartment." She looked at Peter. "If she goes to town on an errand, I could use a credit card to get in and—"

"Breaking and entering. That's a felony."

"Then don't tell anybody, will you?"

"I won't need to tell anyone. You're not going to do it. You're already in enough danger with Ajax. I don't want you snooping around Dante's old place seeing things that might endanger you further."

"Huh?"

Peter seemed oddly impatient. "Look, I just saw the paper today. The news isn't good."

Alyn stared at him. "Show me it."

He handed her a wrinkled edition of *The Washington Post* he'd been reading. The headlines drew her in immediately.

BONE NOT JACQUELINE'S

THE MYSTERY MAN WITH THE BULLDOG

NEW YORK—Yesterday an unidentifiable man left a bone and a piece of paper with the name of cereal heiress Jacqueline Blum at the front desk of the 29th Precinct. "I don't know. We were busy and I took it. I thought it might be someone's lunch," said Detective Howard who was on duty at the time. According to him, he opened the brown paper bag to determine its contents and found a jawbone and the paper with Blum's name on it.

The lab sent the bone back immediately and declared the jawbone not human. Upon further research Detective Howard found out that the bone was actually the jaw of a bulldog.

The precinct immediately labeled the incident a prank; however, questions remain, such as why anyone would want to play such a trick. Animal rights activists have already said they will pursue charges in court if the mystery man who left the package is found, in order to determine how the dog died . . .

Alyn's head suddenly ached. She didn't finish the article. "It's nothing we didn't expect."

"Yes, but now the moment has come when Ajax knows he's been fucked. This is the dangerous time. I don't want you doing anything risky." Peter stared down at her. "If I think the Dantes' apartment needs searching, I'll do it."

"With me in tow." She locked gazes with him, daring him to refuse her.

His mouth turned into a hard, grim line. "Fine. Come along if you insist. In the meantime, I need to get a call to Masterlife."

"Why?" she asked, puzzled.

He rubbed his chin.

She could feel the stress on him like a tightly bound rope.

"I want to make sure it's me and only me handling the Jacqueline Blum case."

She suddenly found herself at a whole new threshold of fear.

Locking gazes with him, she said, "You think maybe Ajax would go to them? Would they do something that was not in-house? Would they take an offer that was approached to them?''

"All I know is that I want to make sure I'm the only one working for them on this.''

"Can you find that out? Will they tell you?'' she asked, her stomach lurching with terror.

"I'll know who to call.''

* * *

Giselda left Blumfield for Potomac Village the next morning. Alyn watched the hand-me-down diesel Mercedes-Benz roll past the guesthouse headed for the main gate.

Alyn slipped on her shoes, grabbed a coat, and she and Peter took the Explorer back to the mansion.

Giselda and Hector's apartment was tidy and plain. About what one would expect of a working class couple hired on to be majordomo and housekeeper. They had no Renoirs over their bed, no jewels stuffed under the mattress. The only thing unusual in the entire place was the open luggage lying on the bed, waiting for the contents. The Concorde tickets were nowhere to be found. Alyn surmised they were probably in Giselda's purse.

"She's definitely packing up,'' Peter said as he surveyed the luggage on the bed.

Alyn stepped over to it. "Mmmmm. Louis Vuitton. Nice stuff.'' She went to Giselda's closet. A wardrobe of plain serviceable black dresses hung there. "I'll bet she's not using that luggage to pack these things.''

She went back to the bed. The only article of clothing they could see was a bit of peach silk pouring from the edge of the cosmetic case. Alyn lifted it out and looked at the tag. The nightgown was made by Vivienne of Switzerland.

"Expensive stuff—if you can get it,'' she commented.

She peered in the bottom of the case. What she saw startled her.

"Peter,'' she gasped. She reached into the case and held the object out to him.

"A Beretta. That's some sexy handgun for a plain old housekeeper," he said.

"Oh, take it. Please, take it," she begged, the metal seeming to burn her hand.

He took it and studied it for a moment.

Alyn held her breath. Finally she said, "Isn't that the kind of gun that killed Ferrucci and Hector Dante?"

"We'd have to have a ballistics test on it. But I'd say chances are."

"What are we going to do? Turn Giselda in? But for what? I can't say I ever liked her, but I don't see her having had much to do with Jacqueline's death with Ferrucci and Dante around to do the dirty work."

"Giselda Dante has every right to a gun. We've no real evidence of her being involved in a crime."

"So what do we do? Put the thing back in the case? Pretend we never saw it? Can't we at least take it to the cops and see if it was the gun that killed these two men?"

"What we do is store the information away. It may help later. Right now though, we deny having been here." He tucked the gun in his belt, then pulled out his flannel shirt to cover it. He looked just like a parole officer going to the projects for his weekly visit.

"We can't let her leave the country. Then we'll never get any answers out of her," she protested.

He nodded. "We'll talk with her as soon as she gets back."

"But she won't tell us anything. I think she absolutely hates me. At least she looks at me that way."

"She won't have any choice but to tell us the story."

"What are you going to tell her?"

He laughed. "Why, the truth, of course. I'm going to tell her that we have the gun that killed her husband. In the words of James Cagney, 'She'll sing.' "

CHAPTER TWENTY-NINE

If Giselda Dante was surprised at seeing Peter slouched in her husband's easy chair when she unlocked her door and stepped into her apartment, she hid her shock like a professional actor.

Alyn began to see there might be a lot about Giselda that they had overlooked, misinterpreted, and stereotyped.

"We came for a chat, Mrs. Dante. Would you mind sitting down?" Maybe it was because he had been a cop, but Peter was the kind of man that when he requested something, people gave into it like a demand.

"What is this about?" Giselda asked, her face pale.

Alyn said nothing. She felt the woman wouldn't talk to her anyway. For some reason she was a source of resentment to Giselda, and she could only hope that maybe Peter could discover the source of it. Instead of participating in the interrogations, she chose to sit quietly at her place on a worn leather ottoman.

"Please sit down." Peter motioned to the couch.

Giselda clutched her purse and several packages she must have bought in town. She took a seat on the couch.

"Alyn tells me you're going away. Where are you going?"

Mrs. Dante gave Alyn the angry stare. "I don't remember informing her."

"She saw plane tickets when she delivered the tea."

This announcement didn't make the woman any happier. "I have no place here with Jacqueline gone, and now my husband. I didn't realize I might need your permission to look for another position."

Peter smiled. "Alyn hasn't inherited. Yet."

"Yes," the woman said sourly.

"But you know, here's Alyn who's got a doctorate in veterinary medicine—she probably makes more than you do, Mrs. Dante, even though you manage this extra-large household. And I can tell you, Alyn isn't taking any trips on the Concorde." His voice grew rough. "Where'd you get the money for that? Did Hector have the imprudence to carry a large life insurance policy?"

"It's none of your business."

Peter reached to his belt and pulled out the handgun. He put it on his lap and let Giselda take a long look at it.

The woman seemed to be having difficulty breathing.

Alyn wanted to get her some water, but she figured it would be thrown in her face.

"Mrs. Dante, did you also kill Garry Ferrucci?" He got right down to business. He even managed to shock Alyn.

Giselda began to weep.

Slowly, gently, Alyn handed her the Kleenex box. She waited for each word from the woman like it was bread for the starving.

"Tell us now," Peter urged when Giselda had finally quieted her sobbing.

"I hated Garry Ferrucci. He was nothing but trash."

"I meet trash all the time, Mrs. Dante, and I don't shoot them."

The woman looked up at Peter. "Mr. Ferrucci made Hector do terrible things. Like what they did to that stable. They burned that stable."

"And that bought you a pretty good lifestyle. Why complain?"

She looked at Alyn.

The woman's hatred took her breath away.

"That stupid, stupid woman. Your aunt was nothing. NOTHING, I tell you. But with all her money, she could buy anything she wanted. Even her men."

Alyn didn't want to interrupt, so she sat silently while the woman spat at her. But all she could think of were those thousands of books upstairs. Jacqueline bought them because there were no good men for sale. Giselda Dante didn't know what she was saying.

"They were either robbing her, or she was robbing their wives. She got exactly what was coming to her."

"So you killed Jacqueline out of jealousy?" Peter asked.

Giselda began to cry again. "No. I wouldn't be a part of their schemes. I was not a killer."

"But you are now."

"In anger one night Hector told me he had been her lover. He told me so many things I didn't know, so many hurtful things. I couldn't take it anymore. He said he preferred even a dead woman to me and when the money came through he was going to leave me once and for all." Her tears came anew. "I loved him. I lived for him for thirty-five years. I grew old, and he never did. He never did." She threw her head in her hands and wept.

Alyn's instincts were to help the woman, but there was no helping her. No one could take away the wounds of thirty-five years. After that much time, the pain might never be eased.

"If you killed Hector out of passion, why did you kill Ferrucci?" Peter, as usual, didn't miss a beat.

"I killed Garry Ferrucci because he was trash, and I knew everyone would think it had something to do with Jacqueline. Garry was obvious because I knew when it was my turn to kill Hector they would connect the two, and my motives would be camouflaged forever."

"Garry was just killed as a decoy." Peter laughed out loud. "All the shit that man was into, and he was killed because he happened to be the man of the hour. There's a certain beautiful irony in that one."

"So what happened to Jacqueline?" Alyn finally found her voice. She held her breath as if all the loose ends were finally going to be tied together.

"I don't know."

Even Peter seemed surprised. "What do you mean you don't know? You just confessed to shooting your husband and Garry Ferrucci. Giving any information about Jacqueline Blum's disappearance is only going to help your situation."

"Yes, maybe, but I don't know what they did with her." Giselda looked at both of them with tear-reddened eyes. "All I know is Hector and Garry made her go away. Hector seemed eaten up by the guilt of his actions, but not Garry. He was just waiting to prove Jacqueline dead and collect his money. But then they found out the will and life insurance had been changed without their knowing she'd done it. Jacqueline was dead, but she'd foiled us all anyway. It was then that Garry went to see that man in New York. Hector was afraid of Ajax. He said nothing to me, for fear that I might talk and have Ajax after him. I do know that one night I overheard them talking about putting her in the stable when the concrete was being poured for the new wing. But I overheard all this before she was missing, so I don't know what they might have actually done with her."

Alyn was sickened. Her aunt had been upstairs, perhaps getting ready for bed, while down below there was talk of hiding her cold stiff body in the concrete of the new stable. Jacqueline Blum's judgment had been terribly misguided, but it was a lack of friends and people she could trust that had turned her into a fool. She had had no one to turn to, so she did the best she could with the ones around her; she summoned the courage to believe in another person once more, only to see her phenomenal courage prove to be her downfall.

"Hector said they were in love." Giselda placed her head wearily in her hands. "I hate them both. They got what they deserved."

Alyn didn't know why she wanted to comfort the woman but she did. Giselda's pain seemed so real and so close to home, Alyn had to voice her thoughts. "I know almost nothing of my aunt, but from what I do know of her, I think she would have hated the way he treated you."

"Then why did she take him from me?"

"Do you know that for certain? Or was that just your husband trying to inflict wounds?"

"Jacqueline was rich. She cared nothing for me."

Alyn shook her head, still unable to believe it. "She was a woman, watching her youth and opportunity get washed away by time. I don't know what went on between her and your husband, but she wasn't stupid. She wouldn't have liked the way he treated you, and she must have seen it. Even I saw it the day I was here. I don't know if this helps or hurts, Mrs. Dante, but you may have killed your husband based on a lie. I don't think Jacqueline would have had an affair with him, if only because in many ways she probably saw herself in you.''

Giselda looked around the room as if reliving the many memories. None of them probably very good.

Out of tears, she turned to Peter and said, ''What are you going to do now? Go to the police? Tell them on me?''

Peter looked at her hard. ''We'll see. First, you have more information, and we'll need that.''

''Information about what?''

''Ajax. We need to get to him before he can get to her.'' He nodded to Alyn.

Giselda sat tight-lipped.

''Did Hector or Garry ever mention a safety deposit box?'' Peter asked.

The woman seemed like she was trying desperately not to speak, but finally she said, ''I can make a deal with you. You let me leave tonight on my flight, and I will help you get Ajax.''

Peter straightened in his chair.

''How would we get him?'' Alyn demanded, still sore on the subject.

''He's coming here. I heard from him last night. He wants to meet with you, Alyn, to agree on sharing the inheritance.''

Alyn smirked. ''I'll bet. Define 'share.' ''

''What could you do to snare him?'' Peter demanded.

''I can tell you when and where to expect him. That should give you a head start.''

''Give me all your information.''

''But—'' Alyn interjected.

Peter gave her a sharp look.

''This woman has admitted to killing two men. We're just going to keep our mouths shut and let her leave the country on the Concorde?'' Alyn was incredulous.

''To save your life, yes, we might just do that.'' Peter turned back to Giselda. ''Tell us everything.''

Giselda nodded. Then she began.

CHAPTER THIRTY

We love women in proportion to their degree of strangeness to us.
—CHARLES BAUDELAIRE

Alyn stared at the dim stable wing that sat half-finished. Here it was, Jacqueline Blum's resting place.

And there was nothing to be done about it.

"We've got to get the cops to start looking for her." Alyn was near hysteria. She couldn't bear to have so much information and have it be lying dormant while Peter choreographed a final meeting between her and her father.

"You know, when we thought Ajax was Ferrucci's killer, he seemed so important," she implored him. "But now that we know Giselda did them in, he doesn't seem so ominous anymore. Maybe we should just dig her body out of the concrete, put her to rest, and be done with this horrible place."

"Not going to happen, Alyn." Peter stood in one of the octagon corners, his eyes cloaked by shadow. "The only way to put everything to rest is to play it out. You won't be safe from anyone until that jaw is identified as Jacqueline's and the money has been transferred out of your possession into your designated charities. Until the Blum fortune's no longer up for grabs you'll be up for grabs."

"Yes, but Ajax now has no reason to harm me. He didn't kill the men we thought he did."

"Don't underestimate the enemy, Alyn. Your father didn't get where he is in the underground New York scene by hustling bubble-gum to toddlers. Besides, he hired me to off you, remember?''

As much as she didn't want to think about it, she knew his logic was flawless. ''Then let's dig out her body from below us. Let's gather the evidence and put the last man in jail.''

''Meanwhile he's free to pay off Mrs. Dante, hire a hit man and take you and me out of the picture. A jury may or may not convict based on what's buried in this concrete.''

''But they might.''

''Then there's always Masterlife. They do not want to pay this policy. Remember? They don't care if your will says you donate the twenty mil to the little orphans of Rumania, they don't want to lose their twenty mil for any reason. The minute anyone starts digging around here, your life just became worthless once more.''

Alyn sighed and swallowed a ball of tears. She felt as if the whole world were out to get her, and that if she held any worth at all it was on the condition she be dead.

He walked up to her. Slowly, he put his muscular arms around her and held her.

''Do you ever think of the future, Peter? Do you ever see yourself in that house with the picket fence, and the dog and the two kids? I used to want that so much. But now, now it seems like a vision from another planet.'' She buried her head in his chest. The tears were coming back.

''I used to dream of that life. Hell, I thought I'd have it.''

''But it was taken away.''

''Yes,'' he said against her hair, ''it was taken away.''

''If I live through this, I want my dream, Peter. I want to give you back yours, and I want mine to come true.''

His arms grew tighter. His voice betrayed his bitterness. ''Somehow I don't think I'm the kind of man you dreamed of sharing that rose-covered cottage with.''

''No.'' She had to be honest. Her laugh was dark and brittle. ''I always imagined the man I married would be kind of like my vision of my father. Good God!''

His chuckle rumbled in his chest.

''I also figured I'd snare another vet. Maybe we'd go on house calls together. Why do opposites attract?''

His hand swept down her curls, then he tugged on them to tip back her head and kiss her.

Afterward, he whispered, "I didn't think I was susceptible to someone like you. At least not anymore. But then I hadn't met you yet, so how was I to know?"

Her expression darkened. "I want to get past this place. I want to find that rose-covered cottage and live out my life without this haunting me." She drew away from him, walked across the stable floor, knelt, and placed her hands on the smooth cobbles. "I think she's down here. In fact I know it. I somehow can feel it." She looked up at him. "How can we tell without blasting all this out of the way?"

"You know Masterlife doesn't want me to find her."

She met his gaze. "But I want to find her."

The corner of his mouth lifted in a wry smile. "Then Masterlife loses." He pulled her to her feet. Hesitantly, he said, "I called them, you know."

"And?"

He shook his head. "I think they're putting someone else on the case. That's not good news."

Frustration and anger ran through her words. "I don't understand how these things can be gotten away with so easily. How can a huge insurance company like Masterlife think they're not jeopardizing their whole business by determining that my life has no value?"

"That's the problem. Your life has too much value."

"I want to catch them."

He looked down at her. His eyes gleamed. "You want to do it? It might be dangerous."

"I'm already in danger."

"Then we've got to be out with it. We've got to let Masterlife and your father know we're going for the inheritance and insurance. We'll tell them you've changed your mind; you're keeping the money. That way, they'll come after you and we can catch them in the middle of their dirty work."

"So I'll just be a sitting duck."

"No, you'll be a decoy." He grabbed her up again. "Listen, if I can make sure you stay safe, we might find it's better to go out there on the offensive. This way, at least we have some control. Otherwise all we can do is wait around for them to go after us if things go awry."

She thought about it.

It was true. Better to go after them than wait for them to go after her.

She shut her eyes, hating to even picture how things might end. "So do you have any ideas?"

"Yes."

She opened her eyes and stared at him.

"I take a meeting with Ajax. I tell him you've decided to go for the full fortune. I think he'll deal with me, and I think Masterlife will get the other guy off your tail if they think I'm working things out for them."

"Will they believe you?" she asked nervously.

"Yes."

His answer was so quick, it rattled her.

"If you do this, I'm taking a big risk. Not only with my life, but—" she frowned, "—but with my heart."

"You'll have to trust me—"

"I'll have to trust you," she interrupted before his words were even out. She stared deep into his eyes. "I don't really have a choice."

"You always have a choice, Alyn. You could go back to Massachusetts today and forget you ever came here, ever met me."

"But that's where I have no choice." She looked away, hating the vulnerability, hating the confession that she knew she had to make. "I could never forget you. I have to trust you, Peter, because—because I'm in love with you." She took a step away.

He seemed to understand she needed space afterward. He didn't make a move toward her.

"I suppose this is the way Jacqueline went." She laughed darkly.

He didn't seem to miss the irony of her words. "Jacqueline Blum had no judgment."

"She did in the end. She wrote those slimeballs out of her will."

"I'm not Ferrucci; I'm not Hector Dante."

She still didn't look at him. "I know, but that would be hard to get across to a third party. Besides, Jacqueline must have believed in those men at one time. Hell, it's obvious she trusted them way too much.''

''I wouldn't betray you, Alyn.''

She finally met his gaze. ''I want to believe that. I do. But it's a lot of money, Peter. Everyone seems to be willing to deal for a chunk of it. Maybe you're willing too, I don't know. All I know is that I'm going to do what you tell me to do. If it succeeds, I'll have everything I ever wanted, if it fails—'' She inwardly shuddered. ''If it fails, then maybe I got what I deserved—for being too trusting, too needy, too much like a Blum woman.''

''You're not Jacqueline. You're not your mother.''

''But I am a woman with a woman's heart.'' She looked at him. Her expression was carefully controlled.

He would have his chance to prove himself and she would let him take it. If he stayed by her, then she would never have any doubts again. If not, then she would be destroyed, and she would go to her grave just like her mother and Jacqueline had: betrayed and broken-hearted.

* * *

The Plush Pussy was quiet even for a Tuesday night. Ajax sat in his office going through accounts. Business was booming. But even though the profits on his clubs were immense, there never seemed to be enough. He had a Jaguar, a Mercedes, a Warhol and a house in the Hamptons, and the bills piled up faster than he could pay them.

The only thing going for him was Jacqueline Blum—and now his daughter, Alyn.

He knew he should feel more about the girl than he did. There was a curious sort of emptiness in him even when he'd seen her. Maybe it was that he didn't possess a soul; he'd certainly been accused of it many times. But he didn't think that was it. What it was, he thought bitterly, was that he was a man who'd never quite gotten a break. He'd always been handsome, intelligent, and certainly cunning. At the age of twenty-eight, it had been relatively easy to seduce the youngest Blum daughter. He'd had her totally.

But then everything had come out against him, and he never seemed to be on top since.

Now he had a daughter—a real walking breathing human being—to remind him of the failures.

And that was why he felt nothing for the girl.

But she just might save him after all. He had to get the right deal, and once it worked out, he would finally come out the big winner.

He picked up the phone and dialed the number.

"This is Ajax," he said into the receiver. "I've thought about your deal. We forget the life insurance and I get twenty percent?"

He listened for a minute.

"Yeah, I know we talked about ten percent. But now I've thought about it. It's twenty."

He listened again. His expression twisted with contempt.

"Hey, knock yourself out. You can hire a guy on the street for five thousand. Fuck, I know that better than anyone . . ." He went to hang up the phone but was stopped by the cry of protest.

Ajax smiled.

He put the receiver to his ear. "That's right. That's right. Twenty percent and I'll work this out for you." He suddenly snapped in anger, "And you just remember who you're speaking to. You want the old broad to stay hidden—well, I'm the only one who can make sure of it, 'cause you God damn know I'm the only one on this earth who knows where she is."

He hung up the phone.

Then he chuckled to himself.

Who would have ever guessed things would work out this way. He'd always been accused of having no soul. But then came along a nice greedy corporation like Masterlife and suddenly, compared to them, he looked like Jesus of Nazareth.

CHAPTER THIRTY-ONE

Today was the day, Alyn thought as she lay in bed with Peter. He slept soundly by her side while a thin finger of dawn spread light upon their bed.

Today they were going to have it out with Ajax.

The meeting—or the sting—had been artfully set up by Peter. Ajax wouldn't know she was in on it until he was being led away in handcuffs. She would look like the perfect victim until the final moment. If things worked the way they were planned. Which they never did.

In silence, she rose and began to dress.

He awoke also. They looked at each other from across the room. There seemed no words equal to their emotions.

Sometimes fear went too deep. At least that was how Alyn saw it.

They drove in the Explorer to meet Ajax in the village. There was a small coffee house in the basement behind Stombock's Saddlery. At the late hour in the morning there would be few people to listen in.

They rode in silence. Alyn's nerves were stretched to the breaking point. She'd hardly slept all night. Even Peter seemed unable to let her go in order to sleep.

But he didn't have the worries she had. He didn't have to think twice about trusting her. She was harmless. A little kitty doctor. But not him. He was hired by big soulless corporations to do dirty work. As much as she told herself she did trust him, all she could think of was Jacqueline and her mother, and how important trust had probably been to them, and how they had probably given themselves the same lectures about to love is to trust and to love completely is to trust completely. She did trust Peter completely.

So she loved completely.

No greater fool could be created by God or man.

They parked in the parking lot. Katrina's coffee house was only yards away. Numbly, she allowed Peter to help her from the car. They walked to the cafe in grave silence.

Alyn could only go through the plan in her head once more.

They would talk to Ajax. Deal with him to find Jacqueline's body. Get him to confess.

Peter and she weren't wired, because, of course, Ajax would probably expect that. What he wouldn't expect was that the two rather frumpy middle-aged women sitting at the table across the quiet cafe would be sitting with amplifying devices in their ears. Joyce had been putting Mabel up in Quincy ever since that day they'd found her terrified, with the jawbone. The caution now seemed pretty wise in hindsight, especially after they'd found out Mabel's apartment had been ransacked.

Now Mabel looked like any other woman waiting in the coffee house for her kids to get out of school so she'd have something to do. No one would ever realize she was taking down the conversation across the room in shorthand.

It was the perfect end for Ajax. To be brought down by two older women he'd never look twice at if they weren't up to their eyeballs in diamonds and life insurance. Joyce and Mabel's testimony would be the clincher. Ajax wouldn't even get bail.

Ajax sat in the corner, sipping an espresso. In his Armani suit, he looked like a young CEO. No one could tell he ruled an empire of sleaze in New York.

"Right on time." He nodded for Alyn to sit down. When Peter made to take a chair, Ajax shook his head. "Not you." He turned to Alyn, "Daddy says to have your pet gorilla park it outside. This conversation is between you and me."

Alyn froze. She thought things might turn bad; she never imagined Peter wouldn't be beside her.

"I want him with me," she gasped.

To her shock, Peter deferred to Ajax. "Maybe you're right."

"No," she protested.

He squeezed her arm. "It's all right. Cut your deal with this piece of shit." He eyed Ajax balefully. "Then I'll meet you outside. I can't help you now anyway."

Alyn watched him walk away. Her heart turned stone cold in her chest. A sudden fear gnawed at her insides.

"So what's this beautiful deal you're going to offer me, Alyn? You know I'll never confess to anything. Why are you bothering?"

Nervously Alyn looked around the coffee house. Joyce and Mabel were in the far corner quietly talking. They looked as average and unnoticeable as two car pool mothers. But their presence reassured Alyn unspeakably.

She looked at her father and wiped the contempt from her expression. "I know you want the estate. I know too I stand in the way of it. I guess I want a deal. You leave me alone. In exchange for my life I release to you my rights to the estate." She opened the brown leather portfolio she carried. Inside were all the documents they needed. She'd signed all of them in front of two witnesses and a notary.

He laughed. "You stupid girl. Haven't you already tried this? But I see you've done as Peter advised—you've once again signed away your rights to hundreds of millions of dollars, just on the promise that I leave you alone. Why, I can't hardly believe it."

"I don't want to die," she said coldly.

"Maybe I don't want you dead," he taunted.

"I know Ferrucci and Dante told you all about Jacqueline's death. I could put you in jail for accessory to murder. But you'd never let me do that."

"You don't know the details on Jacqueline's death, and you haven't a body. Boo-hoo."

"I know she's in the concrete in the stable."

Ajax stilled.

She felt a little triumph. From Ajax's facial expression, she was right on the money.

"You know, they have these sonar devices that can detail a skeleton in a piece of concrete the size of New Jersey. I suppose Hoffa will be found next. But right now, I'm ready to go to the police with this latest tidbit and watch them dig her up if you don't sign my papers."

Ajax laughed. "I *sign* away the right to kill you?"

"These papers basically say if I'm ever harmed, the estate reverts back to me. Take the papers and we can conclude this—"

"Take the papers?" His voice was tight and low. "You lying slut. You sent me out of the Algonquin with a fucking dog bone, and now I'm supposed to believe you? Cut a deal with you? Forget it."

She wondered if he'd ever spoken to her mother that way. He must have. She couldn't believe otherwise.

"You have no choice but to live by my instructions. You haven't any other way to get the money. I'll see you with the Blum fortune but only if I'm left alone."

He smirked. "And I'm to believe you're just too pure and moral and good to want any of that Blum Toasties money? You may be your mother's child, but you're mine also. You've got greed in you like the rest of the world." He nodded to the door where Peter had left. "I mean just look at the size of your boyfriend, Alyn. What? An average cock not big enough to satisfy you? It was never big enough for your mother either."

She slapped him. She hadn't planned on it. It was certainly not helping any of their plans, but the anger in her shot out like a bullet.

His anger was just as unexpected. "Colette did that to me once. She never did it again. Farewell, daughter. Kiss that fortune goodbye." He stood. Lightly in her ear, he whispered, "And kiss that Youngblood fellow goodbye. He's working for me, or didn't you know?"

She looked up at him. Over across the room, she could see Mabel and Joyce's distress. They couldn't hear what Ajax had said, and they knew it was critical.

"No," she said.

"Yes," he refuted. "He was working for two percent. Masterlife offered me twenty. All it took was one phone call and he was in with the program again. You might have changed your will, but twenty percent of twenty million is one sweet number."

"He wouldn't do it. You're lying."

"Am I?" The smile that wiped over his face was like dripping Crisco. "I'm Masterlife's insurance they don't find a body. He's Masterlife's insurance that they don't have another body to pay if they do. Peter and I linking up are worth the twenty percent. We're a fucking bargain."

"I could have inherited the entire estate. Peter knows that. If he'd wanted money, he could have had it all. He watched me sign it away."

"He's a killer by trade, Alyn. Masterlife hired him to put you in jail and keep the body from ever being found. He had no intention of killing you, but when you became difficult, Masterlife had to change plans."

"What are you saying? That he's the one I should be afraid of?"

"I'm saying, meet your boyfriend's new employer." He put out his hand.

She stood. "I don't believe it. I'll never believe it."

"Go ahead, then. Tell him you left me the papers. Even he knows that the Blum fortune is too hard to lay hands on. But Masterlife. They're a guarantee. A sure thing. A cool four million. He has expensive tastes, you know, Alyn."

Alyn felt her heart slow in her chest as if it were beating in quicksand. Peter did have expensive taste—in booze and hotel rooms. He seemed to have made a lot of money but if a freelancer like himself made the kind of money he said he did, then there was nothing unusual in a man living at his means.

But men were greedy.

"There you go. The doubt in your eyes is like a rising storm, Alyn. Smart girl. Don't doubt your instinct. When you go to him, he's going to drive you away. But he's got men waiting for you before you ever get to Blumfield. You're never going to go home, Alyn. You'll be done in by your lover simply because Masterlife said so, and had the money to pay for it."

He was so sure of himself she had to convince herself the words were those of a liar.

"I'll never believe you." She shoved the portfolio at him. "Deal concluded. If I'm harmed you get nothing of the estate. Nothing. Zip. Understand?''

He smiled.

''Just for curiosity's sake, she's in the concrete of the stable, isn't she? That's where they put her, isn't it?''

He met her gaze. He mouthed the word yes.

''How did she die? Do you know?''

He ran a finger across his throat.

Alyn closed her eyes and inwardly moaned. Joyce and Mabel wouldn't have heard that confession either. Now when they went to court, it would be her word against her father's. Another mess fraught with the potential of failure.

She turned and left. Business was concluded. They had virtually no confession, and if the body in the concrete didn't yield any hard evidence, they were screwed.

Peter would be disappointed in her.

She left Katrina's and found him outside waiting for her. He seemed nervous. Every few seconds his gaze darted around the parking lot as if he were expecting something.

He motioned for her not to pause or talk. Even she knew they'd be safer in the car so they got into the Explorer, turned right onto River Road and left for Blumfield.

''Any luck?'' Peter asked when they were past the village.

''The only confession about Jacqueline was in lip sync.'' She looked up at him.

He kept his eyes on the road.

''Masterlife doesn't look too good,'' she continued. ''It seems they cut a deal with him to get rid of me in order to save their twenty million. Joyce and Mabel can probably do something with that. The P.R. is going to destroy that company, thank God.''

''Don't be too sure. Even if they are ruined, the corporation will just metamorphose into another company, and people will never know who they're dealing with.''

''I know.'' Suddenly Alyn felt the weight of the world on her. There was very little she could do permanently to Masterlife. Maybe a few people would go to jail, maybe the company would have to re-form under another name, but it would continue on like the thing it was, a blood-sucking B-movie alien that just won't die.

"He told me you'll betray me. He told me you're working for him and Masterlife."

He whipped his head around to face her. She looked at the anguish on his face.

Anguish that men were casting aspersions upon his character? Or anguish that she knew the truth?

Alyn stuffed the doubts back down inside her. She just wanted to get home, have a hot bath, and for one night quit thinking about all the people who may or may not have it in for her.

"Watch it!" she screamed just as they tipped the hill leading down to Rowser's Ford. A Mercedes 600 sedan was stalled in the road right in front of them. Peter screeched the brakes. They barely stopped with centimeters to spare.

"Christ, I should have known—" Peter never finished his words. From either side of the road four men in dark suits and sunglasses walked toward the car, the dark gunmetal gleam of automatics in their hands.

Alyn looked at them. They weren't policemen. They were Ajax's men. Or Masterlife's. Either way, it was pure animal instinct that told her these men were there to kill. It was the end. The sad, screwed up end. She would be joining Jacqueline in kissing the concrete.

"What should you have known, Peter? What?" she cried out before her door was thrown open and she was ripped from the car.

A thick strip of duct tape was slammed against her mouth. She struggled but razorwire twisted around her wrists and she was thrown into the back of the Mercedes.

The sound of sirens wailed in her ears. For one sweet moment, she wondered if Joyce and Mabel had called the police. Maybe she would be rescued in time, but the hope died as the engine gunned on the Mercedes and they took off.

Behind her, the muffled pop of gunfire errupted. She struggled to a sitting position and looked out the rear window.

"Peter!" she wanted to scream, but the duct tape held firm. Her last view of the scene was that of chaos. A police car had arrived. The men had scattered. Another Mercedes hidden in a drive by

some brush took off, its wheels leaving a long black stripe where they tried to grip the road.

"God damn it. He's in the truck. Go! Go!" The dark-suited man in the passenger seat looked out the rear-view mirror.

Blood from a thousand scratches on her wrists made the leather seats slippery, but she had to know what was happening. She struggled again to her knees and looked out the back.

The Explorer was right behind them.

The men in the front seat of the Mercedes didn't seem pleased.

In terror she watched as the Explorer pulled up alongside their car. The road was hilly. There was more than a good chance another car could be just on the other side of the hill, ready for a head-on.

But the fiend inside the Explorer didn't seem to care. He pulled up along side, and through the open passenger window he aimed an automatic right at the driver.

Her insides screamed though no sound came from her mouth. They were going to die. The Mercedes had to be exceeding ninety miles per hour. If Peter shot the driver, they'd go careening through the passing fields in a ball of fire.

She buried her head in the seat. A shot shattered the windshield. Glass flew over them like an ice storm. Another shot, and the tire blew. She waited for the final crash.

But somehow the driver was still able to control the car. They slowed, but it wasn't enough for the madman in the Explorer. He fired again. And then again.

The Mercedes slowed to a roll. She slipped and slid on her own blood to see what had happened. The passenger seat thug was dead. He slumped back with half his head gone.

The driver was still alive, moaning, slumped over the wheel. A circle on his back grew black. He was shot in the spine. He'd probably never walk again.

Blood was everywhere.

"Alyn."

She looked up through the car window. Peter stood on the other side of her door. But her hands were bound and slashed. She couldn't reach him.

The car door opened. She fell into the matted hay of a pasture. He pulled her from the car. She began to cry.

"Not you. Just tell me it wasn't you who sent them like Ajax said. Just tell me that," she said when the tape was off her mouth.

"It wasn't me," he whispered, lowering himself beside her.

"Please. I want to love you. I do love you. I don't have anything without you," she wept, letting him take her into his arms.

"I know. I know," he said, his voice barely discernable.

That was when she noticed the black spot on his chest, right above his heart.

"My God, Peter, my God," she cried out.

The blood on his chest was a fearful black color. He'd been shot at close range. Already she could see he was pale and weak.

She struggled with the wire holding her wrists. If she could pinch off the artery in his chest wound—if she could elevate his legs—it would all buy him some time until surgery.

She fought with the razor wire until it nearly severed her bone, but it was no use. The wire held and he had passed out.

In the distance, the scream of a siren filled the air.

Until the ambulance arrived she could do nothing for him but lay his head on her lap and sob.

EPILOGUE

It is as absurd to say that a man can't love one woman all the time as it is to say that a violinist needs several violins to play the same piece of music.

—Honoré de Balzac

The postman took his time rolling along the tree-shaded lane. Potomac was the wealthiest suburban village in Maryland, and the houses, part of an old post-war subdivision, stood way back from the road, hidden within the oaks and the elms. The only sign of life was the mailboxes. Each driveway had one. They lined up crooked along the street like drunken tin soldiers.

From the last driveway on the street, two people watched him in a silver Camry, a Budget Rent-A-Car sign where the front license plate should have been. The postman's every move was scrutinized.

"Oh God, do you think he'll miss it? He seems preoccupied." Alyn watched the postman stop and start, and stop and start again until she thought she might suffocate from the anxiety.

Peter took her hand. He was still pale. He'd lost weight, but the gleam in his eyes was back. Last night they'd made love for the first time since he'd come out of surgery. Her pleasure had come deep and hard, and inexplicably she'd begun to cry. Only afterward did she realize how the loneliness and fear had damned up within her. She held him on top of her, unwilling to let him go; he complied, lying still, at peace, his body slick with sweat, his face nuzzled within her hair.

They didn't move for a long moment. In the end, he reached out and pulled her left hand to his mouth. He kissed her palm and sucked on the vulnerable flesh of the inside of her wrist, then he nipped at the base of her ring finger. He asked almost playfully if she would object to wearing a diamond on that finger. His words, his tone, were all light, but the emotion in his eyes was as grave as she had ever seen.

She kissed him back. And she told him she would much prefer a simple gold band and a lifetime with him by her side.

He said it was done.

Now they had only one last detail.

She'd spent weeks with the lawyers. When she inherited, Blumfield was to be donated to Montgomery County as a park. The house, the stable and all the rest of the buildings were to be given in a lot to her alma mater. Their school of veterinary medicine would never have such fine facilities for research and the house would generate endless fundraising.

Alyn had next picked twenty charities of her choice. For their benefit the rest of the Blum money—including the proceeds of the Masterlife policy—would be held in a continual trust. At last, the Blum fortune would be put to good use, and she, the last Blum, could quietly go back to her veterinary practice, and live her life with Peter.

But the house of cards all depended on having Jacqueline Blum declared officially dead.

And that now fell to the postal worker who was leisurely making his way down Bridle Lane.

He stopped and started once more. Arbitrarily, he would get out of his truck and lift up the back hatch to see if there was a package for a particular address.

He did that at the address they were all waiting for.

Alyn could barely breathe.

"Look. He's leaning down," Peter whispered.

Her eyes locked onto the tableau way down the lane. There, clearly, the gray-clad postman was leaning down to look at something at the base of the post box. Suddenly, his shoulders became tight. His head snapped back in revulsion.

"Jesus, he's got it. He sees it."

Without another word, Peter placed the car in drive. They pulled out and headed in the opposite direction.

Alyn took a deep breath.

Peter glanced at her. "Are you ready? There's going to be a lot of attention on you once that postman calls the police, and they truly identify the jawbone Mabel gave us as Jacqueline Blum's."

She looked at him. Their gazes locked. "It'll go away once they know I'm taking nothing. I only wonder if they'll ever officially solve the mystery of what happened to her."

"Ajax will never tell. He'd kill both of us if he wasn't already in jail with the rest of those Masterlife execs on charges of conspiracy to murder."

"There might be an inquest."

"Once they get the note saying to look for her in the concrete of the stables, you can bet on an inquest—especially if they find her there. Are you up to it?"

"Yes. Besides, I don't think they'll make me linger on the stand."

He smiled. "Oh yeah? Who's going to save you from that?"

"Oh, I'll introduce you to him or her in about six months."

Peter almost slammed on the brakes. The car behind them honked. "Do I think—is what you're saying—uh—are you implying—I mean, are you saying that we—?"

"Peter, I'm not spayed, and you're not neutered. I'll let you draw the conclusions."

He pulled the car into a drive. Staring at her as if in shock, he said absolutely nothing.

"If it's a girl, I was thinking about Jacqueline Colette, or JayCee for short. If it's a boy, I thought Peter—"

"I'm going to be a father?"

She looked at him. He wasn't listening to a word she'd said.

"Yes." She had no way to put on the kid gloves. "And I was thinking that Youngblood's a nice name. Better than Blum-Jones."

He reached for her. "Youngblood's a great name. We better see to that wedding."

"I was hoping you'd think that way."

He met her gaze. Sweetly, irreverently, he gave her a deep kiss. "I don't know much about kids."

"Neither do I. But I know a lot about puppies and kittens. We'll manage."

He stroked her cheek. "I love you, Alyn. You've been my damnation and my salvation, and it wouldn't have worked any other way."

"I won't ask for a lot, Peter. Just every minute of your day, every thought that you think, every thing that you do. Is that all right? Because I can't accept less. I've had so much less from men, and so did my mom, and so did Jacqueline. I can't do it except to do it absolutely."

"I love you absolutely." He looked deep within her eyes. "Do you believe me?"

The corner of her mouth tipped in a smile. She touched his chest that was still healing. "I must. Because you have the scars to prove it."

THE FORTUNE HUNTER

BY

MEAGAN McKINNEY

CHAPTER ONE

What is one to do when, in order to rule men, you must deceive them, when, in order to catch them and make them pursue whatever it may be, it is necessary to promise and show them toys? Suppose my books and The Theosophist *were a thousand times more interesting and serious, do you think that I would have anywhere to live and any degree of success unless behind all this there stood "phenomena"? I should have achieved absolutely nothing, and would long ago have pegged out from hunger.*

—Madame Blavatsky

The white-draped specter seemed to float along the floor of the parlor, her ethereal gown waving in the sudden, inexplicable breeze. August in Manhattan provided no cooling winds, but yet, as the ghost girl placed her icy lips upon the cheek of each member of the séance, the Exalted Czarina began to tremble as if chilled by an unearthly presence.

"Go home, sweet spirit. Phantasm, I now bid you to return to the other side." The Exalted Czarina waved her hands across the table where she sat. The phantom paused, then took a slow, elegant step backward as if pulled by otherworldly forces.

Beneath the Czarina's hands, the shawl-draped table began to levitate. The sound of gasps from the audience seemed to raise it higher and higher still, until it slammed violently to the floor. In tandem, the single gaslight in the parlor flared, then extinguished. Cries in the dark accompanied the confusion of gentlemen trying to relight the sconce. But when it was finally lit, the phantom was gone and the table was still.

"Bravo, Czarina! Bravo!" cried a reporter from the *New York Post.* He scribbled something on a pad of paper just as the man from *Harper's* took a shaky sip from his hip flask.

The Exalted Czarina stood. Her young pale face seemed even whiter beneath the pre-Raphaelite cloud of her dark unbound hair. "I must rest," she wept convincingly, her arm draped across her forehead.

The newspapermen shuffled to the door, scrawling and sweating with the same fervor.

"A front-pager if I ever saw one," exclaimed the man from the *Post.*

Another reporter walked up to the table and drew back the shawl as if he wasn't convinced. But he found nothing. Beneath the table were four heavily carved legs and a frightful emptiness in between. "I don't know. I really can't say how this all came about . . ." he murmured before wandering from the parlor.

The Czarina gave a huge exhausted sigh when the last gentleman in the group had left the room. It wasn't easy putting on a display for the press, but it was profitable. Once the articles were published of the night's incidents, she and Lavinia would have a whole wave of the public beating down the door in order to have a chance to speak with their dearly departed. At five dollars a head, it would certainly pay the gas bill and then some.

She leaned back in her chair. The room was in near darkness but if she felt the cold presence of spirits, she didn't show it. Indeed, she felt hot; it was, after all, deep summer in New York.

The Czarina glanced at the closed parlor door, then, telling herself it was all clear, she stretched, knotted her hair upon her head to remove it from the prickly heat of her nape and poured herself a tall glass of water from a nearby silver pitcher. She was just about to unclasp the heavy mantle around her shoulders when she spied a last gentleman still sitting in one of the dim corners of the parlor.

"The séance is over, sir. I really must rest now. It's quite tiring being in communication with the spirits." She stared at the dark form, waiting for him to take his leave like the others.

He stood and joined her in the dim circle of gaslight. He was a head taller than her and the Czarina found herself craning her neck to look up at him. He was well dressed in a black jacket and striped silk vest, and in the dim light his hair appeared as dark as his jacket. He sported a trim Vandyke, all the fashion now, but his gave him a most satanic look. It didn't set her at ease at all to see his eyes flash in anger.

"The séance is over, sir," she repeated.

"You mean the *show* is over."

Her eyes fixed on his face. It was a handsome face. The closely shorn goatee hid nothing. Yet his face was an angry one.

"This was nothing but a genuine communication with the Other Side . . . and it was exhausting for me, sir. You must take your leave as the others have done and allow me to retire."

"How genuine is a fraud?" His black brows came together in a frown. "Not very, I'd say." He touched his right cheek where the phantom girl had in her turn kissed him. "She has cold lips. I daresay they match the temperature of her heart."

"She came from the grave, sir. How else do you expect her lips to be?"

He gave her a sardonic smile. "And where is your famous sister, the Countess? Why was she not conducting the séance tonight? Are her lips as cold? The reporters were disappointed not to see her. As I was."

"She is tired. She has taken to her bed. The spirits take their toll on the body."

"She doesn't sleep well? Could it be that her conscience keeps her awake?" He raised one infuriated eyebrow and gave her a look that proved he thought her less than the dirt scraped from the gutter on South Street. "And how do you sleep, Czarina *Renski?*" he added with naked sarcasm.

"Very well, sir. Very well indeed." She looked nervously to the parlor doors. Suddenly their English butler Rawlings appeared there, and she couldn't hide the relief on her face. "Rawlings, please show Mr. . . . ah, Mr. . . .?" She looked up at the scowling gentleman beside her.

"Mr. Stuyvesant-French. Edward Stuyvesant-French. Remember the name. You'll be seeing a lot of me in the next weeks, my girl."

"Our séances are rarely open to the public, sir. We only make it a policy to have the press here when the demand requires it."

"Then you shall have a private séance for me. I'll pay you well to convince this doubter."

"The spirits don't like to be in the presence of doubters and naysayers."

"How utterly convenient."

"Please, sir. I must go now."

"I'll send a note to you tomorrow with the coinage. You and your sister will have a séance just for me."

"If the spirits are willing, but for now, sir, good night."

Rawlings held the door. Mr. Edward Stuyvesant-French nodded curtly and left with the butler, his tall form dwarfing the older man.

The Czarina flew to the window. Only when she saw the man embark his black hansom cab did she lean against the sill and take a deep breath.

* * *

"He's gone, then? How I hate that man. Why do you suppose we've caught his attention? He's been to every press séance we've held this week." The voice came from the veiled phantom girl who stepped out from behind a screen. Trailing in her wake was a boy no older than eight carrying an enormous palm fan, the source of the mysterious breezes.

From beneath the medium's table, hinges creaked and snapped open and out tumbled a pair of tiny girls, ages four and five, who burst forth from inside two of the hollow, deceivingly heavy, carved table legs.

"Edward Stuyvesant-French is right," the Czarina said, staring after his departed hansom. "Even our famed levitation is nothing but trickery and children playing table legs, but why is it his business to prove it?"

"He's not a newspaperman. He's not a scientist. He'd tell us if he were. We've seen enough of those lately." The phantom girl lifted her white veil and peered out the window at the rain-slicked cobbled streets of Washington Square. "He's taking us personally. I don't like it. He scares me."

Hazel Mae Murphy, onetime resident of the St. Louis Home for Abandoned Children and of late the Exalted Czarina Renski of New York, suddenly laughed. *"He* scares *you,* Lavinia? Just look at yourself. The white greasepaint you wear is really done well. You even frightened *me* tonight and *I* know it's you."

Lavinia Murphy, also known as the Countess Lovaenya, Medium Extraordinaire of Fifth Avenue, touched her cheek and looked at the white smear on her palm. She smiled, her teeth a haunting shade of ivory in the moonlight. "Ice costs a fortune this time of year but it works marvelously in preparing for a kiss, don't you think? I thought Mr. Champignon of *The Herald* was going to wet his trousers when I placed my frozen lips upon his cheek."

"You are wicked, Lavinia."

"Yes. Wicked."

"I don't know how our dear Lavinia thinks of these things." Hazel turned around and looked at the children behind them. The two girls were already half asleep on their feet, and the boy looked to be ready to topple into bed himself. "You did well tonight, my loves."

"You did," Lavinia said, dropping to her knees and giving all three of them a kiss, this time with well-warmed lips. "I'm so proud of you three. You were splendid. Absolutely splendid."

The smallest girl leaned her head on Lavinia's white-draped shoulder. Lavinia stroked the child's hair and lifted her into her arms. "Tired, my little sparrow? Of course you are. It's way past midnight." She smiled at the boy when he took the other little girl's hand. "Jamie, take Fanny upstairs and I'll follow with Eva."

"That man . . . he's sure good and gone now?" Jamie, the boy, seemed to fidget as if something pressing were on his mind.

"So you noticed that awful man too?" Lavinia asked, giving Hazel a sideways glance.

"He's not going to find us out, huh? I mean, if he found us out, would we have to go back to the home?" Jamie stared at the two young women, devastation on his face.

"You're not going back to any workhouse." Lavinia stood with Eva now in her arms fast asleep. "Heavens no. We're not going to even think about that place again. It's 1881, remember, Jamie? I know they don't realize this in St. Louis, but slavery is dead. I hear that applies to orphans as well."

"You and Hazel are old enough that they can't make you go back there. But me and the girls, well, we might get caught. They might find out our name's not Murphy—"

"Well, it *is* Murphy. That's my name and you all shall have it because you're my family now and will be forever."

"I don't want to ever go back there." The boy seemed to grow noticeably paler even in the dim light of the parlor.

Lavinia placed a hand on his head and caressed his vulnerable cheek still plump with boyhood. "I'll never let them take you back there. Never. Hazel and I remember the place too well to ever let you or Eva or Fanny live there again. So no more nightmares, all right?"

The boy mustered a smile. "Promise?"

"I promise. I've done this much to keep us from starving on the streets—why wouldn't I do more if it becomes necessary?"

Content, he hoisted the other sleepy girl into his arms and tottered out the parlor doors with her. Lavinia followed, but Hazel made her pause.

"What if that man does want to cause trouble?" Hazel asked, her face pale and frightened. "I couldn't let them take away Eva—"

Lavinia put her hand up. It was hell on the conscience being a heroine, but she'd done too many dark and dishonorable things to ensure the survival of her "family" to let them be destroyed now. All she really wanted was Hazel to be married and provide a father for Eva. The other two children, she knew, would thrive in the resulting beams of their happiness. With a real father, only then would they have a true family to count upon; and only then would her guilt diminish. The children and Hazel deserved so much. The worst of Lavinia's guilt arose from the idea that they only had her to rely upon, and she was impossibly inadequate.

Her eyes glittered with resolve. "He won't be trouble. I won't allow it. I'll see him out of our paths even if I must handle him all myself."

"He seemed determined. Did you notice the jut of his jaw and the anger in his gaze?" Hazel added.

Lavinia refused to be intimidated. She left the room, saying, "His cheek was like iron when I kissed it. Still, an iron man only makes him a fine match for me, because, you forget, dear sister, after all we've been through, I am a woman made of steel."

* * *

Edward Stuyvesant-French slammed his fist upon the black marble mantel. The drawing room of his suite at the Fifth Avenue Hotel was luxurious to the point of asphyxiation. Heavy brown velvet draperies, maroon leather upholstery and silk tassels the size of wine bottles elegantly finished the room, and yet, the splendid surroundings irritated him. Everything seemed to irritate him.

"Can I get you something to help that snit you're in?" An older gentleman sitting in a plush Turkish chair dismissed Edward's mood in order to contemplate the breakfast tray that had just been laid out by the hotelier. "What you need, Edward my boy, is a good bellyful of Mandan whiskey—that'd take care of the vile brew that passes for coffee in this place, and it'd also wipe out this foul temper."

"They're frauds and I'm going to prove it," Edward vowed.

"Yes, yes, but what will that accomplish? Wilhelm won't care, nor will he believe you." The older man poured coffee into a fancy Limoges cup, then grimaced when he made to drink it.

Edward opened his mouth to retort, but the picture of his friend made him bite back a smile. Cornelius Cook, gentleman adventurer, was the size of a grizzly bear, his fabulous gray whiskers an astonishing contrast to the fragile china cup he attempted to hold to his lips.

Cook put the cup aside, obviously defeated by its femininity. He turned to Edward and resumed the conversation. "They're just a couple of chits trying to make a living. Why bother them? Put the past aside, old boy. That's what I say."

"As you've put the past aside?" Edward's quiet voice belied the heavy meaning of his words.

Cornelius glanced away, his expression distant.

"There are those who say he speaks with Alice in the Countess's notorious parlor." Edward made no attempt to gentle his voice. "And I say this kind of fraud is the most heinous kind."

"He doesn't speak with Alice. You and I both know Alice is gone," Cornelius said quietly.

Edward retrieved an object from his desk and held it up. It was a heavily figured gold locket tied with a wide velvet ribbon the color of a raven's wing. The gold looked almost despairing against the funereal black velvet. "She is gone," Edward said. "This is all that's left. My mother, Alice Stuyvesant-French, has been dead my entire life, and I say no cheap carnival trick is going to diminish her memory by attempting to resurrect her."

Cook stared at the locket swinging in Edward's hand and he seemed pained by it. "But look, Edward, the Countess and the Czarina are just two young women playing at being spiritualists. It's Wilhelm Vanadder you want, not them. Leave the girls alone. Let them have their fun."

Edward spoke through gnashed teeth. "All that 'fun' has built them a town house and furnished it. Have you seen the diamond-and-sapphire ring on the Countess's finger? I saw it once when she took an afternoon stroll. It's enormous. Everyone talks of it. Vanadder gave it to her 'for services rendered.' He gave the ring to her, and it was Daisy's money that paid for it."

"Your father isn't dead, Edward, as much as you might want him to be, and it's not your sister's money until she inherits. As long as Wilhelm Vanadder is alive, he has a right to spend his money on whatever trinkets he chooses."

"He's mad, and worse than that, he's dragged my mother's memory into his madness." Edward's eyes flashed. He dropped the locket on his desk. "I won't have him trumping up these charades of going to speak to Alice when he's only going to that woman for a leg-over."

"You don't know that. The Countess might actually be holding séances."

"It's a sham, and you know it. Those women are nothing but two-bit whores, and if they were just that, I'd leave them alone, but they pretend to be more—and now they've dragged the wrong spirit into their telegraph."

"I saw the Countess just the other day at Stewart's." Cook patted down his whiskers which he did when he was thinking. "She, of course, didn't know I knew of her, or that I was watching her, but she struck me as very polite to the clerk, and very modest in her behavior."

"They claim he talks to Alice when he's with her." Edward looked hard at the man. *"Alice."*

Cornelius said nothing. He merely fingered the dainty cup at his side as if it brought him comfort.

Edward stared at him. "How long have we known each other?"

"A long time, Edward."

"Thirty-five years. It is a long time. It's my entire life."

"So what has our acquaintance have to do with Vanadder and those two wicked females down on Washington Square?"

Edward's voice was harsh, yet hesitating. "Before my mother died, there was talk of another suitor besides Wilhelm Vanadder. There was talk that a good and decent man had been in love with Alice Stuyvesant-French, and that his spirit had been crushed when Alice was caught in scandal with Vanadder."

"There was no such man," Cook answered, his own voice steady but his face taut with irritation.

"Oh? Well, thank God for that. I was afraid for a moment that one noble soul might actually reside in this festering city."

Cook didn't respond; he never moved his gaze from the tiny cup. The scrolls of pink bellflowers that daintily spilled over the rim seemed to fascinate him.

"You know," Edward added quietly, "there was also talk of a deathbed promise, and the kind of love that can last beyond the grave. The gossipmongers said this decent man couldn't stand to lose his dear Alice, not even in death, so in her final moments, before the birth of the bastard who stands before you now, he promised her he would care for it. He would care for this loathsome child of another man who took his love away." Edward stared at Cook, stared until the man lifted his eyes and stared back. "In thirty-five years I never questioned your loyalty, Cornelius," he whispered. "I never had to."

"You've always had my loyalty. You know that."

Edward's gaze was piercing. "You've always been the one I counted on. Even when I was a newborn, and the Stuyvesants filed to reclaim my mother's money, you fought them on behalf of her infant son. And when the Stuyvesants won their suit and shunned this unwanted boy, you took me in and gave me a home. Then, when I was just barely out of boyhood, and vowed to make my fortune in the frontier, you went with me, braving the cold, huddling with the rest of the miners beneath the pathetic shelter of a leaking tarp, enduring the endless meals of beans and pemmican, all the while assuring the foolish young man I was that you had wanted to come along for the sheer adventure of it."

"And it was an adventure." Cornelius finally smiled. "When you discovered that vein of gold near Fort MacKenzie I was never so amazed in my life."

"You were more surprised when I named the lode after you." Edward tipped his mouth in a half smile. "And I recall you were dumbfounded when I gave you half the profits."

"I didn't need half the profits. Now that you named it the Cook Mine and made me the famous one, everyone is curious to know why Edward Stuyvesant-French has returned to his hometown New York dripping in money, but with no visible means of support."

"I don't need to inform them."

"You had nothing to repay, Edward."

"Oh?" Edward frowned. "Yes, of course. I had nothing to repay. This decent man, conjured up by the gossipmongers, didn't exist."

"No, he didn't," Cornelius reaffirmed adamantly.

Edward smirked.

The older man shook his head and appeared to long for the whiskey. "Let's return to the real issue here, shall we? You only want to prove your father's insane for attending these endless séances, but you forget, my man, Wilhelm Vanadder *is* insane and all New York knows it. What's there to prove?"

"That he should have control of Daisy . . . it makes my stomach turn. I should be her guardian."

"Your half-sister has a sad tale to tell, being bound to the chair as she is and having to deal with a tyrant, but I still don't understand how exposing a couple of spiritualists will get the effect you desire."

Edward turned to the mantel and looked at him in the gilded neo-Greco mirror over the mantel. "I'm going to have Vanadder put away and I'm going to use Hazel and Lavinia Murphy to do it."

Cornelius lowered his cup, his eyes focused on Stuyvesant-French. "You mean you're going to have the old guy legally declared insane? In the courts?"

"If the authorities in England could put George the Third away, then I can find a way to put away my wretched father, Wilhelm Vanadder."

"You really hate the old goat, don't you?"

Edward stared at him, his eyes full of anguish and meaning.

Cook eventually glanced away, complicitous.

"It wasn't enough that he failed to recognize me as his own?"

Edward rasped. "Then how about the fact that my own mother perished from the scandal of bearing his illegitimate child?"

"Your mother was society. Look at your name, for God's sake. I'll never understand how Vanadder was able to make your mother fall so far from the pedestal of her birthright." Cornelius's eyes darkened.

"I'm told my father was handsome in his day. He had a way with women that made even a Stuyvesant-French overlook the shiny patina of his new money." Edward looked down as if unwilling to show the expression in his eyes. "Mother must have been convinced he would marry her, he must have convinced her he would claim his son as his own. That's the only explanation that makes sense. Alice misjudged Vanadder's penchant for cruelty, just as Daisy does even now."

"No one ever has proved he was your father, French," Cornelius said, using Edward's nickname.

Edward looked up. He strode over to a tintype encased in a rococo silver frame. "Do you doubt it? Really?"

Cornelius hardened his expression. The man in the picture was the exact double of the man standing before him: the same strong jaw, the same lean, handsome face, the same merciless mouth. Except for the trademark bowler and the old-fashioned Tweedside jacket that dated the era to twenty years before, it could have been the same man.

"He killed my mother. She never recovered from the shame of my conception. She'd been forced by her parents to reject his suit because she was a Stuyvesant-French and he was a nobody with a fortune. Then for one terrible moment she melted for him, and he must have taken great glee in rejecting her when she needed him so desperately."

"Cruel . . . so cruel . . ." Cornelius whispered helplessly.

"Yes," Edward answered, his lips in the same hard line as the lips in the tintype.

"But if you go after Vanadder, all will say you're just doing it to get his money."

"I don't need his money—"

"I know that, but that's not what others will think. They'll say you're doing it to inherit."

"What people will think is of no account. Declaring my father insane on behalf of his invalid daughter isn't the same as declaring him my blood relative. I'll gain nothing from this but the guardianship of my half-sister, but I will pull her from the clutches of his tyranny if I have to use every attorney this side of the Hudson River to do it."

"And if you have to use the Murphy sisters."

"Ah, them. Yes, they're key to the plan. I'll expose them as frauds and make Vanadder look mentally incompetent, or I'll go to my grave trying."

"I pity the poor sisters."

"They're not even sisters, these two little frauds. 'The Murphy girls' ran away from some orphanage in the Midwest, and they've been performing tricks ever since." Edward walked over to a stack of papers sitting on a partners desk. "Here I have their entire history. As they moved east they hooked up with several vaudeville troupes whereby they were kicked out of town after town for solicitation. Finally they showed up in New York and have made a fabulous success of themselves, until they had the great misfortune of becoming my means to an end."

Cornelius's jaw dropped. "You amaze me, Edward. You and your nefarious schemes—how on earth did you dig up all that information?"

"Pinkertons. They were the ones that traced Lavinia Murphy to the orphan asylum in St. Louis." Stuyvesant-French seemed to take great pleasure in recounting the black spots on Lavinia Murphy's character. "It seemed her parents died of cholera on the homestead. She was brought to the orphanage at age five where she remained for eleven years until she left in the middle of the night with another girl of her age, a young boy of four, and two babies. Tracking her whereabouts after that was simple. It's not easy for a pretty young woman to travel with three sisters and a brother and go entirely unnoticed."

"No, I suppose it's not." Cornelius became glum. "Solicitation, you say? At age sixteen? Why, I hate to think of it. When I saw the Countess at Stewart's, I must say it's difficult for me to imagine that strong young woman reduced to such circumstances."

"Now that I'm banishing all myths, Lavinia Murphy's about as much a countess as her 'sister' is a czarina.'' Edward crossed his arms over his chest. ''Their whole business is ugly. Think of the hardened characters we're dealing with here.''

Cornelius softened with remembrance. ''But she certainly is pretty. Not quite the fashion plate with all that blonde hair. Still, I just can't imagine the woman I saw—''

''Don't tell me she's sucked you in, too, with her play of innocence?'' Edward looked down at his older friend as if he'd just turned into an ostrich. ''That's her ploy, you know. She has to appear innocent because a naïve young miss is the best kind of medium to attract the spirit world, according to 'the experts.' '' He snorted in derision.

''She just didn't appear to be a hardened character, that's all I'm saying. She was very polite to the clerk who assisted her and she even carried out her own packages.''

''Then she performs her fraud well.'' Edward thumbed through the stack of papers on Lavinia Murphy. ''But I'll see her exposed. I've got great plans for her.''

''That's her livelihood you're planning to destroy. There aren't a lot of ways for a young woman to make a decent living.''

Another snort. ''Decent? Look, I've told you, there's nothing decent about her. She's a fraud. A criminal. Let her make her money legitimately, I say, or let her make it on her back like all the rest of her kind. That's the only living a woman like her should make.''

''You are indeed your father's son, Edward,'' Cornelius said, with melancholy in his voice.

Edward didn't answer at first, as if the notion had somehow paralyzed him.

''That I am,'' he finally said, his expression hardened as his gaze trained on the tintype.

CHAPTER TWO

If anybody would endow me with the faculty of listening to the chatter of old women and curates in the nearest provincial town, I should decline the privilege, having better things to do. And if the folk in the spiritual world do not talk more wisely and sensibly than their friends report them to do, I put them in the same category. The only good thing I can see in the demonstration of the 'Truth of Spritualism' is to furnish an additional argument against suicide.

—T. H. Huxley

Lavinia looked around the parlor in the town house on Washington Square. It was her triumph. Each satin upholstered Louis Seize chair, each carefully chosen chartreuse Old Paris vase, had cost her her pound of flesh. But now she could gaze across her gleaming home and take reassurance from its opulence. Never again would she be wanting. She had gone from starving pauper to the upper middle class of a prosperous city in only four short years, and more importantly, she'd pulled Hazel, Fanny, Eva and Jamie right up there beside her. The children would never again know the kind of fears that had scarred her in her childhood: the terror of abandonment, the ache of starvation, the ice-cold knowledge that there was no one who cared for her in the entire world.

Lavinia knew she and Hazel would always keep those wounds inside them, but the children were healing. She saw it every time they laughed and chased each other around the tea table, and every time the girls left chocolate fingerprints on their silk dresses. They were comfortable, and, thought Lavinia defiantly, they were at home. At last, they were all at home.

But now all of it—the Princess of Wales pink velvet drapery, the properly worn Aubusson rug, the tarnished Norman-revival gilt mirror, and, more sickeningly, the security each object represented—was threatened. Threatened by a man with no motive and no apparent connection to her.

She eased herself down upon a satin tuffet, her mind enveloped with a vague dread. She would never be able to forget the night she and Hazel had left the orphanage. They'd had nothing but the proverbial clothes on their backs, and rags they were. Now she swished around her parlor in red silk slippers, her icicle blue taffeta day gown making similar whispers, its stunning train of deep scarlet catching all the red highlights in her pale blonde curls.

Indeed she had come a long way from the long hungry nights now burned into her memory. She'd once regretted the impulsive decision to take the children with them; their future was haunted with the specter of starvation. But Lavinia knew what it would have been like for them at the orphanage all too well; she spent eleven years there. As a child it would be endless toil and pitifully inadequate meals, and then, if the girls didn't get out in time as she had, a brutally short lifetime of working on their backs until disease or childbirth stole them away.

So she'd fought back. She'd persevered. She'd done things that a more fortunate, cared-for woman would never have had to resort to, but Lavinia always forced those regrets from her very soul. Her joy was that now she and her "family" had a town house in New York City, servants and a stylish parlor with an exotic canopied Turkish cozy corner that was the talk of the town.

And there were times such as now when all she could think of was how right she'd been to take the children. Eva, Jamie and Fanny were upstairs in their schoolroom with the governess learning things they never would have learned at the home. At the St. Louis Orphan Asylum, the only curriculum was Cruelty and Want. Indeed, the children's futures had worked out beautifully.

But now the letter had come.

She looked down at the missive in her hand, a note hastily—perhaps even angrily—penned across stationery emblazoned with the crest of the Fifth Avenue Hotel: *I request a meeting. Will call this afternoon. ESF.*

Lavinia could almost picture him, Edward Stuyvesant-French,

that dark-haired ogre, sitting in the bar beneath the decadent Bouguereau nude. Plotting her demise.

Yet the reason he should want her demise still eluded her. Perhaps that was what terrified her the most. He was no scientist or reporter whose career depended on exposing such as her. No, he was going after her for other motives entirely. What they were, she couldn't begin to guess, but she could tell from Rawlings' reluctant shuffle up the staircase, she wasn't going to have long to wonder.

"Mr. Stuyvesant-French is here, miss." Rawlings appeared at the parlor doors, looking hesitant and afraid. "He's downstairs. What shall I do with him?"

She plastered on her most brilliant, most confident smile, and said warmly, "You will show him up, Rawlings. Of course."

The old butler stared at her for a long moment, his rheumy gaze darkened with worry.

"It'll be all right," she said with a wry, tremulous uptilt of her mouth. "I promise."

"You promise so much, miss. I think sometimes you're going to drop from the burden of all your promises."

"I haven't let you down yet, have I, old Rawl?" she whispered.

He smiled, but his gray head slumped. "I'll bring him up."

She watched him go, again remembering the old days. In the four years' journey to get to where they were now, she and Hazel had picked up Rawlings along the way. He was an ancient English puppeteer whose fortunes had gone awry with the theft of his puppets. They first met him weeping at the side of the road to Albany. He claimed to be sixty-five years old but Lavinia thought he might be more along the lines of seventy. Nonetheless, they asked the old man to join them in their schemes. Now he buttled for them, and, in addition, he did a fine bit of voice imitation and ventriloquism. He was able to throw his voice to any empty corner and make it sound as if the Queen of England were standing there. Rawlings was a priceless asset in the production of a communication with the dead.

She glanced down at the note in her hand and determinedly put it aside. "Let the lion loose, Rawl. I'll put him back in his cage,'' she whispered to herself as she waited for the demon to darken her lovely ivory-and-gilt parlor doors.

* * *

Lavinia Murphy didn't look as he'd last seen her. Edward almost smirked when she glided up to him, all cold blue taffeta and concealing powder, a display of precise curls cascading down her back.

No, when he'd last seen her she'd been wearing white. She'd had the ethereal masquerade down to a science and she'd beckoned with every muscle in her lithe body. He well remembered that last time. She had worn frozen white but her limbs moved with the hot liquid of a ballerina. Her veiled face had seemed stiff, wiped clean of all expression, yet he recalled her hair was not the studied vain array it was now. Then, it had been wild and full, teasing just by its heavy length dusting her rump. It had swayed like the tail of a mare in heat and that was precisely why they came in droves to see the phantom girl. Hazel and Lavinia Murphy were two of the best paid spiritualists in New York because when one of them summoned a ghost, she was always a beauty.

And last night, when Lavinia Murphy gave her brilliant performance of the ghost girl, even Edward had to admit she'd managed to tap into his own male fantasy of the madonna-whore. As the ghost girl played out her wanton innocence, he knew the powers that could drive men to their knees. And for that, even now, he had to marvel at her.

''Mr. Stuyvesant-French. At last we meet. My sister told me about your attendance at the last séance.'' She neither held out her hand nor pressed it trembling to her bosom. She was neither the cold, calculating businesswoman, nor the sheltered miss. She was, in fact, nothing he could pin down, and, worst of all, a bit of everything most men feared: she had the composure of a businesswoman, the expression of an innocent. And that was exactly why he couldn't wait to rip away the facade. No mere woman should have such power to manipulate. No flesh-and-blood female should possess such merciless knowledge of men.

"Countess." He nodded, his gaze locked with hers.

"What can I do for you, Mr. Stuyvesant-French?" she asked sweetly, her fluid hand motioning him to a nearby *bergère.*

"I've come to request a séance. A private séance."

She studied him for a long moment, and he swore then that her blue eyes appeared violet. For an instant, they seemed to have just enough heat from the color red to astound him.

He took a deep breath. *Fire and ice.* That's what she was, and he was drawn to it. Helplessly drawn. It angered him.

"Sir, we really don't give private séances without a recommendation first, and I'm afraid you have none." She carefully lowered herself to the lady's chair. She managed her wire bustle with more grace than Mrs. Astor. "If we were to make an exception in your case, it would have to be under the most extraordinary circumstances."

"I have extraordinary circumstances." He flipped a silk purse onto the table between them. It was so packed with gold coins it dented the walnut top.

She stared at it, then at him. "As extraordinary as your circumstances are, these aren't the kind of circumstances I meant." With a delicate, achingly feminine hand she pushed the purse back toward him. She had such revulsion on her face he half expected her to hold her nose. "My sister, I believe, spoke with you the night you were here last. She says you plan to expose us as frauds. The spirits don't take kindly to such talk, such suspicion, Mr. Stuyvesant-French."

He smiled. His hand rubbed his jaw. It was a boyish, rueful gesture which never failed to melt the weaker sex.

Lavinia Murphy didn't even thaw.

He decided to change tack. "The spirits you summon here, Countess, surely aren't the kind to cast stones upon a doubter. The phantom I saw the other night was not brought down from her perch in the clouds." He smirked. "Indeed, *she* would know a sinner when she saw one."

"I wasn't at my sister's last séance. I wouldn't know the soul she summoned from the grave that night."

"The girl was much like you, Countess. She pressed her stone-cold lips to my cheek, and now I find I long to feel those lips again.''

Lavinia rose and went to the window. She provided him with a fetching pose of herself framed by the magnificent lambrequins of petal pink velvet; her profile soft and vulnerable, and taut with worry.

''We could not possibly do a private séance for you, sir. I believe you're not telling the truth. I have a gift, you see, given to me by the spirits. I'm able to look into a soul and see the truth that lies within. I cannot find your truth, so I must conclude there is none.''

She was, after all, a cold woman, he thought as he stared at her. A cold woman, and, therefore, an exquisite challenge.

And when she stood by the window in just such a light, he could see red glints in her hair; secret tantalizing flames that were only there in certain moments, a heat that was only made more intense by the chill of her manners.

''Perhaps that's why I've come. To find the truth in my soul.'' He stood and walked to her. He stared until he felt his gaze could bore right through her.

''I'm afraid that's not the service we offer here, Mr. Stuyvesant-French. Now, if you had a dead relative, or a long-lost love that you wanted to summon, perhaps we could help, but—''

He took her hand in his. It shocked him with its warmth. She gave him an all-too-human startled gaze and he smiled in victory. She was in there, all right. Deep beneath the iceberg lay the kind of sweet, hot nymph that lured sailors to the rocks. Maybe it was true what people said about Lavinia Murphy. Maybe all the séances were nothing more than a cover for a high-priced prostitute. In any case, he was now a believer. Whatever her price, it could not be too high.

''Give me my séance, Countess. I leave the coins to you. I'll be back this evening at five and I expect to see my phantom girl then.''

''The spirits tell me this is dangerous,'' she whispered, her eyes wary.

He lowered his head and pressed his lips against her palm. She seemed shocked by his actions, but he swore she fought the urge to curl her hand against the sensation.

''The spirits are right,'' he murmured, and with that, he nodded farewell and departed.

* * *

''I believe it would be best if we simply ignore his arrival at the door, darken the house and wait until he goes away. I don't think this is a good idea.'' Lavinia watched in despair as Hazel counted the gold coins again.

''He left a hundred dollars. Look at this. A hundred dollars!'' Hazel gasped, her eyes wide with awe.

''We must give it back to him. I really don't think we should do this séance.''